Praise for

My Life with Blackie the Greek

"The story of children of immigrant parents achieving the American Dream, on deeper levels this book is the saga of a brave, innovative family—one that confronts a myriad of challenges and obstacles, yet manages to overcome them all. Its characters are not just real, but truly real—people who strive against odds, who often fail but more often succeed, who treat life's adversities for the impostors they are. At core, it is a true yet almost mythic tale of courage and grit, of family and friends, of devotion and love.

The Augers have touched the lives of countless people; this inspiring book will touch new generations, telling them in engaging narrative real stories about real people who have made a real difference. It illustrates Churchill's dictum: 'Never, never, never give up.' It exudes hope. It gives the evolution of a family, a business, personal insights of one remarkable woman, and her abiding religious faith. It demonstrates principles, fortitude, and faith—in all its meanings. In this autobiography about the Augers we actually have an unforgettable account of the life-alerting effect of finding God."

—Gail Berendzen, President, Women of Washington, Inc. and
Dr. Richard Berendzen, author and Professor, American University

"This is a fast-reading story of two struggling children of immigrants who dreamed incredible dreams—and lived to see them happen. Lulu Auger has sketched an incredible rags-to-riches saga that reads like a Horatio Alger fantasy. She weaves a tapestry of 20th century Americana filled with courage, tears, hilarity, suspense, and naiveté. At its root, it is a love story.

World War II separated these two as he, an Army Ranger, was wounded in combat in Italy while she dreamed of his return. From there, this epic tale spirals forward—integrating happenstance, bootstrap struggle, gambling, politics, and famous personalities. Quiet, steady faith in God provides the glue. For both residents and visitors to Washington, D.C., Blackie's House of Beef is now a famous and renowned landmark. But the reader of this memoir will be astounded to learn how it all came to be. Expect to be inspired by this true account!"

—Dr. Vernon L. Grose, author and Chairman, Omega Systems Group Incorporated, Reagan appointee, National Transportation Safety Board, FOX News Contributor, CNN Aviation and Risk Analyst

"A moving account of struggle, perseverance, love, family, and success in the midst of cultural and demographic blending. This is a story about two very unusual people who as a team excelled and achieved the American Dream. We see how an Americanida became more Greek than a Greek, and how she stood by her husband's side to overcome all obstacles. Together they forged friendships, broke barriers, created an ever-expanding commercial enterprise and brought inspiration to those who are privileged to know them. Greek-Americans will be proud of this first-generation achiever and his beautiful Scandinavian partner. I am honored to endorse this publication and its proof, that love conquers all."

—Frank A. Athanason, Col. USA (Ret),
Past National Commander, Military Order of the Purple Heart

My Life with *with*
Blackie the Greek

An Enduring Washington Love Story

My Life with Blackie the Greek

An Enduring Washington Love Story

Lulu Auger

PACIFIC PRESS
Washington, D.C.

To my grandchildren:

In the struggles for achievement you will find your greatest joy of life. May you find the true riches.

Ulysses George Hawthorne Auger III

Constandinos Ulysses Franciscos Auger Economides

Nicholas William Randolph Auger

Bridgette Kathryn Auger

Gregory Ulysses Auger III

James Frederick Auger

Vassiliki Illias Auger Economides

Alexander Robert Auger

Annabel-Rose Auger

Constandina (Chewy/Dina) Francisca Auger Economides

Contents

Prologue

THE ASTROLOGER WHO SAT ACROSS FROM ME was small and his manner intense. His ears lay flat against his close-cropped head and his brown, piercing eyes stared at me relentlessly. A dark presence seemed to hang around him like wisps of cigar smoke.

"Your husband is going to leave you. I am now going to give you the precise time and date."

On hearing these words I flinched as though I'd been hit. Each syllable was a blow to my heart. He had been introduced to me by Jeane Dixon and everything they had predicted over the last year had come to pass. Now he was telling me that my marriage, the dearest thing in my life, was about to end. As I wiped aside a lock of hair that had fallen over my forehead I noticed that my hand trembled. I felt as though I was on a shadowy path that I couldn't get off.

"God, please help me," I prayed silently. Suddenly I remembered a scene from my childhood, back on our small farm in Minnesota. I saw my father kneeling on the floor of our living room with his Bible open on the couch in front of him. Raising nine children during the Depression was not easy, and he always prayed before making any decisions. He said it brought him peace. Thinking of my father brought a tear to my eye, which I hastily brushed away.

I looked up and caught the steady gaze of the man who sat before me. Would I ever again know that peace that Papa had always talked about?

I

The Early Years

I

Just a Girl from Minnesota

HIDDEN FROM VIEW behind the dusty, velvet, lavender-colored curtains, I stared out of our living room window. Down the hill, beyond the old rusted rain barrel and slanting cellar door, golden corn stalks seemed to be waving goodbye to the sun as it set in a glowing red ball.

It was early September 1930, and almost time for the only party that I can remember at our farmhouse in Garden City, Minnesota. Mama said nearly the whole neighborhood from our small town was coming, and excitement and activity filled the house.

She had been preparing all week. Earlier she and two of my older sisters had gone to Mankato for new kitchen curtains, bright yellow linoleum, and a floral oilcloth. Chris, my second oldest brother, was a taxi driver and had come to take them into town. When he got out of the car wearing his jaunty black cap, knickers, boots, and bow tie, I thought he looked like a knight in armor.

While waiting for our mom and sisters, Chris paced restlessly. He gave us long strings of red and black licorice and then patted our heads. Taking out a can of Bull Durham tobacco, he sprinkled some over thin paper. He licked the edges, rolled and lit the cigarette, then inhaled deeply, releasing the smoke through his nostrils. Meanwhile he continued striding back and forth, pausing only once when he struck the match on the sole of his boot. In those days Chris was always in a hurry; but, impatient or not, he was our beloved hero.

Now the party preparations were almost done. Snug in my hiding place I gazed out at the cornfield to the left and the raspberry patch to the right. I could still smell the cinnamon from the bread Mama had baked early in the morning. On the other side of the curtain my sister Myrtle pounded on the piano while Marlin, our younger brother, crunched his popcorn loudly.

The light from the fading sky was still enough for me to see the Harders, our only close neighbors, coming through a clearing in the trees. I knew they would be early, for Lulu always helped Mama. Yesterday they had brought us a huge urn of homemade "root beer" that Old Man Harder had brewed all winter long.

"Old Man Harder" seemed the right name for the man many years older than his wife. He was always bent over and grumbling, ordering us kids out of his way. Most people guessed that he made his living by selling his root beer, or what Papa sometimes called moonshine.

His wife I loved, for I was named after her. Mama told me many times of my older brother Joel running down the woods and across the river in the midst of a severe storm to get Lulu, the midwife who delivered me. I always felt alarmed when I thought that Mama might have died just for me to be born. I couldn't look at Lulu without being thankful. The only thing I didn't like about her was her short, mannish haircut; but when she laughed, she shook all over and her hearty chuckles seemed to transform her and everyone around her.

The Harders had a sixteen-year-old daughter named Cynthia who was fascinating and saucy, and all the boys were crazy about her. Sometimes we would follow her home from school and watch her go up to the apple orchard. There she would meet her boyfriends and smoke cigarettes. With her long blond hair, tilted-up nose, and dancing green eyes, I thought she was almost as beautiful as my older sisters. She seemed to have more passion for life than this little town could contain.

Trailing behind the Harders came the Dolans. We called this couple "Uncle Charley" and "Aunt Ethel" out of politeness, for Ethel Dolan was Lulu's only sister. They didn't belong to our little town but were from Missouri and visited the Harders every summer. Uncle Charley was a real city slicker—his black hair lay flat on his head, shiny and oiled; his white shirt was neat and clean; his bright tie displayed a diamond stickpin; his black shoes were polished to perfection.

Cynthia admired him—too much, I thought. She always bragged to the boys, "You should see my uncle. He's the handsomest man in the world, while you're just little boys!" She'd tease, "I'd marry him if I could. He's no blood relation, you know. He's city and you're all just country."

Cynthia's Aunt Ethel was pretty, and men looked at her more than at her sister, Lulu. To me, Ethel seemed attractive outside but empty inside. Nothing seemed to shine through.

I watched the group approaching and was ashamed to admit it, but hoped Uncle Charley would slip off the footbridge and fall into the river. I didn't want him to get hurt, but just messed up a little.

I tried to think why I disliked the Dolans so much. When I grew older, I realized that when I saw our house through their eyes, it seemed common and ugly. True, it was nothing more than a four-room clapboard house, but it was our home and I wanted it respected.

The Harders and Dolans were out of sight now, but I could almost hear the "clap, clap, clap" on the boards as they stepped onto the footbridge that Papa had formed from iron barrels and wooden planks. They were soon coming up the road and walking toward the house.

"No," I said, certain that if Myrtle heard me she would think I was crazy, "Uncle Charley didn't fall in."

I was sure my sisters Bertha and Maria, now seventeen and eighteen, were upstairs primping. Earlier I had heard them talking excitedly about the evening to come. Now they would be painting their lips, darkening their eyebrows, and powdering their faces. I could imagine them pulling on their flapper dresses and adding many bright beads. Soon their boyfriends would arrive in their roaring roadsters.

I drew away from the window and watched Mama washing herself at the kitchen washbowl. She was hurrying to be ready and was quickly pinning the last of her white hair on top of her head. Tonight she looked clean and neat in her lavender dress with a white collar. I thought she was beautiful.

I couldn't see Papa, but he was probably outside washing his face by the well. Sure enough, there he was, talking with our first guests. From the cool well he had brought up the large jug of root beer from the Harders.

Papa, who was born in Copenhagen, Denmark, looked like a city gentleman tonight in his dark pants and white shirt. Before meeting my mother he had studied to become a Lutheran minister in Copenhagen. But he never returned to finish his degree, and therefore never became a minister but instead was a not-too-prosperous farmer.

Soon my sisters came downstairs. Their dresses were short and bounced up and down as they walked. They met their boyfriends in the roadster that had just driven up. Many more people began to arrive—the Cramers, the Nordstats, and the Thorstons. The old dirt yard didn't look so bad with all these people in it.

Nobody paid any attention to me. I went back into the house and stood watching the rest of the people drive up. Soon everyone entered the house, including my brother Joel, his wife Leona, and Leona's mother Vesta.

Ernie, the Cramers' hired man, started the music with a noisy, twangy thing called a Jew's harp. Leona's brother joined in with the fiddle and Vesta pounded on the piano. The house changed so fast that I was in danger of being stepped on. Myrtle and Marlin had sense enough to get out of the way, but I liked to watch so I lingered in the corner. Soon Uncle Charley spotted me.

"Why don't you go to bed?"

"I don't want to."

"Then I'll put you up here so I won't have your eyes burning into me," he said, lifting me onto the bureau and sitting me down hard beside the kerosene lamp. His face told me that he thought I was a brat.

I sat and watched for a long time. My eyes began to water from the fumes of the kerosene lamp, and it seemed like I was seeing everything through a haze.

The music started again, and Ethel came out by herself. Swaying back and forth, she began to do the shimmy. Everyone stood and watched. Her blond hair, usually carefully coifed, was let free and she whipped it in front of her face. She seemed to be under the spell of the music as she lifted her skirt to reveal her shapely legs.

I looked for Uncle Charley. He didn't seem concerned with Ethel, but was walking toward Cynthia, who looked as beautiful as a fairy princess. He whispered something in her ear and she drew closer to him. The look on his face was odd, like "a fox eating a yellow jacket," as Pa would say. Her eyes turned soft and she snuggled closer.

Ethel beckoned to Ernie, who had a red face and a prominent Adam's apple. With hungry eyes he put away the Jew's harp and came to her. She put her head on his shoulder, entwined her arms around his neck, and pressed her body close to his. Saliva drooled from his mouth and he swallowed many times, closing his eyes.

The other people, deadened from the root beer and the loud music, paid no attention. The soft glow of the kerosene lamp seemed to be hiding everyone behind a filmy curtain. I began to feel sleepy.

Papa must have gone outside, but Mama was busy making sandwiches and talking to some women in the kitchen. She saw me then, lifted me off my perch, and told me to go to bed. I took one more look at the people. The room was swimming and I felt I had seen enough. I started to kiss Mama good night, but she didn't kiss much.

Upstairs, Myrt and Marlin had fallen asleep in the double bed they shared with Mama. I slept in the same room but in another bed by myself. Pa mostly slept downstairs on the leather couch and kept the fire burning during the long winter nights.

I lay in bed listening to the music and studying the pictures made by the cracked plaster where the moon beamed through the window. I may have been only six, but I never forgot that night's party.

A few weeks later I heard Bertha and Maria talking as they got ready for their dates. Bertha said softly, "I hate to tell the kids that we're leaving next week."

As I heard her words I looked into their room and saw several bras and stockings sticking out of a suitcase. I rushed over to Maria and blurted, "Why are you leaving?" Throwing my arms around her, I started to cry.

"Don't feel bad, honey. We have to go make a living."

I sobbed, "Where?"

"To Mankato. Do you remember when Hazel took us to the Saulpaugh Hotel and we had lunch? That's where Bertha and I will be working."

Hazel was my oldest sister and I remembered the outing with pleasure. But no matter what they said, I couldn't be consoled. I cried all night.

On the following Saturday, just a week before school started, we had a family celebration to mark Maria and Bertha's leaving the farm. It was a big gathering, as Mama had given birth to ten of us—nine who survived. Joel and Leona came back, as well as Hazel and her husband Arnie. Our sister Pearl was there with her husband Wally, but Chris had to work and couldn't come.

It was a lovely fall day, so we moved the kitchen table under the cottonwood tree. We had all kinds of food, including a cake that Hazel had baked with molasses, raisins, and nuts, the "poorman's cake."

Hazel was always kind, except when she lined up us three little ones to cut our hair. I wanted mine long, but she said that we had to have the "boyish bob." I was doubly unhappy as I looked at my shorn tresses on the ground and knew my sisters would soon be leaving.

But then Hazel showed us the new clothes she had brought us for school: pink and blue dresses with matching sweaters, thick wool stockings, and rubber boots to wear over our shoes. We all got snowsuits for the cold winter that would soon be upon us.

We gathered around Hazel and hugged and kissed her in thankfulness. She may have been a little cranky, but she was like another mother to us. Without the help of our brothers and sisters, we would have been hopelessly poor during the Great Depression.

Once dinner was over everyone was anxious to leave. Maria and Bertha gathered up their things. They hadn't even left yet, but already the house seemed lonely and dreary. I felt abandoned and knew nothing would ever be the same.

Maria said, "There's lots of food in the house now, Lulu. You'll be okay. Hazel's brought you such nice clothes. And we'll be back—Chris will bring us! We have to make a living, you know. But we'll bring you nice clothes too; you'll see. Be brave now, honey."

I clung to her, crying, and she had to peel me off.

Mama stood at the door, blinking back tears as the girls said good-bye with excitement and joy. As soon as they left, Mama sat down in her rocking chair, masking her sadness. Papa put his hands behind his back and headed for the barn, kicking my tomcat out of his way as he slammed the screen door. The cat's fur stood on end and his tail stiffened.

I went to my favorite window and could see the cars making their way through the woods. I was hoping someone would sound the horn, but it remained silent. They didn't even look back.

Life on the farm continued. After school, we kids picked apples and plums and helped Ma peel them. She also cooked and canned peas, corn, green beans, and tomatoes, along with making watermelon pickles and different kinds of jam—plum, strawberry, and raspberry.

We always had plenty to do. During the summer we'd pick off the bugs from the potato patch. Wearing old straw hats and walking barefoot between the rows of the potatoes, we'd fill our cans with bugs. I didn't like the way they would crawl out onto my hand, so Papa said to put a little kerosene in the bottom of the can to knock them out. When we were done we burned can and all in a bonfire.

We had no electricity or washing machine. Mama used a large tub and washboard, which turned her hands red and raw by the end of the day. We also had no indoor plumbing, but used an outhouse that Pa and a hired man would move from time to time. All summer the hornets and wasps plagued us as they buzzed overhead. The winters brought relief from the pests, except then we froze. Summer or winter, our toilet paper was a big Sears or Montgomery Ward catalog.

Almost two years had passed since my older sisters had left. It was spring again and we could smell the apple blossoms in the air and hear the singing of the robins. We were happy to have survived another harsh winter and were looking forward to summer. We'd spend lots of time outside—eating under the cottonwood tree, playing in the yard, and doing our chores. And we'd see more of the Harders and their annual guests, Uncle Charley and Aunt Ethel.

When school was finished, and the summer was in full bloom and hot and dry, our dog Towser started howling. We felt sure he was about to have one of his fits when his mouth would froth and he'd go crazy. We were told to get out of his way whenever this happened, so today we scrambled into the old Ford that Joel had left in the junkyard. Some of its windows were open, and wasps had formed their nests up in the corners. We kept our heads low, not knowing which scared us the most, the dog or the wasps.

Towser ran all around—through the front yard, up to the orchard, down across the chicken roost, over to the plum and apple trees, and then around the pump and the cottonwood tree. Finally he slowed down and sat panting at the kitchen door. We waited until he fell asleep, not knowing what was wrong.

The next morning, we heard a loud bang. Papa went down into the meadow to investigate and found Towser dead. Old Man Harder was standing over him with a shotgun, saying he'd done us a favor because the dog was rabid. We disliked Old Man Harder even more after that.

A few days later, on Saturday morning, Lulu Harder came up the road, walking slowly and quietly. We missed her usual gay banter as she entered the kitchen, joining Mama with her coffee.

"Alice, I'm so sorry that the old man shot the dog."

"Well, we miss Towser but it's probably for the best."

Lulu was quiet, with her eyes downcast.

Mama asked gently, "You're not just worried about the dog, are you?"

"No, it's not the dog."

Lulu put her head down on the table and broke down weeping.

"Tell me—what's the matter?"

Lulu replied through her sobs, "We had a terrible row this morning. I didn't believe him at first, but the old man was right."

Her cries became louder, and she couldn't continue for awhile.

She began again, "He found Charley making love to Cynthia in the orchard. My own sister's husband!"

Her voice broke again, and Mama put her arm around Lulu to comfort her.

"It was a terrible scene. When the old man kicked them out, Ethel said we were nothing but country hillbillies who didn't know how to live. She said Charley was led on."

Brushing away her tears, she said, "I slapped her so hard that the mark stayed on her face.

"She was always so wild. Nothing ever meant anything to her—not even her husband's doings. But I never really hated her until now."

Mama was silent as Lulu spoke.

"Cynthia won't stop crying. She says she's in love with the bastard, and that. . ." Lulu seemed overcome, and couldn't speak for some time. Finally, she blurted out, "She says she's six weeks pregnant! My little girl. My poor little girl!"

I thought of Cynthia then, lying in the orchard with the boys. I still could remember the way Uncle Charley had looked at her at the party.

Mama cried with Lulu, her arms around her as they stood sobbing together. Words didn't seem sufficient. Cynthia was so beautiful—was that her problem? When would happy times come again?

2

Hard Times

Two more winters came and went, and now we had a new president in the White House. Americans concerned about the continuing economic crisis were wooed by Franklin D. Roosevelt's pledges of a "new deal for the American people" and overwhelmingly elected him president. Roosevelt was confident and enthusiastic, but on the night of Election Day he confessed his fears to his son: "I'm just afraid that I may not have the strength to do this job. After you leave me tonight, Jimmy, I am going to pray. I am going to pray that God will help me, that he will give me the strength and the guidance to do this job and to do it right."

President Roosevelt must have received the strength he needed, for he worked hard his first few months in office to calm the country's fears and implement programs of the New Deal. In fact, in his first hundred days of office—from March to June 1933—he guided over a dozen major laws to enactment.

It was the end of Roosevelt's first hundred days and I was nearly ten when one happy day Mama told us that Maria and Bertha would be coming home for a visit. Occasionally we would see our sisters in Mankato when Papa and Mama would let us accompany them to buy our groceries at the Piggly Wiggly and do some business. But this was the first time that Maria and Bertha were returning to the farm.

Myrtle, Marlin, and I were so excited as we helped Mama straighten up the house. But we were crestfallen when she told us that we were going to have two of our favorite chickens for supper. Calling her a "beheader," we told her she should operate a guillotine.

Mama never paid any attention to us; she just worked quietly. Holding the chicken's body with one hand, she chopped off its little head with the meat cleaver and let it wiggle and bleed on the ground while we cried. Then she dipped the chickens into boiling water, plucked out the feathers, and drew out the insides. When the chickens were boiling they began to smell very good, especially when Mama made a thick white sauce with dumplings and added the vegetables. We soon forgot our beloved chickens.

Chris drove Maria and Bertha home. With whoops of excitement we kids watched them coming up the dusty road in the noisy, black Ford. Hazel and Arnie brought Pearl, Wally, and their four-year-old daughter Patty. She was so beautifully dressed and well cared for that she didn't seem like one of us. I could hardly believe I was her aunt.

Joel and Leona came too, along with their three-year-old son Earl. They had been married five years now and Leona was about to have another baby. She seemed as young as my sisters and was so pretty, with long red hair to her waist.

Everyone seemed to be talking at once and I listened, keeping my eyes glued to them all. Feeling happy and safe, I sighed with joy. I was so content to be part of a wonderfully large family. I also loved seeing the way Leona and Joel treated each other. Joel held Leona's hand, nibbling at her fingers.

Maria and Bertha, decked out in their fashionable sailor suits, seemed older and more city-wise. They had brought Myrtle and me flowered outfits, which we put on as fast as we could. We felt so proud in our new clothes.

Maria said, "Everyone's singing a new song: 'The music goes round and round.'"

Bertha began to sing, and we all joined in. Mama was delighted to have her family surrounding her, and Papa was so happy that he cracked some of his Danish jokes.

After dinner we kids played marbles with Earl and Patty while the adults continued talking under the cottonwood tree. It was a nice summer evening, except for the everpresent mosquitoes.

After a little while Leona asked Joel, "Honey, do you mind if I walk home? Why don't you stay awhile and let Earl play, then you can drive home. Maria and Bertha will walk with me. We want some girl talk."

Joel hesitated and didn't answer her right away. There was fear in his eyes, for Leona had been warned not to have another baby. But she was young—only twenty-two—and carefree. He wasn't too happy for her to walk home, and said so.

But she asked again, "Please let me walk with them. It's not far."

Finally, Joel reluctantly agreed. Myrtle, Marlin, and I didn't go with them because Mama said we needed to help her clean up. I watched the three young women walk toward the barn and onto the path that led in the opposite way from Papa's footbridge.

Only a short time later, when we were helping with the dishes, we heard Bertha screaming hysterically. We rushed outside to see what was wrong.

"What happened?" asked Mama.

Panting, Bertha cried, "Leona slipped on the rocks over the rapids!" Mama gasped.

Bertha continued, "We got her to their house and Maria is calling the doctor." Faltering, she said, "I came back here to tell you."

Joel raced to his car but it was too late. A little boy named Joel was delivered but Leona died, seeming to take her husband's heart with her.

I had seen my mother tired—"bone tired," in her words—and I had seen her blue and unhappy, but I had never seen her as inconsolable as that night when Leona died. Everything seemed to be too much for her: the brokenheartedness of her son, her first and second grandson without a mother, the girls gone. Mama tried to control the tears that ran along her chin. Her usually neat hair had fallen down and needed tidying.

I cleaned the kitchen floor while Myrtle picked up the dishes, trying to cheer up Mama. Marlin came in the house with Lulu Harder. She walked over to Mama and put her arms around her.

"Alice, I know you feel terrible. Like I did when Cynthia—oh! You remember how we cried. But God knows when it's too much for us to bear. Sometimes he rescues us."

Myrtle gave Lulu a cup of coffee as Lulu tried to console Mama. "Remember when I couldn't stand to see Cynthia around the house when she was pregnant? I knew she could never marry the father."

Mama nodded. Lulu continued, "But then Ralph Ingersoll came by. He always liked Cynthia, but felt she was too young and pretty for him." Tears fell out of Lulu's eyes, and she wiped them away on her long gray skirt.

"God will take care of you and your son, too. In the beginning, I felt like you do now. I didn't believe that anything good could come out of all this trouble." Just thinking of it made more tears flow.

"But Ralph was so tender and kind, and Cynthia welcomed him for the first time."

Lulu and Mama reminisced about Ralph accepting Cynthia, their small wedding, and the love between them. They talked about how amazed the family had been that little David looked just like Ralph.

Lulu said, "Just look at what God did! I know he's going to do the same for your son and the kids. They'll be all right."

Mama patted Lulu, saying, "I'm happy for you, I am. I guess in time things will get better."

Mama improved after Lulu's visit, and I saw the value of having a good friend to confide in. Leona's mother, Vesta, took the children and cared for them, and God did work it out, except for Joel's heart. Joel always blamed himself for getting Leona pregnant and never could forgive himself. When he died at the age of fifty, the doctor said that it was a true case of a broken heart.

Myrt, Marlin, and I were very close, especially because we had no other kids to play with. But sometimes we would fight, saying mean, despicable things to each other. We'd use all the terrible words we heard the older kids say.

Christmas came, and I wanted a doll. I had never had one and decided to make my own. Using stiff cardboard for the body, I glued some corn husks for her hair and fashioned a dress using Mama's big needle and white yarn. I colored her eyes brown because Joel's eyes were brown. But one day Myrtle got angry with me and tore up my doll.

When I found the remains I was hurt and angry. "Myrt! Why did you tear up my doll?"

Myrt looked triumphant and said nothing, gloating.

"Well, someday I'm going to be able to buy any old doll I want to. I'll show you!"

I really meant it. Ever since I could remember I had felt a sense of destiny, as though big things were in store for me.

Myrtle obviously had dreams of her own. "Ha!" she replied. "You're not even pretty. You'll never be anything. But I'm going to be a movie star, and I *might* let you be my maid."

I ran to the barn, grabbed my tomcat, and cried myself to sleep in the straw. Papa found me later, still holding Fluffy in my arms. He nudged me with his foot and told me to get up. It seemed that we younger kids were a nuisance to him, since he was nearly seventy. He still missed the older kids.

Hazel bought Mama a battery radio, which she loved playing. On Saturday nights the Grand Old Opry could be heard throughout the house. On one rainy Saturday in February, Gene Autry was singing and strumming his guitar while we kids were setting the table and Mama was frying pork chops and making gravy.

When she reached over to take the potatoes off the stove, the handle of the frying pan caught her arm. The pan fell forward, spilling the hot boiling gravy onto her stomach. She moaned and cried out, grabbing her stomach and stepping back in pain.

Going over to the washbowl, Mama unbuttoned her dress and slowly peeled back her pink cotton underwear. Underneath I could see a red flaming mass.

She went to the cabinet and found the tin of lard. After smearing a big glob on her stomach she placed a clean pillowcase on top of the goo. Putting back her now greasy underwear, she pulled down her dress.

Mama returned to the stove without saying anything and began to make some more gravy with the drippings. We kids were mighty silent at the table. She didn't tell Papa.

That night I had trouble sleeping because I could hear Mama moaning. I thought about the brave people we read about in school who fought battles in the war, and realized that Mama was one of those people.

Whenever we complained, she would say, "Laugh and the world laughs with you; weep and you weep alone." She seemed to live up to that saying. Another of her famous lines was, "Can't means you don't want to." We never had a chance to give up.

When I was nearly twelve, fall came and it was time for the Garden City fair. The fairground suddenly came alive with Ferris wheels, merry-go-rounds, and the popcorn and candy we all loved so much. There were 4-H contests to see who raised the fattest and healthiest hogs, cattle, and sheep, and contests for canning and baking. Mama never joined the competitions, but she loved going to the fair all the same.

Papa had decided not to come with us, so Mama, Myrtle, Marlin, and I walked over by ourselves. When we stepped across the stones where Leona had fallen we all became very quiet.

13

Lulu Harder had agreed to meet Mama at the fair, and we sat at a picnic table right by the place where they were grilling hot dogs and frying hamburgers with onions. The smell was so tantalizing. And when prosperous men walked by us, I liked the smell of their cigars.

Myrtle and I took Marlin's hand and made him stay close to us. We stopped at a counter and paid a penny to throw darts. The man who ran the game looked at Myrtle's face. She was now thirteen and beginning to bloom a little.

"How old are you?" he asked while looking deep into her eyes.

She didn't answer.

He said, "Already your eyes are beautiful."

I didn't like the way he was looking at her so I yanked her away. Later I noticed that she walked a little apart from Marlin and me, wiping her bangs slowly away from her face. She seemed to be thinking about having beautiful eyes.

On the following Sunday the fair was still on, but first we went to the Baptist church with Mama. She liked to sit up front, close to the preacher, while we kids went to Sunday School. Every time we put our pennies in the little collection envelope I thought of Maria. Once, when we came home from church with candy around our mouths, we had to confess that instead of putting our money in the offering we had saved it and bought candy. She told us never to do that again, saying, "That money belongs to God, not to you." We heeded her words.

After church we went to the fair again and all ate at the same stand, ordering juicy hamburgers with fried onions and ketchup. I liked watching Mama enjoy herself so much. Later in the afternoon we went home using the footbridge. When we walked by the Harder's house Lulu saw us and called out, "Hello! Have you been to the fair?"

Mama stopped to chat. Lulu looked sad again and Mama asked if everything was all right.

Lulu answered, "Well, the old man is worried since Prohibition has been repealed—he just doesn't know how to make a living. Maybe I'll have to get on the sewing project of the WPA."

Mama sympathized with her and said, "I may have to do the same. You and I are years younger than our husbands. Maybe they can get old age pensions—I hear they can apply for Relief now from the National Recovery Administration."

They chatted a bit more and then we continued on our way. As we went home we kids skipped and hopped while loudly singing, "Over the river and through the woods, to grandmother's house we go."

Suddenly Mama told us to hush. We all stood still because Mama seemed worried. She kept sniffing like she was smelling something, and then she started to walk faster. We rounded the curve and peered through the trees toward our house. We saw a sickening sight—big billows of flames shooting through the night sky. Our barn was on fire.

Marlin and Myrtle ran on ahead but I was sick immediately and threw up. Mama stayed behind to comfort me, even though she was anxious to get to Papa. Once I was recovered enough, Mama and I clomped over the footbridge and up the old dusty road to the barn.

Mama called out, "James! James!"

We found Papa sitting under the tree. Behind him were his mules Pete and Molly.

He looked up dejectedly and said, "Everything is all right. I saved all the animals."

The fire reflected in his eyes, and I thought how old and tired he looked. His face was smudged with dirt and soot.

He reported, "One of the cows turned over the lantern and the fire spread fast."

As yet, no neighbor had shown up to help and we had no telephone. But the next day some of the Cramers and the Thorstons came by to see what had happened. A few days later some of their hired hands came to help Papa build a protection for the animals. We knew, however, that it would take a lot of money to build another barn.

We kids always brought home the mail from the post office after school. Several months after the fire, Myrtle carried home an important-looking envelope that said "insurance" on the outside.

Papa opened the envelope in front of us and sat down on the stump by the pump. Then he started to pace around the pump, clasping his hands behind his back with the envelope sticking out.

I watched him carefully because earlier that morning when I went downstairs for some water I saw him praying on his knees with his Bible open on the couch. He always talked to God before making any decisions.

That night Papa called us together in the front room. "Well," he said, "I don't think there should be a new barn. The Cramers want to buy this land, and if I sell it to them, we won't have to build the barn. Then we can use that money to buy a house and move to Mankato."

Mama was sitting in the rocking chair. Her coarse stockings had holes in them and we could see where she mended them. Her face seemed thoughtful as she put a loose strand of gray hair back in place. Putting her hand over her mouth for a few seconds, she squinted into the distance a little. She seemed to be thinking carefully before she spoke.

"Well, James, I guess you're right. It would be better to sell."

Papa looked at her gratefully. There were never many words between them and little outward show of affection. But sometimes I could feel their love; it seemed deeper than words. They had worked this farm together, bringing us up as best they could. They had lived through the terrible dust storms and drought of 1933. They had endured hardship and bitter cold, often tramping through the snow to chop wood when our supply of coal ran out. They trusted God to bring them through. And when they leaned on each other, they were doubly strong.

A few days later Mama and Papa went to Mankato, taking along the four-gallon can of sour cream they sold weekly to a creamery for twelve dollars. These sales supplied the money we lived on in 1935.

When they returned we kids had finished the chores, except for milking the cows, which only Papa did. We had been longing for them to come home and were now waiting anxiously to hear their news.

Mama said, "We looked at several houses, but with the help of Chris, Maria, and Bertha, we found a wooden one with two nice porches. It's bigger than this house, and has a sidewalk out front and a large garden."

She continued, "Before we make up our minds, we want to go there again next week and look at two more houses. But I'm pretty sure this is the one. Your big brothers and sisters are so happy we're moving."

Just then the kitchen door opened and Joel came in. We rarely saw him since Leona's death. His face still seemed sad, and I could feel his loneliness. When he saw me looking at him he put his arms out to me. I went to him and he pulled me next to him. He put his arm around me and I snuggled close. With my head on his shoulder, he held me for what seemed a long time.

The unexpected tenderness brought tears to my eyes. He needed someone to love him, too. We didn't exchange words, but he and Papa talked about our moving.

Mama seemed so happy the next few days that her joy spilled over onto all of us. I was rejoicing that I would be seeing my older sisters much more.

Later, Papa made a deal with Mr. Cramer out in the yard, speaking German. A couple days later, Cramer's hired man came and drove all the animals up the hill over to their big farm. Papa loved the animals and had silly names for each of them. He stood and watched them go, the cows swishing their tails from side to side to ward off the flies.

He especially loved Pete and Molly, his mules. They were tied together and frolicked like children. Papa went over to them, bringing their two heads together, and hugged them. It looked like he even kissed them.

I felt sorry for Papa after all the animals were gone. He walked up to where the barn had been, shoulders drooped. It looked as if he were talking to himself. I ran up close to comfort him, but he didn't see me. Just then he turned and nearly knocked me over.

Papa and Mama agreed on the house Mama had told us about and arranged for the move. Sometime later on a blissful spring day, a truck pulled up to where all of our belongings were piled up and ready for loading. We got everything in—the boxes of Mama's dishes and pots and pans, our clothes, the leather couch and the two iron bedsteads, the dresser and the pillows, and Papa's leather chair. It seemed a horrible conglomeration of things.

Just as we were about to get into the truck, I tried to find Fluffy. We all called for him but he didn't come. I began to cry but Papa was eager to leave and wouldn't wait. Mama told me that cats take care of themselves, but I still hated leaving him.

As the truck pulled away I could see Mama turning to take a last look. I looked back too, and I thought of Mama and Papa living there for so many years, and that there, ten children had come from their union.

As we moved down to the water's edge, the house passed out of sight. The driver shifted gears and forded the river. I looked at the footbridge and wondered how many times we had crossed it and how many times Papa had rescued the boards from being washed away by the current.

I wondered too what would happen to the footbridge. But then I knew that the Cramers would circle the other way. Probably next spring, when the ice melted and big chunks came swirling down the river, the boards would be swept away.

My lovely mother, Alice Laura Hansen. She always wore her hair piled on top of her head until it became too much for her to handle. She cried when they cut it short.

My father, James Martin Hansen, came to the United States around 1900 from Copenhagen, Denmark.

Marlin joins the Navy at seventeen in February, 1944.

My beautiful sister, Myrtle Hansen Cochrane. After winning a beauty contest, she was named "Miss Consolidated of the Month."

The Hansen girls: Hazel, Pearl, Lulu, Bertha, Maria, and Myrtle.

The Hansen boys: Christian Peter, Marlin, and Joel.

I graduated at 17 from Mankato High School in 1942.

My brother Chris and his wife, Lorna.

Bertha and me standing by the cellar door in our new home in Mankato.

3

City Girl

THE MOMENT THE SUN WAS UP, I bounced out of bed, trying not to wake up Myrt as I struggled into my jeans and ran downstairs and out the door. I couldn't get over the thrill of the sidewalk under my feet. And I felt the need to be alone and think about the sudden change in our lives. I was a country girl who had come to the city, and I knew that the city was where I belonged.

The small garden to the rear of the house was just the right place for deep thoughts. It sprouted tall hollyhocks and blue wheat flowers, and buttercups grew at the base of the lone apple tree. I loved apples, and reveled in the thought of picking a winesap from a tree even here in the city.

Yet I was so accustomed to seeing our old dirt yard, void of grass or flowers, and of hearing the cows mooing, the rooster crowing, and the ducks quacking, that life here seemed too still. All this quiet took some getting used to.

Then the whippoorwill sounded, and a robin on the elm tree opposite me caught my eye as he ruffled his feathers. I realized that I would always have the singing of the birds. I said to God what Papa always said, "God is a good God." Then I added, "Thank you, God, for bringing us here. I know you did because Papa prayed. God, you are a good God."

I ran my fingers through the grass and thought it made a wonderful coat for the dirt, and how nicely the flowers decorated it. I sunk back to reminisce about the day we arrived here.

What a wonderful surprise it had been to see my brothers and sisters at the door of our new home. They had furnished it fully, buying us used furniture that was better than what we had on the farm, including a dresser with a nice mirror and a dining-room table and buffet.

Mama was so delighted as she looked around the living and dining rooms. But when she entered the kitchen and saw the new table and chairs, she stood staring at them while frowning slightly. Turning to Maria and pointing to the table, she said, "Thank you all, but you can return this. Papa and I have always sat at the old farm table, and so have you kids. It just wouldn't be home without that table. But we can keep the chairs."

Maria watched with disdain as Chris and Joel carried the old chipped table into the kitchen. Mama sat down, ran her hands across it, and set her coffee cup on it with a sigh of relief. She was home.

While we kids were running around, getting acquainted with the house, Hazel was busy cooking dinner at the wood-burning stove. She was fixing Arnie's favorite walleyed pike, caught fresh from the lake, and macaroni and cheese. On top of the new icebox, with a huge chunk of ice dripping below, sat one of Hazel's coconut cakes. Arnie and Papa were in the living room listening to the electric Philco radio, which was tuned to the baseball game on WCCO.

Maria, Bertha, and Chris's wife Lorna were chatting nonstop as they put away some of Mama's things in the buffet and arranged the table. The new dishes had little pink flowers on them and made a lovely setting with the white tablecloth and napkins that Hazel had brought. Hazel called us to tell us to wash our hands and we pumped the handle with glee. The pump caught its water from the rain, and the soap lathered easily.

Marlin had already made an acquaintance with a boy his age named Robby George, whom he brought by to introduce. I thought he was lucky to have found a friend already.

We all took our places at the table with Papa at the head, and I watched him close his eyes to say the prayer. He folded his big rough hands and said simply, "Thank you, Lord, for a safe trip, for this food, and for this home." He didn't seem as tired as usual, and I felt he must be satisfied with his decision to move to town.

We all liked to sing, and when dinner was over Bertha went to the piano. She could play chords to almost any song, and when she started to sing Mama's favorite hymn, "The Old Rugged Cross," we all joined in. Except for still missing my cat, it was a perfect day that I would never forget.

Mama's dream of a new house had come true except for the lack of running water. She was thankful to have electricity, but we still had to endure the hornet-filled outhouse. Papa called the water department and the gas company to see what could be done. But for them to install the long pipes across our wide yard was too expensive.

Papa didn't let that stop him. One morning I saw him dressed in his old blue overalls, carrying a shovel. He had decided to dig the trenches himself. When we went to say goodbye before going to school, we heard him singing, "After the ball is over, after the break of dawn, many a heart is aching, after the ball!" Papa could sing in a wonderfully natural way.

Day after day he shoveled the dirt, with Marlin helping after school. Many weeks later, he called the services and they hooked us up to both gas and water. Mama didn't have to build the fire in the kitchen stove anymore, and we had a small if somewhat inconvenient powder room. The only place we could find to put it was one of the closets.

After settling into our five-room wooden house, I started to feel like just a normal city girl—like the other kids we met. We played ball together, and we'd invite them over to our house to listen to the radio, especially the cowboy shows *Tom Mix and the Ralston Straightshooters* and *The Lone Ranger*, and the adventure show *Jack Armstrong, the All-American Boy*.

It was so exciting to live in the same town with Maria, Bertha, Chris, and Pearl, even though we didn't see them often. When Myrt and I were really lonely for Maria and Bertha, we'd go by the Saulpaugh Hotel and stand shyly by the door, peaking in. One or both were usually working, dressed in their white uniforms with black collars and black lace in their hair. If they spotted us, they'd usually give us a nickel or a dime, but we were seeking their smiles.

One morning in October 1936, Papa was reading the paper about Roosevelt's National Recovery Administration and the lines were deepening in his face. He said, "Alice, the insurance money is gone. And the old-age pension barely covers the mortgage. It says here that you can get a job working on the government-sponsored sewing project."

Mama's face fell, and although she was quiet, I could see from her eyes that she was not happy about the prospect. She had never worked outside of the home and I knew she was protesting inside. But Papa didn't seem too happy about it either.

Just then we heard someone stepping on the wooden porch and rapping the door slightly. Then Lulu Harder walked in, not waiting to be let in. Her short hair was tossed from the wind and her skirt hung down around her ankles with her heavy shoes peering underneath, but to us she looked glorious.

We were so glad she came just then. Mama got up and hugged her while Myrt and I brought her some coffee and doughnuts.

"How did you get here?" Mama asked.

"I took a bus and the driver showed me how to find you. I came to Mankato to sign up for the sewing project. Join me, Alice. It won't be so difficult with you there."

Mama had Lulu back, and now the job didn't seem so scary. They would be together again.

Papa made all the applications and a short time later Mama left for work, wearing her pink house dress and black oxford shoes. The house felt empty without her, and now when we came home for lunch, she was at work. Papa tried to fix our food, but we were hopelessly spoiled from always having Mama with us.

We also hoped none of our classmates would find out that she had to work on the WPA. But she wasn't the only one employed by the Works Progress Administration. Later on I learned that it employed over 8.5 million people during its eight years of existence.

Papa tried his best to cook for us and do the shopping. When we'd come home from school, sometimes he'd have a big bag from the baker just at the top of the Front Street hill. We would watch in anticipation as he'd take out the big sugar doughnuts, jelly-filled rolls, rye bread with caraway seeds, and lots of cookies. The bakery goods were all a day old, and he got them for just a quarter.

But however much he tried, we just couldn't get used to Papa in this role. The wood floors soon lost their polish and dust readily accumulated. Most of all, we longed for Mama.

When Mama came home one day five months later, in March, she winced in pain and looked so tired and drawn. She had fallen on the ice last year and her hip was still bothering her. And she had such difficulty rising so early to catch the bus. Mama had already worked too hard in life, and we were unhappy that she had to continue.

But our oil heater was giving us trouble and was nearly burned out. We needed more clothes and things for school, since Myrt was in junior high school and I soon would be too.

The girls and Chris and Joel would sometimes come to our aid, but they had their own work and problems. Chris was especially preoccupied ever since he found out that his little daughter was deaf. Although Lorna was a strong farm girl, she had contracted German measles when she was three months pregnant and the doctor thought this was the cause for Juanita's condition. And now Lorna was pregnant again.

Papa saw that working was no good for Mama, even though the money she earned was helping the family. He wrote to his Danish friend, Mr. Fisk, to see if he could work for him in Kellogg, a town near Rochester.

Sometime later, Papa received an answer—he was to come. Many people were out of work, but at seventy my father got a job. He drew himself up straight, touched Mama's shoulder, and said, "Quit work now, and I'll be able to send some money home."

Mama hated to see him go, but could no longer carry the heavy load. She packed a little brown cardboard suitcase with his work clothes and heavy shoes, and Chris came in his taxi to drive him to the bus station. After Papa left, Mama sat in his chair and let the tears flow.

Later, a neighbor lady came over and invited Mama to church at her home. Mama told us three kids that we had to go with her, and so on a Friday night we all went to Mrs. Hendley's. She greeted us at the door and directed us to sit on the chairs in her sparsely furnished living room. There were about fifteen of us in all.

A handsome Pentecostal preacher had his big Bible open on a podium as his buxom wife was seated at the piano. We opened our hymnbooks and began to sing, "There's power, power, wonder working power in the precious blood of the Lamb." Everyone sang with all their might.

On the way home, we asked Mama if we had to go back there. We knew she had enjoyed the evening, but we were afraid of being teased by the other kids at school. They hadn't yet found out that Mama had worked on the WPA.

Mama just smiled and volunteered nothing. She kept going each week, although not forcing us to come along. Then one Friday a month later we saw the folding chairs in our living room.

"What's going on?" we asked.

"Mrs. Hendley wanted me to have church here once in awhile."

It was what we feared. Now when the kids walked by our house and heard the singing and clapping, some of them made fun of us, calling us the "holy-roller kids." Mama had made a lot of friends, and though we complained at times, we saw she wouldn't change.

In 1937, when I turned thirteen, a tragedy occurred in Chris's family. Chris and Lorna had barely recovered from the death of their second baby, a little girl named Lavonne, when Lorna became pregnant again. She gave birth to a handsome boy named Dale Chris Hansen, who seemed perfect for the first year. Then suddenly he began to change.

After his first birthday, his physical development and mental capacity went backward and he became terribly deformed. Everything stopped growing except for his head, which got bigger. We all were haunted, and wondered what could have struck this dear little boy. The doctor said it must be some genetic disease, but he couldn't name it.

One day Lorna stood by Mama in the living room with Dale held securely in her strong arms. The little boy's tongue had grown thick and his mouth hung open, the drool sliding down his cheek.

She said, "I'm going to love this little boy and take care of him. The doctor says he can't live more than ten years." Tears welled up in her eyes as she held him tight and kissed his deformed head.

But Chris felt like a cruel joke had been played on him and for a long time seemed mad at God.

We all were upset, especially when we remembered how perfect Dale was when he was born. Mama had a river of strength, however, and didn't seem dismayed. She dearly loved little Dale and more than once said, "Take what God gives and love it. Don't you see how loving this little boy is?"

But she suffered too, although she didn't show it. One day she left her Bible opened and I saw it was turned to Job. She had outlined in red, "Though he slay me, yet will I trust in him."

On a Sunday four months later, Maria brought home a handsome man named Gordon. We hadn't seen much of her lately, and learned from Bertha that he was the reason why. We had just returned from church, so they joined us for lunch. Maria seemed to be bursting with joy.

Over ice cream and cake we found out why. "Mama," she said, "I'm sorry I didn't tell you before, but Gordon and I eloped last week. We couldn't afford a big wedding, and now we're packed for California. Gordon works with the Coca-Cola Company and is being transferred to San Diego. He has to report in ten days, so we have to go right away."

We were all stunned, and I ran upstairs to cry. I loved all my sisters but was especially close to Maria. When I pulled myself together and came back downstairs, the newlyweds were just leaving. I thought my heart would break; I couldn't bear to see Maria go. I just couldn't understand why she hadn't told me earlier.

I cried for many days after Maria left. We were happy that Bertha was still with us, but I knew that she was lonely without Maria and wanted to join her. Within a few months, Maria sent money for Bertha to go to California "for a visit," but Mama believed she probably wouldn't return. The family was being scattered.

Just then we had a letter from Papa, who said he had an ulcer on his leg that wouldn't heal. He had to quit work until it was better and was coming home. We were glad to see him, but Mama had to run up and down the stairs to care for him.

While he was out of work, the heater finally gave way and we had to buy a new one. Papa spent the money for it and now we were near destitute. Maria and Bertha sent some money home in their letters now and then, but even so, we had little left over for food.

In 1938 I was fourteen and going into the ninth grade. One day when Hazel came home she saw me coming down the stairs and exclaimed, "Lulu, you're so skinny! What's the matter?" She hugged me to herself.

Before I could answer, Mama came in from the kitchen and spoke for me. "We've been short of money since Papa got sick and we had to buy the new stove."

Hazel asked, "Why didn't you get word to me? I could have helped." She looked at me as she said, "Why don't you let Lulu come to Lake Crystal for awhile? She can go to school there. One less mouth to feed will help, and we'll take good care of her."

Mama came over to me, and said gently, "Why don't you get your clothes if you want to go. It might be the best thing. Hazel can give you things we can't—things you need."

I did go home with Hazel and her jolly husband, Arnie. She worked as a cook and baker at the cafe in Lake Crystal, and Arnie drove a caterpillar as part of the team building the new highways in Blue Earth County. They had no children and treated me as if I were their daughter.

Once I was established in the school, Hazel said, "Why don't you come to the cafe during your lunch hour at school? You can take cash and help out behind the counter, and that way you can have a nice hot lunch."

At noon, while the other kids went to the lunch room, I'd walk the block to the cafe, put on an apron, and get to work. Sometimes I'd barely squeeze in a fast lunch before dashing back to school. One day the cafe was particularly busy, and when I got back, I was tired. My teacher looked at me and said, "All work and no play makes Lulu a dull girl."

But I liked working in the restaurant, and found the business exciting. I enjoyed meeting people and hearing about their lives. After school, I'd go back to the cafe, sometimes working until Hazel finished up, and then return home with her. Working there gave me a different view of life than my fellow students had.

When my birthday came in October, Hazel and Arnie told me to go to the garage and see what was waiting for me. I didn't know what to expect, but gasped when I saw a beautiful shiny blue bicycle, complete with a silver bell. I didn't even go back to thank them, but just hopped on it and headed for Lake Crystal. I peddled all the way around it, and then downtown and back.

When I returned they couldn't imagine where I had disappeared. I just was so happy and excited to have the freedom to go anywhere I could peddle. They saw how happy they had made me, and knew I loved them dearly.

I continued in the Lake Crystal School until 1940, when I was in the tenth grade. Then I wanted to go home to spend my last two years of high school with Mama, Myrt, and Marlin. Things were a little better now as Papa was back at work and Maria and Bertha were settled in California and could help out more frequently.

In February 1941, Lorna gave birth to a beautiful little girl they named Darlene Ramona Hansen. She seemed very healthy, but so had been

Dale at birth. We all watched her very carefully and worried somewhat.

At six months, Lorna noticed a change taking place in her little girl. She was too frightened to tell anyone, but Mama saw it too. There were signs that Darlene was becoming deformed just like Dale. I was concerned about what Chris might do as he realized his daughter was losing all of her beauty. I watched him closely, for he had always been our hero.

On a hot day in August he came to the house and calmly told Mama, "I'm taking my family to San Diego. Maria says there's lots of work there in the aircraft factories because of the war in Europe. And maybe we can find a doctor there to help us. We want to make a new start."

Chris's blue eyes didn't burst with life as they usually did. It was as if he was completely numb. I watched Mama as we said goodbye to Lorna, Chris, and the three children. Sorrow filled her heart.

Quite a few years later Lorna and Chris learned the name of the affliction—Hurler's syndrome. A blood test would have revealed that they were both carriers—rare as that was—and should never have had children. They loved and cared for Dale and Darlene just the same, but the burden and sadness weighed heavily on us all.

Rumors and fears of the United States entering the war were expressed in every periodical and radio newscast. The whole world seemed to pulsate with change. I was grateful Mama had her church, because otherwise I would have worried about her. More and more she was being left alone.

On a Sunday in early December I took a walk downtown. A young newsboy was holding up a newspaper with the screeching headlines, "PEARL HARBOR BOMBED!"

I went up to him and asked, "Where's Pearl Harbor?"

He said, "It says here that it's in Hawaii. It also says that President Roosevelt calls us to war."

I took the paper home and showed it to Mama. She replied sadly, "I guess Marlin will be joining the navy. Papa said in his last letter that we were going to get into the war."

I went upstairs to be alone and think. I knew things would be different now, and that President Roosevelt was right to call December 7,

1941, "a date which will live in infamy." We had entered a time of great anxiety.

As I lay there, I thought again of my sense of destiny, which I felt even more strongly now that I was a senior in high school. I had tried to explain it to Myrt once, but she didn't understand. I knew I was destined to go somewhere, but where that was seemed a great mystery.

4

Washington Beckons

ON A PARTICULARLY COLD DAY in January 1942, Papa was sitting in his rocking chair next to the oil-burning stove and Mama was having her second cup of coffee. Myrtle and I were finishing cleaning up the supper dishes when Papa called our names. Folding our towels, we went into the living room to his side.

Our father was reading the *Mankato Free Press*, as he liked to keep us up with the events of the world. Since Pearl Harbor there was no end of things to read and discuss. The whole world was seething and changing before our very eyes, but at that moment Papa's mind was on us.

He pointed to a paragraph on the bottom of page four. "It says here that government girls are needed in Washington, D.C. It also has a form to fill out to apply." Laying the paper aside, he put his glasses back into his pocket. "It's the best thing for the two of you."

Continuing in his strong, quiet way, he said, "Myrtle, you can quit your job and leave as soon as you can. Lulu, you can go after you graduate providing you can find work and earn your fare."

Myrtle wrote immediately and received notice to report. Within a month she had quit her job at the telephone company and had her fare. I would be spending a few more months in Minnesota, as I didn't graduate until June.

During the Great Depression our family had known hunger and cold, but we had made it through together. Now that we were growing up it was time for us to make it on our own.

The day came for Myrt to leave for Washington with her friend Marge. I watched her in the mirror as she dressed and preened. Her dark brown hair gleamed and shone—those were the tresses voted most beautiful in the senior class.

"You're really pretty," I said, feeling sorry that she would be leaving and wanting to be close to her.

Myrt looked at me directly, dropping all pretenses. "Am I?" she asked, faltering somewhat. "I don't always feel so. I don't know why." She had a little frown between her eyes that appeared when she was uneasy.

I blurted out, "Just look how well you've done already—you were popular in school, your grades were good, and now you've got a great job. What are you worried about?"

"I don't know," she said. She paused and then asked, "Doesn't it bother you that we've grown up so poor?"

"We're poor, but isn't nearly everyone? I always remember what Papa says, 'This is America. You don't have to stay poor.' I really believe him, and I want to prove that he's right."

Then, wanting to make sure Myrt had no ill feelings toward me, I added, "I'm sorry for the times when I annoyed you, like over borrowing clothes. But we've had great times too—please remember them. I'm going to."

Myrt gave me her sweetest smile that showed no hidden animosity. We embraced and shed a few tears.

She turned back to the mirror, applying her rust-colored lipstick once more. Picking up her winter coat, she grabbed her suitcase and we started down the stairs. As I followed I felt gangly and unsophisticated.

In the living room Mama stood talking with Marge's parents. Mr. Ballinger kept a pipe in his mouth, biting on it, and the smell permeated the room.

I introduced myself and he asked, "Are you going, too?"

"No, not until I graduate in June."

Hearing my answer, his wife asked, "You mean that you will be leaving later—both of you will be gone?"

She looked at Mama, and Mama nodded, not showing any emotion. Mama didn't like anyone to feel sorry for her.

Marge, with kerchief tied around her blond hair and large glasses framing her face, beamed and said, "Louie is going to live with us when she comes." Turning to Myrt, she added, "We're going to need an apartment large enough for the three of us."

Myrt smiled in agreement, nodding her head. They were sweet to emphasize this for me. I kissed Marge on the cheek and hugged Myrt, saying goodbye.

Mr. Ballinger said to Mama, "Well, it's cold out there—four below zero. We better get going before the car freezes up. We'll take the girls up to Minneapolis where they can catch the train. That'll save them a few dollars, and we're going up there anyway."

Mrs. Ballinger draped her scarf around her head and said, "I'll call you once in awhile to see how you're doing."

Mother answered in her usual polite and reserved way, "Oh, that would be very nice."

Myrt kissed Mama, gently touching her smooth forehead. I saw little tears forming in Mama's eyes as Myrt said, "I'll write, I promise. Don't worry about me. I'll come back to see you when I can."

Myrt blew me a kiss as she went out the door and walked toward the car with the others. We had to close the door fast, as the cold air was rushing in. After scraping an opening in the frosty window, we watched the car pull away. Myrt looked back and waved until we could see her no longer.

Mama sighed and went over to her rocking chair, where she opened her Bible. The Psalms were her favorite, giving her peace and solace. I looked at her and thought how pretty she was, with her soft gray hair framing her face.

That day she wasn't able to look to Papa for support, for he was in Kellogg to help out Mr. Fisk who had hurt his back. Papa and Myrt had exchanged their goodbyes over the phone this morning, one of our few long-distance calls.

Suddenly excited about having the bedroom to myself, I bounded up the stairs. Myrt was gone and soon I would be too. Now I had to figure out how to make the money to get to Washington. Papa couldn't help— and I wouldn't ask him anyway.

Propping my head up on the pillows and snuggling under the cozy quilt, I began to devise a plan. I knew right away that I didn't want any boyfriends, as they would just complicate my life. Dating was not important compared with working in Washington.

I had a thought—the *Mankato Free Press*. Glancing through the want-ad section, I found it—an advertisement for someone to be a "mother's helper on weekends." It sounded perfect.

I telephoned the lady and made an appointment for after school on Monday. The next step would be to find a job for mid-June to mid-August, but that would have to wait for now.

"Good!" I said to myself. Having decided my course of action, I dressed in my snow pants, jacket, scarf, boots, and mittens. The front door was closing as I called out to Mama, "Going for a walk! Be right back!"

The frost was glistening and swirling around like silver needles as I pulled my scarf over my face. Just my eyes peered out at the sparkling white world around me. Ah—my hometown in Minnesota! I rolled the word on my tongue. It was an Indian name meaning the land of sky blue water. And so it was, with its ten thousand lakes and more shore line than any other state in the union. What a town to grow up in, Mankato, Minnesota!

Much as I loved this little place, I knew I couldn't stay because it didn't and couldn't contain all my hopes and dreams. Although I wasn't able to explain it, I felt called elsewhere. I was set on a journey and this seemed like my last time to say goodbye to childish things of the past.

I made my way up the Good Counsel hill, slipping and sliding on the ice and grabbing onto trees for support. Finally I made it up to our trysting tree, a gnarled birch where Myrt, Marlin, and our friends had carved their initials. I leaned against the old tree and whispered, "You're going to stay here making this hill beautiful, but I'm going on to I know not where."

Something caught the corner of my eye. I went over to investigate and saw a large cardboard box peeking out of the snow. A toboggan! Jumping onto it, I started down the steep hill, gaining speed while flying over bushes and rocks and narrowly missing the large trees. "Whee!" I cried with delight.

As I approached the bottom I was heading straight for a large prickly bush. Before colliding with it I rolled off into the surrounding snow, saving myself cuts and bruises. For a few moments I lay there in relief, reveling in the winter wonderland. As I watched the frost dart through the air I laughed for joy. It was the happiest of times.

But then the moment passed, and I felt like I woke up. From now on, I vowed, I was going to be serious—and make my dreams come true. It was time to head home.

I trudged back, shoving my hands into my pockets. Through the mitten I could feel a coin—a quarter! Myrt must've left it there yesterday. Putting serious thoughts behind me, I said to myself, "Hey, I should get some ice cream!"

The corner grocery store was open. "Kind of cold for ice cream," I said to Mr. Olsen, "but it's refreshing. How about a pint of strawberry?"

"Sure, Lulu. Your cheeks are mighty rosy, young lady."

I laughed and agreed. "I've been walking up by the Good Counsel hill. The frost flying around is so beautiful."

"Well, you young people don't get cold, but I do. Here you go," he said, handing me the ice cream.

I gave him the quarter, and he handed me eleven cents change. Mr. Olsen had owned this store for thirty-five years and managed it himself again, as his son had just gone into the navy.

"Thanks," I said. "Have you heard from Harvey lately?"

"Yes, he's in Virginia. Can't wait until he comes home."

I noted the emotion in his voice. Nodding quietly, I thanked him and walked back into the cold. Mr. Olsen had done so many kind things over the years. When we and others couldn't afford groceries, he let us charge them, sometimes running up bills as high as twenty-five dollars. He was a good man.

Once home, I smelled Mama's coffee brewing in its blue pot on the stove and enjoyed the warmth of the house. The ice cream looked and smelled delightful as I divided it between two of our best dishes. It had large pieces of strawberries in the good old-fashioned way.

Mama and I enjoyed the rich ice cream together. She seemed happier now, and her quiet confidence was also mine.

Winter turned into spring—lakes and rivers melted, flowers blossomed, and we rejoiced. Making it through another cold Minnesota winter was cause to celebrate.

Meantime, news of the war was heating up. Many of the young fellows in town were joining the services, and I, too, was preparing to do my part. I wasn't interested in going to the prom or other events, because I was working toward my goal. All winter I had cared for a little boy named Paul, earning three dollars a weekend and saving fifty dollars in all. I was careful with my money.

33

On my last Saturday night of looking after Paul, his mother came into his bedroom to say goodnight. She was dressed in pale lavender, the same color my mother loved, and her blond hair was styled fashionably in a french twist. She saw how I admired her.

Calling downstairs to her husband, she said, "Honey—can you wait a second? I'll be right down."

She motioned for me to sit across from her on Paul's stool.

"Little Lulu," she said, using her favorite name for me and smiling. "You remind me of myself when I was your age—ambitious, energetic, enthusiastic. I'd like to give you some important advice that my beautiful grandmother gave me."

Her soft brown eyes were sincere as she continued. "She said to me that a young girl should remember that she will not always be young. She told me not to do anything that would dissipate my beauty: Don't smoke; drink only a little wine. Exercise and eat well."

Then she added, "I must go now, but listen to this advice. Someday, when you are older, you will thank me." She kissed Paul goodnight and went to join her husband.

Her words made sense to me. I didn't mind not having boyfriends these last few months before going to Washington, but I hoped that someday I would have a dashing young man to love. I took her advice and began to read health books and exercise.

In early June, a week before graduation, I answered an advertisement in the paper: "Wanted: salad cook and waitress. Apply in person at Woolworth's on Front Street." My experience in the Lake Crystal restaurant gave me the courage to persuade the sleepy-eyed manager that I was the salad cook and waitress he was looking for.

I had the keys to the dime store and began my days there at dawn. Mr. Reynolds gave me precise instructions on what to do: "Always keep seven dozen cold eggs in the refrigerator. Put them on to boil each morning and save them for the following day. Cut up the cold eggs for egg salad and potato salad. Light the coffee urns. Cut up cabbage, celery, and carrots for coleslaw. Put chicken on to boil for chicken salad."

When lunch time came, I put on a clean pink uniform and went to work behind the counter.

"Give me a strawberry shake!"

I'd dip the ice cream, squirt out the strawberry, add milk, and shake.

"I'd like a banana split."

I'd cut the banana lengthwise, arrange it on a glass dish, add three flavors of ice cream, squirt chocolate on the top, and add nuts.

"How about an egg salad sandwich."

I'd put the bun on a plate, add a little lettuce and the egg salad, and serve the sandwich.

The job seemed easy and came naturally to me, and customers gave me tips. Sometimes they gave me pennies; sometimes nickels; occasionally they gave a dime. I kept all the change and threw it into a pint jar at home. Not only was I saving for my twenty-eight dollar bus fare, but also to buy Mama a nice dress and myself some new clothes.

My last working day was August 13, 1942. Mama met me at the end of the day and we went around the corner to Salet's fine department store. It was so much fun to pick out a new wardrobe. I chose a baby-blue checked dress and a pink dress, both with white collars and cuffs, and my favorite, a navy-blue suit. I also purchased two white blouses and a white sweater. At the stocking counter I bought two pairs of luxurious silk stockings with black seams. My first!

Then Mama picked out her dress in pale lavender with flouncy sleeves. It felt like Christmas as we took our packages home.

The next day was Friday, August 14, a day I had circled in my calendar for months to mark my departure. Now it was my turn to stand before the mirror and primp, fixing my hair and makeup, adjusting my new blue dress, and checking on my silk stockings and first pair of high-heeled shoes. My legs looked so different from when I wore bobby socks and sport shoes.

When Myrt was getting ready to leave, she had been reluctant and a little fearful. I was not. I was happy, as I was sure that it was right for me to go. I gathered my purse, suitcase, and the bag of hangers Myrt had told me to bring, saying, "If you don't, you won't have anything to hang your clothes on."

Before leaving I paused as the memories from my bedroom rushed over me. I said goodbye to the chipped iron bed, the sagging mattress, the small closet, and the dresser and mirror. Next I would say goodbye to Papa.

He was forced to stay upstairs in bed as the huge sore on his leg was back. His leg was propped up on some pillows and he was applying hydrogen peroxide and Lysol directly on the wound, wincing a little and wrapping it with white bandages.

He said, "You're ready to go, Lulu. Here, I have something for you."

Reaching into his shirt pocket, he carefully unfastened the safety pin that always kept the pouch closed. Ever since I could remember this was where Papa kept his money. Every time he took some out to treat us kids or pay household bills he would shield the contents from our prying eyes. This time he didn't bother. Taking out a ten-dollar bill, he handed it to me.

I held it in my hand but didn't want to take it, for I had earned enough to get by. But then I saw the expression in Papa's eyes and knew that his gift was an expression of words that he had never said and probably could never say. The money amounted to a third of his pension.

When I bent to kiss him and say goodbye, he rested his hand on my head. I knew that he was pronouncing a blessing on me. But I didn't know that this was the last time I'd ever see him.

Mama was waiting for me downstairs, and accompanied me on the local bus to the Greyhound terminal. She was wearing her lavender dress, and every time she moved her flouncy sleeves danced around her arms.

She found it hard to speak out, and sometimes I wished I could read her mind. If her pale gray eyes revealed anything today, it was that she knew I would be all right. Though I knew she would miss me, I was grateful that she hadn't bound me, her youngest daughter, to herself. I also knew that with her strong faith she too would be all right.

As I was leaving, Mama said, "I've placed you in God's hands, Lulu," and a little tear ran down her cheek.

I kissed it away and the salty taste stayed in my mouth as I boarded the bus. I waved goodbye until she faded from view.

II

A Capital City

5

"Haven't we met?"

I FELT QUITE GROWN UP as I settled back in my seat on the bus. Our first stop would be Minneapolis, and in the morning we would reach Chicago. No one sat beside me so I was able to stretch out as I made notes in my little diary. After Minneapolis, I fell asleep and slept nearly the whole night.

In the morning, the girl who sat ahead of me turned around and introduced herself. "Hi! I'm Karen. I'm on my way to Washington."

"So am I! I'm going to Washington, D.C. You too?"

"No, I'm going to Seattle, Washington. I want to get as far away from here as I can."

She was quite beautiful with her jet black hair and dark eyes, but she looked sad and hurt. Intrigued, I asked if she had time to join me for breakfast before the next bus left.

We found two places at the counter, and she poured out her troubles.

"I worked in a restaurant in Minneapolis. I made the mistake of falling in love with the Greek boss, and I thought he would leave his wife for me. Then I found out he had many other girlfriends." Tears rolled down her face. "Have to leave this area and start again. I want to get as far away from him as I can."

I tried to comfort her, but didn't know what to say. As we parted, her unhappy face stayed in my mind.

I was still thinking of her when I nearly ran into a young fellow waiting in line to board the bus. His resemblance to the current heart-throb—Johnny Garfield—was startling. Dressed in a beige jacket and an open-collared white shirt, he stood blocking my way, an unruly curl dangling on his forehead. He gestured the curl away, but it sprang right back.

He blurted out, "Haven't I seen you somewhere before?"

Catching me by surprise, I answered dumbly, "Maybe."

We stood looking at each other. Others, irritated that we were blocking the entrance, pushed us along. I went toward the back to my familiar seat. Under my breath, I said, "What was that all about?"

I tried to read the *Chicago Tribune*. Roosevelt . . . Pearl Harbor . . . England and France . . . Churchill . . . Hitler rampaging through Europe. It was all somewhat overwhelming.

I glanced up to the seventh row. "Johnny Garfield" saw me look at him and turned away. I stared out the window as we passed a big flatbed truck loaded with scrap metal. Must be for the war effort, I thought.

We came to another stop and got out for refreshments. I didn't see him at first, but then noticed him gesturing and chatting with another fellow. I tried to pay no attention.

We got on the bus again and I had two seats to myself, as the elderly lady who boarded in Chicago had got off at the last stop. I closed my eyes and fell asleep next to the window.

When I woke up, he was beside me. I looked right into his face, as he was staring into mine.

"More air back here."

"Oh!" laughing to myself. I thought, "What an excuse!"

"So where are you going anyway?" His brown eyes were captivating.

"Washington, D.C."

"Where are you from, the farm?"

I wondered if he was putting me down and didn't answer.

The tone of his voice sounded a little arrogant. "We're coming into Pennsylvania. Say, I'm Turkish. What are you?"

I realized I had never met anyone Turkish before. "My father came from Denmark," I said.

"What does he do?"

"He was a farmer, but he isn't working now. We moved to the city five years ago."

"Oh, so you're a city girl now! First pair of high heels?"

"I've had them awhile," I said, not letting on that I had bought them only last month.

"How old are you anyway?"

"Seventeen."

"Your mama let you leave home at seventeen?"

"I have a job—in the government," I said, still rejoicing at the thought of it.

He seemed to doubt me, saying, "Show me your papers."

I opened my purse and we looked them over together.

"Yeah, you've got a job all right."

Did I notice a little admiration in his eyes?

The bus stopped in Washington, Pennsylvania, where we had to claim our luggage and transfer it to another bus.

My new acquaintance took charge and said, "Give me your tickets. Say, what's your name, anyway?"

"Lulu. Lulu Hansen."

"What else do they call you?"

"Louie."

"Louie. I like that."

I asked, "Well, what's your name?"

"Ulysses."

"What else do they call you?"

"Useless."

"I'll call you Ulysses." I liked the sound of it.

I saw him look up at a sign on the restaurant outside. "DON'T HURRY. WE NEVER CLOSE," it proclaimed in big letters.

Ulysses pointed to it and said, "Someday I'm going to open up my own hot-dog stand."

I noticed a certain conviction in his voice and replied, "Oh, that's how I earned enough money to leave home. I worked as a salad cook and waitress. Well, just for a little while."

He gave me a look that said he didn't think I could be much of a cook. "Do you type?" he asked.

"Certainly, and shorthand too!"

"Learn all that in school?"

"Yes. And I can cook and sew my own clothes."

Then he had a rather apologetic look and said, "Say, I'm not really Turkish, though my father was born in Istanbul. I'm Greek."

"Then why did you say you were Turkish?"

"Just wanted to see what you would say."

He smiled then. He looked great smiling.

As the terrain outside the window began to change, I asked, "Are those mountains?"

He teased me, "You're a real hillbilly aren't you? Never seen a mountain before?"

I didn't reply.

After a few stops, he said, "We're coming into Baltimore. Won't be long now. How about giving me your address and phone number?"

As I wrote it in his little book, I noticed a few other names there too.

"Anyone going to meet you?" he asked.

"Yes, my sister Myrtle. She also works in Washington."

I noticed he kept studying my address. He asked, "You live on Sixteenth Street?" Then he looked again, saying, "Sixteenth Street, Northeast! You wouldn't know it but there's a big difference between northeast and northwest."

We pulled into the depot on New York Avenue. Through the window I saw Myrtle waiting for me, dressed in a new pale blue plaid suit with a blouse that had a frothy lacy collar. She looked great and I said to Ulysses, "See, there's Myrtle—standing right across there by the door."

"Oh, so that's your sister," he said, and for a moment I thought he was going to whistle. "She's very nice looking," he said, turning back to me.

We got off the bus and walked over to her. I introduced them, saying, "Myrtle, meet Ulysses. We've been riding together since we met in Chicago."

Ulysses said, "Glad to meet you, Myrtle." And to me he said, "I'll call you." His brown eyes seemed to hold a promise as he left us, and for a few moments my eyes followed him.

Myrt was saying, "How was the trip? You're probably awfully tired. The train I took was hard enough, but the bus!"

I noticed Myrt smelled of cigarettes. I asked, "Have you started to smoke?"

"Oh Louie, everyone smokes."

"Well, let everyone smoke. I'm not going to."

"How's Mama? Is she all right? How was she when you left?"

"Well, poor Papa has his ulcer back on his leg, and Mama goes up and down the stairs caring for him all the time. It's hard on her." Then I added, "I bought her a new dress before I left—pale lavender, of course. She wore it to the bus depot, and I'm sure she'll wear it to church on Sunday."

Then I complimented Myrt, saying, "You looked so pretty when we saw you out the window. I just love that suit!"

As we started moving to the area to pick up my luggage, Myrt said, "I've got a boyfriend—good old Billy. You'll meet him later."

I knew Myrt and her boyfriends. She never liked one for very long, but tired of them easily. Already she was calling him "good old Billy."

I was hoping to see Ulysses again by the luggage counter, but he was nowhere.

Then I looked among the newly unloaded baggage for my suitcase, but it wasn't there. Nor was the bag of hangers Myrtle had told me to bring, which Ulysses thought was so dumb, saying "We have hangers in Washington." Finally I gave the porter a quarter and my ticket to see if he could find my suitcase. He brought me a small square bag with travel stickers on the outside.

"Here it is."

"But that's not my bag."

"The numbers match, miss."

I said to Myrtle, knowing her quick temper and how mad she would get, "I guess Ulysses got my ticket and I have his stuff."

"Of all the dumb things to do. Now you don't even have any clothes. Come on! We'll get on the street car." She gave a familiar jerk of her head indicating she was disgusted with me. Suddenly, I felt more than a little unwelcome and somewhat deflated.

We arrived at the narrow row house set among other look-alike houses. I followed Myrtle down the steps to the basement apartment. Once inside, she pointed to the couch. "This opens up into a bed, and it's where you'll sleep. Before you go to work, make the bed and fold it up again. Margie and I have the bedroom and I didn't think it was fair to move her out here."

She added, "She won't be home until late tonight. She has a date."

As I looked around, I saw a player piano in the corner, a table and four chairs, a few knickknacks, and a small buffet. A tiny kitchen was on the left with a door leading to the backyard. In between was the small bathroom and the bedroom on the right.

She opened the refrigerator, still giving directions in a short, clipped manner. "This is your corner. You'll have to buy your own groceries."

We then walked to the bedroom and she opened the closet, "This is your space—when you get something to put in it." Disdain again.

We heard a knock on the door, and my heart leaped. But it wasn't Ulysses, it was Myrt's boyfriend, Billy Barton, a tall, skinny fellow. Myrt introduced me to him and he made himself right at home, kissing her on the cheek and sitting down on my bed couch. Oh, how I wanted to lie down on it.

Myrtle brought him a Coke. Then she turned to me, "Well, did you give this guy your address?"

"What guy?" Billy asked.

"She met a guy on the bus. He switched tickets and she lost her clothes. His name is Ulysses."

Billy lifted his eyebrows, went over to the player piano, and put in a roll. He pumped fast with his long legs, singing along with the music. "She'll be coming round the mountain when she comes." He couldn't sing.

Myrtle went into the bedroom and came out dressed in a fitted white chenille robe. Billy whistled. She went into the kitchen and began to make some dinner. I didn't know if I was welcome to join in or not, but I took a chance. "Can I help set the table or something?"

"The dishes are in that little cupboard. You'll also find a cloth and some napkins in there."

We were ready to be seated. Myrtle had only two pork chops, but she seemed willing to share hers with me. A knock came on the door. Billy went to answer it, and I heard him say, "You must be the wandering Ulysses!"

In he came. Billy introduced himself and Ulysses said "Hi!" but I noticed that his eyes were on me.

He came right to my side, saying, "Here's your suitcase." Then he said softly, "Go change into something else, and let's go out. Oh! Here are your hangers!" He smiled. It had become a joke between us.

I went into the bedroom, hung up my things in my little space, washed, put on my new fussy-collared blouse and slightly wrinkled skirt, squirted myself with Myrt's perfume, and did my lipstick and hair. I reappeared feeling amazingly fresh and anxious to go.

I said, "Myrt, Ulysses and I are going out for awhile. Do I need a key?"

"No. Don't be too late though."

She had warmed up to me again, though now she sounded a little apprehensive. She walked with us outside.

Ulysses opened the door of his gray Plymouth 1939 convertible. I smiled at Myrt as we drove off and hoped she couldn't see the triumph I felt.

The top was down, and the wind blew my hair. We were listening to Glenn Miller's great music, and I glanced at Ulysses' profile as he drove. Yep! He sure was a Johnny Garfield look-alike.

We were quiet, just riding and listening to the music. When I couldn't think of what to say, I asked, "Where are we going?"

"To a place called the Fat Boy."

I noticed a sign marking Bladensburg Road and then in the distance the sign for the Fat Boy.

We were soon seated on the top balcony. Ulysses was very hungry and looked around impatiently for the waiter. After ordering hamburgers and milk shakes, he moved closer to me and looked at me pensively.

"You know, I thought about this while on the bus, but I didn't tell you then. You don't know how close we came to missing each other." His eyes held mine for a moment.

"You see, my folks lived at Fourteenth and U. Then we bought a house at Fifth and Buchanan, Northwest. While the move was going on, I told Ma that I would go to Chicago and stay with our old friends the Meltons. Their son, Nick, and I are good buddies."

He paused and then continued, "Well, the night before I met you, I said goodbye to the Meltons. Nick was working and didn't come with me, so I left to catch the bus to Washington. When I got to the station, I was over two hours early." He took a drink of water, and I did too.

"I didn't know what to do with myself, so I decided to take in a movie. There was a drugstore nearby, so I asked the guy if I could leave my suitcase there. He said sure. I went around the corner, took in a cowboy show, and didn't get back until a little after nine. The bus wouldn't have come until 9:45. But the guy at the drugstore didn't tell me that he closed at nine."

As he spoke, I could just see how frustrated he would be.

"There I was, looking right through the window at my case but I couldn't get it. I couldn't believe it!"

"What did you do then?"

"Well, I went back and stayed at the Meltons and caught the bus in the morning. I don't understand how I missed that other bus, but maybe now I'm glad. What do you think?"

He sure was afraid to commit himself. I smiled and said, "Well, I'm kind of glad too." I was more glad than I showed.

He squeezed my hand and kissed me lightly on the cheek.

I wanted to find out more about him. "We've got a lot of catching up to do," I said. "How about telling me about yourself? I'd like to know in case someone asks!" I meant it jokingly.

The hamburgers came, and in between gulps of chocolate shake and bites of food he opened up to me. His life was already quite busy and fascinating.

"You haven't been to any of the places I'm going to mention, Louie, but just listen because I intend to take you everywhere."

Why did I feel so warm and comfortable with him?

He continued, "We used to live in Georgetown at 2919 M Street. There my father ran a lunch place called 'The Expert Lunch,' for the simple reason that he considered himself an expert chef."

He smiled that cute smile again.

"Well, when I was eight or so, he let me run my first little business, selling snowballs. Papa humored me and helped me set it up on the sidewalk." He wiped off the ketchup stuck on his face.

"We lived on top of the store in an apartment. But a lot of people said that our living room used to be George Washington's library. They'd come to see the carved mantle, taking pictures of it. Others would stand across the street with their easels and paint the building. My father is from the old country and thought they were nuts." He paused for another bite of his burger.

"When I was twelve or thirteen, I spent my summer vacations working down at the Northeast Market, at Pete Pappas and Sons. Mr. Pappas was a great guy. But every time I would leave for work, Mama would say, 'Close your ears to all the nasty words they use around those markets, and don't ever let me hear one coming out of your mouth.' There I learned to put the bad oranges on the bottom and the good oranges on the top. I gave all my money, except a quarter, to Mama. She needed it."

He paused for a moment and asked, "Louie, am I boring you? I'm doing all the talking."

"No, please keep on! I really want to hear about you."

He seemed pleased that I was so interested. "Well, we have friends of the family, Theon and his wife Merope. Theon was maître d' at the Wardman Park Hotel, and when I was seventeen—hey, I was your age!" That cute smile again. "He put me to work at the Wardman as a busboy. He didn't favor me over anybody else. In fact, he was stricter with me. In the morning, when all of us guys would report for work, he'd line us up. Our fingernails had to be clean, our shoes had to be shined, and our shirts had to be snow white. Mama kept mine nice." He smiled again.

"Our black pants had to be pressed with a good crease in them and our tie had to be perfect. He was strict, but growing up under a strict boss is the best thing that can happen to a young guy."

He turned to me then and said, "Louie, you'll be meeting all these people—I just know somehow that you will."

I wanted to meet them, and was so glad that he would make me a part of his life.

He went on talking, "After I qualified for that job, I moved around quite a bit. I ended up working at the Mayflower Hotel on Connecticut Avenue. That's where they have the Easter Parade, up by Dupont Circle. All the ladies dress up in their finest, along with their husbands and children. A beautiful sight!"

He paused, took another bite and a gulp, and continued, "I also worked in room service. Boy, the sights you see then, especially the day I delivered the cart to Alice Faye's room! Boy, was she beautiful!"

Then he smiled at me, and said, "You're not as beautiful as you're going to be when you get older. Right now you're just kind of cute." He was being nice to me.

"I wasn't old enough to be a full-fledged waiter. Then I got to thinking—I can't be a waiter all my life. The hours are too long. Maybe I should find a job in the government. Maybe it would be more prestigious." He gestured, rolling his eyes.

"I applied and ended up delivering papers from one office to another. I guess I was the office boy. My boss was a beautiful Greek lady, Ann Papps Commanduras. The first day I went to work I enjoyed it a lot. I had regular hours and I worked from nine to five. I felt like a big shot.

"Then Mrs. Commanduras said to me, 'You don't have to come to work tomorrow, it's a holiday.' 'Holiday,' I said, feeling disappointed. She said, 'The government closes up, Ulysses. It's the Fourth of July. Don't worry, you'll get paid.' I wasn't worried about being paid—I just wanted to work! Mrs. Commanduras laughed and laughed over that."

I could just see him, the eager-beaver.

He continued, "After that job, I went to the Government Printing Office to learn the printing trade, you know, paper hat and all that, running the presses." I nodded.

"That's where I'm working now, but I know what my next job is— I've enlisted. They say if you enlist, you get your choice. Guess the army is the best for me. Can't see myself a sailor."

I couldn't imagine him as a sailor either.

We finished eating and walked hand-in-hand to the car.

"I'm going to give you a glimpse of the Capitol building at night before I take you home. So how do you like my town so far? Are you glad you left the farm?"

I answered with a smile and said, "I'm more than glad." I knew he was teasing again.

We parked with the view of the grand silhouette of the Capitol in the background. No lights were shining.

Ulysses said, "You should see it when it's lit up!"

I answered, "I'll bet it's beautiful. It looks wonderful even now."

It was just after midnight when I came home to the apartment. Margie had just gotten in a few minutes before and was drinking a glass of milk. The white liquid stuck to her upper lip as she said, "You just got here, you've dated, and you're just now coming home! You're the fastest operator I've ever seen!"

I hadn't known Margie all that well in school as she was a year ahead of me. I just gave her my best smile. Her violet eyes were magnified by her thick glasses, but when she removed them, they suddenly looked pink and small.

Too tired to talk, I looked around the room and saw that Myrt had graciously made up my bed. I didn't even wash my face, but lay down and slept, and slept, and slept. This was now home.

6

Could it Be Love?

I SMELLED THE AROMA OF COFFEE and thought for a few moments that I was back in Minnesota with Mama. But when I opened my eyes, I realized I was in my new bed-living room. The white lacy curtains swayed gently in the breeze and I caught the scent of the climbing rose-bush outside the window. I saw it first when Myrt brought me down the stairs—was it only yesterday?

My clothes from last night were lying on the flowered chair, for I had been too tired to hang them up. When I got out of bed, the soft blue rug felt so much better than the hardwood floors at home.

Sleepy and still rubbing my eyes, I walked into our small kitchen. The outside door was ajar, and sunlight and a nice breeze filtered in. I made my way outside to the enclosed garden and the crepe Myrtle tree. Clapping my hands with glee, I spotted a red cardinal up in the purple blossoms of the tree. What a wonderful sight for my first morning here.

I picked Myrt one of the tree's blossoms as I went back inside, smiling at how appropriate it was for it to grow in our yard.

Myrt came out of the bedroom, her face stripped bare of makeup and her dark hair pulled over to one side by a white scarf. Her white robe was partially opened, revealing suntanned legs. She was pretty all right.

"Good morning, Louie. How'd you sleep? We tried to be quiet and not wake you. It's eleven o'clock!"

"I slept so soundly. I sure was exhausted!"

She lit a cigarette, wrinkling her upper lip. Because I knew Papa wouldn't approve, I fought against frowning at her and didn't say a word.

She volunteered, "A cup of coffee and a cigarette in the morning, and I don't have any problems. I'm regular as clockwork."

"Is that right?"

Marge came with her cigarette. She apparently had heard what Myrt said, for she chimed in, "Keeps me regular too." We all laughed.

I saw their box of Wheaties and asked, "Mind if I have some?"

I was crunching away when Myrt said, "Please forgive me for the way I acted when you first came. I felt bad about it all night. I guess it made me mad to think that I was stuck with a dumb kid. But I should have remembered how confident you always are."

She paused for a moment to inhale from her cigarette, and continued. "When I saw you climb into Ulysses' car and the way he looked at you, you seemed to trust him. He has a protective way about him, doesn't he?"

"Well, ever since I saw him getting on the bus, it's as if I've known him for a long time. Even his remark, 'Haven't I seen you before,' makes me think he feels the same way. It seems like I'm in a dream."

Marge didn't agree. "I don't believe in love at first sight. You'll get over it as soon as he leaves. After all, there are plenty of fish in the sea— and you haven't even seen the sea!"

Myrt added, "If you're anything like me, you'll get bored with him after two weeks. As soon as a guy starts telling me he loves me and wants to mess around, I just can't stand him anymore."

She put out her cigarette and looked a little sad as she said, "I'm already getting sick of Billy. In the beginning it was great, but now he's always hanging around."

"I thought you liked him yesterday."

"Oh well, that's the way it goes."

I didn't want her to be depressed, so I said, "Maybe you just haven't met the right guy yet. Time will tell. All I know is that right now I've never been so happy. I'm glad to be here and can't wait to start working. Papa was so wonderful to direct us here."

"Are you always so darn serious?" Marge asked, exhaling smoke through her nose.

"What do you mean?"

"Well, don't you want to play around and just have some fun? This is a big town and there are lots of guys all over the place." Margie gulped her coffee and sat back, holding her Lucky Strike high.

She continued, "Louie, let me give you some advice. Myrt and I have been here for seven months and we're two years older than you. Don't get hung up on any guy yet. Play the field! Find out what there is."

"You don't know me very well, but I'm not the playgirl type. Maybe you're right, that I'm much too serious. Always have been, and probably always will be. And I don't like playboys either."

"How do you know Ulysses isn't a playboy?"

"I don't. But I guess I'll find out."

The phone rang, and since I was the closest to it, I answered.

"Morning, Kid. Sleep well?"

My heart fluttered as I answered, "Like a log."

"Poor me. They called me early this morning and asked me to come into work. I wasn't supposed to report back until Monday, but the Government Printing Office has a special big job the government has to get out today. Hear the presses rolling?"

"Oh, so that's what I'm hearing."

"Yep. Well, I have to get right back. Can I pick you up at seven? We'll go eat and maybe take in a movie or something."

"I'll be ready!"

When I turned around, Margie said, "Look at her face. I do believe she's blushing."

Yes, my cheeks were a little warm.

She added with a little flourish, "What time is he coming? I want to meet him!"

"Seven o'clock. I want you to meet him, too!"

I washed my dishes, made up the bed, and did my laundry and hair. Marge told me where the District Grocery Store (DGS) was and I walked up to the end of the block, past the other row houses. Lots of kids were playing ball in the street and pulling their wagons. I called out a greeting and waved, and they laughed and waved back.

The DGS reminded me of the corner grocery store at home. When I went to pay, I saw the ten-dollar bill from Papa still nestled in the corner of my wallet. "I'll save that for an emergency," I thought.

I wasn't a bit homesick, but I bought a three-cent stamp to mail Mama and Papa a letter. I didn't think I should spend money on a phone call; they wouldn't be worrying about me that much anyway.

I carried my groceries back and replenished what I had borrowed. It felt good to be purely independent.

It was six o'clock before Marge and Myrt were finished with the bathroom and I could take a shower. Saturday night! Me—going out on Saturday night! I remembered back to all the Saturday nights when I took care of little Paul. Then I thought of his sweet mother's advice for taking care of myself and realized I hadn't done my exercises in quite a few days. I would get right back to it.

51

I began to sing:

Thanks for the memories
Riding the bus with you,
Talking with you, too,
Thank you so much.

Thanks for the memories
Friday night in Washington
And Saturday night, too,
Thank you, Ulysses, so much.

It was just past seven when I was in the kitchen and heard the knock on the door. Margie must have been right there waiting for she was already opening it. She was a picture dressed in a tight-fitting red sweater and skirt. Was she trying to impress Ulysses or test him out? I stood to the side and allowed her to pull her little act.

Ulysses stood in the doorway, dressed up in a navy-blue jacket. Impressed, Marge said, "Well! So you're Ulysses. Let me give you a great big hug!"

Before Ulysses could answer, Marge wrapped herself around him and pulled him close. Ulysses didn't seem too pleased. As he disentangled himself, he said coldly, "It's nice meeting you too, Marge."

Marge was smart enough to notice and stepped back. She seemed amazed that he was not one of the pushover guys she was used to. He came over and put his arm around me, just as Myrt walked into the living room dressed in bright yellow. She asked us, "Where are you guys going tonight?"

I didn't know, but Ulysses answered, "To Haje's Chicken in the Rough."

Just then Billy came sauntering in, cracking a crooked but charming smile. I saw the look of love he gave Myrt and felt sorry for him, remembering her remark of this morning.

Marge had plans to go to a party with some friends. Ulysses leaned over to me and whispered, "Say goodbye, and let's go."

As we made for the door, I called out, "Goodbye everyone!"

As soon as we got into the car, Ulysses pulled me into his arms. It was a cloudless and beautiful evening, just made for convertibles. He turned on the radio and Bing Crosby was crooning, "Be careful, it's my heart. It's not my watch you're wearing, it's my heart. It's yours to take, to keep or break. . . ."

This was the Saturday night of my dreams; the night I'd been waiting for. It was worth every moment of all the lonely times and all the hard work.

Ulysses spoke in a serious tone, "Louie, I only have another month here with you. Today I got my report to appear at the induction center and then to Fort Lee, Virginia, on September 17, just before my twenty-first birthday."

I squeezed his hand.

He continued, "The way Margie acted, well, did you say you had older sisters in California?"

"Yes, I have two older sisters there and a brother. Why?"

"Because." Then he stopped and refused to say more about it. "Look, we'll talk about this later. I don't want to right now."

I wondered to myself, "What does he mean about California?" In some ways he reminded me of Papa, like his old-world way of arranging things. I didn't press him, but let the subject drop. He'd bring it up again when he was ready—I knew that much about him.

Sitting close to him, feeling his hand around mine, it was as if we were the only two in the world. His car seemed like a golden chariot that we could keep on driving forever, feeling the breeze against our faces and listening to music—both on the radio and inside.

We made it to the restaurant and ordered our food. When it arrived, Ulysses reached over and broke off a piece of the soft roll. He dipped it in the honey and put it in my mouth. When I ate it, honey dripped on my lips. He reached over and kissed me, saying, "Sweetest kiss I ever had."

He held my face close to his, the honey now on both of our lips. His eyes looked deeply into mine as he said, "I want to teach you some Greek. Say, 'se aga po.'"

I repeated the words, 'se aga po.'"

He smiled that cute smile again and began to eat.

"What does 'se aga po' mean?"

"Well, you'll find out someday." He laughed again, and I smiled at his little joke. He'd tell me in due time.

He was so hungry that he ordered extra french fries, and then reached over and took part of my chicken.

"From here, Kid, we'll drive to Haines Point. Got a lot of memories about that place."

"Is it far from here?"

"No, it's just down by the Jefferson Memorial."

Everything was so new to me. There were so many places to see!

Ulysses continued, "Haines Point is right near the Potomac, and sometimes there are band concerts. Ever been to a band concert?"

"Sure have. Sometimes they're the only thing going on in a small town."

He offered me some of the crisp french fries. He said, "Well, Kid, I never go to a band concert unless I just happen to run into it, like the times in summer when it's so hot that there's no way to cool off. Ma keeps the blinds closed in the house all day to keep out the sun—but sometimes it doesn't seem to help much."

He stopped for a moment with a wistful look, and I thought to myself, "He's already thinking of when he'll be leaving."

He took anther big drink of the orange freeze, ate the last french fry, and continued his story. "That's when Mom and Pop call some of their Greek cronies. The women get organized, fixing Greek pastries and food, filling thermoses with coffee, and buying huge watermelons. They bring their pillows and blankets and we all go down to Haines Point, just like the gypsies. We stay there the night, sleeping on the ground."

I listened with interest.

"Sometimes when there's a band concert, the old folks listen to the music. My three sisters and I run and play with the other kids. Our parents scream after us, 'Be careful! Don't go near the water!' "

Then Ulysses turned to me again, "Louie, say it again."

"Say what?"

"Say 'se aga po.' "

For the fun of it, I said, "Se aga po."

He smiled again and asked, "Want anything else?"

"No thanks. It was all so good." I took my last drink of the orange freeze, and arm-in-arm we went to the car.

We rode along and snuggled close on our way to Haines Point. Suddenly a passing car hit us on the left side. Ulysses' first thought was for me as he tightened his arm around me, saying, "Are you all right, Kid?"

Startled, but certainly not hurt, I answered, "I'm fine."

We had been driving slowly, and it was only a minor bump. The other car pulled to a stop on the shoulder, and we drew right up behind him.

As Ulysses got out to see the damage, he remarked, "I believe the guy is a little drunk."

The young fellow was dressed all in white except for a black-striped tie. He staggered a little as he got out, saying, "Sorry man. I'm late meeting my old lady."

After examining the car, Ulysses said, "Well, it only messed up the paint a bit. I'll let it go, but you better watch yourself."

The fellow made a mock salute, saying, "Thank you, Captain," and sped away in his blue Ford.

When Ulysses came back into the car, I asked, "Do you think you should let him get away with that?"

Ulysses sighed as he said, "Well, in a few weeks I'll be leaving. This car is going to sit for a long time in the garage. When I get back, I'll probably need another one. Now I'm with you, and I'm not going to worry about it." Then he repeated, "Are you sure you're all right, Kid?" He was so loving and seemed to care for my feelings as no one ever had.

I reached over and kissed him on the cheek, saying, "Ulysses, I'm fine."

We reached Haines Point, found a parking place, and walked to the water's edge. A gentle breeze tossed my hair and billowed the pleats of my new pink dress. The light of the three-quarter moon reflected on the lapping water, and it was as if the whole Potomac River were doing a dance just for us.

"Right around here is where my family and friends slept." He pointed across the broad area, and then turned me around to face him, his eyes holding mine in the moonlight. "Never thought that someday I would be here with the one I—well, Kid." He finished his sentence with a kiss.

He removed his blue jacket so that I could sit next to him at the foot of a sprawling elm tree, along the banks of the shimmering Potomac. Though other people were milling around, we were in our own private heaven, the fireflies twinkling around us and crickets singing their special songs.

I remembered Papa's blessings, and thought that God had surely listened to him. Who would have dreamed that I could have found such happiness just a few days after leaving home? I believed in my heart that many more blessings would come.

7

Government Girl

My little windup alarm clock went off, waking me up.

Six thirty! I stretched and rubbed my eyes. I could hear Marge and Myrt in the kitchen drinking their coffee and smoking their Lucky Strikes. Marge was rattling on about some guy named Wayne.

I didn't stop to listen but headed right for the bathroom to take my shower. When I finished, I saw that Marge and Myrt were painting their legs with a dark tan liquid.

"What's that stuff?" I asked.

Marge was amazed, and said, "You've never heard of painting your legs?"

"No, I haven't. It looks great, though."

Myrt called from the bathroom, "Louie, don't wear your good silk stockings to work. People will think you're nuts."

I was just finishing drying myself when Marge came over and splashed my leg with the tan fluid.

"Here," she said, handing me her bottle. "Paint the rest of your legs. It's a lot cooler than stockings, anyway."

When I finished applying it, I said, "Hey Marge, it looks great, but what do you do for a girdle?"

"You wear a panty girdle."

"I don't have one without garters."

"I have an extra," she said. "Here, wear this one."

"But won't this stuff come off and mess up your girdle?"

In the midst of putting on her makeup, Marge answered, "Go have your breakfast and do your makeup and hair. Then, when it's dry, buff it with Kleenexes so that it won't rub off on everything. After you get dressed, I'll draw a seam down your leg."

I did as she recommended, and then she drew a line right down the back of my leg. It looked so real in the mirror.

57

Quickly I slipped into my new navy-blue suit and a crisp, white blouse. Myrt, dressed in white, came into the living room and inspected my legs. "You look fine, Louie, just like all the other government girls! Now, make sure you have your Social Security card and the papers they mailed you."

"They're right here."

"Good. Now listen. Marge and I will walk with you up to the streetcar stop. You'll take a different one from us because we have to go toward Virginia but you need to go to Ninth and F. Don't forget, it's the Civil Service Commission building."

Myrt told me again as we left the apartment walking to the stop, "Whatever you do, don't lose your Social Security card. It's also good for identification."

She took a deep breath, inhaling the fresh air of the morning, and continued, "Another thing, when you come back home, you must get on the streetcar that says Thirteenth and D, Northeast. No other one! You'll have to come home alone, so don't get lost."

I assured Myrt I'd be all right. Then I remembered Marge's comment earlier and asked her about it. "So who was that Wayne you mentioned this morning?"

At the sound of this name, Marge began to boil over.

"Louie! I met him!"

"Who's him?"

She put her arm around my waist and cozied up to me. "You remember how I was all dressed in red the other night?"

"I'll never forget you in red."

"Well, I walked into the party and there was a sailor standing close to the door. His eyes were on me all evening. Finally he came over and said, 'All my life I looked for the girl dressed in red. The girl of my dreams. Then you came walking in.'"

The streetcar was due any second and I quickly reminded Marge of all the stuff she had told me just the other day. Myrt whispered to me, "She's gone nuts!"

My streetcar came then, electric sparks shooting up from the center and the brakes squeaking.

Myrt said, "Get on, Louie. Now don't forget Thirteenth and D, Northeast!"

I gave a quick goodbye and left them. I had to stand up as the car was very crowded and there were no empty seats. I saw other young girls like myself and smiled at a few and they half smiled back. There were signs above the windows: "TALK SINKS SHIPS" and "BUTTON YOUR

LIP. SOMEONE MIGHT BE LISTENING." No wonder everyone is so quiet, I chuckled to myself.

When at the Civil Service Commission I watched people come and go as my papers were being processed. I was so happy to be a part of the busy scene.

The pretty girl who had taken my papers and Social Security card returned and said, "Miss Hansen, you'll be working at the Treasury Department at the Division of Disbursement near Fifteenth and Pennsylvania. Good location, just diagonally across from the White House. You'll be classified as a typist stenographer and your beginning salary is $1,240.00 yearly."

Quickly I figured that I'd earn just over a hundred dollars each month. Inside I was jumping with joy. I smiled and said, "Now all I need to know is how to get there."

She smiled in return. "Catch the streetcar marked Fifteen and G Streets, Northwest, and when you arrive you'll be within a block or so of where you want to go."

I followed her directions and landed in the midst of the most incredible buildings I had ever seen. The sun was shining and the red and gold flowers beside the magnificent Treasury building smiled back at me. It was a picture of the America that represented strength. This was the America Papa talked about during the Depression when we were cold and hungry.

I could almost hear him now, saying, "Hold on. America will come back. We are a strong country—a good country who helps anyone in trouble. God will bring us back because we give."

Then I crossed the street and there before me were the great decorated money temples, the Riggs Bank and the American Security Bank. On the other corner was the National Savings and Trust building, looking very different with its red brick.

The U.S. flag with its forty-eight stars waved to me as I walked up the street. I waved back, remembering school and all of our young hands raised as we saluted the flag every morning, pledging allegiance and saying our prayer of thanks.

I kept walking until I reached my destination, the beautiful Treasury Annex building. Up ahead I could clearly see the White House and across from it Lafayette Park. What a location! I couldn't wait to tell Ulysses.

When I arrived on the third floor I felt shy and overwhelmed. I stood hesitating by the door for just a moment, when a gentleman came up to me, his graying hair falling boyishly across his forehead. He asked, "Are you Miss Hansen?"

"Yes," I replied, taken off-guard by his friendly approach. "I just came from the interview and they directed me here."

He extended his hand saying, "I'm Mr. Thomas, the supervisor. The Commission called and informed me that you were on your way. Follow me, please, and we can get started."

He walked on ahead and I followed, taking in my surroundings. The office was large and noisy. I smiled at some of the workers and they mostly smiled back while their telephones rang and rang. It was like a contained whirlwind, and I was about to be a part of it.

Mr. Thomas paused beside a plain brown desk. "Miss Hansen, this is where you will sit," he said as he pulled out my chair for me. He instructed me, "I've placed you in the stenographic pool. Just means you'll be doing various types of work, not particularly for one person, but for all those who need something special to be done."

He gave me a fatherly smile, "Please wait right here, and I'll be back shortly to get you started."

I began to get settled into my new surroundings when Mr. Thomas reappeared with a huge stack of papers and a long list of names, addresses, and Social Security numbers. Placing them on the corner of my desk, he said in a kindly way, "Now Miss Hansen, please fill in these forms. Here's an extra box of carbon paper. Put a new carbon in frequently to keep the copies clear, please. Do an original and three copies."

Then he smiled again, and patted me lightly on the shoulder, "After you finish, see me. They will need to be proofread." In a little more business-like tone, he added, "If there are any errors, they will be given back to you to correct."

"Certainly, Mr. Thomas."

Mr. Thomas left and the attractive woman next to me said, "Sure glad you came today, otherwise I would have to do all that boring stuff."

What could I do but smile at her and get to work.

"Time's up, Miss Hansen. It's lunch time!"

I looked up with a start, as I had been engrossed in my work. In front of me was a young woman with mounds of curly red hair and a big smile.

I stood up and said, "Hi! I'm Lulu. What's your name?"

She held forth her hand with its orange fingernails. Her face glowed, and was set off by golden freckles and the lime-colored dress she was wearing. "I'm Bridgette. I saw you when you came in. Come and let's have lunch together—I'll show you around."

I was delighted and answered, "I'd love to! Where do we go?"

"We can stroll down to New York Avenue to a place called Nedicks. They have the most wonderful orange drinks and juicy hot dogs. I'm starved, aren't you?

"Come to think about it, I am too. Let's go."

We walked that same fantastic walk I had admired earlier. Bridgette told me about a War Bond rally that was coming up, and then said, "Do you know that the USO is held in the Belasco Theatre, just to the left of our building? That's where all the servicemen meet and dance with all the young girls. You're so cute—you ought to join!"

Immediately I thought about Ulysses and what he would think.

My new friend kept right on talking. "You know, I married my husband just six months after I met him. We only had a week's honeymoon and then he was gone. If I had it to do over, I wouldn't have gotten married. Now I can't have any fun!"

She had the most fascinating laugh, which shook her whole attractive body. Then she looked serious for a moment, causing her forehead to crease, "You know, Harry wanted to marry me so badly. Well, the truth is that at the time, I wanted to marry him too."

As we reached Nedicks she interrupted herself, saying, "Look at the lineup! Oh well, it moves fast." She leaned against the orange building, making quite a picture.

"Do you realize what a perfect backdrop this orange building is for you?"

"Orange is my color, isn't it?" She laughed and continued, "As I was saying, I wanted to marry him too, but I had my doubts because I know myself. I love to have a good time."

Once our table was ready, we squeezed past the diners and sat down in the corner. Bridgette picked up the conversation again. "It could be years before Harry returns. Anyway, that's why I can't go to the USO, but you certainly should. Do your duty for your country!"

We both laughed and then I noticed an odd expression on her face. She said, "Well, we could at least take a peek in the USO once in a while. You know, just walk in and look around—maybe dance a little. That wouldn't hurt anything, would it?"

She was so obvious, and I answered, "Oh, Bridgette, you poor girl. You're having a tough time, aren't you?" I laughed at and with her, and we both knew what she meant.

Just then the young waitress came and we ordered the only thing they sold, orange drinks and hot dogs with everything on them.

Bridgette asked, "How old are you, anyway?"

"Well, in just a few weeks I'll be eighteen."

Bridgette exclaimed, "Only seventeen! You don't know anything about love."

She laughed again, and I thought how she knew nothing of my feelings for Ulysses. I didn't want to mention him to her because I could guess what her response would be.

The waitress cut in, bringing the food and the refreshing orange drinks. Bridgette took a long sip and said, "If you do meet a guy and he wants to marry you before he goes in the service, take my advice and say no. Much better to wait and see if the feeling lasts until the war is over."

Poor Bridgette. She had made a mistake, but maybe she'd be mixed up in any case. I answered, "Thanks for your advice. Perhaps sometime I'll have to think about your comments."

As we finished with our lunch, I asked, "Do we have time to walk up in front of the White House?

"Sure, but we'll have to hurry."

We walked up two blocks to the center of the White House and looked across onto the portico. It looked just as it did in the history books. I thought of Papa—his love of history and his interest in what was going on in the world. This must have been passed on to me too. Here I stood, looking at the great White House where our presidents dwelled, and where even at this moment President Roosevelt and his wife, Eleanor, were making history.

We returned to the office, barely on time. Immediately I set to work, determined to finish the stack of typing before the day was out. My fingers were black from changing the carbon paper, but just before five, I filled in the last form and carried the stack up to Mr. Thomas's desk. He took the papers from me, saying, "Thank you, Miss Hansen. We'll check it and get back with you. Good evening."

I mumbled "Goodnight," and went back to my desk. I was finished for the day.

Now the challenge was to find my way home. I asked directions until I managed to connect with the right streetcar. I climbed aboard and in thirty minutes I was walking the two blocks toward my new home.

Before I went into the apartment, I stopped to pick some more of the yellow roses blossoming by our little window. Only Marge was home and I called out to her in the bedroom. "Margie! You should see the great location where I work!"

She appeared, her face plastered with Pond's cold cream. "That's great! Wayne is coming over pretty soon and I've got to get dressed."

As I arranged the roses in the small glass vase, I wondered what this Wayne would be like who had so captured Margie. I changed from my suit into a blouse and slacks and rested on her bed for a moment. It had been a great day but also a little taxing. My thoughts were on Ulysses. I couldn't wait to tell him where I worked.

Just then the phone rang. I answered, "Hello!"

"Hi, Kid!"

"Ulysses! So good to hear your voice!"

"So how was your first day of work?"

"It was wonderful! I'm working in the Treasury Annex near the White House. It's so beautiful around there."

"You're a very lucky girl. Say, that gives me an idea. Last night I was thinking that we don't have a picture of us. My sister mentioned that there's a good studio located close to you there on G Street. I'm at work tonight, but tomorrow I'll meet you right at the bottom of your steps. Then we'll go together and have our pictures made. What do you say?"

"Wonderful! What a good idea! What time tomorrow?"

"Five o'clock. Be on time!"

"I'll be right there waiting for you."

"Okay, Kid. See you tomorrow."

Marge came out of the bedroom, wiping her cold cream off her face. "Oh, Louie, I can't wait until you meet Wayne."

"I can't believe how you're carrying on about this Wayne after that big lecture you gave me."

She didn't comment but sat down at the dressing table, preparing for her date. She was beautifying every inch of herself.

"Louie, please listen for Wayne. I don't want him to see me until I'm finished."

"Sure, I'll be glad to." I laughed to myself, remembering how she had met Ulysses. I had no intention of doing the same with Wayne.

Then she called out again, "There's some tuna casserole I made yesterday. Help yourself!"

"Great!"

While I was waiting I fixed myself some of the casserole and a little salad. I cleaned up the kitchen just in time to hear the rap on the door. Quickly I opened it, and there stood an all-American sailor, his white cap in hand and an anxious look on his face. He asked, "Is this where Marge Ballinger lives?"

"Yes, this is the place. Please come in."

I could see his eyes were darting past me, trying to catch a glimpse of Marge.

I said, "She won't be long. Here, sit on the couch while I get you a Coke."

He didn't sit, but followed me to the kitchen, cap still in hand. "And who are you?"

"I'm Myrtle's sister. Call me Louie, Wayne, everyone else does."

He walked back into the living room and stopped at the player piano, fiddling with the roller.

I asked, "Where are you from?"

"From Iowa, just across the Minnesota border. Good thing I left or I would have never met Marge."

"Everyone who meets a significant person has a story, but maybe someone bigger than us works it out," I said, reflectively.

He didn't comment but took a drink of his Coke as he began pumping the piano, just like Billy. Marge appeared and Wayne jumped up to greet her. She wasn't shy as she walked right into his arms. They didn't hear me mumble good night, but it didn't matter. I went into the bedroom and closed the door.

Marge's perfume lingered in the air. I lay down on the bed and was glad to be alone. This would be the first time I had a chance to be by myself since I arrived, just four days ago.

So much had happened in such a short time: I had met what might be an answer to a dream of my life. I had a job. I lived in a great part of Washington. And I had found my way home from work, which was no small thing considering my terrible sense of direction. As I thought about the events of the past few days I remembered Mama saying, "I've placed you in God's hands." I felt thankful to think that God may have planned all this.

I tossed about on the bed, laughing about my happiness with Ulysses. What a miracle it was. Then I thought about his leaving. This is what it will be like—the girls would go out, but I'd be here by myself. I thought about Bridgette and the tough time she was having, but then again, I wasn't married. If I wasn't married and could go out but never wanted to, then I would be more happy waiting for him than dating. That was a kind of happiness too. Happiness postponed!

I had been with Ulysses every night since I came, including when we rode with the top down all the way to George Washington's home. Tomorrow we would take the picture. I realized I needed to figure out what to wear.

I jumped up and opened the closet, surveying the contents. I could wear Myrt's pale blue plaid suit if she wouldn't get mad. I dug through the clean clothes bag for the matching blouse and ironed it carefully. Then, just in case Myrt needed a blouse, I ironed one of mine for her and brushed my navy-blue suit for her to wear. I pinned a note on her blouse and suit asking for permission to wear it, in case she came home too late for me to ask. I told her also to wear mine. We both wore the same size six.

I did my hair, polished my shoes, prepared my stuff to paint my legs in the morning, cleaned out my purse, and got myself ready for tomorrow. All finished, I made up my bed, knowing that they'd have to come in and disturb me. I lay there thinking again that this is how it would be with Ulysses gone. I would be alone and they would be coming and going.

When I began to get depressed, I thought about good things like going with Ulysses tomorrow. I thought of Mama, too, and how when I got my first paycheck, I would call her and send her some money.

I heard Billy and Myrt come home about eleven o'clock. Myrt said, "Good night, Billy. Don't come in. Call me tomorrow." When Marge and Wayne came, they crept softly into the kitchen and closed the door, and I never did hear Wayne leave.

Preparing for work the second day was easier. Myrt was sweet about me borrowing her suit, and I arrived at work just on time. Bridgette was absent so I ate by myself in the cafeteria. All the while, my mind was on Ulysses.

When it was five I gathered my purse, closed up the desk carefully, and made my way downstairs. Once outside the door, I stood at the top of the stairs, peering through the people until I spotted Ulysses just as he saw me. He started up, and we met partway, hugging and kissing each other. I didn't mind my fellow workers seeing me with him.

Would I ever go down these steps without seeing his face looking up at mine? I began to miss him already. Every touch was a touch to remember; every word, memorable.

We walked down what I now called my beloved street, made a right turn past the RKO Building and past F Street, made a left and walked past Garfinckel's, where I hoped to be able to afford to shop one day, and down to the Albee Studio. We were surprised to see how packed it was, with all the couples sitting close and getting ready to say goodbye. These pictures would provide hope and inspiration.

We checked in at the desk and the warm, hospitable lady was very sweet to us. "Hello! Welcome! Your name is Auger, isn't it."

Ulysses nodded.

"Mr. Auger, you will need to fill out this form, please. Give me the color of your eyes, and the color of your hair as near as you can describe it—the way you want it in the picture. You do want it in color, don't you?"

"Yes," Ulysses answered. "Two of them."

The lady smiled knowingly. Certainly she had been through this many times before. She gave Ulysses the bill, but before paying he asked, "When will they be ready? By September sixteenth?"

"It can take a month to six weeks."

"A month to six weeks!" I saw Ulysses' jaw harden and irritation in his eyes.

She reached over and patted his hand. "Mr. Auger, I'm going to watch out for these personally. I guarantee that you can pick them up by the sixteenth."

She looked honest and sincere, and I saw Ulysses soften as he said, "I'll be here on that day, but would you mind if I call you once in a while and check up on them?"

She smiled and shook her head, saying that she didn't mind at all.

Soon we were inside the studio and being moved about by the photographer. "All right, Miss. You sit on this side of the piano stool. You, Sir, sit right beside her. Miss, tilt your head toward him."

He pulled a big black cloak over his head, and said, "Now smile." The lights flashed. "Now, smile again. That's it! One more!"

Mission accomplished, we walked down toward Thirteenth Street where Ulysses had parked the car. Just then the dark clouds gave way to a few heavy drops, the wind howled, lightning flashed, and loud thunder roared.

We didn't have coats or umbrellas, so we ducked into the closest place, which happened to be Child's Cafeteria at Thirteenth and Pennsylvania Avenue. We decided to eat right there.

We sat as close to each other as we could. Ulysses was hungry and ate fast, but I was a slow eater. He ate all of his as usual, and then reached over and had quite a bit of mine. I was getting used to it.

Then we shared our desserts. He stuffed chocolate in my mouth and I stuffed strawberry in his. We were laughing and playing—two kids without a care in the world, except for a big war hanging over our heads.

As we walked through the puddles, Ulysses said, "Boy, am I glad I had the impulse to put up the top. This rain came so suddenly, the car could have been drenched."

"You have good instincts."

In the car, we cuddled close and kissed. Ulysses asked, "Where do you want to go?"

"We've driven by the Lincoln Memorial but I'd like to walk up the steps and see Lincoln up close."

I knew he didn't like sight-seeing, not even for me. He smiled my favorite smile and said, "Sure, Kid, if that's what you want."

We arrived and walked up the steps, along with many other couples. There was only a dim light, and Lincoln appeared larger than life. He looked so melancholy, like some of the Danes Papa used to tell me about. The more I stared at him, the more emotional I became, and big tears dropped from my eyes.

Ulysses asked, "What's wrong, Kid? What are you crying for?"

"You grew up here—you take everything for granted. But this is new to me. Look at how wonderfully Lincoln is sculptured, and the expression on his face that shows the suffering of his life. You know he had a broken heart. He married a woman who made his life miserable."

Ulysses couldn't stand to see me crying, so he put his arms around me. "Kid, you're too serious and you think about things too much. Look, he was a great guy, but he's dead."

He held me close, and then said, "Come on, Louie. Let's go!"

I took one last look at Lincoln's sad face as we went down the steps to the car. Ulysses was right. I was just too sentimental.

We sat there in the car, and Ulysses held me close, looking into my eyes and saying, "Louie, se aga po."

"It means I love you, doesn't it? Saying it in Greek is not quite like saying it in English. But maybe that's the way it should be for right now. We're awfully young, and you'll be leaving soon, and well...."

"Well what, Louie?"

"I don't know. Ever since I met you it's as if you've almost taken me over. I don't know if that's good or bad or right or wrong. I think everything needs time. We both need to grow, and we need to know what we really want."

Ulysses answered, "I know what I want, and it's you, Louie. You know, I've never told anybody that I loved them before. I can tell you in Greek, but it's hard to say it in English. I don't know why it is, but I'll try."

He sat for a moment, and then he said, "I loves you, Kid. There, I've said it. I don't know what kind of hold you have on me, but it started from the first moment I saw you."

I looked into his eyes, and then closed mine as he kissed me. I'd always remember this moment.

Over the next three weeks, we spent all of our spare time together. The gas rationing sometimes curtailed us, but Ulysses searched out his buddies who were leaving for the service and managed to wangle some of their gas coupons. We were young and in love but also were cautious and made no commitments. We had a great time sharing our feelings and experiences as well as our thoughts, hopes, and dreams. We were doing the dance of love—but only the dance.

8

The Pain of Separation

SEPTEMBER 16, 1942, WAS THE DAY before Ulysses was to leave for the Army and was five days before his twenty-first birthday. That morning I said to Marge and Myrt, "Today I'm doing all the cooking—and all the cleaning of the kitchen."

"Well, that's good news," said Myrt. "What's going on?"

"Don't you remember? It's my dinner for Ulysses' birthday and farewell. You and Billy will be there, won't you? And Marge, you and Wayne? You promised!"

Marge, sleepy from being out late dancing the night before, leaned back with her cigarette and said cheerfully, "Whatever you want, Louie. In fact, I've been out so much lately that I look forward to some home cooking. What did you find to make?"

"Smell!" I held forth the frying chickens, bought at an outdoor market. "And, look, I got these fresh tomatoes from the lady next door—from her victory garden—and these great cucumbers."

Around half past three I set to work cooking. I was nervous, because I knew that Ulysses was very particular. Well, all I could do was my best. I floured the chicken and put it on to fry while I boiled potatoes, whipped them, and then made mashed potato cakes with onions. Earlier in the day, I had baked a golden cake with chocolate frosting, using up all of my sugar ration coupons. On the top I added twenty-one candles. By 5:30, everything was ready but me.

Quickly I ran into the bedroom and tried to remove all the cooking smells. I put on the same blue-checked dress I wore when Ulysses and I first met. When I was ready I went back to the kitchen, drinking in the fresh air from the open door and relaxing a few moments. Myrt and Billy had left to get a last-minute gift, and Marge was taking a shower before Wayne came.

Standing there, I didn't hear anyone come in the front door until I heard Ulysses say, "Hi, Kid!"

I saw his shining face and a package in his hand. Before I could say anything he took me in his strong arms and we kissed the wonderful kiss between two who are on the brink of saying goodbye. Then he held out the package.

"Here, open it!" His eyes were filled with expectancy.

"This is your birthday, not mine!" All the while I was smiling and unwrapping the box. There it was—our picture, our heads close together and in lovely color.

"Oh, Ulysses, it's just wonderful. Thank you so much." I kissed him again.

Just then Myrt and Billy came along with Wayne, and I showed them the picture. Then I put it on the piano so that I could see it first thing in the morning and last thing at night—and many times in between.

As we sat down to dinner around the small table my mood changed out of the blue. I had been so busy all day that I didn't have time to think about Ulysses leaving, but now I was suddenly overwhelmed. We held hands under the table and exchanged glances.

Everyone ate and sang "Happy Birthday" when we cut the cake, while Ulysses and I were absorbed in the moment and in each other. We tried to talk but the depth of feeling was more than we could manage. Wayne cracked some jokes and Billy got up and pumped the piano. We all sang silly songs until it was past midnight.

When it was time to part, Ulysses and I went out and sat in his car.

"You fixed a good dinner, but I've never heard of fried mashed potatoes before," he said, teasing me. Then he held me close, and said, "Louie, if I'm anywhere in the States this Christmas, I want you to come be with me wherever I am. Besides, I want you to think about going to California, getting work there, and being closer to your older sisters."

I could see his dear face from the light of the street. He was concerned about me.

He continued, "You have a brother there too, don't you? Please think about it. You could make the move right at Christmastime. You could come and see me, wherever I am, and then keep going."

I could see he had been planning this advice to me for a long time. Again, he reminded me of Papa. I said to him, knowing how sincere he was, "I'll think about it. I won't say now if I will or I won't, but I'll think about it."

He seemed somewhat relieved as he answered, "Good girl! You'll come to see it's right. And another thing, please don't go to the USO. In fact, if I could, I'd put you in a box and keep you there 'til I come back!"

He must have seen my expression, for he quickly added, "Don't say anything! I'm only kidding, but you're so young and impressionable."

A little irritated, I said, "Well, I might be young, but don't forget that none of us are that young. We've lived through a Depression and now World War II. It's not exactly kid stuff."

Realizing how serious I sounded, I kissed him lightly on the cheek and assured him, "I may be young, but I'm not as impressionable as you might think."

"Don't get mad, Louie! It's just that I worry about you." He pulled me to him, and I felt safe and warm in his arms.

He said, "Maybe I'll get to see you before Christmas. But we'll be together then if at all possible—unless they ship me out or something."

Then he drew my face close to him and said, "Christmastime—promise?"

"If it's at all possible, I promise."

We sat silently, listening to Artie Shaw's "Stardust" on the radio. Ulysses said, "Se aga po, Louie."

"Se aga po."

"Say it in English."

"I love you, Ulysses."

Our tears mingled. It was time for me to go. I opened the car door and Ulysses walked with me, our arms tight around each other.

At the door, we had our last kiss. He said, again, "Se aga po, Louie. We'll be together at Christmas!"

We kissed again, and he said gently, "Go inside."

I left his strong arms and entered the apartment alone. I grasped his picture, numb. Just a month and a few days since we met, and now he was gone.

The girls must be asleep, I thought as I opened my bed quietly and put on my pink pajamas. I took the picture in bed with me, sobbing. Nothing would ever be the same. But then I thought of the letters we would write and about being together at Christmas. Finally I fell asleep, out of sheer exhaustion.

Fall came in all its splendid colors. Golden leaves sailed to the ground and piled up in the gutters and sidewalks. Tall sunflowers and brilliant chrysanthemums decorated my walk to the trolley stop. Ulysses had left for the Army ten days ago, and I was anxiously waiting for a letter from him.

The first thing I did each evening when I got home was to see if there was any mail. I couldn't write to him, of course, until he sent me his address. But I did compose letters to him in my head every night before going to sleep.

I thought of him all the time. Whenever I came down the steps at work, he was there. Going by the restaurants we had visited filled my mind with memories. Sometimes a man walking down the street would resemble him. My heart would leap, but of course it was never him.

"Ulysses, my darling, where did you go? Where are you right now? Ulysses, maybe today!" Coming home, once again there was no mail on the table. Dejected, I sat down on the couch. "It shouldn't take ten days to write a letter," I thought.

I went over to Ulysses' picture and held it close. Maybe it was just a dream. A month of being together and that was it.

As I was brooding, Marge came in from the bedroom and held up some letters. "Sorry I didn't leave these on the table," she said, with a teasing grin.

"You mean there are letters! How could you do this to me!" My eyes were not on Marge but on the envelopes. One was from Ulysses and the other from Mama.

Carefully I opened up Ulysses' letter. He had written "Rush" on the back of the envelope. I tried to quiet my pounding heart as I read:

> Dear Kid:
>
> I'm in some strange world here, with some strange people. They can't even say my name. They never heard of the name Ulysses, not even Ulysses Grant! Anyway, already they've changed my name. "Hey, you with the black hair, hey Blackie!" They must be listening to Boston Blackie on the radio. To top it off, some of the other guys called me "Radio Joe," because I won all their radios in a crap game. But, finally, they're all calling me Blackie. Here I am in a strange world, and renamed twice.
>
> Louie, I'm so glad that I met you and that I have you to hang on to. By the way, even though these strangers are calling me Blackie, I never want you to. You know, I'm not a

writer or a poet, or anything like that, but this morning when I woke up, it just came to me, these words, "There's a picture in my heart of you that always will remain." There you were, right before me. You know, I'm not the lovey dovey type, but this is the longest letter I've ever written. It's like I'm talking to you, like we did when we were together. Let's never lose that, Louie.

Se aga po, a million times. Stay away from the USO. Keep thinking about what I told you regarding California. Remember, Christmas—we'll be together if at all possible, unless I can figure out a way beforehand. I just might!

I'll be mailing you a birthday present. Watch for the package. You've got my address now so please write me right away. I can't wait to hear from you. Aren't you glad we have each other's pictures?

Se aga po,
Ulysses
XXXXX OOOOO (Kisses and hugs)

I held the lined pages close, sighing deeply. I could see the painstaking way he formed every word. After I calmed down a bit, I read Mama's letter:

Lulu and Myrtle:

Thank you for the letter and the dollars you sent. It's good news when I hear that both of my daughters are working and doing well.

The leaves are turning again and we are heading for winter. Papa's leg is nearly healed. He can walk on it now. Today, he walked to the bakery on Front Street hill and brought home some day-old rolls and doughnuts. They were good and you know how Papa likes them in the morning with his coffee.

We're all right here. Please write often. Whenever we receive a letter from any of you, it cheers us up, especially Papa. Won't be long until February when Marlin leaves for the navy.

Love,
Mama

So in one day, I heard from the people who were dearest to me. I was glad to be home alone tonight, to write letters and fix my fingernails. I sat down to write, but the sore throat that had been plaguing me all day began to be acute and my forehead felt feverish.

"What's the matter, Louie?" Marge asked. "Was there something upsetting in the letters?"

"No, they were wonderful. It's this sore throat."

She came over and felt my forehead. "Come, get into our bed. I'll get you some good ol' Campbell's chicken soup."

One moment I felt flushed, and the next I felt chills. I climbed into bed with a sigh.

Marge brought me the soup. "You're such a mix of goodness and rascality," I said as I held Ulysses' letter, reading it over and over.

"I can see you've had it bad for this guy as soon as you met him. I must be a nut, too, for I feel the same way about Wayne."

Marge sat on the stool and finished her makeup, adding, "War is such a terrible time, but if you have someone in your life to love, someone to share the horror with, it almost makes it bearable."

"You're getting so wise."

"Here, take some aspirins."

"I can see why Wayne loves you, even though you're such a brat," I said, holding my throat and feeling very tired.

Marge made a face at me and went to answer the door.

Before she and Wayne left, Marge came in to say, "I'll call the doctor in the morning and ask him to come by and see you. I'll bet you've got strep throat. I'll suggest he brings some sulpha. It's a new medicine and it's really good."

Once alone, I tried to write Ulysses but couldn't concentrate and finally gave up. At ten P.M. I took another two aspirins and got into my bed, shivering one moment and sweating the next.

When morning came I could barely whisper. I croaked to Myrt, "Call in sick for me, will you? I hate to be absent."

Her dark hair fell across her face as she said, "Sure, Louie. As soon as I get to my desk, I'll call for you. Don't worry, everyone gets sick once in awhile."

The girls left for work and I lay in misery. The only other time I could remember my throat aching like this was when I was a little kid when Marlin had to have his tonsils out, so they decided to take out mine and Myrt's too. After our operations in Mankato we stayed at Pearl's house and our older brothers and sisters took care of us, entertaining us with stories and bringing us ice cream. No such lovely company cheered me today, except for my letters from Ulysses and Mama.

In the afternoon, I answered a knock on the door.

Standing there was a short man with a thick gray beard. "You must be the sick girl!" he said. "I'm Dr. Schaeffer. Miss Ballinger told me to come by."

"Please come in. I'm glad you're here."

Just the chill of getting up caused me to sneeze and shiver. "Young lady, don't go around barefoot!" he said, scolding me. "Now, sit up on the bed and let's take a good look.

"Say ahhh. I'm going to take a culture but it looks like strep throat."

He reached into his black bag and brought out a small glass bottle. "This is sulpha. It'll nip it in a couple of days. Great stuff." He jotted a number on the notepad, saying, "Here's my phone number. Call me if you need me. And call me when you get better, too. I'll want to know how the sulpha worked."

He was like a kindly grandfather as he patted me on the head and assured me that I'd be all right. I wanted to pay him but I didn't have any cash, until Papa's ten-dollar bill came to mind. I whispered, "How much do I owe you?"

"The household call and medicine will be five dollars."

I thanked him in a whisper as I paid him.

He said, "I'll let myself out now. If you get up, wear a warm robe and slippers. Drink lots of liquids. Call me if you need me!"

I moaned and groaned and tossed with fever and chills until Friday morning, the third day of being sick, when I finally woke up with an appetite. The girls had already eaten breakfast and were at work. Their leftover coffee smelled delightful, and with it I fixed scrambled eggs and toast with grape jelly. The sulpha was successful; surely by Monday I'd be back at work.

After breakfast, I snuggled up in the chair and wrote my first letter to Ulysses. I put a three-cent stamp on it and left it in the slot of the door for the mailman.

I was so relieved and happy to return to work on Monday. As I was putting my purse away, Mr. Thomas said, "Miss Hansen, you're back. Good! Looks like you lost a few pounds—are you sure you've recovered?"

"Oh, good morning, Mr. Thomas. Yes, I'm fine and anxious to get to work." I smiled at him, and he gave me several jobs to do. The day sped by quickly.

The moment I returned home, the telephone rang and Marge called out, "Louie, telephone!"

"Hello?" I answered.

"Is this Louie?" the strange voice asked.

"Yes, this is she."

"I'm Margaret, Ulysses' sister."

"Margaret! What a surprise!"

"Ulysses wrote me a letter and asked me to call you. He tells me that your birthday is October fifth and he would like me to take you to lunch. Could we meet at the Reeves at Twelfth and F, about two o'clock on Sunday?"

"Sure, I'd love to. I look forward to being with you."

"Yes, me too. I'll wait for you inside. Don't worry, the way Ulysses described you, I shouldn't have any trouble recognizing you."

I was thrilled at Ulysses' thoughtfulness. I hadn't met any of his family yet, though I felt I knew them from all the things that Ulysses had said.

A day before my birthday, I came into the apartment and found a package waiting for me. It looked like a shoe box. When I opened it, I found that Ulysses had sent me a pair of brown and white red-soled saddle shoes, size 7 1/2B. Inside was a little note, "You don't need to grow up too fast, Louie. I'll bet you look great in saddle shoes. Se aga po."

"He's an original!" I said to myself.

The next morning, on my eighteenth birthday, I was dressing to meet Margaret when Myrt asked, "What are you doing today? Do you want to go out with Billy and me?"

"I didn't tell you, but Ulysses' sister called and we're going to have lunch and spend the afternoon together. Thanks anyway."

"Oh, that's nice. Being with his sister is kind of like being with him, huh."

With my paycheck I had bought a cerise skirt, hat, and matching gloves. I wore them with a black turtleneck sweater and felt very well dressed as I walked into Reeves. A young girl, just a little older than I, came toward me and I recognized her immediately. Margaret looked quite a bit like Ulysses with the same black wavy hair and big beautiful brown eyes.

We embraced, and she said, "Ulysses had told me all about the two of you. He's kept it a secret from Mama and Papa though, because, well, it's like him to do that until the right time comes. He's never brought any girl home to Mama, except the Greek daughters of friends, but I'm sure that Mama will know that you're special when he does bring you."

I remembered that my neighbors growing up had said that Greek people want their children to marry into their own heritage. That's probably why Ulysses hadn't taken me to his home.

I changed the subject, "I know about Mr. Theon and Merope. I know about your house in Georgetown—George Washington's library. I know about the family sleeping down by Haines Point." And I blushed a little as I said, "I also know what 'se aga po' means."

She laughed at that, saying, "If you knew my brother, he doesn't sling those words around easily."

After we had our lunch, we walked down by the Washington Monument. As we strolled along I mentioned, "You know, Ulysses wants me to leave here and go to California. I'm thinking about it and trying to figure out what to do. Probably I'd not have much trouble getting work."

"Have you ever been to California?"

"No, but my sisters moved there when I was thirteen."

"Then you haven't seen much of them, have you?"

"No."

"Well, then, maybe you should go and get to know your family."

Her answer made sense to me. Maybe Ulysses was right after all.

We walked under the beautiful trees along Constitution Avenue when some bird droppings fell right onto my hat.

I wasn't superstitious, but Margaret said, "Toop. Toop."

"What does that mean?"

"Why, that means that you'll have good luck."

I had never heard of such a thing and we laughed and kept on walking.

Five days later, when I had just returned home from work, someone knocked on the door. I hadn't even had time to change my clothes when I answered the door. I gasped as I saw Ulysses in his army uniform.

"Ulysses! Am I dreaming?"

"Hi, Kid. Guess what? They must've lost my papers. All the other guys keep shipping out and they keep skipping over me . . . so I took a chance, caught the bus, and here I am. I can't stay late, but I just had to see you."

Why talk! I ran into his loving arms. We were in a tight embrace when Billy and Myrt came in the door.

"Ulysses, how'd you get here?" Myrt asked with amazement.

"I went AWOL. I took the bus, and I don't have a car or anything. Nor did I tell my folks."

Immediately Billy volunteered, "Here are my keys—use my car. What's the latest time you can stay?"

"I have to catch the midnight bus without fail, and then hopefully I can sneak back in."

I didn't want to waste any of our precious time. "Ulysses, just let me freshen up a little. I'm so happy, I could die!"

I was shaken as I fixed myself up. I started to put on the saddle shoes but didn't since we were going out to dinner.

Ulysses' bright brown eyes gazed into mine. He looked so wonderful in his uniform as he wrapped his arms around me; together, we went to Billy's car. We ate corned-beef sandwiches and strawberry cake at the Blue Mirror restaurant while listening to "I Only Have Eyes for You" on the juke box.

Then we walked over to the Casino Royal and danced together, swaying in each others' arms.

"What have you got, Kid, that makes me miss you so much," Ulysses whispered in my ear.

"Whatever I have, you must have it too, because I miss you the same way."

We clung to each other as we sat down and ordered another Coke. The room was so crowded with servicemen and their girls.

The music started up again. It was Hal McIntyre's "This is the army, Mister Jones/No magazines or telephones/You had your breakfast in bed before/but you won't have it there any more. . . ."

Ulysses whispered in my ear, "Are you going to fix me breakfast in bed someday?"

"When the right time comes, I promise you I will."

We danced on, but the night was slipping by fast. Ulysses looked at his watch and said, "Time to go. We'll barely make it for Billy to get me to the bus on time."

In the car, I sat as close to him as I could, but we didn't talk much. The electricity was racing through both of us and we knew our time together would soon be over.

We had just thirty minutes for Billy and Myrt to run us to the bus station, and we cuddled the whole way there. At the Greyhound station, Ulysses' bus to Fort Lee, Virginia, waited. The bus was filled with servicemen but I believed there was only one AWOL.

Before he boarded, I said, "Ulysses, please let me know as soon as you can what happened when you get back. I love you, darling. Thank you for taking the chance to come and see me. I'll remember this forever."

He held me close, my head on his army uniform.

Billy and Myrt had to pry us apart, and Billy had to put Ulysses on the bus. It took off immediately.

In the car, I started to cry. Myrt said, "What are you crying for?"

"Cause he's probably going to get into a lot of trouble."

"If I know Ulysses, he'll work his way out even if he is."

It took a whole week before I heard from Ulysses.

Dear Louie,

Well, I did get in a lot of trouble and the Lieutenant really has it in for me. Rumor has it, though, that we're being shipped to Camp Campbell, Kentucky. If that's so, then you can come at Christmas on your way to California. I've been confined to quarters, but it was worth every moment.

Se aga po,
Ulysses

By Thanksgiving, Ulysses was in Camp Campbell and I was making up my mind to go to see him and then keep going to California. Ulysses wrote from Kentucky.

Louie,

I asked a fellow where I could get a room for you in Nashville, just across the way here. He gave me the name of a lady and I'm going to make arrangements for you to stay there Christmas Day. If the Colonel will let me, I'll pick you up, and we'll be together in the afternoon. I inquired

79

and that's the most time I will have, since I'm not very popular.

That did it. I wanted to go see him. I talked it over with Myrt: "Ulysses wants me to leave here and go to California to be with Maria and Bertha and the family. What do you think?"

"Well," Myrt said, taking a long drag on her cigarette, "I certainly don't intend to leave here. But, then again, I just might have to go to get rid of Billy. Well, you go ahead, and then let me know how it is out there."

I only had a month to prepare. I notified the office. They were used to people coming and going and I'd just be replaced.

Bridgette went regularly to the USO to dance "harmlessly with the boys." I finally told her about Ulysses and she thought I was nuts. But I didn't care.

I needed fifty-eight dollars for my bus ticket to San Diego with a stop at Nashville. The day before I left Washington, I strolled around downtown ending up on Connecticut Avenue by the Mayflower Hotel. I was fascinated by all the elegant and busy people coming and going. I walked through the swinging doors and into the lobby, and then down the long foyer. I gazed at the wonderful antiques as I walked straight through to the other street. Why did I find this place so compelling?

Returning home to the apartment, I felt a little melancholy and torn when I walked down the steps. When I opened the door, there were Billy and Wayne and Myrt and Marge. They had dinner waiting. Billy started pumping on the piano and Wayne sang:

> You can bring Pearl, she's a damn nice girl, but don't bring Lulu.
> She's the kind of smartie that breaks up every party.
> You can bring Pearl, she's a darn nice girl, but don't bring Lulu.
> I'll bring her myself.

Wayne ended with a loud note.

Billy said, "Lulu, we barely got to know you." Then he looked directly in my eyes, like a big brother. "Are you sure you're doing the right thing?"

"Well, I'm not really that sure, but I do know one thing—my heart is with Ulysses. We promised each other to be together at Christmastime. I think I'd better follow my heart. Don't you?"

Billy scratched his cheek and said, "Well, go ahead, but please don't give Myrt any ideas about leaving."

I looked at Myrt and she winked at me, and I remembered her earlier remark.

Myrt and Billy drove me to the Greyhound bus station, the very one I had arrived at just over four months ago. I waved goodbye out the window as we headed for Nashville.

When I reached Nashville, I took a taxi to the address Ulysses had given me, as I knew he couldn't meet me after all. We drove through the lovely tree-lined boulevards and stopped at a stately white house with Christmas lights decorating a lone pine tree.

Mrs. Henry made me feel so welcome with her freshly baked pecan cookies and tea, and then she showed me to my room. I fell asleep instantly until I was awakened by a rap on the door, as the maid said, "Telephone."

"Hello?"

"Hi, Kid. You made it all right! Gee, it's nice to think you're just a few miles from me."

"How are you?" I asked.

"Well, I've been pretty cooped up since being confined to quarters after going AWOL. And the Lieutenant won't give me any special leave for tonight, like I hoped. I told him about your being here tomorrow and finally, he gave in and said I could leave at three but have to be back at nine o'clock sharp. I'm borrowing a guy's car and I'll be there right after three or as long as it takes to get there."

I slept soundly as I dreamed of being reunited with Ulysses.

After Ulysses picked me up on Christmas day, we found a small cafe with a view of the Cumberland River and a pretty park that ran right down to the water's edge. The cafe was decorated for Christmas with lots of bright lights and a big star on the top of the tree. A few snowflakes started to fall and Bing Crosby was singing, "I'm Dreaming of a White Christmas." We were together, just as we had dreamed.

Ulysses said, "Kala Xpristouyena. Merry Christmas. Say it, Louie."

"Kala Xpristouyena." And I added, "Se aga po."

"Se aga po."

A sign jutted out on the street from a small hotel. As we sat holding hands, the sign would go off and on, seemingly beckoning us with "HOTEL HOTEL HOTEL." The thought of going in there was on both our minds. Ulysses said, "Wouldn't it be nice to be together for a few hours?"

I was tempted, but said, "Our time isn't yet, remember?"

"Yes, you're right. I think too highly of you to take you in there. We'll be content just as we are, but it would be wonderful."

It was hard to resist his eyes and we snuggled even closer.

The waiter came. We ordered roast turkey and all the trimmings as we cuddled together.

Tommy Dorsey's band was playing, "I'll be seeing you/in all the old familiar places."

Ulysses said, "That's right, kid. I'll be seeing you everywhere."

He kissed me and said, "Remember when we were on the bus, when you were asleep there by the window with the sun's rays across your face."

The song continued, "I'll be looking at the moon/but I'll be seeing you."

I said, "I'll always remember how the moon shone down on the convertible—that beautiful haunting August moon."

Reaching over, Ulysses kissed me and put my coat around us.

We lingered the whole afternoon and into the evening right there in the booth until Ulysses looked at his watch. "Thanks for coming here to be with me, Kid. Isn't it awful but I have to go. You know, everyone is a little afraid of the future, but don't you be scared. You're going on to California and we'll be together again. Nothing can keep us apart."

We stood at the front door of Mrs. Henry's home at exactly eight o'clock. Ulysses had one hour to get back on time. We lingered there as long as we could. As he wrapped my coat around me, he said, "Do me a favor and don't wear brown. Myrt can wear brown. But black is your color."

It struck me funny that at our serious time of parting, he was criticizing the color of my coat. I started to laugh and then he laughed too. He was always telling me where to go and what to do.

We kissed again, and then he said, "Louie, I want you to write me every single day—I don't want you to miss even one day. Put your hand up and promise me that."

I didn't know if I'd be able to keep that promise, so I said, "I'll try."

Ulysses let me in the door and I stood with it open while he drove away, taking my heart with him.

III

California Girl

9

Return of a Wounded Soldier

As I stood before the vastness of the Pacific Ocean, I thought of my father staring across a field of wheat as it waved to and fro in the wind. One day as he stood gazing at it, I stared out too, hoping to see what he saw. He said with yearning, though not particularly to me, "It's like the sea in Denmark." I reached up and took his big, rough hand as a tear stained his suntanned face.

I wished Papa were standing there with me now—to feel the ocean's spray on his face, taste the salt in the air, and hear the cacophony of seagulls. I was so lost in thought that I didn't hear Myrt come up behind me.

"Boo!"

"You rascal—you surprised me! What are you doing this far up the beach?"

"Ahh," she said, "I woke up so happy to be here in California! The last few months have been great. I thought of you living up just a mile, so I decided to come see you. Besides, I wanted to tell you that Marge and Wayne got married and are living in Chapel Hill."

"Is he still in the navy?"

"Yeah, he got a stateside job. Lucky dogs."

"Guess that red outfit she wore to impress Ulysses really caught her man."

Myrt chuckled, and changed the subject. "What were you thinking of, standing there so still?"

"About Papa, and how he missed the sea in Denmark."

"What makes you think that?"

"Just something he said once."

Myrt's face was more animated ever before. Her blue eyes, so like Papa's, matched the water and the sky.

"How 'bout Billy," I asked, "Is he still writing?"

"All the time. It drives me nuts."

"Oh well, another gal will come along and then he'll forget you."

"How about Ulysses?"

"I meant to call and tell you—I got a letter yesterday. Let me read it to you."

I fished it out of the top of my bathing suit and read,

> Well, Kid, they finally got to me. I was hit at Venafro, near Monte Cassino, but don't worry, I have all my parts—all eager for you. I'll be coming home on a hospital ship. I'll let you know.

Myrt frowned as she said, "So he's been in Italy, huh? Mmm— nearly a year and a half since he left."

"I know. In some ways it seems like such a long time since I was with him in Nashville. But then in other ways it seems like only yesterday." I sighed.

"Well, I'm experienced with these guys who return from overseas. You remember—well of course, you gave the ring back for me."

"Talking about Robert?"

"Yeah. When he left, he was a clean-cut guy. I thought I loved him. But then when he was sent home just six months later, he'd changed completely."

"Is he the one who had the bad ear from an explosion?"

"Yeah, that's the one. When he got back, all he wanted to do was to go to bed with me. His morals were shot and his mouth was filthy."

"Gosh, Myrt, you didn't tell me that before."

"I know—I kept it to myself. But that's why I asked you to give the ring back, because he wouldn't take 'no' from me. Nor would Derrick. Should've just written them the 'Dear John' letter." Then, with a quizzical look on her face, she said, "You know, Ulysses might come back like that. What would you do then?"

I left her question unanswered as I asked, "Why did you accept their rings and get engaged in the first place? Why not just date them?"

"I don't know. I look at the poor guy telling me how much he loves me, how beautiful I am, and how he can't live without me. Then he surprises me with a ring." She gestured with her cigarette. "Oh, hell, Louie. It's happened to me twice plus Billy. Think I'll just lay off men for awhile."

She was growing too serious for such a dazzling day. "You're all of twenty-one now," I said. "The right one will come along, I just know it."

"Well, I don't know. Maybe I won't want anyone anyway." Thinking about it made her tired.

"Are you working the swing shift?" she asked.

"No, are you?"

"I was, but I'm working days now. I feel so much better, too. Hope I never have to work the graveyard shift again. Getting to bed at eight in the morning is so hard."

I started to sing the silly ditty that was so popular, "Milkman, Keep those Bottles Quiet."

Myrt, used to my habitual singing, said, "You know that lady with the five children who lives next to Maria? She's become a riveter. She says it's a good living. Each morning she goes off to work wearing blue overalls and carrying her lunch pail. Guess she'll have to stay home when the men return and want their old jobs back."

I thought about working in a factory, and didn't like the idea very much.

She turned to leave, and then remembered, "Hey, by the way, I meant to tell you—I was walking along the street the other day when a guy snapped my picture. He's going to enter it in the 'Miss Consolidated of the Month' contest. I probably won't win, but if I do, I get time off, my picture in the paper, and I'll promote War Bonds for a week. Sounds like fun!"

"Sure does! Hope you win!" I called out as she left, walking down the beach toward her apartment.

A couple of months later, at the end of March 1944, I received a letter from Ulysses. It still showed an APO number, but it was written on notebook paper instead of the standard VE issue.

> Hi, Kid.
>
> Just got off the U.S. Shamrock Hospital Ship and I'm here in Walter Reed Hospital for a little while before they send me someplace else.
>
> Say, I got notice that on April 26, Mrs. Roosevelt has invited some of us Rangers to the White House for dinner. If you were here, you could come with me. Anyway, I'll let you know how it goes.

I sat down on the couch and read and reread the letter. If he had invited me, I would have gone. I was disappointed and a little hurt, and tried to put him out of my mind.

Three months later a letter came postmarked Camp Crowder, Missouri.

Hi, Kid.

They sent me here and can you believe they're shooting real bullets over my head and training me all over again. They call it "rehabilitation." Believe me, it doesn't work.

Finally I got through to them and they have given me two weeks R & R. Is it all right if I come to see you? I can spend about ten days. Please write me right away. If you can't see me, or don't want to, I'll understand.

Louie, I would really like to at least see you, if it's OK.

P.S. I'll be coming on the train. XXXOOO

When I read and reread the letter, I whooped with joy, dancing around. "He's coming! He's really coming!" I shouted, skipping around the living room.

My roommate Mildred came out of the bedroom. "What's the matter, honey? What's going on?"

"Ulysses is coming!"

"You mean that guy you've been mooning about?" she asked in her soft Texan accent.

"That's the one," I said.

"Let me read the letter, honey," she said, extending her hand. "He can sleep on the couch. Helen won't mind—she's had so many men sleeping all over the place."

"Okay, if you two agree, that part is settled."

"Well, what else are you so nervous about?"

"I don't know, except that he's so particular about everything."

"He can't be as particular as you, Sugar. You must be two peas from the same pod."

The next day, I called Myrt at work. Before I could tell her my news, she blurted out, "You won't believe it, but I met a guy bowling. His name is Weldon and is he cute! He's three years younger than I am, but I don't care. He's so much fun!"

"Hey, not so long ago you said you were laying off guys for awhile. Anyway, what I called to tell you is that Ulysses is coming! I want you to come to the train station with me to meet him. Will you?"

"Boy, I wouldn't miss it for the world. When's he coming?"

"He'll let me know, but it'll be soon."

"Great! Hey, do you want to meet Weldon?"

"Sure," I replied.

"Wait at your desk and I'll bring him by. He's picking me up here."

Myrt and I were both secretaries in the same building but worked in different offices, so we seldom saw each other during the day.

While waiting for Myrt and Weldon to come, I busied myself arranging the typed figures on the cost-plus-fixed-fee contract between Consolidated and the government. Tomorrow morning I would go to the Ditto room and run off the copies. The Ditto machine was the latest technology, doing away with carbon copies. The only drawback was that it colored our hands deep purple.

Just as I finished, Myrt and Weldon arrived. I looked into his charming face and noticed his dancing green eyes gazing right back into mine. With a laugh and an extended hand, he said, "Hi Brat."

"Hi, Weldon. Is that a nice thing to say when just meeting me?"

"Yeah, I can see you are one."

"Myrt, how can you stand this guy?" I said, teasing him. "He must have something I can't see."

She smiled and pushed her hair away from her forehead. I could see he aroused an interest in her—at least for now.

She said, "He's really coming, huh? He hasn't forgotten you?"

"No, he hasn't! I'm so excited I can hardly do my work!"

Weldon asked, "Who is this Ulysses?"

I answered, "Myrt'll tell you about him, but I'm hoping that you both will come with me to pick him up."

Weldon said, "Sure, if she wants to, but who is he?"

Myrt answered me, "Of course we will." To Weldon, she said, "You've just got to meet him. He's the guy Louie met the day she left home. She's been waiting for him for a long time. He's been overseas—he's an Army Ranger."

It was agreed; they would come with me.

I had a hard time concentrating the next two weeks, and my boss said I was absentminded. He was right. I thought about Ulysses whenever I could, planning my clothes and thinking about the places we would go.

I wanted to look my best for Ulysses, so I stayed in the sun to keep my tan. I also added lemon juice to lighten my hair and fixed it a dozen different ways, trying to find the best one.

I worried and couldn't sleep. "Dear Lord," I prayed, "Please help me to act naturally and to be myself when he comes."

August 3, 1944, finally arrived—the day for us to go to the train station. When I got into Weldon's car, I panicked. "Myrt, will Ulysses even know me?"

"He'll know you. Don't worry."

As we walked toward the depot Myrt took my arm. Long minutes went by, and then the train came to a screeching halt. The doors opened, and people poured out. One by one they came down the steps. I looked into the faces until I spotted him, complete with Ranger patch on his shoulder and a black beret on his head.

My heart was pounding and I was damp with perspiration. I kept inching toward him through the crowd, and then when he was close enough, jumped right into his arms.

"Ulysses! I can't believe you're really here!"

His brown eyes looked into mine as he said, "You look swell, Kid. You're growing up!"

Myrt kissed him and Weldon called him "Useless," and we all made our way to the car. Ulysses and I held each other while Weldon carried the luggage.

Just before I got into the car, Myrt handed me my purse. "Bet you didn't know you threw it!"

"Thanks," I said, "What's a purse at a time like this!"

She gave me a look that said, "You must be nuts."

My heart was racing as we sat together in the back seat of the '42 Chevy. Weldon loved to talk and asked Ulysses many questions. I was silent as I tried to manage my thoughts and feelings. Who was this stranger—the guy I'd think nothing of throwing my purse for? Who was this person who wore the black beret so rakishly? This fellow who has been in Italy and North Africa? Would he behave like Myrt's boyfriend? He had seen much that I had not, and he seemed so much older.

He nervously lit a cigarette and the smoke rushed out of his nostrils. He didn't smoke before. While they all talked, I watched the tops of the palm trees as we raced by them. I was glad I could be quiet, for I needed to catch up to myself.

Just then, Ulysses reached over and covered my hand with his broad, square hand. He seemed like a more mature man now and I felt intimidated. Then he stopped talking to Weldon and whispered, "Are you glad I came?"

"You know I am. I took off the whole week to be with you."

"Good girl," he said, and a flush came over me.

It was nearly five-thirty. The sun was setting, making the sky a glowing red. A cool breeze came off the water as we unlocked the door to my apartment to drop off his luggage. We didn't linger long, joining Myrt and Weldon again to make our way up the coast to La Jolla.

Weldon wanted to go to a small Italian restaurant but Ulysses said, "Please, I don't want any spaghetti. Just the thought of it makes me sick."

"Why is that?" Weldon asked.

"Because of a dumb mistake I made once. I had three cans of C rations. It was dinnertime and everyone else was eating so I started to open a can just a little, but then I decided I wasn't hungry. The next day I ate that can but it had spoiled, making me sick. Guess I poisoned myself."

After dinner was over and we drove back to the apartment, Myrt said to me, "You know, he really is quite a guy."

I agreed. I was warming up to him as the night wore on. When we kissed goodnight, cuddling close together, it was as if my heart went right into his.

Morning came. I wasn't sure how I could sleep with Ulysses just a few feet away, but sleep I did. In fact, I didn't even hear the girls leave for work. It was ten o'clock!

I washed my face quickly, brushed my hair, put on a bathing suit and covered myself with a light robe, and peeked into the living room. Ulysses was all tangled up in the white blanket, an arm dangling over the side of the couch.

I made us some coffee, using the same coffee grounds the girls had used and adding two tablespoons of fresh coffee on top, as it was scarce. In the middle of fixing the breakfast tray, I heard, "Louie, where are you?"

Oh, how my heart raced. His beard was beginning to grow and his disheveled hair was a curly mass. I said to myself, "Slow down, keep calm, and don't get carried away."

"Come here, Kid!"

He drew me to himself and we kissed passionately. Sorely tempted, I disengaged myself from his arms and said, "Here's a bathing suit. Let's take a morning swim and then have breakfast."

His strong hand gripped mine as we entered the rushing water. Sun-bleached surfers were not far away, gliding gracefully on the waves. We went further in, the tide threatening to pull us under. Ulysses shied back, saying, "Better watch my head!" I remembered that he'd had a bad concussion.

Refreshed, we started back through the sand, my carefully combed hair now wet and stringy. No matter. My love was here beside me— the dream I had dreamed so often in the last two years.

"Hey, Kid, I'm hungry. How about some breakfast?"

"Okay, it's nearly ready. Here's a towel—I'll bring it out."

As I went in, Ulysses called out, "Scramble my eggs well and make sure there's no runny stuff in there."

After breakfast we took a straw mat out onto the sand. Ulysses' lithe, muscled body was white next to my brown skin. As we lay close, it was as if the sun were wrapping us in a warm blanket. Ulysses drew close to me and began to share things he had never told anyone else.

He spoke of the guys in the outfit, of the dangers, fears, hopes, and homesickness. Of the "Dear John" letters and how they upset and worried the guys. Of the ladies in the towns, and the nurses and their liaisons. Also of the bravery and courage of the Rangers and the way they admired and loved Colonel William Darby.

Then he said, "Sometimes, just for the hell of it, some of us would get leave and go into the strange towns and take a look around. Well, one day Nick Bartoni—hey, he was from Minnesota, too! Well, in Casablanca, we went to the medina in the old part of town. It was all so strange and so different. We saw a huge building, with a wall around it. Then we noticed two carved doors—each about ten feet across—that were open. We didn't see anyone around so we went in.

"We noticed that there were many small rooms, and suddenly dozens of women came out all covered from head to toe. We couldn't even see their faces. They pulled out long knives from somewhere and came after us, forcing us up against the wall. We couldn't understand a word they were saying. I'm sure we could've fought them off, but if we did, we probably would have been court-martialed. They were about to kill us for invading their privacy.

"Then we heard men marching outside. It sounded like an army. They were coming closer and closer as we stood tensely against the wall. Fortunately for us, it was the French Foreign Legion patrol. They could see the women with the knives through the opening and rescued us. A tall swarthy Frenchman said, 'Americans, huh? Don't you know better than to enter these places? Get back to your outfit, tout de suite!' He didn't have to tell us twice."

"Wasn't a bordello, was it?"

"We didn't know, and never found out."

"All these things going on," I mused, "and here I was in this country, praying for your safe return."

"Well, I came back, didn't I?'

"Yes, but what about the shrapnel and the concussion?"

"Well, you've probably never heard of Monte Cassino. It's an ancient monastery high on the mountain overlooking Venafro, Italy. The Nazis captured it and had their headquarters up there. All of their heavy guns were shooting down on us.

"It was November last year—November the 13TH. During a lull in the battle, someone came to tell a buddy of mine, Steve Metrick, that the CO wanted him. Steve wanted me to go along with him. It was chow time, so I said, 'You go and I'll save you space in the chow-line.'"

Ulysses paused then and I saw him try to fight back the tears forming in his eyes. His voice cracked as he said, "I turned to go one way, and he turned to go the other. Just when he turned and passed a doorway, a Jerry shell came out of the blue. It hit him, the impact breaking every bone in his body. I watched his body crumble before my eyes."

He was quiet for a moment, and then said, "It barely missed me. I ended up with a concussion and shrapnel. Makes you wonder why I lived and he didn't. We were only a few feet apart."

Telling me about Steve drained Ulysses and put him in a melancholy mood. He added, almost in a whisper, "We promised that if anything happened to either of us, we'd go tell the folks." He moved his head over onto my lap. He was too tired to talk more and closed his eyes.

Sensing this, I began to sing to him. "I don't want to walk without you, Baby/walk without my arms about you, Baby."

He fell asleep, and his rhythmic breathing made me reluctant to move. I searched his face that was young in years, but now old in experience. He was still a Johnny Garfield look-alike. That little curl on his forehead was cut very short, but it was still dangling there.

I listened to his soft breathing and pondered about him and me. Where would this all end? I knew we needed time, but what is this sense of destiny I felt? Do all lovers share this feeling? I didn't hear Myrt speak this way with any of her loves. Or anyone else for that matter.

I looked at his closed eyes, now deep in sleep. I was determined not to disturb our relationship over petty things. I would stick with it until I knew which way it should go. "Lord," I prayed, "please help me to know the right way."

A Convair PBY plane zoomed over the ocean with the thrust of its engine reverberating in the sky. It startled Ulysses and his whole body trembled. I patted him, assuring him everything was all right. He settled down again, secure in my arms.

After awhile, I grew very thirsty, so with one hand I molded a lump of sand under the mat and fashioned a pillow for him. I released him gently and laid his head on the mound.

When I returned with some Cokes, he had awakened. He looked more rested.

"Where'd you go, Kid? You left me alone."

Holding the glass to his lips, I said, "Have a drink!"

Eagerly he drank. When I bent to kiss him, he slipped a piece of ice from his lips to mine. Close in his arms, I asked, "You feel better now?"

"Yeah. Seems like I just want to sleep all the time."

"Are you hungry for anything?"

"Just more of you!"

As he embraced me, I said, "Ulysses, you never made it clear to me what happened after you left me in Tennessee. I know you couldn't explain it in a letter."

"Well, Kid, that whole deal is how I got into the Rangers. You see, after you left, it wasn't long before we were shipped out. We ended up in North Africa. You remember that lieutenant who had it in for me after I went AWOL? Well, aboard ship they asked for volunteers. They chose me right off the bat, my name beginning with an 'A', and they named me mess sergeant."

He paused to take a sip of Coke. "Anyway, on this ship the lieutenant would come in after hours and ask for something special. When he did, I pointed to the rules on the wall poster. I didn't bend any of them for him. Boy, did he have it in for me after that. As soon as we landed, my buddy Nick and I were arrested to quarters and put in a six-foot pup tent.

"While we were in the tent, we could hear a fella outside apparently recruiting for the Rangers. I was so anxious to get away from this lieutenant that I called out to him and asked if I could volunteer for this Ranger outfit. The lieutenant was double glad to get rid of me, too. He said, 'If you can pass the physical, go ahead.' Nick volunteered too."

He took a drink of the Coke, wiped his face with a piece of the ice, and pulled me down to him, saying, "That, Kid, is how I got into the Rangers."

We lived precious moments there on the beach. He was different in a more mature way, but he was discerning and respected my feelings.

The next day, we decided to take the bus into town. We got off at Broadway, San Diego's main street, landing in a sea of sailors and marines.

"Why didn't you tell me all these guys were here?" Ulysses asked. "I'd have never sent you to San Diego!"

I just laughed, and then asked, "Are you up to walking? I want to show you where I worked all the time you were gone."

"Sure, Kid."

We passed Lindbergh Field and saw signs for the war everywhere: "TALK SINKS SHIPS," "UNCLE SAM NEEDS YOU," and heavyweight champion Joe Louis saying, "WE'RE GOING TO DO OUR PART."

Ulysses asked, "Is this the way it is, with all these signs everywhere?"

"Yep. And look at the camouflage over this whole area. From the air it's supposed to fool the enemy and appear to be a desert scene."

We had reached the building we called "The Rock" because it lacked windows. We stood outside in the concrete courtyard, the place where most of us gathered for morning coffee and sometimes lunch.

"Ulysses, I wanted to come here with you because so many mornings I've stood out here sipping coffee, thinking about you and saying a prayer."

"Well, Kid, I'm here now and believe me, I ain't going back."

I reached up and kissed him. Standing here with him was a dream come true.

We started to walk back toward town. Just as we passed by Lindbergh field, a B-24 took off with a deafening roar. Ulysses, trigger-trained for self-preservation, dove down into the gutter of the roadway. He was on his knees with head down, his hands covering his ears. When he realized where he was, he quickly got up and brushed off his uniform, saying, "Sorry. For a moment I thought I was back in Italy."

I comforted him, realizing that while his body was in pretty good shape, his mind needed a lot of restoring. Shakily, he lit a cigarette and we kept walking toward town. I held onto him and felt his body still trembling. Up ahead we saw a sidewalk cafe and whiffed the tantalizing smells of hamburger, onion, and mustard. It would give us a welcome break.

After a lunch we decided to duck into the theater next to us, where *Casablanca* was playing. Ulysses said, "Seems like a long time ago that I was right there."

It was an extraordinary film, and left us in a serious mood. Afterward we took another long walk toward the zoo and then had dinner in a crowded French restaurant. Only out of necessity did we let go of the other's hand.

The next few days we grew brown in the sun, talking, sharing, and getting to know each other better. On Thursday, I got an urgent call from the office. "Miss Hansen, please come into work tomorrow. Two girls are out sick and we have an emergency report that we have to get out. We really need you."

Reluctantly I agreed, leaving Ulysses alone in the apartment. I hated to leave him, but the day went by quickly as we were so busy.

When I returned home, only Ulysses' clothes were there. I hunted all over but couldn't find him. Finally I walked to the bus stop, lingering there. Soon the doors opened, and Ulysses got off the bus.

"Well, you found your way around," I said.

"Yeah, I went downtown. Got a little tired of the sun. Let's go inside—I got something for you."

He pulled me close to him on the couch and handed me a small wrapped package.

"Open it!"

Hastily, I tore off the pretty gold and pink paper and opened the tiny box. In it was a gold ring, encircled with roses.

"It's not a diamond, Louie, and I couldn't afford one anyway. Just wanted you to have something on that left hand of yours. Let's call it a friendship ring."

He put it on my finger.

He had surprised me completely, but the words "friendship ring" caused my heart to sink a little. I said, "Thank you, Ulysses. It's really beautiful." I put it to my lips and kissed it, saying, "I'll always cherish it."

Haltingly, he said, "Kid, well, you know it's more than a friendship ring. Maybe some day it'll be something else."

His brown eyes showed promise and sincerity and that was enough for me.

I said, "Tomorrow night's our last night. Myrt and Weldon want to know if we'll go dancing with them at a place called Pacific Square. Frank Sinatra was there not long ago. I wasn't going to scream when I saw him, but I must admit I let out a little sound."

I smiled at him, and he hugged me and said, "If you want to go, Kid, it's okay with me."

Weldon and Myrt picked us up and we drove down Pacific Highway and parked on the large lot. We could hear the music from outside the large dance hall. Tommy Dorsey's band was filling the night air, and as we entered, Helen Forrest was singing "Long Ago and Far Away." As Ulysses held me close in his arms the words of the song seemed perfect: "Just one look and then I knew,/that all I longed for so long ago was you."

Ulysses whispered in my ear, "Louie, about that ring. You know what it might be someday, don't you? Right now, I don't know what I'm doing. I'm not even discharged yet, but will be soon. I need to spend time with my folks and sort things out."

I could feel his breath on my ear as I said, "Don't worry—we've got plenty of time."

I had danced with others and felt them close. But when I was dancing with Ulysses I never wanted the music to stop.

On our last morning together, Mildred took our pictures under the palm tree. Ulysses had gained seven pounds and looked wonderfully tanned and much better than when he came.

I hated to see him go, but it was not a sad goodbye. I realized that this was an interlude in our lives and that he needed more time before he would come to himself.

10

Wedding Bells

A WEEK AFTER ULYSSES LEFT, Myrt called. "Louie! I won the contest!"

"You did? Wow, that's great! Congratulations, you deserve it!"

"I can't believe it," she said breathlessly. "Come shopping with me, will you? I need a new dress for my pinup picture."

We arranged to meet at La Dona Dress Shoppe just off Broadway. Having arrived early, I browsed in the window of the lingerie store next door, where a white negligee and gown caught my eye. The ensemble was different from most because of its delicate hand-embroidered roses, which seemed to match the roses on my friendship ring.

I went inside to take a closer look. It was even more beautiful than I had realized.

"I'd like to try this on," I told the friendly woman behind the counter, "but I'm meeting my sister next door. Could you hold it for a little while?"

Through the window I saw Myrt approaching, hair flying in the breeze and yellow suit sparkling in the sun. I went to congratulate her again.

We looked through the racks of dresses together. I thought to myself, "Myrt might not be able to pick her men very easily, but when it comes to clothes, she knows exactly what she wants."

She selected five dresses and went back to the fitting room. While she was trying them on, I slipped next door. The gown and negligee fit perfectly. I just had to buy them.

"How much is this?" I asked, holding up the combination.

"Fifty dollars."

"Fifty dollars!" I said, "That's expensive!"

"It's all handmade—just look at the workmanship."

I agreed that it was lovely.

"I'll need twenty dollars to hold it, and five dollars a month."

I grew flustered thinking about how tight my money would be, especially as I must always send money to Mama. But then I thought back to when I bought my riding outfit. When lunchtime would come I'd go into a drugstore and order a cup of hot water. I'd sit next to a ketchup bottle and some little dishes of oyster crackers, which I'd make into my free meal. I knew I'd have to do it again, as well as stopping in at my sisters' for dinner a few times.

I said, "Here's the twenty dollars. Please hold it."

When I joined Myrt again, she asked, "Where've you been?"

"Next door to see what they had." But I didn't explain what I had just done.

"That black dress looks great!" I said. "The low-cut bodice, whew! And I love how your legs look with that sheer at the bottom."

"I think this is the one," she said to the cute salesgirl. As she paid for the dress, she said to me, "I really can't afford this dress."

"Well, you can always join me at the drugstore for ketchup and crackers."

A few weeks later, I received a letter from Ulysses from Camp Crowder, Missouri.

> Had a wonderful time, Kid. Thanks for everything. Now they're talking discharge. I'll let you know—I'm still tanned—and feel good!
>
> Don't take off the ring.

Then about a month later Ulysses sent me a birthday card and said that his discharge date would be October 25, 1944. He was going back to Washington, D.C. to spend some time with his folks and return to his printing job. I thought of him often, but tried to get on with my life.

A month later, I was sitting at my desk when I felt an excruciating pain in my right side. The last few days I hadn't had an appetite and felt strange. But it had been nothing like this pain. I called Myrt and she helped me get to a local Seventh Day Adventist hospital not far from work.

They examined me, and although there was some mention of appendicitis, they took no action. Maybe they didn't work on Saturday, I thought. In desperation, I called my brother Chris and explained the situation.

After contacting his own doctor, he called me back. "Get your things together and leave your robe on. I'm coming to get you."

In a short time he arrived. A man of action, he picked me up and carried me out of the room, down the elevator, and right out the door. The staff was short-handed and no one saw me go.

His doctor was waiting at another hospital, and as soon as I was in the elevator he gave me a shot. That's the last I remembered until I woke up with a bandage on my right side.

The doctor had been in my room, checking on me. He said, "Got the appendix out just before it broke."

I murmured a prayer of thanks under my breath. I was so glad I had called Chris.

After five days in the hospital, I received a call from Maria, who told me that I would be discharged the next day. "I'll come and get you before ten o'clock," she said, "and I'll take you home with me until you recover."

The next morning, Maria and her two little girls, Shirley and Phylis, showered me with love. Her pain from her recent divorce didn't stop her from reaching out to me. I was so glad to belong to a large family.

I had been at Maria's three days when she received a telegram. I waited expectantly and a little apprehensively as she gave a dime to the man with the worn Western Union cap. Telegrams were expensive and only used in times of major importance.

She opened it quickly, and I saw her face turn white. She handed it to me, tears streaming down her face. I read and reread it, unable to speak. Strong Papa, always there, was now gone. Maria called Chris, Bertha, and Myrtle, and then came to my side so we could cling together. Marlin, in the navy, still needed to be notified. The rest of the family was in Minnesota with Mama.

I wanted to go along to Mankato, but the doctor said it was too risky and wouldn't allow me to go. I stayed with the two little girls while my brother and sisters took turns driving nonstop to Minnesota.

After I was left with Shirley and Phylis and my aching side, reality set in. Papa had died. When I thought of him, I remembered strength. In my mind, I returned to his last act toward me, giving me money he should not have spared and placing his hands on my head to bless me. I vowed never to forget his words of encouragement and his faith in God and America. He believed in the American dream, that success could happen. Even though he was gone now, I hoped that I could prove him right, no matter what it took.

On a day in the middle of March, I got home from work, took off my shoes, sat in the big chair, and looked across at the couch where Ulysses had slept. He hadn't written me since New Year's, and I was a little depressed. Was I wasting my young years? Why had I bought the lingerie? Where was he now, and what was he doing?

Just then Mildred came out of the bedroom, holding a letter. "Look what's on the envelope!"

I sprang from the chair, taking it from her hand. It was Ulysses' handwriting! It said "Louie, look where I am!"

With a gasp, I tore open the letter.

> Kid. Came to LA with two guys, Gus Plakus and Stanley Valanos. You don't know either one. What a trip! When I see you, I'll tell you about it. We're staying at the YMCA—no room anywhere else.
>
> Found a job as soon as I got here at the Pacific Press, printing the *Life* and *Time* magazines.
>
> Can I come to see you week after next? Tell me where and I'll tell you when. Se aga po.

I thought to myself, "Well, I'll be darned. Just when I'm ready to give up on the guy, he turns up. So he's in LA! I wonder what all this means."

I wrote him right back, but instead of inviting him to the apartment, I told him to meet me at Maria's house.

He surprised me by his quick reply: "Louie, I've got it all figured out. I'll be coming up the street between five and five-thirty, if I beat the traffic and if it isn't foggy."

Immediately after work on that Saturday, I took the streetcar up past the zoo to Maria's. When I opened the door, I said, "Smells good. What are you cooking?"

"Mama's favorite. Chicken and dumplings with fresh green peas from my garden."

"Ulysses will like it."

It was now 5:15. I touched up my lipstick and said, "I'm just going to wait outside for Ulysses. He should be here any minute."

The sun was low over the mountains and the famous cool breeze ruffled my hair as I stood in the front yard. Soon a black Chevy came along, and then I heard, "Kid! I found the place!"

His brown eyes were sparkling, his black hair shiny and wavy. He complimented me on my new dress, which was chartreuse on one side and black on the other.

Keeping my distance, I said, "You must've been awfully busy in the past few months."

"Well, Kid, when I got to Washington, the printing company gave me my old job back. I saw a lot of friends, and my family gave me parties. It was good to be home again for awhile."

He paused, looking into my face, and said, "Guess I got to missing you a little bit." His eyes spoke more than his words.

He kissed me full on the lips then and held me close. I started to forget my irritation.

"Come in the car for a few moments."

"So what made you want to come to LA?" I asked, wondering how he would respond. "And how did you get here?"

"Well, Kid, me and a couple of guys, Gus Plakus and Stanley Valanos, were having a beer at a hangout called Buck's Bar. Out of the blue, Gus said, 'Why don't we go to California?' Stanley said, 'Yeah, why don't we?' It sure sounded good to me, so I offered my car but said we'd need more money. We talked about it, and before the night was over we agreed that if each of us came up with a hundred dollars, we'd make the trip."

Ulysses paused to light his cigarette.

"By the end of the week, we had all the money. I borrowed on my car from a loan shark. Have to pay him back at eleven dollars a month. Anyway, we set out. First, we used up my hundred, and then Gus's. That took us to the California border. When we got there, we told Stanley it was his turn. He turned his pockets inside out and said he didn't have any money. Boy, did Gus and I get mad."

"What'd you do then?"

"Well, if you only knew Stanley! He charmed his way through it—got some girls to buy us dinner, and some guy to give us gas, knowing we were all veterans. We were flat broke when we finally got to LA. Stanley called his brother, Connie, who sent some money and then flew out a week later to get his clothes. Stanley had taken most of them with him.

"Fortunately, Gus and I found work immediately at the Pacific Press. We were able to get rooms at the YMCA because we had jobs. Stanley found some kind of work too—he's got his eye on Hollywood."

I interrupted him, "I wish we could stay here and talk; it's been so long. But Maria's been cooking all day, so we shouldn't keep her waiting."

"Listen, Kid. I'm going to be seeing a lot of you from now on. We'll never stop talking. Let's go meet Maria."

As we entered the house, Maria gave Ulysses a big hug and kiss. I noticed Phylis and Shirley had picked red bougainvillea blossoms for the centerpiece, and now Shirley was placing the warm rolls on the table and Phylis the butter. Maria brought in the chicken and dumplings, which Ulysses eyed hungrily. Everything was ready.

Later on in the evening, Maria asked me, "Are you really interested in this Ulysses?"

"I am. He makes me feel complete inside."

"You're both so different."

"He's strong, Maria. Reminds me of Papa. Yeah, I do like him. There's something that gets lit in me the moment he's near."

Maria loved me and wanted the best for me. She didn't say anything else.

About eight o'clock the front door opened and in came Myrt and Weldon. Myrt proudly held forth her left hand, which sported a diamond and ruby engagement ring. Ebullient Weldon saw Ulysses.

"Useless! You're back! Say, we're getting married in June. How about being our best man?"

I saw Ulysses' bewilderment. He looked at me as if to say, "Is it all right?" I nodded my head, and Ulysses shook Weldon's hand and said, "Swell!"

Our reunion at Maria's was the first of many nights together. Ulysses continued to drive back and forth to see me, staying at my apartment at least two or three times a month. I wondered if I was moving in the right direction after all.

I was sitting at my desk on April 12, 1945, when the loudspeaker announced that the only president I had ever known, President Roosevelt, had died of a cerebral hemorrhage. Now Harry Truman would become the president. I leaned over on my desk, crying, when I received one of my rare phone calls. It was Ulysses.

"So the big man died, huh!"

I was sniffling.

"You're crying aren't you? Sentimental again!"

"He's the only president I've ever known."

"Kid, don't take it so hard. The country didn't fall down."

A month later, on May 8TH, excitement was in the air. It was VE Day and the Germans had surrendered in Europe. Again, Ulysses called me. "Kid! I'm driving down. I don't have much time—got to get back to work—but have to see you."

We intended to go dancing, so we met at Convair. It was bedlam outside: Horns were honking; people were screaming; couples were kissing; Pacific Square was packed. The celebrations were everywhere, and we couldn't dance. All the confusion gave Ulysses a headache.

"Can't we go to the apartment and make a sandwich?"

"All I have is bologna."

"Good. I love it."

We made our way, inching along through the heavy traffic, waving, yelling, and honking at all the other revelers on the roads and sidewalks.

Eating our bologna sandwiches, we reminisced about the lonely, fearful years. Ulysses said, "When Italy surrendered in August of '43, it caught me sitting on the commode in the men's room. I kept hearing all the church bells ringing like crazy. I asked someone what happened, and they said, 'Italy's surrendered! It's over!' And now the Germans have surrendered too, Kid. We're together!"

He paused, with a wistful look in his eyes. "Can't help but think about the guys who didn't come home." He had many fellow Rangers to remember. We found out later that of the fifteen hundred original Rangers, only ninety-nine returned home. But the war wasn't over yet. There was still Japan to conquer, so victory was not yet complete.

About midnight, Ulysses said, "Damn boss, Otto. He drives me crazy, he's a regular slave driver. Have to go, Kid. It's a long drive back up the 101A. Hope there's no fog."

We said goodbye at the door. Ulysses said to me, "One day we won't be kissing goodbye. We'll just be right together."

I went to bed singing.

The second Saturday in June 1945 was Myrt's small family-only wedding at Maria's house. In the children's room I dressed in the yellow bridesmaid's dress and sang "Happy the Bride the Sun Shines on Today."

I fastened a yellow rose in my upswept hair, thinking back to the day Myrt left Minnesota, so unsure of herself. Today, just three years later, she seemed radiant and confident.

Yesterday, Mama had arrived. The rest of the family and I worried that Papa's death might have left her devastated, but she seemed as calm and serene as ever. Mama always seemed to be standing on a solid rock. In a way, her serenity was a mystery to us.

I went into the flower-laden living room and saw her drinking her coffee. She was dressed in her favorite lavender, her pale gray hair upswept with the same curly tendrils caressing her neck. Bertha was there too, practicing the bride's song and complaining how out of tune the piano was, while her husband Jay sat reading the *San Diego Union*. Shirley and Phylis, dressed in pink frothy dresses and black patent shoes, were playing hopscotch out by the front door, waiting for the wedding to begin.

I could see Ulysses out in the backyard dressed in his dark blue suit, sprawled on the chaise under the shade of the lemon trees. Earlier he had said to me, "I'm going to stay out here until all the fussaria [troubles] are over and the Reverend comes. Call me at the last minute, cause I'm not coming back into the house."

Just then Myrt, who had been finishing dressing in the bedroom, came in. She was glowing in her lace wedding gown.

Kissing Mama, she said, "How do I look as a bride?"

"If you're marrying the right man, you'll always look beautiful—just like you look today."

"I hope I am, Mama. He makes me very happy."

Mama hugged Myrt, and Myrt kissed her on the forehead. Maria came out of the kitchen with a large tray of ham and cheese sandwiches with colorful pieces of fruit. On the other end of the table was a pink and white wedding cake.

Chris and his wife Lorna came in. Pearl and Hazel weren't able to be with us, and Marlin was still in the navy.

Then, through the window, I could see the Lutheran pastor arriving with his large black Bible. Right behind Rev. James came Weldon's parents and his sister Marlene, who was dressed in a pink bridesmaid's dress. Except for the photographer, we were all present now. I went to tell Ulysses.

"Everyone's here, Ulysses."

He pulled me down to him and kissed me.

"You just messed up my lipstick!"

"Let me mess it up again." He kissed me again just as the late photographer arrived through the back way and snapped our picture.

Inside, the minister had everyone lined up. We took our places and the photographer went to work.

Bertha, her dimples showing as she smiled, began playing the wedding march. She was right, the piano was out of tune. Chris took the signal and went back to the bedroom. Soon Myrt appeared, Chris's arm about hers, as she slowly entered, her eyes on Weldon and his admiring eyes on her. Ulysses and I stood on either side. Mama sat in her comfortable chair, watching all of us with a smile.

The minister began, "We are gathered here together in the sight of God and man to join this man and this woman in Holy Matrimony. If there is any reason why this man and this woman should not be married, speak now or forever hold your peace."

It was quiet for a few seconds and Weldon couldn't help but clown around, stretching his neck over to see if anyone would step forward. Ulysses nudged him. I worried, wondering if he would ever be serious.

As the minister spoke on, the two little flower girls gazed upward at Aunt Myrtle and soon-to-be Uncle Weldon, who was now trying to look serious. With his curved-up mouth and mischievous eyes, it wasn't easy.

"Do you, Myrtle Hansen, take this man to be your lawfully wedded husband, to have and to hold, in sickness and in health, for richer and for poorer, till death do ye part?"

Myrt cleared her throat and said, "I do."

It was Weldon's turn.

"Do you, Weldon Cochrane, take this woman to be your lawfully wedded wife, to have and to hold, in sickness and in health, for richer and for poorer, till death ye do part?"

My eyes were glued on Weldon. I was hoping to see the serious side of him. His face turned pink, and he looked at Myrt as if he were on his knees imploring her to understand that he did love her. He looked deeply into her eyes and with sincerity said, "I do." He made me very happy.

Phylis handed him the small gold ring at the right signal. Weldon put it on the bride's hand carefully, saying "With this ring, I thee wed."

The minister finished with, "I now pronounce you man and wife. You may kiss the bride."

Bertha struck the final cord on the piano as they kissed. We all gathered around for congratulations, more kisses, and plenty of food and punch.

Lorna had played in a local dance band in Mankato and couldn't resist going over to the piano. She caught the mood and began to play, "Roll out the barrel/we'll have a barrel of fun. . . /Roll out the barrel/we've got the blues on the run."

The way she played we couldn't help but sing. We sang every song we could, with Weldon as the best singer. I forgot all about the bride until she stood before us in a rust-colored suit. We all stopped singing.

Weldon went to her and whispered something in her ear. Myrt blushed and Weldon said, "Thank you all for everything. We're leaving now, driving to Mexico. Only have a week's leave."

Myrt kissed Mama and waved goodbye to the rest of us. Off they went with pink and blue ribbons flapping in the wind and tin cans jangling behind them. What a day!

Chris and Lorna took Mama home with them for an extended visit. It was time for us to leave too, so that Ulysses could get to work at midnight. We said goodnight to all.

When we got to my apartment we stood by the palm tree overlooking the ocean. The moon lit up the breakers as the sea danced about, and Ulysses said, "Did those words the preacher said today mean anything to you?"

"No, not much."

He said, "Ptseftis," meaning liar.

We kissed and he held me close there in the moonlight.

"I'm so tired of running back and forth between here and LA. Hope there's no fog on my way home."

I sighed, thinking of him driving all the way back to LA.

He looked out across the water and said, "This would not be a good night for a landing. It's too bright."

No matter what was going on, the war experience was always with us.

"See you next week, Kid. Se aga po."

As I prepared for sleep, I relived the day, thinking also of Papa. I wished he could have been there with Mama. When it came to the singing part, he could have outdone Weldon.

II

From One Coast to Another

MYRT AND WELDON CAME BACK from a wonderful week in Mexico and seemed so happy to be married. The summer passed by uneventfully, until one day I'll never forget—August 6, 1945.

During the ten o'clock coffee break, Ophelia, a fellow secretary, suggested we get some coffee and doughnuts. As we stood enjoying our refreshments, we heard a beep on the loudspeaker signaling a message to follow. We stood silently as we waited for the news.

It was announced that the crew of the Enola Gay, a B-29 bomber named for the pilot's mother, had bombed a faraway place called Hiroshima with something called the "atomic bomb." We had never heard of this terminology before; it was a surprise to us and to the world.

As we listened further, we heard that thousands had been killed and that the Japanese had been warned to surrender. If they didn't, a second bomb would be dropped on Nagasaki in three days.

We were all stunned as we laid our coffee aside.

Ophelia remarked, "Doesn't it feel like the end of the world is coming? It just sounds so eerie."

I was silent, shocked by the news.

She continued, "Did you hear what they said about the 'mushroom cloud'?"

I nodded. The world had suddenly changed, and we could feel it.

Three days later the second bomb was dropped on Nagasaki, killing thousands more. The Japanese surrendered a week later, on August 14, although the war hadn't yet come to an official end.

Ulysses and I continued to see each other at the weekends, with him driving the ninety miles down Highway 101A from Los Angeles. When he visited at the end of August, the fog was so thick that he couldn't see a foot ahead of him.

He was visibly shaken when he came through the front door. "Louie, I can't stand that trip anymore. I had to drive while hanging outside on the running board."

I tried to comfort him, thankful that he had made it safely.

He continued, "On Labor Day weekend, you take the train and come and see me."

I looked at him, and he could read my mind. "Don't worry—I'll have the landlady get a room for you."

I agreed to go.

I took the train to Los Angeles on a remarkably hot day, and Ulysses was waiting for me at the station. I was wearing a pink silk dress and beige shoes with no stockings. Still it was stifling. The car must have been at least a hundred degrees inside.

As soon as we drove off, Ulysses said, "We've got to find a place to get a cold drink."

I could stand the heat quite easily, but Ulysses had more difficulty. His face was dripping with perspiration and his shirt was wet. We held hands and drove down Lascienga Boulevard until we came to an outdoor root-beer stand, where we had huge, frosty glasses of root beer brought to our car.

We drank eagerly, and when Ulysses had nearly finished, he looked across at me and stared for awhile. Then he lifted the glass to his lips and drank more, looking like he wanted to say something.

I didn't speak, but worried about him for a moment because his eyes were so bright and shiny.

Then he said, "You know, I think I'm drunk, but I just looked at you and I think we're supposed to get married."

He surprised me so much that I nearly dropped my glass.

"What did you just say?" I asked incredulously.

"Kid, I think we ought to get married. I've had all the freedom I want and I think I want to marry you. What do you say?"

"Are you drunk?"

"I think I am. This cold root beer must've gone right to my head. Just looking at you there, I think we ought to get married."

"Get married!" I repeated.

I was silent, thinking how strange it was that what I had been longing for had finally come, but now it seemed such a surprise and I wasn't sure. Then I thought about my life. The war would be over any day now and I'd probably lose my job. I sensed such a feeling of change in the air.

I looked at Ulysses again, who was still staring at me, waiting for an answer.

"Are you sure?" I asked.

"Why ask if I'm sure? I'm as sure as any drunk can be."

So there in the hot car, drunk on ice-cold root beer, I accepted. It must have shocked both of us, because we rode around in silence. The thought of getting married really sobered us up.

It was the beginning of an era, but also the end. Two days later, Sunday, September 2, 1945, was called VJ Day when the war officially ended aboard the USS Missouri, which was anchored in Tokyo Bay. World War II was now history.

When I returned home from seeing Ulysses, at first I kept silent about our engagement so I could ponder our decision. But later, at Maria's house with Mama and everyone present, I made a little speech.

"Mama, I'm going to marry Ulysses. I know that he's Greek and a little bit different. But then again, he's not so different. Papa was a foreigner and you married him, which makes both Ulysses and me first-generation Americans. When Ulysses speaks Greek, it's like Papa speaking German, or Danish or Norwegian. I'd like you to feel happy about it, Mama."

I didn't worry about what anyone else thought, but I did want her blessing.

Mama, quiet as always, was silent for quite a few moments. Then she said, "Lulu, I told you I put you in God's hands."

That was all she said. In other words, although she might not trust my judgment, she trusted God.

I was thankful for such a wise mother. I continued my speech, "Just before Christmas, I want to take everyone out to dinner to celebrate. Before New Year's Eve, I'm going up to be with Ulysses."

Before they could look shocked, I added, "He lives in a rooming house, and he's getting me a separate room there until we get married." It was drilled into us that nice girls didn't.

"Since none of his family can be at the wedding, we've decided that it will be just the two of us. Ulysses tried to get permission for us to be married in the Greek Orthodox Church, but because I'm not baptized in it, the priest can't give us permission. We'll get married quietly instead."

Mama didn't look worried, but was as peaceful as always.

Ulysses came down at Christmas, and we enjoyed a goodbye celebration dinner with my family. With a mixture of feelings, I realized that it was a real turning point in my life.

On December 31, I took my heavy suitcases to the train station. While waiting to board, I called Myrt.

She said, "If I ever saw anyone fall for a guy, it's you! I get the feeling that your life is not going to be too easy. But I bet one thing, it will never be boring. You're mighty ambitious. Don't forget to come see us sometime."

She seemed to be choking back tears.

Then she added, "Much as I love Weldon and I'm happy, I doubt if I'd ever get so excited as to throw my purse for him."

In busy Los Angeles, I stepped off the train and into Ulysses' waiting arms.

"The landlady got you a room across the hall from me. We'll be sharing a bath! Don't mind, do you?"

I was shaking as I shook my head. It was all so intimate and exciting.

We drove to Mrs. Handley's large stucco house. A widow, she supported herself by renting rooms. When Ulysses introduced us, she said, straightening her apron, "Had to turn away a lot of people to save this room for you, but Ulysses is such a gentleman."

Behind her back, he looked at me as if to say, "Sure fooled her, didn't I?"

I laughed and took his hand, and we went to my new gray and pink room. It wasn't bad, but I was used to the fresh ocean air. This room was musty and reeked of cigarettes.

Ulysses caught me in his arms and whispered, "I love you."

I soon forgot the smell.

As I started to unpack my things, Ulysses lay across the bed, his eyes on me. Then in a slightly apologetic voice he said, "You know, Louie, we could go to Washington and get married there. But if we did, they'd make such a fuss. You'd be surprised the fussaria [trouble] it would create."

"I'm happy just the way it is."

"Listen, Kid. When we can afford it, we'll be married again in the Greek Church. I promise you."

"Please don't worry. It will be wonderful to be just the two of us."

"Hey, it's New Year's Eve tonight—1946 already! What do you say we just go out for a little dinner? We're together, that's all we need."

I didn't care about big celebrations. It was so thrilling just to be with him.

Since we didn't have a church in which to marry, the next day we looked up chapels in the Yellow Pages. We found an interesting one at Hollywood and Vine, the Marriage Manor, which we called.

"Do you have a marriage license?" they asked.

When we said that we didn't, they instructed us to get one at City Hall. They also told us to get our blood tested. After sorting out the details, we made a date for January 9TH.

The day before our wedding, we told our kind landlady that after tonight we would need only one room, because we were getting married.

She was very happy and said, "I've got some wonderful flowers from the garden. I'll give you a large bouquet."

I asked, "You wouldn't have any roses, would you?"

She looked very excited. "I sure do! My son is a nut on roses. He's the one who grows them and takes care of them. Also, I'll put a pretty pink coverlet on the bed. Ulysses' room is the biggest, so you'll be moving in there, right?"

I nodded.

"What time is your wedding?"

"Two o'clock."

"When you return, I'll have it all fixed up for you."

I hugged her, thanking her.

Then she added, "I'll move your things for you. Don't you worry about anything."

I went to bed with excitement, but Ulysses had to work the graveyard shift from midnight until eight in the morning. Otto, his boss at the printers, haunted him.

The next morning I got up early and dressed carefully. I wanted Ulysses to sleep as long as he could, so I didn't go over and wake him.

Around twelve thirty, he knocked on my door, having slept barely five hours.

I kissed his sleepy eyes as he asked, "Aren't we supposed to be there at two o'clock?"

He was unshaven and looked tired and disheveled. His hands were black from the ink of the presses.

"Go and dress, honey. I'm finished with the bathroom. Don't worry—we'll make it on time."

While he dressed, I straightened my purple skirt, fussed with the bolero jacket, and fixed the collar on my white blouse. Lastly I adjusted my big black hat and pulled on my white gloves. I was sure about Ulysses, but nervous thoughts were going through my mind. Was I ready to give myself away? To change my name? Would he always cherish me? Would I appreciate him?

I checked to see if my seams were straight, thinking "This is it! Oh, Mama, you should be here with me."

In less than fifteen minutes, Ulysses came back. What a transformation—his plaid suit fit beautifully, his white shirt was immaculate, his tie perfect.

I picked up his hand. "You got most of the black out."

"Yeah, used the brush. Well, Kid, you're not going to change your mind, are you?"

I smelled his nearness when he kissed me and thought of all the things that drew me to him, even when we first met. If I walked away now, where would I go?

"No," I said, firmly resolved. "I'm not going to change. I'll keep the vow we're going to make."

It had just stopped raining as we made our way to the Marriage Manor. When we neared the chapel, the sun peeked out of the clouds. As we entered, a kissing bride and groom were just leaving, and Rev. Grey was waiting for us.

"You must be Mr. Auger. And you must be Lulu."

We nodded.

He adjusted his glasses and took out a fancy form. Ulysses handed him the marriage license and the blood certificates.

He said, "That will be five dollars for the marriage fee and five dollars for the witness."

The photograph Ulysses arranged for us to have taken at the Albee Studio just before he left for the Army in 1942.

Ulysses in the U.S. Army Rangers. He served in the First and Fourth Battalions and fought mostly in Italy. Of the 1500 original Rangers, only 199 returned home. (James Altieri, Darby's Ranger's WWII.)

The wounded soldier comes to visit me in California in the summer of 1944. Here we are at Mission Beach, soaking up the sun. He shared much of what he had experienced in the war, and we drew close together.

Our wedding day!
We were married on
January 9, 1946, at
the Marriage Manor in
Hollywood, California.
Just the two of us.

The family I married into, the Augers. Ulysses and me, with his parents, Sophia and Gregory. In front, Diana, Margaret, and Harriet. This photograph was taken at the baptism of our first son, Gregory II, in 1949.

Ulysses gave him ten dollars, and Rev. Grey filled out the form.

"My wife plays the piano," he said. "What song would you like?" I looked across at her, and my mind went blank. I just said the first song that came to mind, "Some Sunday Morning" from *Oklahoma!*.

Rev. Grey directed Ulysses to the back of the room. Some fellow took my arm and the other attendant took Ulysses'. We came toward each other, and when we were directly in front of the minister, he began to read the familiar words.

I looked into Ulysses' eyes, which for a moment seemed a little wild. I didn't know how I appeared, except that a deep and contented feeling came into me.

"Do you promise to take this man, Ulysses, for your lawfully wedded husband, to have and to hold, in sickness and in health, for richer, for poorer, till death do you part?"

I said, "I do."

He repeated the same to Ulysses.

Then Ulysses slipped the little gold ring that I had been wearing for over a year back on my finger. I looked into his brown eyes and it was as if I had truly come home. This is where I belong, I thought, and this was my father's blessing when I left Minnesota.

We left the chapel laughing, happily wrapped up in each other. From there, we lunched at Frank Sinatra's uncle's place. On the door was a sign reading, "Closed on Tuesday for no damn reason at all." Good thing it was Wednesday. We ordered sirloin steaks with steak-fried potatoes and a salad. There wasn't any cake so we had lemon-meringue pie—my favorite.

We sat staring into one another's eyes.

With a mischievous look, Ulysses said, "Louie, let's go home."

Once there, we saw the pretty pink coverlet and the two vases of pink and yellow roses from the landlady. The room had been aired out, and smelled inviting.

A few tears came in my eyes.

Ulysses came over to me, "Sentimental again, huh?"

"This is the real thing. It's like I've been dreaming, and now it's real. It's kind of scary."

He held me, and then went in the bathroom. After just a few minutes he came out wearing a gold bathrobe with a horse head on the pocket. He smiled at me as if to say, "Your turn."

I went in, taking my negligee and gown with me. Mama had told me, "After you get married, it's right with God and man."

I smiled at the mirror as I put on the lovely lingerie. With some nervousness but excitement, I put a rose in my hair as I splashed on perfume. My husband was waiting.

We fell asleep for a few hours, and when Ulysses woke up, he said, "I feel awful, but I didn't want to spoil it for you—I have to go to work."

"You're leaving me!"

"Louie, you know Otto. I tried to get out of it but he said, 'I told you to wait until your day off. I don't accept any excuses, not even getting married.'"

I choked back my tears and tried to put on a bright face for my husband. After all, those of us who grew up poor after the Depression were thankful for every little thing. So he had to work on our wedding night; well, at least he had work. He'd come home, and we'd be together from now on.

Nevertheless, when Ulysses left, I lay in bed and cried and cried. My tears weren't because I was unhappy, but just from the fact that it was done—we were married. That was finished, and now would come the real part, the living together.

A few days later, Ulysses finally had a day off. We rode up Figuroa Street and saw a little French restaurant where we decided to eat.

From our table, we could see a rather nice apartment house through the window. We were hoping to find a different place to live, for how long could we cope with one room and no kitchen?

I said, "Isn't that an interesting apartment house? Nice windows."

The French owner of the restaurant came over to us, a woman with strong features who appeared to be in her forties. At my age, that seemed old.

I asked her, "Do you think there are any apartments for rent over there?"

"Mon cherie," she said, with a delightful but thick accent. "What a question. There is not an apartment for rent in the whole of Los Angeles."

Without asking permission, she pulled up a chair and gazed at us intently. Looking at Ulysses, she said, "My friend, you look like a real Greek god."

Then she leaned toward me saying, "Listen, I tell you the truth. If I didn't like the two of you, I wouldn't say a word. But I know of a couple who live in that first apartment on the left, where you see those nice windows. Today the woman moved out and took everything with her. Her husband drinks all day. Soon he'll come home and he'll be furious."

She left for a moment and went to take cash from some customers. When she returned, she said, "Give me your phone number. I'll call you if the fellow leaves. He'll have to—he doesn't even have a job."

Ulysses and I looked at each other and nodded to her.

She continued, "I'll tell the landlady about you. She comes in here all the time. I'll call you if there is a chance you can get the apartment."

It seemed like an impossibility, but we left feeling some hope.

I was just finishing dressing a few days later when the landlady knocked on the door. We had a phone call.

"Is this Lulu?" the French woman asked in her thick accent.

"Yes," I replied.

"This is Madame Fenand. Come right away—I have the apartment for you."

I choked back a squeal of delight and thanked her. We drove to her restaurant in a big hurry, and when we entered the little cafe, Madame spotted us.

"Shh! Don't say a word!" she said. "There's a long line of people waiting for that apartment, and if they hear how you got in, I might lose my customers."

She walked us across the street and introduced us to the manager, who took us to room 103. It was a studio apartment—just one room with a large closet, a full bath, and a small kitchen—and the rent was fifty dollars a month. It seemed like a miracle to me. We quickly agreed to it.

While Ulysses was at work the next day, I looked at the advertisements for furniture sales. One in particular looked enticing, which said "Whole house of furniture for sale."

On Sunday, we drove to the lovely home. A terrible sadness seemed to hover over the couple as we spoke. I could feel their deep sorrow and finally couldn't stand it any longer.

"Is anything wrong?" I asked.

The wife's eyes brimmed with tears. "We had a little boy who was three years old, but he was run over in the street. We're moving away and not taking anything with us. We just can't stand the reminders of him."

My heart went out to her. I couldn't imagine losing a child like that.

We made a deal with them, furnishing our whole apartment for just two hundred dollars, including silverware, glasses, dishes, utensils, and linen. Within a few days we were all set up. How blessed we were while others were desperately trying to find a place to live.

After we were settled in, Ulysses wrote to tell his mother of our marriage.

> Dear Ma,
>
> Sit down and take out your false teeth. I don't want you to swallow them.
>
> Louie and I were married on January 9TH. Please tell everyone. We couldn't get married in the Greek Church.
>
> I called Father Daniels and asked him, but he said "no." I would have to get permission from the Archdiocese in New York. I didn't want to wait that long. Louie and I will get married again in Washington at the Greek Church. We are very happy and finally found an apartment.
>
> Me agape [With love],
> Ulysses

We loved our little apartment, and enjoyed our first months of marriage. Now I really had to know how to cook and bake. Ulysses' favorite was custard pie, but only when it was very cold. Also, washing and ironing clothes took up my time. On weekends we went to the movies, but Ulysses worked a lot and seemed tired all the time. The war experience had left him drained, and he suffered many headaches and backaches.

Then in April the pressmen went on strike at the Pacific Press, and Ulysses wasn't working. Out of necessity, I called my old job in San Diego to see if they would give me a reference to work at the Convair Plant in Downey, California. Immediately I got a job as Secretary A with my same salary, $1.35 per hour.

One day in July when I came home from work, Ulysses said, "Remember that hot-dog stand I said I wanted to open? What do you say that we head East and give it a go?"

I was taken aback at first, but then realized what Ulysses had been up to in the past few months. While I was at work, he had found a Packard grill at the junkyard and attached it to our old Chevrolet. He had worked hard on what we now called our Chevy-Pac, but what I hadn't understood was that he was fixing it up for the long journey across the country.

Before we left, I called my family to say goodbye.

"Didn't I tell you?" I said to Myrt, "I knew it all the time—call it a sense of destiny or whatever—but this is the way it has to be." Then I choked back a tear. "I miss you all already. Please kiss Mama for me. I won't forget to send her money."

"Don't worry about Mama. We'll all be looking out after her. She seems very happy with Chris. They go to church a lot, and you know how she loves that."

"Yes, she does. Thanks, Myrt. I'll be fine, too. I can't explain it, but I have a great feeling of adventure, like there's something waiting for me. I know there will be hard times, especially without having my family in Washington, but I'll get by."

The day we left was a hot August day in 1946—exactly four years since I had first landed in Washington. I was coming in again, but it was different now. We were married and on our way. I hoped Myrt was right—that I'd never be bored.

IV

In the Business

12

The Hot-dog Stand

IT HAD RAINED HEAVILY IN THE MORNING and even messed up my new shoes as I made my way to work. I was back in my beloved D.C. and was anxious to leave the office in order to meet Ulysses at our cafe, the "hot-dog stand" as he liked to call it.

At my new job in Washington, I was assistant to Kathy, the main secretary. Today was Friday and therefore payday for the construction workers. It had been a busy day and we hadn't even stopped for lunch, as the paychecks had to be delivered to the job sites by three o'clock. But now it was nearly five, and we were feeling more relaxed.

The buzzer sounded, and Kathy answered it. She turned to me, saying, "Mr. Cladny would like you to come into his office a moment."

I was very fond of this kind and shrewd boss. He was about fifty, with a thick stock of gray hair, and very friendly. But for some reason, when I entered his office today his eyes avoided mine. He nervously removed his glasses and put them away, and then took them out again and put them on.

After what seemed like a long silence, I finally asked, "Mr. Cladny, is there something you wish to speak to me about?"

He then turned and said, in an apologetic tone, "Mrs. Auger, I'm afraid this is your last day here. I really don't want to let you go, but I guess under the circumstances, I have to."

He handed me my final check.

I started to ask under what circumstances, but thought that wasn't appropriate. So instead I said, "I'm sorry if I haven't done my job well."

"Oh," he stammered, "It's not that at all, it's just . . ." He looked confused and awkward, so I took the check, thanked him, and said goodbye, going to my desk. I wanted to tell Kathy what had happened, but I was too emotional and didn't want to burst out crying. I picked up my few things, mumbled goodbye, and walked out with tears running down my cheeks.

I liked working, and we needed the money. As I walked to the streetcar I relived the scene in Mr. Cladny's office. I had never before felt the sting of being fired, and it was humiliating.

I reached the Minute Grill just after five thirty, and saw that Ulysses was very busy. The whole twenty-nine–seat restaurant was filled with a payday crowd who were drinking, eating, laughing, and celebrating.

Ulysses spotted me and came by my side. "Hey, what's the matter, Kid? Why aren't you smiling?"

"I'll tell you later when you're not so busy."

I saw an empty coathook and hung my red jacket there. Ulysses motioned for me to come over to where five men were squeezed into a four-person booth.

Ulysses introduced me saying, "This is my wife, Louie."

They made a motion to stand up but I signaled them not to, as I reached my hand out and was introduced.

Harvey Peters asked, "How come we haven't seen you around before?"

Ulysses answered, pulling me away and saying, "You'll be seeing a lot of her now."

Then he took a second to ask me, "Are you all right?"

Before I could answer, someone grabbed his arm and pulled him away.

I heard Harvey shout, "Hey, Lucile. More beer over here!" In the same breath, he turned to one of the guys and said, "I've got to get home to my wife or she'll get mad." Then he laughed and said, "Well, she can only get so mad."

Lucile brought the beer and the guys continued joking and talking.

Someone put a nickel in the Wurlitzer juke box owned by our friend John Deoudes, and the singer's voice added to the noise of the clanging of the pinball machine and the shouts of the three fellows who were playing it. Just back from the service, they seemed to be having the time of their lives. They were each wearing the little ruptured-duck pin, the symbol of the returned serviceman. They were young, just like we were, hoping to make a living and start their families.

Lucile seemed to be getting behind. Ulysses was in the kitchen so I stepped up to the cash drawer. Just then he came out with a sizzling hot dog.

"Hey Blackie, got a new cashier?"

"Meet my wife, Louie."

A fellow who was alone picked up his cup and signaled for more, so I brought him some more coffee. Then someone wanted to pay, so I rang up the cash. It all came back to me—I had done this before.

Just before six thirty, the place began to empty out. Another week had finished.

Ulysses, now anxious to clean up and leave, said, "That's it for the day. Can you count the cash and register it in the book while I go straighten out the kitchen?"

I removed the money from the drawer and counted it, leaving twenty-five dollars in the kitty. Our sales were $135.75. The paid-out cash was $60.26.

Charlie, the dishwasher and clean-up man, mopped the floor. Lucile attended to the booths and put the condiments away. When everything was finished, Ulysses came to sit with me in the "office," which was the small booth near the cash register. Now we had a moment of quiet.

He looked across me and with a mischievous look said, "Got fired today, didn't you?"

Surprised, I asked, "How did you know?"

His face contorted as he said, "Now, Louie, don't get mad. You know how we borrowed two thousand dollars on Mama's house to get started. Well, the loan was hard to get because a lot of the returning GI's come home, borrow on their folk's home, and end up losing it."

He paused to light his cigarette. Perspiration glistened on his forehead. "We can't let that happen," he continued. "We've got to put everything into taking care of this place so we can pay our bills."

He exhaled the smoke fiercely through his nostrils, right into my face.

"Listen, Kid, I told you before you took that job that you could only work until I got the place going. It's going now but you didn't want to quit. So this morning, I called your boss and told him that if he didn't fire you today, I was going to come down and climb his frame."

For a few moments I didn't know what to feel or say. I don't get mad easily, but do more of a slow burn and try to get a hold of the situation. Immediately I thought of dear Mr. Cladny being forced to fire me and saw why he had such difficulty in doing so. I now understood perfectly the "circumstances" he was under.

"You could have talked to me and explained—you didn't have to do it this way! You know it hurts to get fired. I cried all the way over here."

It didn't seem to bother Ulysses a bit. His mind was on the business and I could take it or leave it. I sat pouting, feeling sorry for myself that he didn't seem to care. His eyes bore deep into mine.

I was caught. Would I walk out of here or would I make a stand? As we stared at each other, I thought of my ambition—even as a child—to be a success. I remembered my mother asking me what I wanted to be when I grew up. I could just see myself, a mere eight-year-old, replying without hesitation, "I want to be in business and I want to write a book."

While glaring at Ulysses I also remembered my father and mother having just such a standoff. Mama usually gave in, saying "a woman has to be a helpmate for her husband." Could I be as my mother was?

As if he were reading my mind, he asked, "Well, are you coming in Monday or not?"

"You actually called Mr. Cladny and said that to him?"

He didn't answer, but just gave me his ice-cold stare. Of course he had.

After a moment I replied, "Well, if I do come in, what am I going to wear? I don't want to mess up my few good clothes."

He must have had it all planned out, for he said without a pause, "I think you should wear a white blouse and a black skirt. Those Greeks who run their greasy spoons go around in dirty brown suits and sloppy ties, and expect customers to like 'em. Well, that's not going to be us."

Even though I agreed outwardly and knew I would come to work, I still trembled inside. I could see that it was not going to be easy to work beside him, except for my dream of success. If I always kept in mind the final goal, I could transcend the common everyday annoyances. I had seen it in my mother and father during the Depression as they set their wills to make it through the hardships. I was so grateful for the pattern set before me that I couldn't hold back the little tears that squeezed out of my eyes.

This naturally domineering man, whom I had willingly married, made me realize I would have to fight hard to stay myself. I vowed that throughout my whole life, I would remain me inside, therefore free.

The next day's bright sunshine filled me with more hope. Ulysses was already dressed, wearing his beige sport jacket with the Ranger patch sewn on the sleeve. He was fighting another war now, the war of business.

His Saturday-morning routine was to go to the restaurant and with Charlie he would "GI" the place, as he called it. With hot water and ammonia they would scrub the entire restaurant—the floor, the tile walls, the kitchen, and everything.

Following the cleaning job, Ulysses would go down to Pete and George Pappas's market, the same place he had worked at as a kid. He had arranged for them to save all the vegetables that would normally be thrown out over the weekend, and buy them for a nominal amount. He figured he saved about $30.00 a week, and we were able to serve fresh vegetables.

After kissing me goodbye, he took a last sip of coffee and said, "Kid, you go buy the blouses and skirts and I'll meet you at the store about one. We'll take in a movie or something."

I agreed.

After tidying the bedroom, I left the house about ten o'clock and caught the streetcar down to Garfinckel's department store. This was my first time to shop there, the place of many treasures. I had a few dollars in my pocket and wanted to enjoy a little freedom.

After walking through the revolving door I stood still for a moment, taking it all in. To my left, I saw gorgeous silk scarves, leather purses, lace collars, and lots of interestingly shaped hats—all accessories for the well-dressed lady. To the right, I saw the perfume counter and the displays of cosmetics, powder, creams, lipsticks, and rouges. Beyond them were silk and rayon stockings, and close by jewelry only to dream about.

When I had my fill of looking at the beautiful things, I took the elevator to the very top floor. There I stood by the mannequin encased in a gorgeous white wedding dress. Now I'd never wear such a gown, but when Ulysses and I got the time, we would be married again in the Greek church. I could still dream.

As it was almost twelve o'clock, I hurried to find what I had come for. I found skirts on sale, and bought two for less than twenty-three dollars.

Now for the blouses. I asked where the most reasonably priced ones were, and made my way through the sea of colorful dresses until I saw the sign marking the sale. I found a long-sleeved one with ruffles at the neck and sleeves, but knew the ruffles at the wrist would get messed up from the dishes. Then I found one with ruffles only at the collar for nineteen dollars. I bought it as well as another one with a pointed collar.

I was now outfitted for work. My new clothes, worn with a smile, were all I needed. "Lord, help me to smile," I thought.

I left the store and walked past Schwartz Jewelers, where a sign caught my eye. I didn't intend to buy anything, but was intrigued by their sale on men's gold watchbands. I had just enough money left to purchase one I particularly liked. On an impulse, I bought it for Ulysses.

After my shopping, I barely had time to get to the Minute Grill on time. When I arrived, Ulysses had just finished putting away the vegetables and was nearly ready to go.

He was tender to me as he said, "Kid, I need you down here with me. Why should you work somewhere else when our business needs you? I need you to type the menu—you know the cook's handwriting looks terrible. And you can do the daily worksheets, take cash, and help the waitress."

I softened, grateful that he understood what I was giving up.

"By the way," he continued, "I hired a waitress. Remember 'Olive Oil' in the cartoons? She looks just like her. You'll see her Monday when you come. So what did you buy?"

"Two blouses and two skirts."

"Let me see. How do the skirts fit? You don't look good in large skirts."

He held them up, saying "You bought them at Garfinckel's!"

"Well, I figured I should get the best so that they'll last. They were on sale and are a little out of style. They're wearing big skirts now—full and long ones."

"Forget the full skirts. They're not for you. So you spent all your money, huh?"

"Yeah, I did. But I also bought something for you," I said, handing him the gold watchband.

He held it in his hands, examining it closely.

"How come you bought it?" he asked. "You know I don't have a watch to go with it."

"I know you don't now, but I get a feeling that it won't be long before you will."

"You like to dream, don't you, Kid?"

I nodded, for I knew I was a dreamer. But being a dreamer and hopefully a doer made life a lot more interesting. Mama always said, "Whatever you do, do your very best—as unto the Lord."

I looked around at the restaurant and wondered where it would take us.

On Monday morning, we went over to Twenty-second Street for my first full day's work at the restaurant. Jenny, the new waitress, greeted us. Sure enough, she was an Olive Oil look-alike. Her dark gray-black hair was pulled back into a bun, her face was snow white from the powder that extended into her hairline, and her dark red lipstick was smudged onto her yellow teeth.

I put my jacket on the hook, tucked my purse under the cash register, and sighed. This was certainly different from a nice, neat office. Still, I was here, and I would make the best of it.

Where's the typewriter? Oh, over there—an old Royal all covered with dust and debris from lack of use. This was the kind of machine we used in high school. It was slow going, but it worked, particularly after I unstuck the keys with some oil.

I went into the small pungent kitchen to see George Lekas, the cook. He was no taller than I was, and Ulysses said that he was as nervous and hot-tempered as most good cooks. His mustache was similar to Hitler's, but I hoped that's where the resemblance ended. He was delighted that he didn't have to write out the menus anymore.

Under the shelf I found a stack of menu paper furnished by the National Boh Beer Company with their logo across the top. I began to type:

```
Specials for today:            September 30, 1946

Hamburger steak and two vegetables       .40
Spaghetti and meat balls                 .40
Chicken and dumplings                    .45
Swiss steak                              .50
Hot roast turkey sandwich and
```

In the midst of typing, Ulysses appeared over my shoulder. "Well, what do you think? Here, I brought you some coffee and the jelly doughnut you always like."

He bent over and kissed me on the cheek. "Bet you never got a kiss at the construction company!"

"No, but the pay was good."

"Well, don't expect any here. We'll be lucky if we can pay the rent and the notes."

Gosh, I never thought about salary. Now I wouldn't have any and I had just spent my paycheck.

At lunchtime most of the customers whom I had met on Friday came in. They remembered me and began to kid me.

"Came down to check up on the old man, huh?"

Those who didn't know who I was made remarks like, "What's your name, Cutie Pie? Where'd you come from?"

At the end of the day, I said to Ulysses, "Well, so far it's a lot more tiring than the office. And putting up with the men's remarks isn't so easy."

"You'll get used to it, Kid. They don't mean anything by it—it's just their way of being friendly."

The next day, a young fellow wearing the ruptured-duck pin delivered pies from Connecticut Pie Company. He brought two fresh cherry pies, a lemon layer cake, and two french-apple pies filled with raisins. He also brought a lemon-meringue pie, which reminded me of our wedding day.

Ulysses took the pies from the box and gave me the sales slip. We paid cash for everything, for Ulysses was afraid of credit. He feared we might get behind and never get caught up again. I counted out the $3.15 and made an entry to the Connecticut Pie Company.

After the pie delivery came the bag of linen, filled with white towels for the kitchen and torn ones for the counter use. There were also white aprons for Ulysses, the chef, and the dishwasher. For this I paid $1.77 out of petty cash.

Then a rash of wholesalers came in. First was the Coca-Cola Company, with a bill for $3.40. Then the ice man delivered a huge chunk of ice, water dripping everywhere as he placed it on top of the Cokes and the beer with tongs. I handed the strong-looking fellow $1.50.

Capital Cigar and Tobacco brought in boxes of cigars and two-cent mints. This was the biggest payout at $11.04. Cigars were popular with the mechanics, and nearly everyone wanted a mint after lunch.

By eleven-thirty, with menus typed and us at our posts, we were ready for the customers. We were aptly named the Minute Grill, for most of our people only had thirty minutes for lunch.

Right on schedule, the hungry customers poured in and we dashed about in restrained confusion. In that two hours or so of rush we did the bulk of the day's business. At two o'clock, I checked the register. So far, including breakfast, our sales were $116.00. Our paid-outs amounted to $44.06. Before closing at seven o'clock, we expected to pick up another twenty dollars or so in sales.

Sometimes good ideas dropped right out of the blue. One day Mr. Dawson, a quiet man who worked for David Lawrence at *U.S. News*, stopped by for a cup of coffee. We were just getting things together to close up and go home.

As he sat sipping from his cup, he said, "You know, Blackie, in mid-morning and then again in the afternoon, we sure wish we had a cup of coffee and maybe a snack. Do you think you could arrange it?"

Blackie said he'd think about it. And indeed he did—Mr. Dawson's idea had sparked an interest in him, and he pondered it all night. He couldn't even sleep but tossed and turned, finally waking me up.

"What's the matter?" I asked.

"You know, Mr. Dawson had a good idea. Tomorrow I'll go over to Gichner Iron Works. Henry will understand what I want. I'll need a cart, a huge thermos of coffee, and some holders for paper cups and cream and sugar. And I'll need a place for the doughnuts and sweet rolls."

After a deep yawn, he added, "You'll have to stay in the restaurant while I push the cart around."

Satisfied that he had most of the details worked out, he finally fell asleep, and eventually I did too.

On the way to the restaurant the next morning, all Ulysses talked about was the coffee cart. As soon as he could, he walked up the alley to Gichner Iron Works where Al Horning, a German who had come over just before the war broke out, was assigned to work with him. Al had a good understanding of what Ulysses wanted. They made a drawing and set to work on it.

By Friday morning, the cart was welded together just as Ulysses had envisioned. It was Al who wheeled it down the alley and brought it through the back door into the already crowded kitchen. Ulysses and I went to see it.

With a laugh, Al said, "Blackie, how do you like the rubber tires? We were afraid that if you didn't have them, your cream would have churned to butter by the time you got back from the route."

"You did a great job," Blackie said as he examined the cart from top to bottom. He placed the big coffee thermos into its groove, and it fit perfectly.

On Monday morning, we got to the restaurant a little early. We were excited about loading up the cart. About nine forty-five, it was filled and Ulysses was ready to go. He wore his beige Eisenhower jacket and had a streetcar conductor change-maker and at least twenty dollars in singles.

I stood out by the kitchen door and waved goodbye to him as he took off pushing the heavy cart. His plan was to go to Mr. Dawson's office on Twenty-fourth Street and then figure it out from there.

Meanwhile, all the routine of the business went right on. I prepared the menus and received the wholesalers, one of whom delivered his Greek groceries in an ambulance. Harry Magafan, fresh out of the army, had bought the vehicle for three hundred dollars through the GI Bill. He filled it with Greek cheese, olives, and olive oil and went around to his customers in his own distinct style.

About eleven o'clock, Ulysses returned. The sweat was running down his forehead even though it was cool outside.

"Boy, was it something. Everywhere I went somebody wanted something. I could hardly pour the coffee fast enough. First I went to Mr. Dawson. He introduced me around his office, and then sent me to some other offices. Then I went to the Weather Bureau, and then I came around to the Capital Cadillac. Akers caught a glimpse of me, and looked the cart over. He thought it was a good idea."

Mr. Floyd Akers, the owner of Capital Cadillac Company, was a large bulldog of a man who was very stern and carried real authority. However, he was an excellent businessman and one we wanted to emulate. He liked the idea of the coffee cart and allowed us to go through his shop.

Several months later, on a cold winter's day, the telephone rang. I went to answer it and heard my mother-in-law's voice.

"Mama. It's you! What'd you say?"

She answered, "Papa is cooking dinner for you and Ulysses. Will you come?"

Ulysses had stepped out but I answered for both of us. "Sure, we'd love to."

"Great. You work too much—we never get to see you."

"Yeah, I know. I'm sorry. Sometimes when we get home we just sneak upstairs, exhausted."

When Ulysses returned, I said, "Your Mama called and wants us to come to dinner. Papa is doing the cooking. I said 'yes'—I hope that's all right with you."

"Sure, Kid. We live with them but hardly see them."

"So Papa does the cooking, huh?"

"Oh, he's the expert chef. If you don't believe it, just ask him."

"Well, that dinner he cooked when we first came from California was sure good."

We locked up the restaurant. Winter had truly come and I was shivering. The heater in our Chevy-Pac was not working very well.

"Move over here, Kid. Don't you remember how you used to snuggle up so tight that I could hardly drive?"

I squeezed over and put my hand on his leg.

"Someday," he said, "I'll buy you a nice fur coat."

"Now, who's the dreamer?"

"Well, you'd look great in it."

"It's sweet of Mama and Papa to cook dinner for us, don't you think?"

"Papa likes you."

"I'm so glad, even though I'm not Greek."

Ulysses smiled. He had made his choice, and I was it. His pat on my arm told me so.

"When did Papa come to this country?" I asked. "My father came about 1900, I think."

"Papa must have come about 1917, or something like that. He's got so many stories that we don't know what to believe."

He continued, "It seems that Papa came from Turkey with his brother, Nicolas. Papa called him the Professor because he wore glasses and was always reading some book. At first they stayed together. But Papa was like a wild horse and wouldn't stay put. He went from New York to California, working in every restaurant he could. He must've learned something because he got the title 'chef' from somewhere."

Ulysses paused for a moment and then continued, "He wound up in a small town in Pennsylvania—Pottsville—working for a family named Arsanakis. They ran a small restaurant and had a young daughter, Sophia. Papa was nearly thirty. You should see a picture of him then—thick coal-black hair, worn like a pompadour. Anyway, he fell for the young girl and eloped with her. Can't you just see the poor family? Not only did they lose their daughter, but they lost the chef too!"

We both laughed, for when a chef leaves, it's a catastrophe.

"They came to Washington. Pop got a job, and I guess things went along pretty well for awhile. Then they had a fight. Mama was still a kid, so one day when Papa was at work she caught the bus and ran home to her mother. Boy, I can just see Papa fuming now. Mama was pregnant and the baby was due, and I suppose she wanted to be with her mama.

"Anyway, knowing Pop, he probably went crazy. He got a Greek friend of his who was rumored to be in the moonshine business. This guy had a big black touring car and even had a shotgun. Anyway, Mama was in the hospital, and had given birth to me about ten days before. Papa snatched baby and mother and brought us back to Washington. And that, as the story goes, is how I got into this town!"

"Quite a story. I believe it!" I said.

Ulysses stopped the car. We had arrived home.

"Papa's an interesting character all right," I said, as we got out of the car and walked up the steps, musing about Ulysses' parents. When we entered the house we were still laughing, which always delighted Mama. She didn't seem to care if I was Greek or not as long as her son was happy.

The house smelled wonderful. Mama had baked bread and made baklava and Papa had cooked string beans with lamb and potatoes in a tomato sauce. He had also made a big Greek salad with olives, feta cheese, tomatoes, and cucumbers.

There were seven of us around the table. They were all kind to me, but I was still the stranger. We'd be speaking English and then something would trigger the conversation and it would turn into Greek. Then someone would think of me and they'd speak English again.

As I sat there, I became lost in my own thoughts. I remembered how Maria had pointed out how different Ulysses' world would be. But I had willingly joined him, and therefore also his family. I needed to enter in fully because I didn't want to spend my life feeling like an outsider.

I looked across at Papa. He still had a lot of hair, only now it was gray. His dark flashing eyes had a look in them that sometimes was very kind but at other times made it seem like he could smash something.

Yet he seemed very fond of me, and sometimes I wondered why. Would I ever fit in? I had no family of my own here, and no friends to turn to or sort things out with. I looked toward Ulysses and he smiled, speaking to me with his eyes.

I smiled back, and sighed. If everything was all right between us, then I shouldn't worry about fitting in—that would happen all by itself.

When I came out of my deep thoughts, I noticed that Harriet, Ulysses' twelve-year-old sister, seemed uneasy. She was fussing with her hair, twirling her pigtails, and looking agitated.

I leaned close to her and asked, "What are you so worried about?"

Still twirling her hair, she answered, "My English homework. My teacher is so mean—she yells at us in class. And the more she yells, the less I understand what she's talking about."

"I'll help you," I said. "English was always my favorite subject."

"Do you mean it?" she asked, with wonder in her voice.

"Of course I do," I said with a smile.

As soon as dinner was finished, while Margaret and Diana cleared up the dishes, Harriet and I found a table in the corner and worked on her studies. From then on, it became a ritual. If I wasn't home in time to help her, she left her homework for me to check.

Harriet became a dear little sister to me, and I became an accepted member of the family.

13

Hoping against Hope

ONE COLD AND WINDY DAY in November 1947, Ulysses and I were enjoying George's chicken noodle soup and talking over our customers' complaints about the lack of beef on the menu.

They had reason to complain. Although the Office of the Price Administration, or OPA, had stopped rationing certain items such as sugar, gasoline, and coffee, the prices of scarce goods had skyrocketed. Meat was in great demand but in short supply, and often there was none to buy. The customers wanted steaks and roast beef, but all we could find were hamburger and swiss steak, which was tough meat that was nearly pulverized to make it edible.

"Well," I said, thinking about the hungry men, "they probably got more meat in the service than they do here at home."

"Yeah, I know," Ulysses responded. "You remember Tom Sarris and his brother-in-law, Chris Kariakos? They got hold of a whole beef, and they're going to let me have a side of it. I'm going to go there now to get it for tomorrow."

As soon as Ulysses left, I noticed a distinct change in the demeanor of the waitress. The old-time Greeks had a rather derogatory name for them, which Mama had just told me about. She had said, "Watch out for the Americanitha's."

I had asked her if I was one, for I thought that this was the name for all girls who weren't Greek.

She had replied, "No, that's a name for the waitresses who are always flirting with the boss and trying to . . . well . . . you know! Watch out for them!"

I wondered if Mama was speaking from experience. I remembered the young girl I had met on the bus, who had fallen in love with her boss at the Greek restaurant.

Now I looked across at this Americanitha. Her complexion was perfect, without a blemish. She sat in the booth and didn't bother to close her legs. I busied myself with the paperwork and tried to ignore her. We were in the lull between lunch and the afternoon snacktime for the people at Colonial Storage.

Lucile was studying me for what seemed a long time, and then asked, "Don't you do anything else? I've been here for over a year now, and you've never taken off a single day."

Her tone said she thought I was a fool.

For a moment I didn't answer her. She was waiting for my reply, still sitting there with her uniform hiked up. What she didn't understand was that she was talking to a dreamer with a vision.

Finally I merely answered, "My day will come."

The afternoon crowd showed up then and we got busy, and the spell was broken.

It was a little after five when I heard a bang on the kitchen door. Charlie Hooks opened it, and in came Ulysses needing help with the heavy gunnysack. Blood was dripping everywhere and was all over the white apron he had tied on to protect his clothes. Together he and Charlie placed the meat on the cutting board as the blood formed a small puddle on the floor.

Ulysses looked as if he had experienced a narrow escape. He said, "Well, I've got the meat and it's good and fresh. But I don't think Chris or Tommy will ever eat another piece of meat. As Chris was butchering it he was telling me about getting it from the farmer. I guess the farmer took the cow and hit her on the head with a sledge hammer. She wasn't even dead when several guys hung her on a hook. Then the farmer began to cut into the hide and pull it right off with the poor cow still moaning. Tommy got sick."

I'd never seen Ulysses become so emotional over an animal.

He continued, "Finally the poor animal died. The farmer kept the hide and gave Chris and Tom the meat. They packed it in ice and brought it to Chris's garage, and there he cut it up into pieces and divided it with me. I put down an old oilcloth in the trunk, and started driving back here. When I got to Eighteenth and Columbia Road, the police stopped me."

I waited in anticipation as he nervously lit his cigarette.

"Well, for sure I thought they were stopping me because of the meat. But the cop said, 'You're driving with California license plates.' I showed him my license and told him that it hadn't expired. He told me to get it changed right away anyway.

"When I drove up here and parked, I saw the blood running out of the trunk. Lucky they didn't notice it! At least I've got plenty of meat for a little while."

Charlie made room in the refrigerator. While they were putting it away, Ulysses said, "I wonder when there'll be enough meat in this country to order what we need. At least when those damn mechanics come in here bellyaching tomorrow, I'm going to shut them up with some real meat."

I knew Ulysses. It hurt him to get the meat this way, for it was through the black market.

A few months later, when Blackie returned from his afternoon run with the coffee cart, the telephone rang. I recognized the voice—it was Tom Sarris.

"Yeah, well, I'll be right over," I heard Ulysses say.

He wiped the perspiration off his face as he said, "Kid, I'm going to Tom's for a little while. Think you can handle it here?"

"Sure. Go ahead."

As he kissed me before leaving, again I felt the pains that had started earlier in the morning. They were stronger now, but I didn't mention it as I figured Ulysses would just be gone an hour or so.

He said, as we parted, "You know, Tommy's got his used-car lot. Our Chevy-Pac may not have long to go—maybe I can find a good used car. Here's the number where I'll be."

The pains came and went, and then around four o'clock the waitress got an urgent phone call and said she needed to leave for an emergency. I wondered if I should let her go, especially considering the way I was feeling. Ignoring my common sense, I told her to go ahead.

Now there was only me and the new dishwasher, Charlie's younger brother, Robert Hooks, who came and worked every night after school. Later he would become a famous TV star, but then he was very young and inexperienced. I attended to the few people who came in and ordered coffee and ate the remaining doughnuts. All the time I was watching the clock, hoping I could make it through.

Just after five, I noticed that the coffee needed making, as some of the Cadillac fellas would soon be coming in. I put the fresh grounds into the large urn and then lifted up the boiling water and poured it over the grounds. Just as I finished pouring it, I felt a strong jolt in my stomach as a sharp pain ran through me. Gasping and stifling a cry, I grabbed the counter to steady myself and dropped the empty water pail. Mike, a Cadillac mechanic and good friend, saw me standing there trembling in pain.

"Mrs. Auger, is there anything I can do for you?" he asked.

"Yeah, there is." I tried to smile. "I have to go to the ladies' room for a few moments. If I'm not able to come out for a little while, could you take care of things here?"

I was embarrassed to ask him, but the pains were acute and I had the dreadful feeling that soon I would be very messy. Without another word, I dashed into the ladies' room.

By myself in the tiny area, I understood what I had suspected—I was having a miscarriage. We had lost our first baby. I didn't dwell on it, as the pains were so severe that I had to swallow a scream. I grasped the door handle and held on until some of the cramping subsided.

Then I remembered where I was and that I had left poor Mike alone.

I leaned out the door and called for him, while noticing that he had made quite a few sales and had piled the money in front of the register.

"Do you see that telephone number up on the register?" I asked. "Could you please call it and try to reach Ulysses? And could you hand me my purse and my raincoat?"

He immediately gave me my belongings. After a few minutes, he knocked on the door. "Mrs. Auger, your husband wasn't at that number. They don't know where he is."

"Thank you, Mike."

I got myself together as best I could, although I looked like a ghost in the mirror. Finally I could emerge, and saw that all the customers had left and Robert was finishing up in the kitchen.

Thankfully, Mike was still there. I said, "I hate to ask, but do you think you could take me home?"

He was slightly reluctant, but he said, "Sure Mrs. Auger, but let me try that number again."

Again, Ulysses was not there.

The drive took about twenty-five minutes, and the pains still were going on when we arrived home. Mama answered the door, and when she saw me standing there with a strange man, she blurted out, "What happened? Where's my son?"

I thanked Mike and entered the house, trying to explain. "Ulysses went to visit Tom Sarris, and I guess he forgot about the time. I had a miscarriage, and Mike helped me close up the store and then drove me home."

"You had a miscarriage! Oh, Mama mou!"

She seemed more nervous than I was in waiting for Ulysses. After I took a shower and cleaned up, she fixed up the bed for me. Never were the soft sheets more welcome.

"Tomorrow, I'll take you to my Dr. Nathanson," she said, fussing over me. "She'll look you over."

"Thank you, Mama."

I fell asleep immediately. When I awakened, Ulysses was kissing my face repeatedly.

"What happened?" he asked. "You never told me you weren't feeling well. And I didn't know that you were pregnant!"

"I didn't really know myself but it's okay. It's probably the best thing right now. I'll be all right. Mama is going to take me to her doctor tomorrow."

"I bet you wonder where I've been."

"Yes—do you want to tell me?"

"It's no secret, Louie. I went to the used-car lot with Tommy—and didn't find anything. Anyway, Tom said we should go see Harry Triantis. So we went over to the guy's house, and his mother had cooked big macaroni fried with burnt butter. We were eating and talking with a neighbor who had lost his leg during the war. He was a little drunk, and was Greek-dancing with his wooden leg. He seemed to get around so well that I couldn't feel sorry for him. Made me know how lucky I am to have come home in one piece."

He kissed me again and said, "Sorry I wasn't there with you. When I looked at my watch, it was seven-thirty and I called the restaurant but you weren't there. Then I called Mama and she said you were asleep."

He hugged me close again and said, "How come you didn't tell me you had pains?"

"Because I didn't realize how serious it was. Anyhow, I'm glad you're home. Seems so blue without you. You're going to have to thank Mike—he really helped me. He took the cash, waited on customers, and brought me home. Since I couldn't reach you, there was nothing else I could do, except take a taxi. And I wanted someone with me, not a complete stranger."

"You make me feel bad, Kid. You went through that all by yourself."

"Yeah, well, I'm okay." I changed the subject quickly. "I was also worried about leaving the money in the register, so I scooped it up and put it in my purse. You'll have to count and register it. And the register tape is there, too. And all the paid-outs are listed and I left twenty-five dollars in the kitty."

"Good girl. Well, you take it easy for a few days. Get checked out tomorrow with Mama. Don't worry. We'll have lots of babies."

Ulysses fell asleep, but my mind was running wild. I was so tired that it was easy to feel sorry for myself. I was losing track of what it was like to have a close friend—to just go out with a woman and talk.

Then I remembered my dream of success, and tried to focus on that. Still, nagging doubts entered my mind. I didn't have any salary, and didn't any money for clothes like when I worked for someone else. I looked over at my worn and messy shoes and wished for a new pair. Then I remembered that my stockings were ruined and wondered if I had any more. And my beautiful nightgowns were frayed. I was letting the blues get to me.

I looked across at Ulysses, breathing deeply in sleep, his thick black hair framing his face. I realized again that each person is virtually alone and cannot look to another to fulfill the hollow place in one's heart. Only God can do that.

I thought of home, and living through the Depression. Then I mused on what it felt like to have a good job and buy food and clothes and be able to give to Mama. And I thought of the war years, now over for nearly two years.

Then I rose up in spirit. I vowed not to allow myself to be depressed, for I was determined to have victory in my life. Today had been a setback, but in a few days I would be better. I was certain of it.

I got up and brushed my teeth again and said my prayers. I was determined not to allow myself to get down for too long. Life was ahead of me, and I wasn't going to waste it.

The next day, Ulysses' mother took me to see Dr. Nathanson. She said that I had had a pregnancy of the tube and that it surely could never have come to term. Indeed, she said, I could have had a great deal of trouble and was very lucky. Otherwise I was basically very healthy and checked out well. I was relieved, although still drained and tired from the experience. But in a week, I was back at work.

Days and weeks sped by and were more or less the same. We developed a routine at the restaurant and home, including Ulysses' daily runs with the coffee cart. The men he served at Capital Cadillac, *U.S. News and World Report,* and the Weather Bureau also became our customers in the restaurant.

Sometimes on Friday nights we'd go to the Blue Mirror and enjoy a strawberry shortcake and take in a movie. And every Sunday it was necessary to go to the Minute Grill, even though it was closed. We couldn't afford to leave the gas burning under the coffee urns all weekend, so we'd close them off on Friday nights and then light them again on Sunday.

By spring in 1948 we were able to move into a basement apartment. We knew we couldn't stay long as it wasn't much and the smell of the upstairs cooking was unpleasant. Apartments were still hard to find, but we noticed a new apartment house being built on upper Fourteenth Street.

We took a chance and filled out an application, and were surprised and delighted when later we were notified that we were accepted. The apartments wouldn't be ready until the following March, but at last we would have a nice place to live by ourselves.

In May, the boss of the mechanics at Capitol Cadillac invited us to go to the Chesapeake Bay for crab fishing. We had a wonderful time, and made it a habit over the summer. One weekend when we were staying at Doggetts' small clapboard hotel we were enjoying fresh fish for breakfast. Usually I savored the taste, but this time the smell bothered me. I wondered if I could be pregnant.

It wasn't just the fish, for I really was pregnant, and this time I didn't keep it a secret. In the beginning I didn't show much, but during the last few months I felt like a walking house. I couldn't afford fancy maternity clothes, so I went to Sears and bought colorful artist's smocks to wear over a maternity shirt.

As we approached the time of the birth, everyone kept making jokes about when the baby would come. Ulysses made a game of it by sticking a piece of paper on the back of the register. The guys wrote their name and their guess of the weight, the date, and time of the baby's birth. Whoever won would get a free lunch. It was fun and the customers were like my family, caring for me and cheering me on.

We were able to move into the new apartment on March 1, 1949. Everything was clean and new, and it felt spacious and fresh after our cramped basement surroundings. We were thrilled to be in our own place.

A couple of weeks later we went over to Mama's house to see her new black-and-white television that the girls had bought. We were watching Milton Berle when I began to notice some pains in my abdominal region. I sat still, not wanting to be embarrassed by a false alarm. But the pains increased, and suddenly I stood up. When the others saw the expression on my face, they got to their feet too.

"I think you'd better call Dr. Hogan," I said to Ulysses.

It was no false alarm. I'll never forget the sight of our first baby wrapped in a little blanket and placed in my arms. Little Gregory had so much dark hair that a nurse had tied a blue ribbon in it. Dr. Millwater pronounced him perfect, born on March 13, 1949, and weighing seven pounds and thirteen ounces. It was Mike who won the free lunch. He had guessed seven pounds, twelve ounces on March thirteenth.

My already full life became much busier. Mama, now called Yia Yia, agreed to watch her grandson while I worked. During the week I would get up and dress Gregory and then take him by bus to Mama's house. After leaving him there I would catch another bus to the restaurant, trying to make it by ten o'clock. I'd work through lunch and then pick up the baby and have dinner ready for Ulysses when he came home. It was tiring but I was young.

On a beautiful fall day in September, I dropped off Gregory at Mama's house and made my way to the restaurant. The birds were singing as if it was their last day before flying south and I felt fully alive. Finally it seemed that we were getting somewhere. I still didn't receive a salary, but once in awhile we had a few dollars left for me to buy a fresh blouse or a new skirt. Today I was wearing new black shoes.

I came in the restaurant singing, "Kiss me once, and kiss me twice, it's been a long, long time."

It was ten-thirty, and I had no time to waste. I got out the typewriter, finished the menus, and greeted the friendly mailman when he came in.

"Got a registered letter for you today!"

"Registered letter!" I exclaimed, wondering what it contained.

"Yep. Sign right here."

"Okay, Kevin. Thanks."

I noticed that it was from our landlord. I read and reread the contents, trying to grasp what it said. Our property was being sold for eighty thousand dollars, and we had the first option to buy. We had just thirty days to come up with the money or we were out.

As I stood in shock, Ulysses came in from his rounds with the coffee cart. Without a word, I handed him the letter. I stood beside him silently, knowing what an upheaval he would feel.

"Eighty thousand dollars!" he exclaimed.

I nodded, feeling dejected.

It felt like a bomb had exploded in our midst. Everything had been going along well: We were happy; we had our little boy; we had a business. We might never get rich, but we could survive and be our own boss. But now, like a sudden death, the business was about to come to a halt.

Ulysses said, "Even the army wasn't this bad. You mean we've done three years of work and we can lose it all just like that."

That night, both of us slept fitfully. But in the midst of tossing and turning, I prayed and summed up the courage to hope. We seemed to be naturals in the restaurant business. How could we lose it all now?

I reminded the Lord of my dreams as a child. Why did I have them if they were just to be empty? I couldn't let myself hit bottom—it was too painful, and I was too much of an optimist. For deep in my heart, I hoped that some break would come.

In this state of sometimes hope, sometimes distress, I thought of the restaurant across the street. Called the Sea-Land Tavern, it was larger and in a better location than our Minute Grill. And it was for sale.

"Oh Lord," I cried out, "Could you have that place for us?"

With a renewed sense of hope, I fell asleep.

In the morning, I said to Ulysses, "You know that place across the street—it's just right for us. Maybe we can find a way to move over there."

"Yeah, right," he said. "It would take ten thousand dollars. What am I supposed to pay with, buttons?"

He was so distressed throughout the morning that he even found it difficult to be nice to the customers. Finally he said, "I'm going down to the *Washington Post*. Maybe I can get a job as a pressman again."

"Go ahead," I responded. "Maybe it'll ease your mind to know there's something else you could do."

Just then, Mr. Akers's chief financial officer came in for a cup of coffee.

Blackie saw him and said, "Watch the lefta [cash] while I go talk to Mr. Moore."

Mr. Moore listened intently while Blackie spoke, looking intrigued. As he stood up to leave, he said, "Don't say or do anything until I talk to Mr. Akers."

While we waited to hear back from Mr. Moore, that evening Ulysses paid a visit to the *Washington Post*. When he got home, he said, "Well, when I got there, the pressmen were sitting on the steps eating their supper. I saw the shop steward and asked him if he had any openings, showing him my union card. When I showed him the card, he didn't hesitate for a minute. He just shook his head no, saying, 'You left a strike-bound plant. Nobody in this city will give you any work.'"

I could see Ulysses was devastated, and tried to comfort him. I thought again of the restaurant across the street.

Two days later, Mr. Moore came back into the restaurant and motioned for us to come sit with him. As he spoke, I noticed how meticulously kept his fingernails were. His navy-blue suit and striped tie made him appear the epitome of the evolving postwar businessman.

With no foolishness or hesitancy, he said, "Mr. Akers had Mr. Jones of Sandoz Realty Company look up all the particulars on this place and the place across the street."

Ulysses and I passed a glance between us. I could just guess what he was thinking.

Mr. Moore continued, "Would you be interested in the place across the street?" he asked.

Hope, blessed hope, suddenly filled us. I didn't gesture, but Ulysses twisted his neck in his characteristic way, trying to hide his excitement. He replied, "Of course we would."

We talked a bit further with Mr. Moore. As he left, he said that he would get back with us.

That night we were too excited to sleep, not daring to hope at one moment but believing it would happen the next.

The next morning Mr. Moore called the restaurant and left word that Mr. Akers would see Ulysses at one o'clock. As we served the customers, our hopes would rise and fall. I knew in a deep way that I really loved this business and didn't want to lose it. Yet I also knew that we wouldn't lose it—I was trusting as Mama always did.

One o'clock came. I was busy with the customers as Ulysses waved goodbye on his way to Mr. Akers's office. In just a few minutes, he was back.

He called out, "The old man is going to pick me up in four minutes in the limousine. I better go wash my face."

When he came out, I asked, "Shouldn't you be wearing a jacket?"

"How can I? I don't have one."

He quickly borrowed the chef's dark blue jacket. It was too small and smelled of the kitchen, but he squeezed into it. Through the front window, I saw Mr. Akers's big black limousine pull out front, his chauffeur at the wheel. Blackie went out and I saw him get in the back seat and drive away.

Fortunately I was so busy when he was gone that the time went quickly. Around two thirty, Ulysses returned, cigarette in hand. By the look on his formerly dejected face, I knew it was good.

He slid in the booth, saying, "Well, Kid, we got a big break. Boy, that Akers is some big man. When I first got in the limo, he asked me how old I was and did I have any money. Then he asked me what my name was, cause he only knew 'Blackie.'"

I smiled, thinking how his nickname had really caught on.

He continued, "When we got to the American Security Bank, I followed him in. He introduced me to a guy named Siddens, who then took me to a nice fellow named James Willett.

"Akers came back and whispered something in Willett's ear. Next thing I knew, papers were being typed up. Apparently the big guy had arranged everything in advance through Mr. Jones.

"Then Mr. Willett asked me if I had a lawyer. When I told him we didn't, he wasn't fazed. He just pulled out the yellow pages and found the name of a lawyer close to the bank in the Woodward Building. He located a guy named Cumberland and even got him on the phone. Told him I'd be right over."

"Well, did we get it?" I asked anxiously.

"Hold on—I'm telling you. I went right over to the lawyer's. As I entered the office, I met a young fellow named Don Cefaratti, who took me into Mr. Cumberland's office. He said he would get in touch with Akers's lawyer and would handle the whole deal for two hundred dollars."

"You mean we've got the place across the street?"

"Yes, little dreamer, we did. Let's go over and take another look."

Arm in arm, we walked across Twenty-second Street to the Sea-Land Tavern. From the outside it didn't look bad, but inside it was a makeshift cafeteria. The operator wasn't meticulous or tidy and merely spread his apron over the food at night. Even though there was refrigeration underneath, it wasn't appetizing or sanitary.

Blackie whispered so that the owner couldn't hear, "I'm gonna rip out all this stuff and put in a nice neat counter across here." The owner had been forced to sell because he couldn't pay the rent, and he wasn't pleased to be leaving.

We went back across the street in a jubilant mood. It was Friday night and soon our payday customers would be coming in for a quick beer. Blackie told everyone what had happened and even though we couldn't afford it, we gave them free beer. We wanted them to rejoice with us, and celebrate we did.

I stood behind the counter, watching all the antics. Harvey grabbed Lucile and they danced to the jukebox music, which was playing the Jersey Bounce. We laughed and sang.

That night I wrote a letter to my mother.

> Dear Mama,
>
> Hope you're well and happy in California. We just came through a business crisis but I remembered how you always held steady and believed that what was right would happen. I felt that same strength. Thanks for your example in my life.

I enclosed our monthly check to her, and mailed it off.

When we told Ulysses' family about what had happened, Papa, now a papou (grandfather), was holding his grandson. He said, "We always believe in the old country that every child brings much tihi, huh Mama?"

By tihi he meant luck. We agreed.

Settlement day came thirty days later. Our deposit of $750.00 was made out to Barbara Walker, the property owner. On our purchase day, October 26, 1949, the remaining $9,250.00 check was signed over to her. We and the bank were now the owners of a property that had changed hands seven times in the last five years. We were hoping— and determined—that it would never change hands again.

14

Life over the Shop

WORLD WAR II WAS BARELY OVER when the newspaper editorials started to be filled with fears of "communist subversion." Eastern Europe had fallen to communism and Chairman Mao Tse-tung had just formed the People's Republic of China. Then we discovered that Russia had the atomic bomb and that Russian spies were in our midst. Financier Bernard Baruch called this period "the Cold War" and Winston Churchill pronounced the iron curtain to have descended.

With Europe in dire need, the United States developed the Marshall Plan to give aid to Europe. When I read about the Berlin Airlift, I remembered what Papa had said: "America gives, and God will always bless her."

I also remembered Papa saying, one night as we sat around the dinner table, "I might not live to see it, but one day the Jews will again have a country of their own." Indeed, he wasn't alive, but it happened on May 14, 1948. The United States was the first country to recognize Israel.

Against this backdrop of increasing world changes and tensions, we found that at home we had a few battles of our own to face. We idealists thought that winning World War II had ended the world's problems, but the fallacy of that statement became obvious in what we saw around us.

There were shortages everywhere. Shortages mean opportunities, but at the time we didn't realize just how opportune our timing was.

On our opening day at the new Minute Grille, now spelled with an "e" at the end for effect, our name in neon lights could be seen from far away. Underneath was another sign taped to the window. It read, "OPEN: UNDER NEW MANAGEMENT."

It was about eight in the morning when we first stepped into the completely revamped restaurant. Ulysses had gutted the old hackneyed cafeteria, and across the far wall was a new counter with eight stools. The walls were wallpapered in a pattern with old cars, in honor of Capitol Cadillac. The place looked bright and clean.

We probably would have felt a little proud if we weren't under the same kind of lease situation as before. Here we also just had a three-year lease, and after that we would be under a month-to-month lease with a thirty-day cancellation clause and no option to purchase. The property was owned by Cities Service Oil Company, which is now Conoco.

But today, we laid all worries aside for we were excited about our new restaurant. I was twenty-four and Ulysses was twenty-seven. I dressed in my usual white blouse and black skirt but Ulysses took off his pouthia (apron), and dressed up a little in a tan manager's coat.

I looked out across the street and noticed that someone had painted "KILROY WAS HERE" on the window of the old Minute Grill. How appropriate! Soon Mr. Akers would be tearing it down for his used-car lot.

Our first customers were Mr. Pratt and his son from Pratt's Service Station on the corner. On the same side of the street was a dental lab, and some of the young students came in. And all of our customers from across the street showed up. We were filled and immediately placed an advertisement for a new waitress.

Cook George was still with us as well as the same kitchen cleanup fellows. We were air cooled, meaning fans. Air conditioning was yet something to dream about. We now seated sixty people, instead of the twenty-nine across the street.

I still typed the menu on the old Royal typewriter and painstakingly got the figures right. Roast turkey was sixty cents, seventy-five cents with coffee and dessert. Roast beef sandwiches were forty cents. Soft shell crab with two vegetables, fifty-five cents.

We raised our prices only slightly to make up for our now doubled rent and the increased note payment, but coffee was still a nickel and pie ten cents. Those who wanted to splurge could spend an extra nickel for ice cream.

We began to see new customers. The well-dressed Cadillac salesman who rarely came in the old Minute Grill now became our regulars. Many Cadillac customers relaxed with us while they waited for their cars to be repaired. And the bosses began to come and we catered to their special needs. Mr. Akers always had a western sandwich—ham, onion, and tomato fried with an egg—and Mr. Moore liked a ham sandwich on white bread, cut with a clean knife with no odors. Edna, our new waitress, looked after them to make sure they were well cared for.

We got to know the Cadillac salesmen quite well. One of the top ones was Bill Ballas, of Greek descent. He made a joke out of everything, but we learned that underneath he was quite serious about his work and family.

One evening he brought in his attractive wife, Janet. I had left my five sisters in California, but she instantly became like a sister. We didn't get to speak very long that evening, but I felt a bond with her and found out later that she felt it too. I now had a needed close friend.

Friday nights were still the best for business, but one Friday evening I saw seven of our regular mechanics walk right by us on their way to another place. In the midst of being busy, I ran out to see where they were heading.

"Harvey!" I called out, "Where are you going?"

They stopped, and Harvey replied, "You're getting too fancy over there, and all the bosses are coming in. It's just no fun for us anymore—you understand. Across the street used to be 'our place'."

I felt bad that they didn't feel comfortable. We weren't fancy; it was just that our clientele was changing.

A few weeks later, Ulysses went to the restaurant to check things out during the quiet of a Saturday. I had a lot to do at home, like cleaning and laundry. Saturday was the day I had Gregory to myself, and I wanted to get my work done quickly so I could spend every moment with him.

I was nearly done with my chores. Little Gregory was asleep in his crib, his rosy cheeks so precious. After folding the last of the clothes, I'd put Gregory in the stroller and we'd go for a walk.

I had to go down to the lower level to take the clothes out of the dryer. Should I leave him for just a few moments? I stood over him debating, but he didn't stir. I hated to wake him up.

I reasoned that it would just take a second to run down and get the clothes. I caught the elevator and rushed to get them out of the dryer. When I got back to the elevator, it was long in coming. It took all of three minutes before I opened the apartment door. I put the basket down and ran to Greg.

I was shocked to see that in just those three minutes, he had somehow pulled his soft yellow blanket over his face. I unwrapped him and saw that he wasn't breathing. I gasped, shaking him, but he didn't respond. On the way to the telephone, I yelled in a panic, "Gregory, come back! You're all right!"

I dialed the operator and somehow managed to ask her to send the rescue squad.

I cried out, "Lord! Help! Bring him back—please, dear God. I give him to you! Bring him back, please!"

I opened the apartment door and stepped out in the foyer where a maid was working across the hall. She saw the baby and yelled, "He's dead! He's dead!"

I said, "Don't say that—God is bringing him back!"

Just then, he began to whimper and opened his little blue eyes for a moment.

"Lord, thank you!" I said. "You're giving him back to me, just when I gave him to you."

He seemed just fine now and was breathing normally. The rescue squad came, and they checked him over and said that nothing was wrong.

It was a beautiful day outside. I was elated that he was fine, but drained from the experience and still shaking. I fed him and then took him in the stroller to the market. He was back to his cheerful, smiling self, and seemed oblivious to what had just happened.

I wasn't, however. Every few minutes I'd stop the stroller and make sure he was still breathing. I'd lean close to him and kiss his chest, which he thought was a game. We laughed and played together, and I gave thanks that he was fine.

Then I thought, suppose something happened when a maid was there—maybe he would have responded differently. I shuddered at the thought. I wanted to stay close to Gregory and not leave him as I had been doing. Besides, I was exhausted from the long bus ride to Mama's with the two transfers, along with juggling work at the restaurant with trying to care for our family at home.

I thought about the apartment over the restaurant. It was ugly and run-down, but it had possibilities. We had to make a decision anyway, for our lease was up on the Fourteenth Street apartment.

Later when at the restaurant I took Ulysses upstairs. I said, "You're so good at fixing things up. Don't you think you could make this livable up here? Look, there's two bedrooms and a living room and dining room, and a very large but sparse kitchen. If we could get a new refrigerator and add a couple of shelves for dishes, we could manage. What do you think?"

Ulysses nodded, but didn't say anything. I could tell he was thinking.

We looked out the window onto a slanted tin roof. "Couldn't that be blocked off on the end?" I asked. "Gregory could play there, and maybe we could put up a clothesline to hang out the clothes."

Ulysses had a real knack for remodeling, and loved a challenging project. I noticed a very interested look on his face as he said, "Yeah, I think it can be done."

He called up Slim Powell, the fellow who had helped him remodel the restaurant. They went to work the very next morning, and within two weeks they had torn out the old bathroom and completely rewired the electricals.

I went to a drapery place and found some wonderful material except for a flaw running right down the center. Regardless, I bought it and sewed four pairs of draperies. When I hung them a certain way, the flaw was not so visible.

We ordered green carpeting and moved in our blonde furniture from the Fourteenth Street apartment. I remarked to Ulysses, "Well, I've always heard of the Jews, Greeks, and Italians living up over their businesses. Now we've joined them."

"Yeah," he responded, "but this is better. It'll save us paying rent and the old car is almost shot anyway. I don't know when we can get another one."

It was comforting to know we were close to Gregory. The little roof wasn't much for him to play on, but he was small and seemed to enjoy being out there while our newfound housekeeper, Nellie, hung the clothes. Because the roof was slanted, he had a great time sliding his little cars and trucks up and down it.

Every afternoon, about two o'clock, Nellie brought Greg into the store after his nap. I'd usually be working on the cash or the books. Seeing him all dressed up and on his way to play at Dupont Circle was the highlight of the day.

Soon after coming in the door, he'd say, "Mama, can I have some ice cream?"

"Sure, what kind do you want?"

"Strawberry."

"You don't know your grandmother, but she always likes strawberry, too."

Then he'd kiss us and wave goodbye on his way to play in the sandbox.

Business continued along. One morning Ulysses and I noticed a well-dressed and prosperous-looking middle-aged couple come in. They sat at one of the center tables and ordered coffee. From the sounds of it, they were arguing over the color of their new Cadillac.

"But darling," she said, "I won't be happy in a black car. Please—I want the blue one."

As she said this, she pushed her fur coat off her shoulders, revealing a lovely blue silk dress. Blue was obviously her color.

Her words didn't faze him one bit.

"No!" he exclaimed, loud enough so most people could hear. "We're going to get the black one and that's final."

He wasn't smiling and stared down at his coffee cup. She seemed to accept it, for she patted his arm. They made up and ordered two french doughnuts.

After that, Ulysses and I would joke, and I'd say, "but darling, I want the blue one." If the day ever came when we could argue over the color of a car, we would have gotten somewhere. We didn't even own a car that we could count on.

Next to us the Wall's Mattress Company was moving to a new location. Blackie was intrigued with the shop and said to me, "I think we should take over the lease to this place. We just might need it in the future, and if someone else takes it, we'll be sorry."

We took the risk in 1950. But right after we signed the three-year lease, business took a dive. North Korea attacked South Korea and it was a shock to be at war again. Truman was president and General Douglas MacArthur was in charge of the forces defending South Korea.

Here we were with business going down and an extra two hundred dollars to pay out each month. We even had to borrow on the $5000 insurance policy that John T. Pappas, the insurance agent we inherited when we bought the Minute Grille, convinced Blackie to take out for Gregory's education. We scrimped and saved to pay out the

$13.29 each month, but soon we were not able to make the payment or the rent. Blackie said to John, "I'm short $80—I can't make the rent."

John said, "Look, I'll let you borrow on the insurance policy."

"What! I can do that?"

John said yes, and made it possible for us to meet the rent that month.

While they were talking, an idea popped into my head. We had to do something quick. I turned to Blackie and said, "You know I like to sew. Maybe we could open up a cleaners next door."

"A cleaners? How do we do that?"

"Let's look into it."

It couldn't hurt to do some research, so I inquired and found out that we could send clothes out to be cleaned wholesale. I visited several cleaners to learn what the setup should be.

When we had it figured it out, Ulysses had Slim come and build a six-foot counter for me. Behind the counter, he installed a long pole with a hook to hang and bag the clothes. And he placed shelving for the shirts and other laundry, as well as a long rod to hang up the cleaning when it came in. We named it the Shanghai Cleaners, putting up a sign.

It went pretty well at the start, but we needed more business. I made up some pamphlets and found someone to hand them out around the neighborhood over the weekend.

On Monday morning, I had customers waiting by the door. I promised to hem skirts and cuff pants for $1.25. I was kept plenty busy.

I also found out that there was such a thing as reweaving. If a person got a hole in a good article of clothing, it could be reweaved. I arranged for this to be done, but lost several times when the customer failed to pick up the item and I still had to pay for the reweaving. After that, I learned to charge for it up front.

With all these services, I was able to pay the rent and had a little left over. I had to hire some part-time help so that I could keep up with my sewing and spend some time at the restaurant.

When we lost our bookkeeper we hired a husband-and-wife team, Connie and Helen Valanos. After about a month, Connie came into the restaurant one afternoon. I could tell he didn't want to alarm Ulysses unduly.

He said, "You know, Blackie, according to your statement, you won't be able to stay in business very long. Your food cost is 125 percent."

"A hundred and twenty-five percent! It can't be!"

"It's true. Look here—figures don't lie. I've got all your canceled checks right here," he said, laying out the checks before Blackie.

"Coca-Cola, $90.00. Connecticut Pies, $55.00. Wilkins Coffee, $80.00," he said, adding up the paid-outs for the month.

Blackie laughed, "You just don't know my system. I guess you'd call it kiting checks—call it what you will. I'm using the wholesaler's money. Here's what I do. All deliveries come cash-on-delivery. I don't have the cash, so I give them a check and use the next day's date. I cover the full amount, only I add on a few dollars. Then they are forced to give me change."

Blackie tapped out his cigarette and lit it with the new lighter I had given him. I noticed Connie studying his face.

He continued, "The change they give me adds up. For instance, now I've got nearly thirty dollars. I wait until after the busy part of lunch is finished, about 1:45 or so. I take what I can spare above the kitty, add that to the other money, and write out a deposit slip.

"Then I run fast to American Security at Fifteenth and L. Usually I catch a cab or maybe my old car decides to work. Mr. Clary, the fellow at the bank who locks the doors at two o'clock, has gotten used to me. He lingers outside the door. At two o'clock on the dot, I come dashing in. I get there in time to make the deposit and breathe a sigh of relief. I've been able to cover the checks so they don't bounce. The next day I do it all over again."

Connie went away, shaking his head and saying, "Guess I can't figure according to the checks, huh?"

In April of 1951, the war in Korea had reached a climax. MacArthur wanted to march further than Harry Truman thought he should, and he also spoke out to the news media without permission from the president. Truman got frustrated and fired him.

Most of the country admired the general and looked forward to hearing his farewell speech on Capitol Hill on April 19TH. Ulysses and I decided to make the most of the interest, renting a black-and-white television set and placing it on the small bar.

When the customers came in at lunchtime, they were thrilled with the idea. While they ate their meal, they were transfixed by the whole affair. Television was relatively new and this was a first. When the general got to the end of his short speech, many just stopped eating and even stood up.

We all listened to the end of his speech: "I still remember the refrain of one of the most popular barrack ballads of that day which proclaimed most proudly that, 'Old soldiers never die, they just fade away.' And like the old soldier of that ballad, I now close my military career and just fade away—an old soldier who tried to do his duty as God gave him the light to see his duty."

There was hardly a dry eye, but the war didn't end there, and life in the United States went right on.

In September, Blackie was turning thirty. Nine years had passed since the birthday dinner that I had cooked for him, Myrt and Billy, and Marge and Wayne just before he left for the army. To celebrate his thirtieth, we invited our friends Bea and George Cokinos and Catherine and Mimi Sclavounos to have dinner with us.

We all sat together in one of the booths, laughing and enjoying ourselves. During coffee, George gave Blackie a small package, a gift for his birthday.

Blackie's eyes lit up as he opened it, for it was an eighteen-carat Swiss watch. He said to me, "So you knew I'd be getting a gold watch, huh?"

We told them the story of the gold watchband I had bought Blackie with my last paycheck five years ago. We went upstairs and removed the leather band and attached the gold band. It looked grand!

One day the next spring I was in my cleaners when a man brought in some cleaning and a pair of pants for me to cuff. As he handed me the clothes, the smell made me nauseated. I'd been through this before—something was going on.

At the same time, even though the war wasn't yet over, business in the restaurant began to pick up. The need for the cleaners was diminishing.

I said to Ulysses, "I think we should sell the cleaners."

"Who the hell would buy it?"

"Well, let's advertise and find out."

We placed an ad in the *Evening Star* and waited a week with no response. Then on Saturday morning a man walked in. I was busy, for Saturdays were my best days. The man stood in the center of the cleaners, looking at its size and measuring the windows.

"I'd like to rent this space," he said, "but not for a cleaners. I'd like to make it a cut-rate appliance outlet."

I was tagging clothes and paused to look at him. I called Ulysses at once, and we arranged to make a lease for him. As soon as I could, I would put up a going-out-of-business notice. What clothes people didn't claim would be given to the Goodwill around the corner.

When I knew the cleaners would be closed, I felt a certain rest coming into my spirit. My feet felt like lead—I was bone tired. I locked the door of the cleaners and went upstairs, hoping to nap before making dinner. Gregory was playing with his little truck and Nellie was anxious to go home. She didn't do any cooking on Saturday.

Just as I got upstairs, the phone rang, and a familiar voice said, "Louie! It's Janet Ballas. I fixed a big plate of spaghetti and meat balls and a nice salad. Can Bill and I and the girls come tonight?"

"You mean you cooked dinner?"

"Yeah, I did. Can we come?"

"That sounds wonderful! Please do."

"Well, I know how tired you are."

It was a real treat. Bill and Janet came with their two daughters, Joy and Wanda, who played with Greg. I had indeed found a friend.

Two weeks later was my last Saturday at the cleaners. Mr. Carter was already moving in his wares and wanted to get started. His cut-rate store was a novel idea, and he was very excited about it.

While I was counting up from a good day of business, Ulysses came in with a new friend he had met.

"Louie, this is Nick Antonelli. You know, I told you I met him through Warren Brokow."

"Hello, Nick. Very nice to meet you."

I noticed Nick was tall and thin and about the same age as Blackie. He was becoming quite well known in the city for his real-estate deals and parking lots.

Nick asked, "Can you close up and come for a ride?"

I started to say no, but Blackie said, "I'd like to go by Nick's house. One of these days, I've got to see if we can afford one."

I protested that I should stay open for the customers to pick up their items.

"C'mon Louie," Blackie said, "close up. If they haven't come for their clothes yet, they won't be coming."

"I really shouldn't."

"It's okay. Go change and get Gregory. I'll stay here until you come down."

I gave in. It was the loveliest of May days so I put on something pink. We rode in Nick's blue Thunderbird out Massachusetts Avenue to his modern, well-furnished home.

They had a nice backyard with trees and a swing. Nick's daughter, Lee, was outside playing and Gregory joined her. I went out too, and sat on a comfortable chaise lounge. The housekeeper brought me lemonade and cookies.

As I sat there, basking in the warm sun, I realized I had forgotten what it was just to sit still and watch the kids play. I hadn't remembered how trees and flowers could refresh one's spirit. I thought again what my Lake Crystal teacher said when I was working during school lunch, "All work and no play makes Lulu a dull girl."

But how could I take more time for myself when our business and family demanded so much? I sighed, thinking of my dream of success.

Time seemed to be flying by. We were well into 1952—an election year with Truman as the lame duck in the White House. "I like Ike" Eisenhower was running on the Republican ticket, and was the winner. The hot thing on television was "I Love Lucy" with Lucile Ball and Dezi Arnez. Lucy was pregnant, just like me, and every time we watched the show I found myself identifying with her.

Gregory was now three and needed a nursery school. We found a good private school at Sheridan Circle and Massachusetts Avenue where we enrolled him.

The first morning I walked him to the school it was a lovely September day, and the birds were singing a sweet song. Gregory was all dressed up in navy-blue pants, a white shirt, and a gray jacket.

"I'm gonna like school, Mama."

"I know you will, honey. You already know your alphabet!"

I knew he'd be all right. He was a gregarious little guy who made friends very easily. He loved to talk—so much so that his Papou sometimes gave him a dollar just to stop asking questions. He fit in well at the school, even though he was just three.

On a rainy Saturday morning Ulysses went downstairs to the restaurant. Around noon I called him through the intercom that Mr. McGee from Executone had installed, but even with repeated tries there still was no answer.

Finally, I took little Gregory to see what was wrong with Daddy. When we peered through the windows, we saw him lying on the floor. We quickly opened the door and Gregory ran to him.

"Daddy! Daddy!"

Holding him close, Ulysses said, "It's all right. Just help me up."

His back was bent way over and he could barely make it to sit down in the booth. He had been complaining of constant back pain for some time, but I had never seen him like this.

"You should go to the Veteran's Administration," I said. "Maybe they can help you."

He made a gesture, holding his head in his hands. "Hell, my back hurts and my neck aches. I'm tired out. Why don't we just give up and get out of here."

Whenever he mentioned quitting, it did something to me. It was like the dream in me flared up. I said, "We can't give up—we have to keep going! I know we're going to make it." I caressed his arm. "You're just tired, honey," I said.

He did agree to go to the VA, saying, "Maybe I can get my pension. They're supposed to be paying me thirty dollars a month in disability."

After his appointment the next week, he returned looking miserable and mad.

"What's happened?" I asked.

"Hell, they kept a bunch of us waiting and treated us like dogs. We had to fill out form after form and it took them an hour to find my records. Then they sent me to some damn psychiatrist who asked me all kinds of questions. The guy said that the pain in my back was all in my head."

He paused to take a drink of Coke and I noticed his hands were shaking.

"I got so mad, I hit the guy hard where his hand lay on the desk. I asked him if that was all in his head. He tried to grab me but I ran out before he caught me. I'm sure he wanted to send me to the mental ward."

He shook his head, saying, "We'll never get the pension money now."

I said, "We've gotten along without it so far. Let's just forget it and move on."

Strangely enough, Ulysses' back improved right after the episode at the VA. Good thing, because it was time for our second baby to be born.

It was 2:30 A.M. on a chilly January night when the pains came. I lay in bed wondering what to do. It would be a shame to wake up Gregory and take him out in the cold. Besides, maybe it was a false alarm. If only I could just go to the hospital, I would be safe there and then could sleep.

I looked across at Ulysses, who was sleeping soundly. I crept out of our warm bed and found my clothes and my small suitcase, which was all packed. I wrestled into my stockings and shoes and put the maternity skirt around me. For a small person, I sure got big when I was pregnant. When I put the worn flowered smock on, I hoped it would be for the last time.

I looked in on Gregory and kissed his cheek goodbye and then called a Yellow Cab. I left a note for Ulysses and went down by the front door to wait for the driver so they wouldn't be woken up.

I checked into Doctor's Hospital and slept solidly all day. Nurses and the doctors came and went but Dr. Hogan had instructed them not to bother me until the time came. That evening, at 10:18 P.M., Ulysses II was born. He was a hefty baby, weighing eight pounds and two ounces.

When I finally saw Ulysses, he was standing before me holding our second son, a little black-haired boy with a blue ribbon in his hair. That day the headlines read "President Eisenhower Inaugurated." And the day before, both on television and in real life, Lucy Ricardo gave birth to her son, Rick Jr. I found out later that 70 percent of Americans watched the episode—far more than those who tuned in to watch the inauguration.

A week later, baby and I checked out of the Doctor's hospital. At home, Gregory was anxiously waiting to see his little brother. When I carried him up the stairs, he asked, "Are you sure he isn't a plastic doll?"

I smiled and let him take a closer look.

Gregory's little bed and Ulysses' crib fit snugly in the small room. Ulysses and I stood and gazed down at them as they slept. How wonderful it was to be home, and how sweet it was to have my family.

15

"How 'bout some beef?"

ALONG WITH THE BIRTH OF OUR SECOND SON in January 1953, an idea was born. While I was in the hospital with our new baby, a friend of ours, George Jones, took over the cash register. At the close of business one day, he suggested to Blackie that they visit a restaurant called Hodges. He wanted Blackie to taste the roast beef sandwiches there, freshly cut from a round of beef.

I heard about their excursion later, and I could tell that Ulysses was pondering something. "We went into this dinky place," he said, "and there was a man carving sandwiches from this big round of beef. You know, the upper part of the leg." He slapped his thigh.

"I ate one, and it was so good that I ate another one. It was just as good. I ended up eating four of them!" He handed me one. "Here. Taste this."

I wasn't the least bit hungry but I took a bite. "You're right—it's really good. And it smells appetizing even though I'm not hungry."

We began to think beef. It would take many months and a lot of work to plan, figure it out, and finally make it successful.

On a Saturday morning in hot August, Ulysses said to me, "Get dressed—Bernie Goldstein is coming. I'm going to lay it on the line with him about the beef."

In the restaurant circles, Bernie Goldstein of District Hotel Supply was said to know more about meat than anyone else in town. While waiting for him to come, Ulysses was nervous and restless. He paced the floor, adjusted the furniture, was cranky with the kids, and picked up their toys with frustration. Finally there was a knock on the door.

"Hi, Bernie. Come on in!"

"Whew, Blackie! Kind of airless in here. Why don't you get a fan?"

Blackie was in no mood for small talk. "Look," he said, "I didn't bring you up here to talk about the air. I brought you up here to discuss meat."

Blackie motioned for Bernie to sit down at the table. I gave them some cold orange juice.

Blackie launched into his idea. "I want to sell roast beef sandwiches. At first I'm going to experiment and I want your help. I'm going to start with a round of beef, and I want it fresh every day. I'm not going to sell any day-old beef."

Bernie nodded.

"I know that meat men are the biggest thieves in the world, and with the kind of meat I'm going to sell, even a penny will make a difference. When I start out there probably won't be any profit at all."

Blackie lit a cigarette and offered one to Bernie, and they filled the room with smoke.

"I've also talked to Tony Auth of Auth Brothers for a bid. I'm going to put you two against each other—the best beef and the best price wins. I'm gambling on this beef, so it's got to be good or I'm sunk."

Bernie sat back. He was an attractive man with thinning hair, a penetrating voice, and a winsome laugh. He answered, "Gotcha. I know exactly what you want and I won't disappoint you. I'll do the best I can for you—I think it's going to work."

Bernie left, perspiration running down his face. His parting remark was, "I'll get you all the figures, and we'll work it out. It'll be great!"

Blackie made quite a few trips to Hodges because he liked the sandwiches and because he wanted to figure out how the big round got cooked in the middle. He talked to Slim and asked him to make a two-foot copper tube to run through the center of the round. This would be a conduit for heat, and it would also make the meat easier to handle.

Bread was another important part of the sandwich.

Ulysses said to me, "Get the Charles Schneider Baking Company on the phone. I want to explain to them what I want."

I called the company, and the next day a representative of the bakery came. I heard Blackie describing what he wanted. "Listen, I want a crisp roll on the outside, but I want it soft and great tasting on the inside. I don't want any of those rolls that are made by machine."

"I've got just the roll for you," the young man said. "Look—they're benchmade all by hand and baked in special ovens. They'll be just what you want. I'll bring them by for you tomorrow."

"One more thing," Blackie said, "I want them to have poppy seeds. Poppy seeds give a guy an appetite, and go together with beef."

The following day, they brought in a dozen perfect benchmade rolls, which tasted good. Now that we had the bread and the meat in process, we needed to figure out the setup for the beef.

We thought the logical place for it would be the small liquor bar, which customers saw as soon as they entered the front door. Working with Slim, Ulysses took the top off the bar and replaced it with a carving board. Over this two-inch piece of wood, they set glass pie cases not only to protect the meat, but to give customers a view of the carver as he worked.

The day that Bernie Goldstein delivered two huge rounds of beef really emptied our cash register. Bernie took them into the kitchen with Blackie. They placed one of the rounds in a huge baking pan and refrigerated the other one for the next day.

The meat filled the whole oven, and went on to cook at six in the morning. The kitchen was burning up with smoke and the heat of the oven set at 500 degrees.

It seemed incredible that we would bake so much meat and not even know if it would sell. We were all nervous, and no one more so than Blackie. A couple of days with this kind of expense and we wouldn't be able to pay our notes.

The meat cost sixty-two cents per pound after it was roasted and there were at least four sandwiches to the pound. We were planning on selling each sandwich for forty-five cents. We didn't do any advertising—in truth, we didn't know how to. Nor could we afford an advertisement in the paper. We just put the large piece of meat out in the front for everyone to see.

People were hungry for meat, and there it was. Our first carver was Bob Dalton, who wore a red kerchief with his white chef's outfit. At our instruction, he gave away plenty of free samples to customers who loved the meat and wanted more. When we saw how our patrons reacted, we knew that we had something right.

We also sent some free sandwiches over to the mechanics, and they were delighted. After their first taste, they did away with their lunch pails and instead sent over for a roast beef sandwich and a Coke for fifty cents. Such word-of-mouth advertising immediately began to build our sales. We had customers from the Weather Bureau, the Navy Department, and our friends at the businesses around us. And these customers told their friends.

The first day we gave away or sold almost half the round of beef. The day after, we sold another half. Every day our sales increased but the day-old beef began to pile up and we had no place to put it.

About this time, Blackie began meeting with some of his friends every Wednesday for lunch around one-thirty when business died down. They named their fledgling group the One-thirty Club. One day they met at the Old Athens Restaurant, whose owner, Mr. Chritsodemas, had also joined the club. Blackie told him of his problem of the left-over beef and he agreed to buy it for ten cents a pound. It wasn't nearly enough to cover the loss, but enough to keep us going. Pennies counted!

At the very time we started selling the beef, the World Series was on. We knew that the guys at Capitol Cadillac were real baseball fans, and that Mr. Akers didn't allow his employees to listen to the radio as they worked. Since we were located directly across from them, we took some heavy blue chalk and wrote the score on the front of our windows as the game progressed. The fellows appreciated it. Also, to oblige our customers, we rented two small black-and-white televisions so that they could view the game.

Business turned out to be so good during the week that people asked us to open on Saturday also. Downtown was the place to shop, for there weren't any department stores to speak of in the suburbs. After shopping, people wanted to stop by for roast beef.

We thought about it and decided to open. It meant working the staff on Saturday also, but most of them didn't mind. Again, without advertising we just opened up, and word of mouth brought people in— men, women, and children.

One Saturday, a well-dressed mother came in with her cute young son. He was wearing a little tweed jacket, but the Woodward and Lothrop tag was still hanging down the back of the coat. Blackie walked over and yanked on the tag, pulling so hard that the jacket tore. The tag said $23.76, so we refunded the lady right then and there. So much for that day's profits.

After beef took over the Minute Grille, nothing was ever the same. Our three-year lease was now up and we were on a month-to-month one with a thirty-day cancellation clause. It was nerve-racking, but we kept right on doing the best we could, hoping and praying that there'd be a way to save us.

We were actually losing money at the same time as we were growing. With our precarious lease, we couldn't borrow any money from the bank. So to make ends meet at Christmastime, Blackie drove to Gateway Finance in nearby Virginia where he borrowed three hundred dollars at 19 percent interest. We'd be paying it off for the rest of the year, but it allowed us to renew the beer license and to take care of the Christmas bonuses.

We were often late in paying our bills. We had received one notice from the gas company and two cutoff notices. Then one day a young fellow wearing the gas company jacket and cap came in to turn off the gas. It was about one thirty, and lunch was tapering down. I was busy with the customers, so Blackie sat him down and served him lunch.

They were talking, and I noticed that Blackie kept looking at the clock. When it was ten minutes to two, he left the man still eating and came up to the register.

"Louie, make out a check for the gas bill for $48.00."

I wrote out the check and handed him the deposit for the day as he prepared to do his run to the bank.

"I've got to go now, but as soon as Dan over there finishes eating, give him this check. He won't have time to take it to the bank today, and with this deposit, it will clear tomorrow."

I smiled. He had pulled this trick before—one more way to keep the bill collectors happy.

It was on a Thursday in the summer of 1954 when Mr. Carter came over from next door with a distraught expression on his face.

"I've got to tell you—I tried my best. I needed to buy more merchandise to sell, but I didn't have enough money for it. So I used the sales-tax money. But today they came to collect and I didn't have their money. Now they closed me up."

The dear man had tears in his eyes. It was a shame, for he was such a hard-working person. They cleared out all of his merchandise, and now we had the room again. Ever since the Korean War had ended in July of 1953, our sales had increased. We needed the space to expand and wasted no time.

On Friday night, after the close of business, Slim Powell set to work with Blackie. They worked all night long, breaking through the wall of the store next door. Because we were open on Saturday, they hung a painter's cloth over the opening while business went right on.

Inside the new room, we painted the walls a bright persimmon. I went to my favorite second-hand drapery shop and purchased a bolt of matching fabric for the windows. We worked the whole weekend. By Sunday, the draperies were finished, a new dark blue rug was in place, the walls were painted, we had rented tables and chairs, and we had new tablecloths, napkins, and some new tall plants. Voilà! The room was ready for business.

When our customers came in on Monday morning, they were surprised to find another room. Some swore we had had it all the time. Blackie's farsightedness had paid off.

Though our business was good, problems threatened to overwhelm us. We lost our cook of many years, George Lekas, but Peter Young of Ted Louis's famous restaurant was still with us.

One day he came out of the kitchen and addressed Blackie. "You've got to do something about the kitchen. It's so smoky from all the baking of the beef and the frying of the potatoes that I can't breathe."

"What you need," Blackie responded, "is a gas mask."

He immediately went to Sunny Surplus and bought several masks. Our kitchen looked like a combat zone, but at least our people could breathe.

We did what we could to keep our employees happy, for good employees like Chef Young were hard to find. The shortages were everywhere, causing many enterprising people to start various businesses. And other businesses were expanding, including Deiners Flooring next door to us. They needed larger facilities and were moving away.

They had an employee by the name of Cleveland who was a little mentally retarded and had a dangerous streak. If he got mad over something, he would break off any convenient bottle and come after the offender. Mickey Deiner said Cleveland didn't want to leave the neighborhood and that he was a good worker if he was handled right. Would we take him on?

We made him our dishwasher and cleanup man when our regulars were in school. One day we were extremely busy and were running out of dishes. I rushed in the kitchen and demanded that Cleveland bring some clean dishes out right away. He didn't like my tone of voice and came at me with a broken Coke bottle.

I yelled, "Cleveland! Put that bottle down now and get to work!" Thankfully, he obeyed. He was representative of the chaos under which we worked.

We were surviving from the cash register but had only a very small profit. Our kitchen was impossible and we needed walk-in boxes desperately. Slim built a small one of cinder blocks in the backyard that helped, but what we needed was a whole new kitchen.

It was a beautiful, crisp autumn day in 1954 and the golden leaves were chasing one another down the broad avenue. I was at the cash register, watching them scurry by. I could see Blackie, too, for he was standing out front with George Cokinos and Mimi Sclavounos. They were pointing to the top of our building.

I put my jacket over my shoulders and joined them as I heard Blackie ask George, "So what do you think—should we order a big sign for up there, or should I take the money and enlarge the kitchen?"

"Think you ought to put up the sign," replied George, still looking up.

The night before, Blackie and I had discussed the dilemma of a new sign or a new kitchen. We hoped a large new sign would attract enough business to enable us to expand the kitchen through our regular everyday sales. With our precarious lease, borrowing was out of the question.

Our new sign covered the width of the building—it was so large that nobody driving by could miss it. It read "Blackie's House of Beef" and featured a cowboy roping a steer. Our customers had changed our name, for to them we were "Blackie's." We took down the Minute Grille sign and sold it to an ambitious young man who planned to open his own restaurant.

Now that we had decided on the logo as a cowboy roping a steer, we had a direction and began to think western. We stayed on the lookout for wagon wheels, pictures, or anything western for decoration. On weekends, we'd borrow a car and take the kids out to the country to visit antique houses. Those were the fun times.

As weeks passed, the sign did attract customers. And with more and more word-of-mouth recommendations, our business grew.

Although our sales were increasing, we were still a little hesitant about spending the money to enlarge the kitchen. While pondering the decision, Blackie heard of a consultant from the May Company who gave business advice. Since he had a good reputation, Blackie decided we should confer with him before making the big move. The fellow charged twenty-five dollars an hour, and we were barely taking in forty dollars an hour, but we made arrangements to hire him anyway.

He came in on a Monday, a fairly young man who chain-smoked Lucky Strikes and spoke in a clipped, educated accent.

After exchanging introductions, he said, "You go on about your work, and I'll sit here and observe everything. I'd like to be free to go into the kitchen and see what's happening there. And let me examine your daily worksheets for the past few months."

Mr. Jackson got a cup of coffee, went into the kitchen for a few moments, and then sat in a booth puffing on his Lucky Strikes. Blackie got increasingly irritated watching him and said, "I must be a nut to pay this guy to sit there and smoke cigarettes."

After three hours, Blackie couldn't take it anymore. "That's it," he said. "I'm gonna pay him off right now. Hell—I bet I know more about this situation than he ever will."

We walked over to Mr. Jackson and Blackie asked, "Well, what do you think?"

With rather lofty tones, the consultant answered, "I'd like to spend another day observing."

Blackie's face turned red and for a few moments I thought he would explode. Through clenched teeth, he said, "Nope, can't give you another day. Fact is, I can't give you another minute—my cash register is nearly empty. But at least you can tell me what you think."

The fellow lit yet another cigarette and replied, "Well, you're only on a month-to-month lease. You might just as well go ahead and remodel the kitchen. You've taken a chance thus far and you could win. I'll send you a written report."

We paid him his seventy-five dollars and Blackie was mad the rest of the day. More than once he said, "I paid out seventy-five dollars for a guy to tell me what I already knew. I must be a dumb fool."

From our small beginning, we began to grow. Our lunch business increased and we were now selling three rounds of beef with no advertisement other than word of mouth. There was a hunger for the meat that civilians had been denied during the war years.

We were so busy that we had hardly a moment to daydream, rest, or pull ourselves together. One day a few weeks later I looked down and noticed that my stockings were torn. As I was walking down Connecticut Avenue to buy some more I caught a glimpse of myself in a store window. I looked horrible—the exhaustion was certainly showing. Something needed to be done.

Blackie and I talked about it and decided to hire a cashier and find a company to print our menus. With the help of Slim Powell, we built a cashier's cage out of wagon wheels that looked like a small horse-drawn cart. Then we hired a young girl named Anne as cashier and employed Menu's Daily for the menus. I felt relieved.

I now had a little time in the afternoon to spend with the kids. We enjoyed walking up to Dupont Circle where they would play in the grass. On the way there I'd look up at the John Robert Powers Modeling Agency, which always intrigued me. One day I decided to go in and find out what they did.

The young woman behind the desk explained, "This is more or less a finishing school. We teach ladies which clothes are best for them, and we show them how to do their make-up, hair, and all those things that make them attractive."

Then she added, "Of course, some women become models but that's not our primary purpose."

I thanked her, and the kids and I headed for Dupont Circle. There I sat on a park bench and watched them play while I figured out how I could afford the course. I needed to look my best and learn what was my most flattering style.

Later I was able to pull together enough money to pay for the course, even though I wasn't receiving a salary. I made arrangements for Nellie to walk up to the circle with us, and while she looked after the children, I would spend a few hours at the agency.

I was told that simple, classic styles were best for me. Although I couldn't afford the wardrobe they recommended, I knew I could sew my own clothes and found ideas for new outfits from dress-shop windows. The only catch was that I had to stay up most of the night sewing.

I knew that my appearance had improved when one day the boys and I walked along Connecticut Avenue and Gregory said, "Mama, your face looks just like the faces in the window." I stopped and gave him a big hug.

A couple weeks later Blackie's mother accompanied us to Dupont Circle. The boys loved her, and she adored them. But when we walked a little distance, she began to complain about a pain in her left thigh. I asked if she had gone to a doctor, and she said that she had. He said it was rheumatism and that she should take aspirin for the pain.

I was concerned for her but was too exhausted and caught up in the business to give it much thought. I was sure in my heart that if we kept going—and if the lease didn't end—that someday we'd be successful.

As the weeks went by, we were pleased that our new sign did attract customers. While the business was picking up, we started building the kitchen, paying for everything right out of the cash register.

We were gambling with big money this time—the government's. It was late October and the liquor and beer licenses would soon be due, and then the income taxes by March fifteenth. We hoped and figured that if we could open the new kitchen, the extra sales generated by it would cover the taxes.

Blackie worried about it day and night. "It's going to be real tough," he said. "If we fail to finish it and have to interrupt business, we'll be in a terrible jam." His jaw was clenched and his tone was as much a command as a plea. We had to stick together.

Blackie went from restaurateur to builder. I watched the concrete slab being poured and the cinderblock walls being erected, this time with work permits. A large walk-in box was built to accommodate the meat and a new large Blodgett oven was installed.

Blackie's dream was a big white kitchen with a red quarry-tiled floor. Our new kitchen wasn't yet his dream, but it was a grand improvement. And we had managed to put it in without a loan while also scraping together enough money to cover the taxes.

We were so entwined in our work that we seemed almost devoid of feelings separate from the children and business. Every moment of our time was taken up.

It was close to Christmas. We had plenty of opportunity—people were begging for us to be open in the evening—but Ulysses was always tired and upset. The slightest thing seemed to throw him off. Also, he was unable to get a good night's sleep. In a way, I became nurse as well as his wife because I understood his war background, nervous energy, and need for phenobarbitol.

The last weekend before Christmas, Chef Young approached me with a worried look. "Mrs. Auger, your husband is standing out in the backyard. He looks kind of funny to me."

Alarmed, I went through the kitchen and found Ulysses without a jacket, standing amidst the garbage cans and leaning against the back-yard fence.

There were tears in his eyes and his hair was disheveled. He was trembling and shaking from the cold. I put my arms around him and he came with me up the back steps, through the storage room, and into the hallway to our apartment. The boys saw him and stared wide-eyed.

"Daddy's all right," I said as I walked him back to the bedroom. "Go and play, boys, okay?"

I had feared this might happen. Ulysses hadn't been sleeping well and was more irritable than usual.

As I undressed him, he said, "We need another walk-in box. Got to age the meat properly. Hear me? Get someone here. Get Slim."

"Sure, Ulysses. You lie there and I'll get someone. We'll get the walk-in box."

I left him and went immediately to the phone, biting my lower lip and struggling to speak plainly. "Dr. Winik, you're the doctor of the Auger family. I'm calling about their son, my husband. Do you think you could come over to our apartment? He's very ill—not physically, but emotionally. He's all tired out. Do you think you could come right away?"

He came within a half-hour. As I walked him up the steps, I explained how Ulysses had not been sleeping and how nervous he was.

"Probably he should go away somewhere," he said.

"Oh, that's not possible—we just don't have the money for that. Look, if you could give him something to let him rest, I'll take care to give it to him and will keep him at home in bed."

"Let's go see him," he said. "If I agree, I'll tell you what to do."

Nellie was dressing the children to go play. I kissed them good-bye as the doctor and I walked down the hall to the back bedroom. Ulysses was out of bed, trying to dress himself while mumbling about the meat.

Dr. Winik knew him and had cared for his father. He said, "Hello, Ulysses. Please lie down on the bed for me."

Ulysses obeyed, but insisted that he was all right and asked what he was doing there anyway.

"Just a moment, young man," Dr. Winik said. "I just want to check your blood pressure. That's it, lie down there.

"Mrs. Auger—please get us a glass of water."

I brought the water, and Dr. Winik handed Ulysses two pills and told him to take them. The doctor talked to him for a few moments, and soon Ulysses just lay right back and went to sleep.

Outside in the living room, Dr. Winik said, "I think maybe you're right. Fill this prescription and give him this medicine night and morning. We'll just keep him sleeping, and you can feed him. He'll be drowsy, but you can probably handle it. Feed him, give him the medicine, and don't let him go to work. How does that sound?"

"Good. It's all we can do, anyway."

"Yes. He's young, and I think he'll snap out of this. He's been taking the phenobarbitol. I just increased the dose a little, and along with these sleeping pills he's sedated pretty heavily.

"Here's my telephone number," he continued. "Call me night or day if you run into any trouble."

"I will. Thank you so much."

"He's suffering from sheer exhaustion. Only rest is going to help him."

While Ulysses slept I went down to the business. It was mine for a week, and Christmas week at that. There were so many decisions to make, such as who would cashier for me. I called our former book-keeper, a thin, kindly man, and he promised to take cash between twelve and two o'clock.

I used our many tricks to keep ahead of the bill collectors. I dated the checks ahead and asked the wholesaler to hold it for an extra day so that it could be covered. Guts, float, and a lot of hard work kept us going.

As it was the week of Christmas the staff were expecting not only their paychecks but Christmas bonuses. I couldn't go to the Gateway Finance as Ulysses had the year before, so I had to get along without the three hundred dollars.

I knew we had a hundred dollars in the register. In two days I would need to pay the bonuses, as it would be Christmas Eve. But when I went to the register at two o'clock, there was no money there. There was only a returned check for a hundred dollars.

"Gus!" I cried. "What happened? Where's the money?"

"Well, the meat delivery fellow brought the check back, because he wanted cash instead."

"Why didn't you ask me? I had it predated for a reason. Look—I really appreciate your helping me, but I've got to have that hundred dollars!"

"I'm sorry, Louie. I'll get you a hundred dollars. Ulysses can pay me when he gets better."

Where he got it from, I don't know. But I knew that this juggling we did so skillfully enabled us to keep going. I watched the cash register very closely after that. Money was a commodity like meat or anything else. We learned creative ways to keep our head above water even when we were short of cash.

The stress had taken a toll on Ulysses, who was still sleeping under medication, but I was getting exhausted too. The whole burden of the business came down on my shoulders that week, and I didn't have Ulysses to counsel with. Nor could I enjoy Christmas week with the children. Nellie took care of them, and we had to instruct them to stay away from Daddy's room.

There were times that week when I was trying to be friendly with customers but the tears would come into my eyes. I tried to brush them away, keeping my worries to myself. Customers, I knew, needed smiles.

On Thursday, the day before Christmas Eve, Mr. Akers came in for lunch. His expression usually conveyed his wealth and social prestige, but today he was a man of understanding. In his deep and unusually tender voice, he said, "Don't worry—he'll be all right. And you're doing a good job here too."

His words comforted me, and I appreciated them.

We were selling a whole beef now, and in spite of everything, we somehow made it through that Christmas week. When Christmas Eve came on Friday, I was able to pay the bonuses. After all the customers went home early and the staff had left, I took a moment to sit in the front booth and cry with relief.

When I locked the door and went upstairs, Ulysses was still asleep. This was the night I was to cut off his sleeping pills. First, however, the boys and I had something important to do.

Nellie had them dressed in their warm clothes. Gregory bumped his red wagon down the stairs and then the three of us traipsed through the snow to get a Christmas tree. Earlier I had bought their gifts and hidden them away, back in the room where Daddy was sleeping.

I kissed and hugged them, now able to give them my full attention. "You boys have been so good," I said. "You didn't bother your Daddy all week."

"We did a little, but Daddy yelled at us so we left him alone then," Gregory said.

Ulysses II was nearly two years old and could really get his point across. He said, "We were quiet, Mama." He put his finger to his lips and whispered, "Shh!" They were very sweet to their tired mother.

The boys chose a little Christmas tree, which to them seemed very tall. We loaded it on the red wagon and then bought some new trim and bulbs. When we reached home, we lugged it all up the stairs.

It was about six o'clock and dinner time. We went to the back bedroom where Daddy was just waking up. He lay there, his brown eyes shining, looking very rested. We all piled into the bed, and for the first time all week I felt relaxed and happy. I had what I wanted, my own dear family.

After a time we enjoyed the wonderful food Nellie had prepared— her famous Southern fried chicken, corn bread, salad, whipped potatoes, apple sauce, and a big orange pumpkin pie. We ate and laughed. Our boys couldn't understand why their Daddy had to sleep all the time.

After the children were in bed asleep and we had the tree decorated, Ulysses and I drew close to each other. I tried to make him understand where the week had gone.

Somehow after this week of sleep, Ulysses emerged stronger than ever. Miraculously, no further treatment was needed. However, all the challenges were still there waiting for us. Our month-to-month lease was like walking a tightrope. We were unable to borrow money for expansion but we were determined to grow anyway.

Undaunted by the impossible lease picture, I knew we'd just keep striving toward our goal. We were living above the family business but we were happy and close-knit. The dream I had inside was bigger than the lease, bigger than the problems, bigger than Ulysses and me. I knew we just couldn't give up.

V

Struggles but Success

16

Moving on Up

I GOT A CALL FROM MARGARET in January 1955. Her voice was strained, and I was having a hard time believing what she was saying. "You and Ulysses need to come—Mama's very sick."

"What's wrong?" I asked.

"Well, you remember how Mama's leg hurt but the doctor advised her just to take aspirin? Her pain kept increasing so finally we took her to another doctor."

Her voice broke but she continued, "The tests showed that she's got bone cancer and that it's spread throughout her body." She sounded hurt and disappointed in us, and I hardly knew how to respond.

Ulysses borrowed a car from Joe Rinaldi, one of the Cadillac salesmen, and on a clear and sparkling day we drove to Mama's house in Tacoma Park where the family had moved a few months before. The boys were laughing and playing in the back seat, unaware of the seriousness of our visit.

We entered the modern house and saw Mama lying on a rented hospital bed in the living room. We tried to hide our shock as we greeted her—we could barely believe how fast she had deteriorated. Her eyes were sunken and her once beautiful hands were bony and blotchy. She was just fifty-three-years old.

I hugged Ulysses II close to me. Gregory, who was older and more aware, shrunk back as his father went to Mama's side.

"My son," she said, "You came."

It was devastating just to look at her. I saw Papou sitting in the dining room, his brooding, tear-stained face staring out the window. I gathered the kids close to me and took them to Papou's side. At once, his face brightened and he embraced them, saying, "Ela [come], let's go outside."

Mama died on February 19 and was buried on Washington's birthday. The restaurant was closed that day.

The following day, Blackie went down to business and I looked around the apartment for the kids. We had lived there for six years, and it showed. The kids' toys were scattered over the worn green rug, and the furniture was nicked and scratched.

More disturbing than the state of the apartment, however, was the lack of fresh air and space for the boys to play. There wasn't any grass, and nowhere for them to pull their wagons. Looking around, I felt a little despondent.

I heard little noises and saw the backs of their shoes peering out from under the curtains. "You little rascals," I said playfully, "Are you hiding from Mommie?"

Ulysses held his favorite toy, a yellow duck. Gregory had a long face, as he was old enough to understand that his Yia Yia had died. It was a sad day.

I held them close and said, "I promise that someday soon, we'll move away from here and you can have a yard to play in."

Gregory asked, "Will there be swings?"

"Yes, honey, there will be swings."

Business was booming. It was as if we had enrolled in a college, although we didn't have any professors to teach us. We just worked and figured out things as we went along.

We didn't really choose to open in the evenings, but responded to the demand in late 1955. Customers were staying later and later for the hot roast beef platter; the young people loved the roast beef sandwich with potatoes and gravy; and everyone adored the roast beef sandwich on the hard poppy-seed roll.

Also, Pete, our baker, made outstanding desserts, such as cheesecake and pies, the favorite being banana cream. The customers ordered them to take home along with bags of sandwiches.

After yet another customer asked about us being open in the evening, Blackie said, "We can't go on this way. We'd better make up our minds which way we're going."

I heard him dial the phone and ask for Bernie.

"Hey Bernie, I'm thinking of opening in the evenings. I want to serve prime rib and some good steaks. Come on down and let's talk about it."

The next day, Bernie came prepared. He was a good man to work with because not only did he understand what we needed, he acted. He brought with him a standing rib roast, several New York steaks, and a fillet mignon. He said our broiler would need to be at least 850 degrees.

Blackie took nothing for granted, weighing and studying the meat. He evaluated and checked the cost, calling Bernie's competitors, the Auth Brothers. Then he called the gas company to calibrate the broiler to see how hot they could get it.

We tested the New York steak by eating it for dinner. It was very good. We now had the product, so we decided to open in the evenings.

I asked, "What about prices and menus?"

"Call around and see how much prime rib and steaks are selling for," Blackie replied.

I searched through the restaurants in the yellow pages. There weren't many beef houses, but I found several, such as Fan and Bills, Hendrix Steak House, and Cannons. The price of the prime rib varied between $3.95 and $4.95 for a complete dinner.

We fixed up a menu of prime rib, salad, baked potatoes with sour cream and chives, green peas, and a small salad. And we had bleu cheese and crackers on a silver platter for the customers just as they sat down. This was all included in the price of $1.95. We were aiming to sell quality beef at an almost giveaway price.

On opening night Blackie and I stood by the cash register, looking forward to our first dinnertime crowd. We didn't have any fanfare or advertising except a little sign that said, "Open evenings until ten thirty."

"Well, Kid," Blackie said, "This is it. What do you think?"

"I think we're going to make it big," I said with a smile. "The timing is right."

"Always the dreamer, aren't you?" he said as he kissed me on the cheek.

A few nights later, Jean, a lovely lady who was a reporter with the *Washington Daily News*, came into the restaurant with her husband. I could tell that her husband was hesitating when he saw the booths and the counter. But Blackie and I were right there and started talking to them. We invited them to have dinner with us in the Eldorado Room. After awhile her husband warmed up to us, and the two of them became our greatest boosters.

In fact, a few weeks later Jean sent a restaurant columnist to us named Don Hearne. He later wrote a column that built us up highly. From just this one mention, our business grew almost faster than we could handle.

Even though we had just enlarged the kitchen, we were still running out of space. And the toll of too many hours—night and day— was wearing on us. We decided to get some more help and hired a manager, George Papadeas. We also needed someone to cover the front desk, so we hired a silver-haired Greek fellow named George Changuris. He had a calm personality and could be trusted never to lose his temper even if a customer did.

After hiring George Changuris, Blackie said to him, "Look, George, it's too confusing to have two George's working here. I'm gonna call you Sam. If you don't like that name, better tell me quick. Once I program a name, I can't get it out of my head."

George, ever the gentleman, nodded his head "yes." From then on he became Sam at the front desk.

We also hired some more waiters, including a few students from the nearby Georgetown University. They became so popular that customers often invited them to their homes for Sunday dinners. One of them was Al Bauknecht. Whenever Blackie had a difficult customer he'd ask Al to take over. Al had good "bedside" manners and could assuage the unhappiest customer. And when we hired a young busboy by the name of Panayotis Nafpliotis, we never dreamed he'd eventually become the official dentist of King Hussein of Jordan. Born in Cairo, Egypt, he was of Greek descent and shortened his name to Peter Neff. He worked as a busboy and then became a waiter.

Peter became friends with one of our regulars, Dr. Bernard "Steve" B. Brody, who became known as the father of modern pharmacology with his discovery of acetaminophen (Tylenol) and many other medicines. Dr. Brody would come in, sprawl out his papers on a table, and work for hours on his projects while enjoying a thick cut of roast beef.

When Dr. Brody found out that Peter had a degree in chemistry, he was intrigued and wanted Peter to come work with him. Peter did go for awhile, but the life of a reclusive researcher was too isolating for him. Instead, he left Dr. Brody and went to dental school. Later, Peter established dental institutes in Washington, D.C. and Jordan. We were thrilled to witness another instance of the American dream becoming a reality.

In January 1956, just three days before our tenth wedding anniversary, we received a call from our friends Irene and George Pappas.

Irene asked, "Say, how about coming to New York with us?"

I had never been to New York, although Blackie had. Actually, during the ten years of our marriage, we really hadn't been anywhere except the Chesapeake Bay. The suggestion was more than intriguing.

I asked Ulysses, "Do you think we could go to New York with Irene and George?"

"Go to New York? Are you crazy? How am I going leave this place?"

"It's only for one night—we can leave on Friday and come back on Saturday. It's our tenth wedding anniversary, you know."

"Are you sure it's only for one night?"

"Well, Irene says she wants to go and have dinner, and then the next day she's picking up a fur. Then we'll come right back."

"Our tenth wedding anniversary, huh?"

"That's right. Ten years have flown by."

"Well, get them on the phone."

I was about to dial when the phone rang. I answered it, "Hello? Oh, hi Jimma!" Jerry and Jimma Strong had a popular radio show and were now doing our advertising.

She said, "We've got four tickets for the Broadway show, *Oklahoma!*. We were going to use them, but found out that we couldn't. Would you like them?"

"*Oklahoma!*—wow! Are they for this weekend?"

"Yeah, they're for Friday night."

"Can I call you right back? Please don't give them away until you hear from me."

I couldn't believe our good fortune. I turned to Blackie and said excitedly, "Jerry and Jimma just said that we could have four tickets to *Oklahoma!* on Broadway."

"I'm not interested in any Broadway show."

"Oh, come on. It'll be wonderful."

He scowled and then softened, saying, "Well, call and ask Irene and George. If they're interested, I suppose we could go."

I was thrilled that he was actually contemplating the idea. George answered the phone and as soon as he heard my voice, he asked, "Are you guys coming with us?"

"Well, we're just thinking. Listen, someone is willing to give us four tickets to *Oklahoma!*. Would you two be interested?

"Would we! Irene just loves Broadway shows."

I turned the phone over to Blackie, and heard him say, "Well, maybe we can spare one night. What time do you want to leave on Friday? No, I can't leave until I make a deposit at the bank. How are we going to go?" He paused, and then said, "By plane! Well, I guess that'll be all right."

It was settled. We had never left our children before, but I called Blackie's sister, Harriet, who was excited about staying with them. She asked Papou to be with her as well.

We worked right up to the last moment, making a deposit just before catching the plane. But our flight was running late and we had trouble catching a taxi once in New York, so we went directly to the Mark Hellinger theatre, bags and all. They obliged us by storing our suitcases for us.

"Oh, wow," I said to myself. "Here I am watching *Oklahoma!*, and they are singing the very song from our wedding, 'Some Sunday Morning.' "

What a show—I'd never forget it. As we left the theatre carrying our bags, I was nearly overwhelmed by the majesty of the city. I sang to myself, "How you gonna keep 'em down on the farm, after they've seen Broadway."

We went into Sardi's restaurant nearby and squeezed into a booth. We ordered the Kosher sandwiches and pickles, which were crisp and good. We found out where they bought them, and decided to order them for Blackie's.

Now dining had become sampling—a place to taste and learn. We ordered the cheesecake as well, but realized after tasting it that Pete made very good cheesecake. We felt a small measure of confidence.

The Plaza Hotel felt like wonderland to me. I loved all the polished furniture in our two-bedroom suite with its connecting living room.

We slept soundly, and the next morning ordered breakfast in our robes as we sat looking out onto Central Park. I hoped we could take a ride in a horse-drawn carriage next time.

We then prepared to go to Christie Brothers, the famous New York furriers. I was thrilled that Irene was going to get a fur coat. While watching her parade around in her black walking coat, Blackie came up behind me and placed a blond mink stole around my shoulders. As he did, he kissed me and said, "Happy anniversary, Louie."

He surprised me as I was sure we couldn't afford anything. I looked at him blankly and he said, "That's why I stopped at the bank."

"What! Really!" I was stunned. "Oh, thank you, Ulysses. I just love it."

It was time to leave and we reluctantly headed for the airport. Once in Washington we went straight to the restaurant, which was completely packed. Blackie thought it wouldn't run without him, but it was doing fine.

.

We were now selling more than three rounds of beef during lunchtime and we finally had some profit to build on. We were filling up in the evenings and there usually was a line of people waiting for tables. This created a problem during the rainy times, as the customers had to step out the front door into the downpour.

We decided the solution would be to erect an awning. I called the Third Precinct to find out if awnings were allowed, but no one seemed to know.

One day a few weeks later we got our answer when Captain Emory came in for a cup of coffee.

Blackie said to him, "I've drawn up an awning I want to have made, but I don't understand about the permits or if it's even legal. I don't see any other awnings around."

The Captain seemed to favor the idea. He said, "All I can tell you is to go ahead and get the awning up. I'll give you a temporary permit, and if nobody complains, what's temporary might become permanent. There's an ordinance that forbids restaurants from putting up awnings, but it's in the works to change, so you go ahead. I'm retiring anyway, so I'll go along with you. You might as well be the first."

We installed a black awning with our name on it, and nobody ever complained. It became permanent.

On a Saturday night in the spring of 1956, the boys and I were upstairs peering through the draperies and watching the people streaming into Blackie's. Businesswise, it was a happy feeling, but personally it was a lonely time. I somehow knew that the struggling phase of our life was over and didn't know what to expect next.

Gregory was now seven and Ulysses II was three. As we stood looking out the window, I was profoundly struck by an overwhelming sense of the need for change in our lives. I looked at Gregory and noticed tears in his eyes, though he probably couldn't articulate why. I began to cry too.

The restaurant business is all consuming and there is no such thing as working from nine to five. Being open in the evenings was dividing us as a family, since by the time Blackie came to bed, the rest of us were asleep. Then in the morning I had to get the kids up early to prepare their breakfast and take Gregory to school.

Blackie and I talked it over and agreed that it was time to find a house. We decided that our apartment could be turned into an office for the business. This decision was reinforced when the neighbor's girl-friend slashed his throat and left him lying on the sidewalk in a pool of blood. Thankfully the fellow lived and the restaurant was closed at the time. And although we could see him from our window, the boys didn't know about the incident. But the remembrance of the man lying there was a grim reality that the world was changing rapidly, heading in an uncertain direction.

I contacted Ruth Hildebrand, a real-estate agent whom I had met at my beauty shop, and explained the type of house we were looking for, preferably in the American University area. Meantime, Blackie arranged to take out a GI loan.

A short time later, Ruth called me and said, "I think I've found you the perfect place with a nice fenced-in yard. It's an English tudor with beautiful stone and brick, and there are even swings in the back."

We took the children to see the house on a bright and sunny day. We were filled with anticipation at just the thought of being able to own our own home.

Ruth met us at the Davenport Street house. At first glance, it seemed like a palace. There was a huge oak tree out front with violets and buttercups blooming at its base. Close by sat an inviting white wrought-iron bench. The walkway was angled up to the front door.

We fell in love with the house, with its open porch, cozy base-ment with fireplace, and roomy bedrooms upstairs. The only disap-pointment was the kitchen, for it was old and rusted out.

After Blackie and I looked the house over, we couldn't find the boys anywhere. Then we saw them through the kitchen window out in the yard, swinging on the swings. They looked so happy and so at home that tears welled up in my eyes.

Blackie, not noticing my tears, asked, "So what do you think? Should we keep looking or what?"

"This house is everything I ever dreamed about. The kitchen's not good, but it's fixable. And everything else is perfect. I don't really want to look around if you're happy. Just look at the kids! They love it already."

Blackie started talking to Ruth about the arrangements while I joined the boys in the yard. As I walked out to them, the smell of the tomato plants reminded me of Mama and our garden in Minnesota.

The grass was so green and fresh that I lay right down. The boys came and joined me, laughing and giggling. It seemed obvious that we belonged here.

We enrolled Greg in the second grade at the nearby public school. Ulysses II was ready for nursery school, so we placed him in the Holy Cross nursery, a fine Catholic school some distance away.

Nellie was at home during the day to care for the house when I went to the business. Gregory was close enough so that he could walk home from school, but we arranged for Ulysses II to take a taxi from Holy Cross to Blackie's each day. He loved to go to the restaurant and work behind the bar concocting Shirley Temples. When I finished cashing out at about three o'clock, we'd come home together.

One day I was in the restaurant, speaking with a favorite customer named Jack Thomas who worked for the State Department.

He asked, "So how would you like a dog?"

"A dog! You know, I promised the kids a dog when we moved to the house and they've been nagging me ever since. What kind is it?"

"It's a black and white mongrel—just a mutt. We're being transferred to Japan and can't take him, but I'd like to find him a good home. He's just six months old."

"What's his name?"

"We never really named him. My wife doesn't like dogs much and she just calls him 'the mutt'."

I couldn't help but laugh. "Well, I like him already. But how do I get him?"

"What time are you leaving here tomorrow?" Jack asked.

"Three o'clock."

"I'll bring him by right at three."

I told Blackie about the offer of the dog, and he agreed that it was okay. I didn't tell the kids, as I wanted to surprise them.

The next day, Ulysses II was behind the bar at the restaurant when Jack brought in the dog. The mutt was on a red leash, but when he spotted Ulysses II, he pulled right out of it and ran over to him, licking him.

"Ulysses, what do you think? Want to take the dog home for awhile?"

"What do you mean, Mama?"

"Well, this gentleman says we can have him if we'll take good care of him."

"Do you mean it, sir?"

"Yeah, I mean it."

"Oh, boy! Wait till my brother sees him."

We put the dog in the back seat of the car and he jumped around all the way home, Ulysses trying to hold him still.

When we got home, Gregory was waiting for us. The dog leaped out of the car and ran right to him. When their father saw our puppy, he said, "Let's call him Cheesecake." The boys and Cheesecake had a great time together.

A short time later, Ulysses II came home from school and said, "Don't call me Ulysses any more. The kids are calling me BJ." This stood for Blackie, Junior. We started calling him BJ.

The next day I received a telephone call from the Mother Superior at his school. She wanted to see me as soon as possible.

When I arrived at her office, she motioned for me to sit in the chair across from her. She was cordial, but I could see that something was disturbing her.

"Mrs. Auger, are you aware of just how worried and upset your son is about certain things?"

"Well, not really. What do you mean?"

"He was sitting in class and seemed so preoccupied. I went over to him and asked him if something was bothering him. He seems very worried about a lease and keeps mentioning a parking lot."

"Oh," I said, "He probably heard us speaking about our business being on a month-to-month lease. And we've been buying property on the corner for a parking lot. I suppose he understands how concerned we are about the lease, and he must have picked it up. We'll speak to him about it."

"Well, I can understand that. When one's livelihood is threatened, it can be a great worry." She wiped her handkerchief across her forehead and continued, "Now, is it true that after Ulysses leaves here, he takes a taxi to the restaurant?"

"Yes, we've arranged that with the Yellow Cab Company."

"But is it true that he works behind the bar with the bartender?"

I answered, "There's really very little business in the afternoon. He spends his time preparing Cokes, or if he's hungry, he has a sandwich. At three o'clock, I take him home with me. He's only there about forty-five minutes."

She seemed satisfied with my answer. Then she said with uplifted eyebrows, "He tells me that you're going to get married."

"Oh, Sister David, we are married. It's just that lately we have been talking about the need to be married in the Greek Church. We had a ceremony in California years ago, but we haven't taken the time to have our marriage blessed by the Greek priest. We've been making plans to do it pretty soon."

The smile and relief that came across her face was quite visible. When Ulysses finished at the school, he was one of the two children who impressed her the most.

On the business front, we began to pursue the Cities Service Oil Company, trying to convince them to sell us the restaurant property. Our sales were now into the hundreds of thousands of dollars, but without a long-term lease, the restaurant was worth virtually nothing.

We were assembling the row houses surrounding us, particularly on the corner across from Blackie's, in our quest to keep the restaurant. We reasoned that if we could obtain enough property, we might be able to trade corners with Cities Service. Or if that wasn't possible, perhaps we could move the restaurant across the street.

Driven by our desire to buy up as much real estate we could, Blackie's became one of the biggest front offices in Washington, as the real estate people used to call it. When they saw open real estate, they headed our way.

With the upsurge in our income and living conditions, strange things began to happen. We started to receive threatening letters and phone calls. The letters said we ran a lousy restaurant and that the food was horrible. Who were we, they asked, to think that we were capable of success? But we were under too much pressure to think we were any-thing special. We grew a little despondent with each letter and crank call.

Gusti Butinelli, owner of Gusti's restaurant on M Street, was able to shed some light on the troublesome letters and calls, having lived through it himself.

"Let me give you kids a piece of advice," he said. "It isn't your ene-mies you need to watch now, it's your acquaintances. They resent you for being successful. Don't make any friends for awhile, but just sit back and be natural, and you'll find a new level."

We looked across the table at each other and nodded.

"Tell you something else—share the success with each other. You've earned it, so travel and see other good restaurants. I've learned one thing, that you have to converse with your customers, and especially here in Washington. Our clientele have traveled all over the world and have experienced the best."

He paused, taking a sip of his drink. "If you really want to be tops, get out and get around. Travel to other cities and look the restaurants over. You'll pick up ideas. You know, people might forget the whole country they visited, but they seldom forget the city where they've had a good meal."

We had a lot to learn and a lot of growing to do. Just a few short years ago, we were struggling to pay the rent. We still faced challenges now because our real estate was expensive, but it was a different feeling. Having acquired property, we now had something to fall back on—even with the difficult and worrisome lease.

After our dinner with Gusti I mulled over his words. It's true that Ulysses and I were facing challenges, like the crank calls. But I was sure the future was opening up, for our life was changing rapidly. I needed to write the family and tell them all the things that were taking place, and assure Myrt that my wish had come true. I never had time to be bored.

In the spring of 1958, business was tremendous. The standing line never ceased, even though we were adding new rooms. In fact, Ulysses had invented an electronic seating coordinator—a panel with flickering col-ored lights—that would notify Sam our maître d' not only when a table was ready, but when it was *about* to be ready.

Ulysses and I were together by day but didn't see each other very much since he mainly worked in the office upstairs while I managed the restaurant downstairs. Then I would go home around three o'clock for the kids returning from school, but Ulysses continued working through closing time, which was about eleven o'clock. As a result, the boys and I had dinner alone every night except Sunday, when the restaurant was closed and their daddy was with us.

I assured myself that we weren't the only couple who had to make adjustments and sacrifices. The fifties was a start-up time for many new businesses, with returning servicemen channeling many of their dreams, drives, and frustrations into their careers. I spoke to other wives who felt alone while their husbands were searching for success.

As far as my husband was concerned, being busy seemed the very medicine he needed after the war. He was so occupied and tired that he seldom had time to think about the past—or even his frequent back pains and headaches.

Sometimes he'd be very late in coming home. I'd worry about him and ask why he was so late. He'd reply, "I can't run the restaurant all night long and then just come straight home. I need time to unwind."

These years were the beginning of the lonely years, and I didn't expect them to end any time soon. Even so, I tried to make the most of them, spending most of my nights writing a novel I dubbed *The Pink Rose*. I wasn't concerned about getting it published, for it helped me express my feelings.

Every time I started to write, I became sick to my stomach. Finally I went to an internist and explained what was happening. His answer was, "I think it's healthy—you're probably getting the deep things out of you. Keep writing until you're no longer sick." I followed his sometimes difficult advice and finally got to the point where I could mostly relax and think more clearly.

One Sunday in April, Ulysses said to me after breakfast, "What do you think, Kid, should we see if we can be married again in the church?"

I was thrilled beyond words. I set to work, calling Father John Tavlarides at the Saint Sophia Greek Orthodox Cathedral. He said I would need to take instructions in the church, so I made the arrangements, took the course, and was baptized a Greek Orthodox believer. We fixed the wedding date for May 28, 1958.

About ten o'clock on the eve of our remarriage, Ulysses called me from the restaurant.

"How's business tonight?" I asked.

"Really good. We finally have everyone seated. Just thought I'd remind you about tomorrow—got my clothes laid out?"

"Of course I do. I've got my dress ready, too, and the kids' shoes polished. Hope you get home early to get a little rest."

"I promise to come right home. Can you have a little sandwich ready for me? It seems I can never sit down and eat here unless I run over to Aldo's and get a plate of spaghetti."

As I lay in bed, waiting for Ulysses to come home, I relived the first time we were married. Even in my memory I could feel the excitement again. This time was far different—the stars were gone from my eyes. Life wasn't perfect, but it was good. We were seldom bored because of our involvement in the business. And I was determined to take life as it was and enjoy it.

Sunday came with the scent of honeysuckle in the air and the wonder of having two fine boys with us the second time. As I looked into Ulysses' brown eyes and said "I do" again, I felt that something great was bound to happen and that we were on our way.

Ulysses put the same little gold ring on my finger, but this time I also put one on his. He wore it Greek style, on his right hand.

After the ceremony, we drove out to Normandy Farm in Maryland. The kids enjoyed the ducks and the peacocks while Ulysses and I held hands and walked around. There would be lonely days to come, but this was one of the best to remember when they did.

17

"We've made it!"

THE FABULOUS FIFTIES WERE COMING TO AN END—the time of the hula hoop, Howdy Doody, Davy Crockett, and slinky, the kids' favorite new toy. Crooners such as Frank Sinatra, Perry Como, and Vaughn Monroe were all the rage with songs like "You Are my Sunshine," "Don't Fence Me In," and "Racing with the Moon."

Our film stars were Marilyn Monroe, Grace Kelley, and Elizabeth Taylor, who made her debut in *National Velvet* at twelve years old. Heartthrobs were James Dean, Gregory Peck, and Burt Lancaster.

On the serious side, we had the hydrogen bomb and fallout shelters along with racial tensions in Little Rock. The great civil rights leader Martin Luther King, Jr. rose to prominence, and in 1955 Rosa Parks refused to move to the back of the bus. A year earlier, Dr. Jonas Salk developed the polio vaccine at the University of Pittsburgh and the next year, inoculations against polio began.

Television played up everything in our living room, the faces of the famous and infamous looming large before us. We became instantly familiar with them, and some became our heroes.

At Blackie's, we had a reservation for Fidel Castro for a party of eight. We seated them in a small private room as they wanted strict privacy. At that time, Mr. Castro was considered a hero after he ousted the dictator Fulgencio Batista. The U.S. Government seemed to support him, but when he returned to Cuba he began his anti-American rhetoric. Turns out he was a communist.

On January 7, 1959, two days before our thirteenth wedding anniversary, we received a call from Fishbait Miller, the popular Doorkeeper of the House of Representatives.

"Blackie," he said, "you and Lou come to the opening of Congress tomorrow. President Truman is going to pay a surprise visit, and I want him to sit next to Lou."

I was thrilled, and thought back to the day in California when I heard that Roosevelt had died and Truman was president. It seemed a long time ago.

The next day we went to the Capitol, and Fishbait seated the former president right next to me. Truman remarked that he had never observed the goings-on from the gallery before.

As we sat there watching the proceedings, he kept asking Fishbait who various members were, saying he didn't know too many faces anymore. He swore a little when the new Minority Leader, Charles Halleck, was introduced, saying, "I don't give a damn for him." And when Blackie clapped for Halleck, Truman looked disapprovingly at his hands.

He seemed to be trying to catch the eye of Joe Martin, the former Minority Leader from Massachusetts, and said, "Doesn't he look sad."

As Truman left he said he hoped we had enjoyed it as much as he did. He didn't want to get tied up signing too many autographs, but he gave me his just the same.

A short time later, we decided it was time to expand again. We were thinking about a theme for the new room when a friend came by the restaurant, John Maragon. He suggested that we invite Ramon House, the marshal of Dodge City, Kansas, to the room's opening. What a great idea, we thought, especially because Congressman Usher Burdick of North Dakota had just given us some western mementos. These included an original picture of Sitting Bull and some of his rifles.

We decided to name the room "Boot Hill" after the legendary cemetery in Dodge City where in the 1870s many buffalo hunters, drifters, and others without money were "buried with their boots on."

Marshal House was happy to come to Blackie's with his whole posse, so we made plans for a party. We invited some friends, hired a photographer, and served lots of steaks and roast beef. But we weren't prepared for the excitement that arose when the marshal and his posse appeared complete with cowboy hats and boots and a real six-shooter.

Kids stared and grabbed onto their parents as the colorful contingent made their way to the Boot Hill room. Marshal House shook hands with many people and patted the heads of curious youngsters, including our sons.

During dinner, the marshal entertained us by answering our questions. Blackie asked, "How'd they get the name Boot Hill?"

He answered, "Well, back in the late 1800s the cattlemen would drive thousands of head of cattle across the plains over the Texas Trail into Dodge City. The animals were driven right through the town, and you can just imagine what those cowboys were like after spending months at a time on the trail. They'd come in to spend their paychecks at the local saloon and would meet up with gamblers, gunfighters, and buffalo hunters. Gunfighters were anxious to show how well they could shoot, and they made their fame and reputation—and sometimes met their death—right on Front Street. In fact, so many died that they had to have a cemetery, which they named Boot Hill."

Someone asked, "When did the cattle drives end in Dodge City?"

Marshal House answered, "The Sante Fe Railroad came in about 1884 and the animals were then rerouted out of the city. Things began to simmer down a little bit, but not much. The killing went on until law enforcement came in with such two-gun marshals as Wyatt Earp and Bat Masterson."

Before the marshal left he invited us to Dodge City for the Round Up Rodeo. We made our plans and outfitted ourselves in full western garb, prepared to look the part.

A couple months later, in the spring, we arrived in Dodge City and were wined and dined at Miss Kitty's Longbranch Saloon, complete with can-can girls. The next day a dozen of us rode in the local rodeo. I could ride fairly well, but when the horses cantered and bunched up together, I found myself hanging on for dear life. Blackie was a much better rider, and was relaxed enough to tip his hat to the cheering crowd.

Never had I seen so many cows up close, who stared back at us as they chewed their cud. The marshal invited Blackie to brand a steer, so he took the branding iron, bit his lip, and stuck the hot iron on the animal. I was glad the marshal didn't ask me.

We returned to Washington tired but happy. We had a tie to Kansas which we'd always cherish, and lots of mementos for the walls of the new room.

A short while later, in early summer, I had the urge to move again. We had been at the Davenport Street house for three years, but it no longer felt right to me. I thought of what Mama said to me once, "If you have a strong sense of something and you are a Christian, it's probably inspired by God."

One morning I tried to broach the subject of moving with Blackie.

He listened with a scowl and said, "What are you talking about? We just got this place fixed up!"

I tried to explain my sense of the timing. "I know—it's just that when I was downstairs this morning, I had the strong feeling that we should move again."

"What are you, some kind of nut?"

"No, I love this home, but there's no room to grow here anymore. Would you at least consider what I'm feeling?"

"No. I'm not going think about it and I don't want you mentioning it to me again."

He wouldn't talk about it anymore, so I tried my best to forget about it too.

But a few days later, I felt that strong urge again and knew I had to approach Blackie. I dreaded doing it, but waited for the right moment.

That time came a few weeks before Easter when the kids and I returned from Sunday school, just when Blackie was waking up. I fixed his breakfast, scrambling his eggs well done and preparing his favorite toasted rye bread with orange marmalade and Casseti Greek cheese.

While the kids played out on the porch with their new ducklings from Nellie, I took the breakfast tray to him along with the *Washington Post*. Once he was satiated with food and rest, I broached the subject again.

"I'm sorry, Ulysses, but I just can't let it rest."

"Can't let what rest?"

"Well, I think we should look for another house."

"I told you to forget it!" he said, scowling.

He returned to his reading, but being a stubborn Dane, I just stood there. On the surface it did seem a little ridiculous since we had just spent a lot of money installing air conditioning and new electrical wiring. But deep down I knew that it was right.

He was tired and annoyed and didn't like thinking about what I was proposing. Finally he gave me a seemingly impossible task. With resignation he said, "Okay. If you can find a house five minutes from the restaurant with trees and a stream, I'll take a look at it. But in the meantime, don't talk to me about it."

I kissed him full on the mouth and went out of the door triumphant. I was determined to find just such a place. I started singing loudly, "Oh, what a beautiful morning. Oh, what a beautiful day!"

The next week, following Sunday School and Blackie's breakfast, I took Greg and BJ in the car along with their little ducks, saying "Let's go find a stream where the ducks can swim free, should we?"

They scrambled into the car and I drove down Massachusetts Avenue, staying within five minutes from the restaurant. To my delight, there was a winding road with several small picturesque bridges crisscrossing it. Under the bridges ran a bubbling stream.

I parked the car and the kids grabbed their new pets. Together we stood on a small bridge, surrounded by a forest of trees with colorful wildflowers growing profusely alongside the road. High above, the birds were singing and I spotted a lovely cardinal on a pine tree just before us. For a passing moment, I thought we had landed in paradise.

Greg broke my revelry. "Mama," he asked, "can we let the ducks swim free?"

Before I could answer, they tossed off their shoes and socks, rolled up their pant legs, and plunged into the stream with ducks in hand. I watched them with pleasure as they laughed gleefully as the little ducks took off down the stream.

They followed their pets, splashing and running as fast as they could and not minding the cobwebs and spiders under the bridge. Finally, they grabbed the ducks and Greg fashioned a dam out of some meshed wire while BJ held them tightly, squashed in his little hands.

While watching the boys, I took in my surroundings and noticed several houses under construction at the top of the hill. Perhaps that was our house up there—we were five minutes from the restaurant and there were trees and a stream. Could it be?

I didn't want to hurry the kids too much, but after awhile I said, "Kids, we'll be coming back again soon. Right now we have to go home to Daddy, but first put on your shoes and let's take a look at the houses being built up the hill."

Reluctantly they scrambled out of the stream, complaining all the time. We drove up to the houses and saw four in a row, with two completed and two still under construction. I liked the one at the end by the cul de sac, an English Tudor.

Out front stood a short gentleman who was the builder himself. He introduced himself as Mr. Gianetti and seemed very kind, offering to show us the houses.

At my command, the boys controlled themselves as we looked carefully at each room. What intrigued me most was the wrought-iron balcony that opened out from the master bedroom. I stood on it, looking over the tops of the trees and glimpsing the glistening stream below.

I whispered to myself, "Is this it? Is this the house?"

I turned to Mr. Gianetti, "Are you going to be here very long today?"

"Until around five o'clock."

"I'll try to bring my husband by."

"Do that."

My heart was racing as we drove home. It seemed to be too good to be true, but maybe there was a chance.

Once home, we all went up to the bedroom, standing before Blackie with shining eyes. He wasn't quite ready for our exuberance but listened anyway. The boys climbed up on the bed and hugged him as they told him of the ducks swimming in the stream.

"Please come with the kids and me," I said. "We've got something to show you."

"Well, what is it?"

"I don't want to tell you, but just drive where I want you to, okay?"

With resignation, he said, "All right. I guess so."

We all went to the car, and I said, "Drive over to Connecticut Avenue and then turn off where I tell you."

"Are you sure?" Blackie asked. "You know you don't have any sense of direction."

"I'm sure. Please just do it."

"Okay," he said with a sigh, "I'm too tired to fight you."

I directed him to the house coming from the back way. I didn't want him to see the trees and the stream until I could take him to the balcony and prove that I'd found what he wanted.

As we drew nearer, he said, "What are you doing in this neighborhood? Nothing here but expensive homes and embassies."

"Just keep going and you'll see."

We arrived and I introduced Blackie to Mr. Gianetti. This time the kids stayed outside and played while I immediately took Blackie up to the bedroom. I opened the balcony door and drew him outside.

"What do you see?" I asked.

"A lot of trees. And is that water down there?"

"It sure is; it's a little babbling brook."

"Hmm."

"How far you think we are from the restaurant?"

"About five minutes, I guess."

"Well," I said triumphantly, "I found it. Now what?"

"What do you mean, you found it? What are you talking about?"

"You know, you said I needed to find a house with trees and a stream that was five minutes from the restaurant."

"Are you nuts? How much you think this thing costs, anyway?"

I avoided answering his question as I took him up to the attic and then showed him the other three bedrooms. All was well until we came downstairs to the kitchen.

"Call this a kitchen?" he said. "Those cabinets don't belong here."

I showed him the living room and dining room, the library and powder room. Downstairs, there was the third full bathroom, a lovely recreational room, and a maid's room.

While in the furnace room, he said, "I'd take those kitchen cabinets and move them down here, and put new cupboards upstairs."

I couldn't believe it—he was already figuring things out.

To Mr. Gianetti, he said, "What kind of price do you have on this house?"

"Fifty-five thousand dollars."

He looked at me as if to say, "Are you crazy?"

But the idea of the house got a hold of him, just as I was sure it would if it was right.

Not too much later, Blackie met a real-estate agent name Joe Donnelly and told him about the house in question.

Joe responded, "Gianetti is stuck with those houses. I know he'll work a deal for you—he'll probably even take your present house as a down payment."

It turned out to be the right house in the right place at the right time. Mr. Gianetti worked it out for us, and eventually we were able to buy the two adjoining lots.

As the house of my dreams was still under construction, we weren't ready to move into it until just before Labor Day. On the last day of August I was there doing some cleaning before we moved in. While on the balcony wiping down the French doors, I was singing along to

Rosemary Clooney's "This Old House." Through the music I heard the phone ring, so I went to answer it while nonchalantly sitting on the pink rug.

I heard Myrtle's tearful voice and asked her what was the matter.

"Louie, it's Mama."

"What's wrong?"

"I should've told you right away. A couple days ago, she had a slight stroke so we put her in the hospital. The second day she felt pretty well and regained her speech. I was with her again yesterday, and she seemed so peaceful but it was as if her thoughts were far away. Looking into my eyes, she said, 'Myrtle, I want you to take me to Minnesota when I die and bury me beside Papa.'"

I inhaled deeply, wondering what Myrt was going to say next.

She paused, and then added, "You should've seen her glowing face when she said that. Anyway, I assured her that whenever it should happen, that I would take her to Minnesota and that you would be with me too."

"Of course I would."

"Well, last night, Marlin and Chris and all of us gathered around her, and Bertha sang her favorite song, 'The Old Rugged Cross.' We talked and laughed together, enjoying the evening. Just as we left, Mama said very softly, 'I'm going home.' Chris said, 'Yeah, probably tomorrow, Mama.' She said, 'Not that home.' We just kind of brushed off her remark, and we all left her."

"What are you trying to tell me, Myrt?"

"Mama had a premonition."

"Of what?"

"Louie, Chris got a call very early this morning. Mama died in the night."

"Died! Did you say Mama died?"

"Yes—don't fall apart. Remember how many times Mama used to say, 'Don't mourn for me. I'm going to a far better place'?"

For a few moments I couldn't speak, and then finally I murmured, "Tell me what I should do now."

"Well, Chris took immediate charge of everything. He's arranged for a service here in San Diego tomorrow. Then the next morning, I'll leave with Mama on the train. We'll arrive in Mankato on Thursday. In the meantime, you call the airlines and let me know when you'll arrive. I'll get there early, so I'll arrange for the car."

We hung up and I was left alone with my thoughts. Sometimes I cry easily and sometimes I find it hard to cry at all. Right now the tears wouldn't come. There was so much to think about, and all right in the middle of moving.

I called Ulysses and asked, "Are you busy?"

"Busy ain't the half of it. What's the matter?"

"I just heard from Myrt. It's Mama—she died in the night."

"Oh, poulaki mou [my little bird], I'm sorry to hear that. When do you have to be in California?"

"I'm not going there. I'll be meeting Myrt in Minnesota. Mama wanted to be buried beside Papa."

"You go ahead and do whatever you have to do. But you know that I can't go with you."

"I know. I've got everything boxed and labeled for moving so you and Nellie and the kids will just have to do it all."

"We can handle it. We'll just put things away according to the boxes. By the way, when you get back our new bed should be ready. Got a call from Wall's Mattress people this morning."

He was trying to cheer me up by mentioning our new round, pink bed.

The last thing Ulysses said to me before I boarded the plane was to bring Myrt back with me.

On the plane to Minnesota I had plenty of time to think. I had only been back there twice, the last time when Gregory was four and BJ was just nine months. I chuckled to remember Greg's excited shouts that "Grandmother's cooking my pajamas!" When I had gone to investigate, I saw that Mama had the big copper boiler on the stove, as was the old custom. In it was all the wash, and on top were Greg's pajamas. Mama had sat in her rocking chair and laughed and laughed. It was my final visit there with her.

I thought about how my life had been moving along ever since I left home at seventeen. Actually, except for the children and now our new home, our life revolved around the business. Ulysses had just finished remodeling the restaurant kitchen for the third time and finally had his dream.

Business was going well, and we were always trying out something new. Our latest thing was broadcasting live every Friday night on WGMS, a Washington radio station, in the Black Angus room. I was looking forward to bringing Myrt back so that she could see the progress we had made in thirteen years.

As the small commuter plane touched down in Mankato, I caught a glimpse of the town of thirty thousand. Though it was my hometown and would always be a part of me, I wasn't sorry I had left it.

Myrt, cigarette in hand, was waiting for me in the small airport.

"It's so good to see you," she said as we embraced.

"Was it a hard trip?" I asked.

"It was a little, but since it's what Mama wanted, that made it easier."

We clung together, letting the tears for Mama flow as we walked to the little red Ford Myrt had rented.

"What happens now?" I asked.

"A hearse met our train and they've taken Mama's body to the Lake Crystal funeral home. We'll go there in the morning, and then follow the hearse to Garden City. I booked us into the Saulpaugh Hotel tonight. Remember going there to visit Maria and Bertha?"

"Sure do. Hey, we should take a last look at the old house. We may never come this way again."

"Good idea. Let's drive up there while it's still light."

We drove up the Broad Street hill where we had walked so many times before. We passed the limestone quarry and the familiar gas station where we often filled our bicycle tires with air. We turned right onto a pretty street where little wooden houses stood doll-like, occupied by neat Germans and Scandinavians.

To the right stood our former house, improved now by the addition of white aluminum siding. As I glanced at the slanting cellar door, I reminisced, "Remember when the radio would blare out that a twister was coming and we'd barrel down to the smelly basement? We never knew if afterward the house would still be standing or not."

We went back to where Mama always planted her garden. I was thrilled to see the tomatoes and hollyhocks growing profusely in the black loam soil. Then we walked up the few steps to the wooden porch and stood on the spot where Papa had fallen with a heart attack. I could tell Myrt was thinking about him too as we knocked on the door.

A middle-aged lady in a faded green apron answered, and Myrt spoke first. "Hello. We're sorry to bother you, but we grew up in this house and wondered if we could just come in for a moment and look around. Our mother just died, and, well, you understand."

"Oh, you must be the Hansen girls. Come right in. Of course I remember your mother. We bought the house from her—lock, stock, and barrel."

We stood in the living room where we saw our old baby grand piano that the girls had bought from the second-hand store for $35.00. I walked over to it and struck a chord. It was just as off-tune as ever.

"Would you mind if we spent a few moments up in our old bedroom?"

She was a very neat and fastidious housekeeper and said she didn't mind at all.

Upstairs, Myrt and I stood in front of the tilting mirror on the mahogany dresser, the very mirror in which we always searched our faces when dressing, the very mirror in which we gazed before leaving home for the last time. And now we stood before it again, both years older, married, and with children.

Myrt, looking squarely into my eyes in the glass, said, "You left the family and you've been far away from us since the day you left California. Has it been worth it?"

"Some things just have to be. Remember what Papa used to say, 'Lulu has a bee in her bonnet and she has to keep moving so it doesn't sting her'? Strange, but his words seem to sum me up. But I like to use the word 'destiny.' I feel there's a long way for me to go yet, and I'm barely getting started."

I paused reflectively, and then continued, "I feel at home with Ulysses. It seems hard to explain but we click in a funny way. In business, I know what he's going to say before he says it. It's something like the way Papa and Mama used to work together on the farm. They were a team, like Pete and Molly."

"You're too much for me, Louie."

We stood in silence, each in our own thoughts. Then we made our way downstairs, passing Papa and Mama's empty room. After thanking the lady, we headed for the Saulpaugh Hotel and what we hoped would be a good dinner.

I was glad when I awakened to see the sun shining through the heavy brocade draperies, for Mama always liked the sunshine. We drove the twelve miles out to the Lake Crystal funeral home, where the casket would be opened for me to say a proper goodbye to Mama.

At the funeral home I stood with a rose in my hand, looking down at the face of my beloved mother. It was as if she were in a deep sleep and would wake any moment. Her hands were crossed and I could see her worn wedding band of fifty-seven years still on her arthritic finger.

While placing the pink rose in her hands, I thanked her for allowing me to leave her and follow my dreams. I kissed her still unlined forehead and a few of my tears spilled onto her as I said my goodbyes.

We followed the hearse to the grave site high upon a grassy hill. In the streaming sunshine, we laid Mama to rest beside Papa. They both believed in that great "gettin' up mornin'" when the Lord would return and they would be raised up.

We felt peaceful when we left, for we had fulfilled Mama's desire. They were together in death as they had been in life.

Myrt came back to Washington with me, and Ulysses picked us up from the airport. He said, "Welcome, Myrt. You haven't been here in a lot of years."

"Hi, Useless. Thanks for wanting me to come."

"You don't have much time to dilly dally," he said, " 'cause I want you and Louie to be at the broadcast tonight to greet Vaughn Monroe. I get so busy I can't pay any attention to these people when they come in."

Driving home, Ulysses said to me, "Hope you appreciate all the work I did getting everything ready for you to come home."

"I know you did a good job," I said, reaching up and kissing his cheek.

At home, Ulysses said, "Well, I need to get right back."

"No—please don't," I said. "I want you to show us what you've done."

"Well, all right."

He opened the front door. The kids heard us and came running in from the yard, breathless and sweating.

After a sweet embrace with them, I asked, "How are your rooms? Sorry I couldn't be with you on your first night. Meet your Aunt Myrtle."

She bent to kiss them, but they shook her hand and managed to say, "Hello, Aunt Myrtle."

Gregory said, "Mama, we got friends here already. There's Charles Wishart from England and Roger Barry. Can we go play ball again?"

"Sure, go ahead."

In the living room, I said to Ulysses, "Everything fits so wonderfully. You did a great job."

"Even got food in the refrigerator. Nellie was a real help. Well, gotta go back to the business. Now remember, don't be late. Nellie will stay with the kids."

"Ulysses, let's look at the round bed before you go."

"Well, guess I can spare another moment. Let's go see it."

Upstairs in the corner bedroom sat the bed made especially for us. It was pink and round with a pink upholstered headboard. I lay across it, wanting to stay in it and fall asleep.

"What do you think, Kid?"

"We've got ourselves a bed!"

"Now I really need to go." He kissed us goodbye and reminded me one more time not to be late.

After Ulysses had gone, I opened the balcony door and told Myrt to step outside to see the view below.

"Wow! This is great. You ought to set up an easel. You could do a lot of painting out here."

"I might get around to that someday," I said, wondering when I would ever have the time.

We went back in and Myrt lay on the bed, saying, "You've always liked fancy things. I remember you taking a Montgomery Ward catalogue and cutting out the furniture, setting it up in a cardboard box. You'd dress up dolls and make fancy clothes for them. Now you've got a beautiful house and fancy clothes. We're so different—I like my one-level house that I don't have to worry about."

I interrupted her musings. "Say, we better figure out what to wear tonight. Oh, I hate to tell the kids I have to leave again."

"You must like meeting all these celebrities. I wouldn't care about them."

"Well, they're part of our business, and after you meet them you realize that they're no different than anyone else. As Mama would say, 'Some are just more needy then others.'"

We dressed and reluctantly said goodbye to the boys. I told them, "Tomorrow's Saturday. We'll be with you all day."

We walked into the restaurant at 6:55 P.M. There was a lineup for seating.

Myrt said, "This is like a zoo with all these people."

"It's music to our ears," I responded. "We're still on a month-to-month lease so we have to do everything right from the cash register. Without all of these customers, we'd be nowhere."

We stood in line for a few moments, unable to push our way through. Finally we were able to walk into the Black Angus room and were greeted by Mr. Parker, the maître d'.

"Parker, meet my sister, Myrtle."

"A pleasure. It's your first time here—welcome. Here's your table right close to the broadcasting area."

"Thank you. By the way, did Mr. Monroe come in yet?"

"No, not yet, but Stan is waiting for him. He only has a few minutes before he has to broadcast. He already has the 'WGMS ON THE AIR' sign lit up."

"I'll go stand by the door and route him through. Myrt, sit here for a second while I see if I can find him."

As I stood waiting for Vaughn Monroe, I thought of how he was known as the glamour boy of the forties. Now he had two big hits, "Til There Was You" and "Racing with the Moon."

I saw him coming through the door, a very tall man with electric blue eyes and a friendly smile. I introduced myself and asked him to follow me. I brought him immediately to Stan Hamilton, who stood up quickly, shook his hand, and went right into the broadcast with him.

I joined Myrt at the table. She asked, "How long does it last?"

"Thirty minutes."

"How come you've got it broadcasting from here?"

"Well, it's good publicity for us. And it's a great radio station with a wonderful broadcaster."

Ulysses found us and sat with us, his eyes roving everywhere to keep track of what was going on. He asked Myrt, "Well, what do you think?"

"What a business you've got here! But do you always rush around like this?"

"Have to," he said.

While Ulysses and Myrt got reacquainted, I went around to the tables to talk with some of the customers. One little lady caught me in the foyer and said, "Do you know why you do the business here?"

"No, I don't know," I said modestly.

"Because you don't try to fool the public."

No, we wouldn't even know how to fool the public, I thought.

When the half-hour broadcast was over, I returned to the table. Blackie had just seated Vaughn.

"Blackie," he said, "my wife runs a prime rib restaurant in New Jersey. Know what she does—she partially cooks one or more prime rib and keeps them for emergencies. When she sees there's a sell out, she pops the partially cooked one in the oven, so she's rarely out of beef."

Blackie looked my way and said, "What a good idea—I'm going to start doing it. Don't mind if I call it a 'Vaughn Monroe,' do you?"

"Don't mind a bit," he said with a smile.

Since Vaughn was also in the restaurant business, we had a fine time exchanging stories. Blackie recounted one about setting up a table for a colonel and his party of eight. He said, "The colonel was hanging over my shoulder as I was trying to get the table ready. Finally I grew impatient and told him to keep his shirt on. The next day I got a call from him. He said, 'Blackie, there's a short, stocky black-haired fellow working downstairs who was extremely rude to me last night. You ought to fire him.' I told the colonel I'd take care of it and fire him immediately."

We all laughed together, enjoying ourselves.

At the end of the evening, Myrt commented, "He's just an ordinary guy, isn't he?"

I agreed.

The next day, Myrt and I decided to take a picnic down to the Tidal Basin. After gathering the kids in the car, we first drove to the little row house on Sixteenth Street, N.E., where we had lived when we first came to Washington. I had never been there since moving back.

Myrt said, "Gee, if I'd married Billy, I'd be here with you."

"You didn't have the passion for him," I responded.

From there we drove to my favorite spot, the Jefferson Memorial looking out over the Tidal Basin. We ate our lunch, rode the pedal boats, and enjoyed the wonderful setting.

While sitting in one of the boats, Myrt said, "I'm glad you're happy here, but I can't wait to get back to California."

The next day we said goodbye to Myrt, who returned to her life in San Diego. And I resumed my busy life at the restaurant and our wonderful new home.

18

Owners—At Last

In November 1960, on a cold and blustering day, Blackie was frustrated and depressed. Nearly nine years had passed with no lease, and he felt like we weren't getting anywhere. Without a lease our restaurant was worth virtually nothing, except for the furniture, fixtures, and equipment—and that wasn't worth much if it had to be moved.

Our precarious position was a constant worry. If we were to be canceled by Cities Service with just a thirty-day notice, we wouldn't be able to pay the many mortgages on all the property we had acquired.

I poured Blackie a second cup of coffee, which he gulped with a troubled look as he stood to leave for the restaurant. Just then the phone rang.

He answered it, and when he turned around to tell me about the call, his face had changed completely. "It was the office—I'm supposed to call Mr. Cayhill at Cities Service. What do you think he wants?"

"I wonder," I said. "Wouldn't it be something if they wanted to sell the property? He's going to retire soon, remember?"

"I'll call him right away," he said with determination.

While Blackie was on the phone all I could hear him say was "yes" and "okay." Then after a pause he said, "All right—I'll be there."

When he hung up the phone I asked, "Well, what'd he say? Tell me exactly."

Blackie seldom remembered anyone's precise words, but he'd probably always remember Mr. Cayhill's. He answered, looking at me intently, "He said, 'Blackie, would you meet with us regarding the sale of the property? We can meet here at my office on Thursday if that's all right with you.'"

It was almost too much to take in. We had been under the thirty-day lease for twelve years and had been praying, figuring, using influence, and spending every dime to buy up the surrounding property in an effort to protect our asset. And now the unreachable might just be within our grasp.

Feeling the weight of the upcoming meeting, Blackie said, "I need to get down to business."

I was optimistic but cautious as I said, "I think everything is going to work out fine."

As Blackie got to work, I wondered if Mr. Cayhill was planning on doing us a great act of kindness before retirement. He was well aware of our predicament and just might help us. I felt a spark of hope and began to sing my favorite hymn, "Joy Comes in the Morning."

The night before the meeting, Blackie tried to guess how much they would be asking for the property. He went down into the recreation room with pencil and paper to make estimates on how much they would ask per foot.

The next morning, Blackie took a newly invented felt tip pen and copied the numbers in his left hand. He figured how much it would be for fifteen dollars a foot, sixteen dollars a foot, and so on, writing almost up to his wrist. During the meeting he was careful not to let anyone look into his palm, for he didn't want them to realize how far he was willing to go to buy the property.

When the group met at Arlington Towers and after all the small talk was finished, Mr. Cayhill faced Blackie squarely and said, "We're prepared to sell you the property for fifteen dollars a foot."

Blackie surreptitiously glanced in his left hand. Fifteen dollars a foot came to $350,000. Without trying for any reduction, he said, "That's fine."

Mr. Cayhill asked, somewhat incredulously, "You're not going to give us an argument?"

Blackie nodded. For what these good businessmen didn't know was that our sales were now in the hundreds of thousands, and once we signed, the value of the restaurant would go from zero to close to a million dollars.

Our next obstacle was the financing. Blackie made an appointment with our friends John and Pete Kalavritinos, who had opened the first Greek-owned bank in Washington, the Republic Savings and Loan.

"Well, guys," he said, "I think I have a chance to begin to grow and establish myself. Here's what has happened. Cities Service is willing to sell me the Twenty-second and M corner for $350,000. That's Blackie's and the gas station on the corner. The deal won't be finalized until I hear from the head office, but I want to be ready when they call. I'd like you to loan me $350,000."

*We moved to the sunny side of the street in Washington, D.C. after purchasing
the Sea-Land Tavern in 1949.*

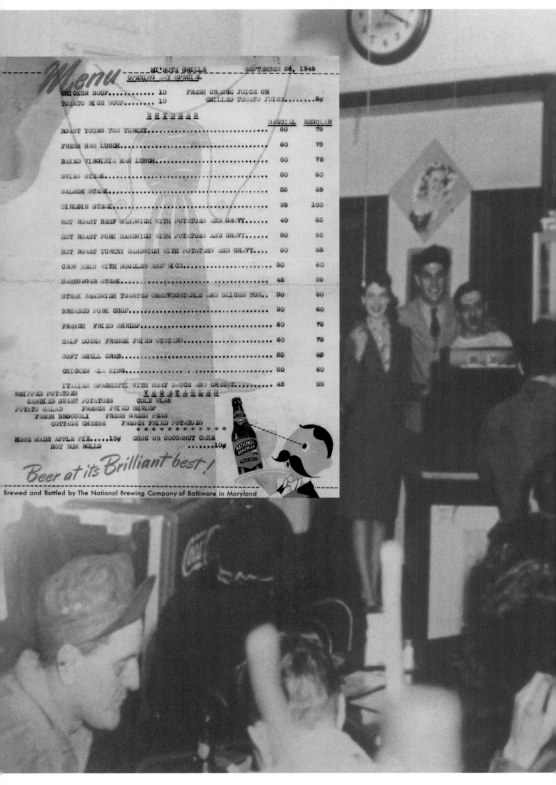

Our humble beginnings in Washington, D.C. started with the Minute Grill in 1946.

The new Minute Grille (above) began to flourish in the place that has been our location for over fifty years.

We changed our name to Blackie's House of Beef in 1952.

Blackie's House of Beef in 1970, before we built the Marriott Hotel over it.

Pete, always the joker, said, "If that's all you want, sure, you can have it right now."

John took the more cautious approach, and together with Pete looked over our sales, the measurement of the land, and the possibilities. In the end they said, "The value is there. You can count on us—we'll be glad to do it."

We were overjoyed yet somewhat apprehensive as we waited for the final papers.

We were still waiting on January 19, 1961, the day before the inauguration of John F. Kennedy. At forty-three he was the youngest person ever elected president of the United States. A popular candidate, he was the talk of the restaurant throughout the day.

It began to snow in the early afternoon, and although it was piling up on the grass, bushes, and trees, the streets were still clear. Little kids passing by could barely form snowballs as they scuffled and played, snow sticking in their hair. Some of the Cadillac customers nervously sipped coffee as they waited impatiently for their cars to be repaired, hoping to make it home before the great predicted snowfall would make driving impossible.

I had become engrossed in checking the cash and making entries in the ledger and didn't notice the weather for some time. Then Blackie came up behind me and said, "Look at the snow coming down! It's covering everything, even the street."

"Oh dear!" I said, a little surprised at how fast it was accumulating. "I'd better get going before the streets get too slippery."

"Don't drive—stay here with me and we'll go home together. We'll close early, for we probably won't have any business with this snow anyway. Call and see if Nellie can stay with the kids until we get home."

I called home. Nellie said the kids were already out playing in the snow and that she could stay the night.

Around four o'clock we made plans to close the restaurant to allow our staff to make it home. We weren't sure when to close, as we still had a few customers. We sat waiting for the right moment when some more people came in, making it impossible to close.

We continued to watch outside as it grew dark, and soon noticed that the traffic was slowing down to a crawl. Some cars had failing batteries and others got stuck. The snow didn't stop, but grew heavier.

A little later, we saw cars being forced over to the side of the street and heard the grinding of engines from stuck automobiles. Inevitably the motorists couldn't move. Twenty-second Street had become a huge parking lot, stretching up to Pennsylvania Avenue and Washington Circle and beyond.

The drivers remained in their cars for awhile and then, as if on cue, began to head our way. Dripping from the melting snow, they entered with astonished looks at being interrupted from their journey. The many travelers—mostly people we hadn't seen before—instantly filled the restaurant.

Once the customers made telephone calls and visited the rest rooms, a sense of camaraderie prevailed. They didn't complain if we ran out of something or if the service was a little slow. And since we were shorthanded, they even pitched in themselves. The restaurant took on the air of a big party.

Blackie went into the kitchen and told the chef, "People are pouring in. Get out some more steaks and increase the salads. Put some more potatoes on to bake. And get out the Vaughn Monroes and start roasting them. I think we're going to need them!"

Every time we looked up, more people appeared and simply crowded in. Strangers spoke to strangers, and after awhile there weren't any strangers as people shared tables and soon were laughing together. For the most part, everyone seemed eager to celebrate Kennedy's inauguration the next day.

We had installed a noisy but interesting United Press news ticker in the foyer of the Black Angus Room during the Kennedy/Nixon debates. It made a continual clicking noise, except when a bell would ring to indicate a bulletin. The news at the moment was the big snowstorm, and of course, Kennedy about to be sworn in.

As the evening went on we began to run out of supplies, but no one objected when we had to serve dinners without bread. Then when we were completely out of beef, we sold ten-ounce tops for $2.95. Before the night was over, our new friends drank up everything we had. What a grand, unexpected, and unplanned party it was—and we got paid for it.

It was one o'clock before we left for home, and four A.M. before the chef and his assistant finished cleaning the kitchen and preparing for the next day's business. I cuddled close to Ulysses in the Cadillac as we slipped and slid over the road. He reached over and lovingly patted my bulging stomach, saying, "It wasn't too difficult for you tonight, was it?"

"Actually, it was one of the best times we've had in the restaurant. They were such pleasant people."

The sand trucks and snowplows converged ahead of us, forcing us to pull off to the side of the road while they careened around us. Because of the importance of the next day's activities, the city was determined to open all the thoroughfares.

Temporarily halted on the side of the road, Ulysses asked me again, "Are you sure you're okay?"

"I sure am. Our little souvenir from the European trip is doing just fine."

Last August, although still uneasy about our thirty-day cancellation lease, we decided to join some friends on a trip to Europe. We went first to Copenhagen, my father's hometown, and then to Paris, Rome, and Athens. It was a whirlwind time, but the best part was arriving home and finding out that I was pregnant.

Finally the convoy of snowtrucks passed us, and we were able to continue on our way home. We made it eventually, and fell into bed exhausted.

The following morning we decided to take the boys with us to the restaurant to celebrate, for the schools were closed due to the snow and the next day was BJ's eighth birthday. As we drove in we commented on how well the city had cleaned up the streets. They didn't want anything to stop the inaugural proceedings.

Business was quite good, and we joined the customers to watch the television as President Dwight D. Eisenhower, one of the heroes of World War II, stepped aside and the young John F. Kennedy took the oath of office. With his beautiful wife Jacqueline next to him, he uttered the line that would be remembered for years to come, "Ask not what your country can do for you—ask what you can do for your country."

An era had ended, and the new frontier promised by Kennedy had begun.

The month of April crept into Washington as soft and beautiful as a kitten entering a child's room. It brought with it the delicate cherry blossoms surrounding the Tidal Basin and Jefferson Memorial, the purple magnolias growing alongside the broad avenues, and the pink and white dogwood blossoms in front of many homes. Washington seemed to be singing a special love song this spring.

The city was filled with celebrants of the cherry blossom festival, filling Washington's restaurants and hotels. We were no exception, with long lines of waiting customers every day.

In the midst of the burgeoning spring beauty, our daughter Dina was born on the eighteenth of April, weighing seven pounds and ten ounces. She had a head full of beautiful blonde hair, on which the nurse had tied a pink ribbon.

What made the season extra wonderful was that two days before her birth, the final papers came through from Cities Service. No contracts were ever received more enthusiastically or signed with more flourish. Simultaneously, we heard that the Kalavritinos's bank had approved the financing for purchasing the property. Finally the tense years of living on a month-to-month lease were over. We were owners! And not only of Blackie's but also of the gas station next door. Papa was right—every baby brought much tihi (luck).

I didn't want to leave little Dina, so I was happy to be a stay-at-home mother for a time. Blackie, though, had many plans for the new corner property and put them into effect immediately.

After securing permits to tear down the small buildings on the property, he called the Federal Wrecking Company of Bernie and Nate Gitelson. He had used them many times before, and they were familiar with him getting permits on Friday, tearing down and cleaning up the area on Saturday, and being ready to go by Monday.

Blackie said to Nate, "Have your guys tear down all those shacks on the corner where Cities Service was as soon as you can, except for the grease rack room. Leave the far wall and the brick exterior with the bulletproof window intact."

Nate said, "I'll send Leroy right down to you and you can show him what you want done."

The next morning, Leroy and his crew used their big wrecker's ball to demolish everything Blackie had ordered. By Monday morning, the whole corner was cleared and the debris was carted away. Blackie had wasted no time.

The following Saturday he was up before the sun. Through my sleepy eyes I saw him and asked, "Where are you going so early?"

"Didn't I tell you about the six bricklayers I'm meeting? I'm going to put a wall around the property where we tore down the buildings. Then I'm going to put up a courtyard. Everybody's copying us with the western look, and I'm sick of it. We'll make it look like New Orleans."

When he came home that night, tired and disheveled, he said, "We began to lay the bricks about eight this morning. I didn't let anybody stop working. I had the coffee brought to them, because I knew if they left, they probably wouldn't be back.

"A funny thing happened this afternoon. We were about three bricks up the line when two winos came by on their way to the liquor store. I remember them because they spoke to some of the guys." Blackie paused and grabbed one of the warm cookies I had just baked. He continued, "About four hours later they came back, and by then we had gone up the line about five feet.

"One of the Sneaky Petes said, 'Where'd that wall come from? It wasn't there before.' The other guy said, 'You're drunk, man, that wall's been there all the time.' 'No,' the first guy said, 'You're the one that's drunk—there weren't no wall there before.' And they argued all the way down the street."

Blackie grabbed another cookie and said, "Tomorrow I'll take you to see it. Next week we're going to do the brickwork for the New Orleans room."

Soon after the courtyard was finished, we met DeLesseps Morrison, the former mayor of New Orleans who had just been selected the U.S. Ambassador to the Organization of American States. He was charming and well liked by everyone, and called Chep by his friends.

In thinking about opening up the courtyard and New Orleans room, Blackie and I decided to celebrate with plenty of food, music, and dancing. Since it was a New Orleans courtyard, we invited Ambassador Morrison as the honored guest. He was immediately enthusiastic.

The evening of August 29 turned out to be clear and not too hot. Blackie was nervous as he circulated around the restaurant checking to see that everything was perfect. He kept the food hot and replenished, made sure the strolling violinists kept playing, and confirmed that our staff was attentive and mannerly.

Ambassador Morrison and I stood at the garden gate welcoming the guests with a smile and a hello. Many well-known and respected people came through our wrought-iron gate, including nearly all the ambassadors, many senators and congressmen, and successful businesspeople.

It was a great night and a wonderful party. We were serving a different clientele from when we first started out, but I felt at home with all our customers—from the mechanics to the rich and famous.

When the evening was over, Ambassador Morrison called me to one side. "Lou, I'm stuck," he said. "I've been dating ZsaZsa Gabor, and I wanted her to be the Queen Venus in New Orleans. Well, the ladies who head the Royal Crewe of Venus are persnickety. They think she's beautiful, but in view of her notoriety they don't want her to represent them."

I nodded, wondering what he was getting at.

"They gave me the job of picking the queen, and now they're after me because I haven't come up with the right one yet. When I saw you I got an idea. Would you consider being the queen?"

"Chep, I've never even been to New Orleans. Why would they want me?"

"They'll want you, don't worry. What do you say?"

"Well, if Blackie says it's okay, it's all right with me."

Blackie and I talked it over and decided that I should go ahead. It was arranged—I would finally get to wear a gorgeous white gown.

When I arrived in New Orleans, I was met by the beautiful Lynn Planche, a former Queen Venus. We instantly became good friends. She took me around, including to the evening's get-acquainted party. I was a little nervous, especially as I would be the first queen ever from Washington.

The next day I was measured for the white satin gown on which thousands of rhinestones would be sewn by hand. I was fitted for another gown as well; this one was a pale lavender—very much my mother's color—to be worn at the party before the day of the parade. I returned home with excitement for the event, still six months away.

Meantime, our business kept moving ahead steadily with something exciting always happening. Often we had celebrities coming in, such as Jimmy Durante, James Garner, Julius LaRosa, and Jonathan Winters. Being in the capital city, we also entertained many people working in some fashion in the government, from ambassadors to members of Congress to the many staff working in agencies and on Capitol Hill. Some were regulars, including Senator and Mrs. Hubert Humphrey, Senator and Mrs. Robert Dole, and the director of the FBI, J. Edgar Hoover, and his friend Clyde Tolson.

In December we saw the hundred-year anniversary of the Pony Express mail service between Sacramento, California, and St. Joseph,

Missouri—a distance of roughly two thousand miles. The riders would carry large sacks of mail and travel from one city to another as fast as they could. When one rider became tired, another would grab the pouch and keep riding. The service ended on October 24, 1861, when the first transcontinental telegraph line was completed.

Now, a hundred years later, some young riders were dramatizing the occasion with a horseback journey across the nation. When they arrived in Washington they went to the White House and from there rode to Blackie's. Customers—and we—were astonished to see the rough-looking riders enter the restaurant.

They asked to see Blackie and then presented him with two fine but worn leather saddles. The spokesman, Mickey Finn, said, "On behalf of the memory of the Pony Express riders, we present to you these saddles, which we carried all the way across the nation. Your restaurant is now a repository of western Americana."

Blackie thanked them, took the saddles, and hoisted them up above the beef-carver's stand. We enjoyed a nice lunch before they moved on, leaving us with memories of those who dared to ride long and hard in celebration of our nation's past.

My second trip to New Orleans for the final fitting came a few months later, in February of 1962. The big show followed on March 4TH.

When my day came, I was dressed in a sparkling gown with rhinestones that glittered with my every move. Earrings dangled from my ears, the tiara glimmered on my carefully coifed hair, and rhinestones twinkled about my neck. I sparkled from head to toe.

As I stepped into the carriage I felt like Cinderella. The sun was shining and my dress was shimmering as we made our way along the parade route. The crowds lining the streets were cheering as they yelled, "Throw me something." The little pages tossed them beads, trinkets, and specially made doubloons.

We rode through the streets to City Hall, where Mayor Schirro greeted me with a glass of champagne. We toasted the crowd of fifteen hundred people and then I was to break the glass. It wouldn't break! I tried three times before it finally shattered. The people laughed, cheering and clapping.

Once the parade was over, it was time to prepare for the ball. Before the stage curtains opened, they attached my ruche, my head-dress that encircled my hair like a halo, along with the huge—and heavy—train with its sequins glittering along the sides. The train was mounted on small wheels to help me walk, but it still wasn't easy to move. The gown's strong straps cut into my flesh, but I did my best to smile as the curtain went up and the music played.

The evening didn't finish until four in the morning. We were still going strong as we joined other revelers at the Morning Call cafe to enjoy doughnuts and coffee.

The next day I was interviewed on television and then on radio with Herbert Moore. Following the broadcast, he said he was moving to Washington and was planning on publishing a magazine. He asked if I would like to be a columnist for him, which had long been my dream. I wrote my "Woman on the Go" column for many years.

Our experiences in New Orleans were something to treasure, but we were looking forward to returning to our business and family. No sooner did we arrive home when George Panagas, a hard-working real-estate broker, came by the office. He said, "Blackie, the building across the street from you is for sale. Do you want it?"

"Which one?"

"The Colonial Storage Building."

Blackie had a gleam in his eye. This building housed a moving and storage company owned by two brothers. They were good customers of ours, but Blackie had a complaint against them. Many times he had asked them not to park their big trucks in front of the restaurant, but they paid no attention. Blackie's would be completely obscured for hours at a time.

"How much does the landlord want?" Blackie asked.

"The building and ground are $135,000."

"Will they come down?"

"Probably not."

"Yes," Blackie said, "I want to buy that building. They've parked in front of our place long enough."

Blackie was thinking about how to finance the purchase when Leo Bernstein came into the restaurant. We had known him for some time, as he was one of the many Cadillac customers who came in for coffee while they waited for their cars to be repaired.

Blackie walked over to him and said, "Leo, I want to buy the building across the street."

"How much are they selling it for?"

"$135,000."

"How bad do you want it?"

"Bad."

"Who's the agent?"

"George Panagas."

"Tell him to draw up the papers," Leo said, "and my Guardian Federal will take care of it."

The deal was made. The moving and storage company moved out, and we leased the building for a time.

Not long after that acquisition, George Panagas came back to us again, telling us that the long building next to us was for sale. With Leo Bernstein's confidence in us, we were able to buy this much-needed property also. It would become the home of the future cocktail lounge and would give us the space for the kitchen expansion.

Meantime, our friend Nick Antonelli was doing well with his PMI parking lots. He was in the process of building a beautiful building at 1730 M Street, N.W., which was rumored to be the future location of a new bank. One day Blackie mentioned to me the talk of the new bank and said he wished he could qualify. But that's all he said. As it was August and we were into the summer doldrums, I didn't think much of his remark. Everyone was talking about going somewhere, and we were thinking about it too.

Blackie had read about the Space Needle restaurant in Seattle and the great fair that was going on there. When he was a teenager, he had attended the 1939 World's Fair in New York and it had made a tremendous impression on him. He'd like to go to this fair too. We spoke to John and Vivian Kalavritinos, and they were in the mood to accompany us.

So on a hot day we entered the Statler ticket office to inquire about airfares. A pretty girl was at the desk, busy writing up a young man's flight. We waited for awhile, and then Blackie interrupted her, asking, "Miss, how much are four tickets to Seattle?"

She mumbled something about being with him in a few minutes.

Blackie kept looking at the big map in back of her. He said, "From Seattle we could go to San Francisco and even to Hawaii. Hmm. How about Bangkok?"

He turned again to the young woman at the desk. "How much is a ticket to Bangkok?"

She replied, "Bangkok is halfway around the world. If you want to go to there, you might as well just keep going around the world."

Blackie turned to me, "What do you think, want to go around the world? Let me call Nick."

He reached Nick Antonelli from the pay phone, and Nick said that if he could settle the property on Connecticut Avenue he'd come with us. I called Vivian Kalavritinos and she said they'd love to go around the world.

Blackie went back to the desk where the girl was still talking with the fellow. Blackie said, "Give me four tickets for around the world—maybe five."

The salesgirl came to her senses and pressed a buzzer for another person to come out while she attended to our itinerary. We planned to travel from Seattle to San Francisco, Hawaii, Tokyo, Hong Kong, Bangkok, Calcutta, Tehran, Beirut, Lebanon, Istanbul, Greece, and finally to Rome before heading home.

While they were writing up our trip, Blackie called Nick again. "What do you want me to do? I just ordered four tickets for around the world."

"Get me a roundtrip ticket to Seattle and back for my daughter and me. I know I can go that far with you. As for around the world, keep calling me at every stop and if my deal comes through, I'll join you wherever you are."

We decided to take in the World's Fair first with the older kids, and then Nick would accompany them all back to Washington. John and Vivian took their two girls, Alexis and Christina, and left their baby Jack with his grandmother. We took Gregory and BJ and left one-year-old Dina with her nanny, Carmen. The ten of us boarded United Airlines for Seattle.

On arriving, the kids didn't want to rest and neither did we. We reached the fair via the Monorail, a glorified streetcar running at seventy miles an hour. Once there, we thoroughly enjoyed ourselves, going on the rides, eating, laughing, and holding hands. When the rains came, we didn't care; we just got wet and kept going until dinnertime in the Space Needle restaurant.

Soon it was time for the children to return back to Washington with Nick. We said tearful goodbyes as they left, for we wouldn't be seeing them for at least a month.

We visited Hong Kong, where we looked over into Red China, which was such a mystery. In Bangkok we ate curry and watched a Siamese boxing match and then went on to Calcutta, where our taxi driver dodged sacred cows running loose.

After Calcutta we landed in Tehran and were met by Nasser Tehranni, a former waiter at Blackie's when he was studying at Georgetown University. He took us to the desert in search of camel caravans. When we came upon a gypsy camp with ten camels, he bargained and arranged for us to ride the animals. Except for the odor of the unwashed beasts, it was a great experience.

Our next stops were Beirut and Cairo, and then onto Istanbul. At every stop along the way we called Nick Antonelli to see if he had closed his deal and could join us. In Istanbul he surprised us, saying the deal was finished and that he could meet us in Athens. Once at the airport we greeted him with hugs and made our way to the hotel, all five of us squeezed into a taxi.

The next morning was scorchingly hot, the sun beating down unmercifully as we climbed the Acropolis. We envisioned how it must have looked centuries before, and on the way down we paused on Mars Hill, where the Apostle Paul told the Greeks about "the unknown God."

On our last day in Greece we hired a car to take us to Volos, and Nick accompanied us as we drove a hundred miles outside of Athens to visit Blackie's Aunt Frosso. The roads were winding and narrow, and I caught sight of many signs that warned of falling rocks.

When we had visited Aunt Frosso two years before, we noticed that her small house had just a well for water and no electricity. While there, Blackie had made preparations for her to put in electricity and running water, and now he wanted to see how it had turned out.

Aunt Frosso was about seventy-five and was strongly built, looking very much like Papa. She was pleased to have a nephew to look out for her and greeted us with open arms.

After lunch in town, Blackie addressed her in Greek, "Thea Frosso—where do you shop?"

She answered, "Come, I'll show you."

We walked down the narrow streets to a small grocery store and saw large gallons of olive oil, barrels of vinegar, gunny sacks of beans and rice, and staples of every kind, such as toilet paper and bath soap.

Blackie said, "Pick out what you need."

After Thea made her selections, Blackie whispered something to the owner. He had a satisfied smile as he began loading gunny sacks of rice and beans, four large metal containers of olive oil, and packages of soap, toilet paper, and other household items into his delivery truck. It seemed enough to last Thea Frosso for a year.

We made it back to Athens a little tired, but after a night's rest we were ready for the enchanting city of Rome. We visited many historic places, including the coliseum that had been filled with the blood of the martyrs and the jail where the Apostle Paul was imprisoned.

Amid the breathtaking beauty of the city there was poverty too. In one of the parks we came across a little homeless girl who was selling pictures and flowers. With her smattering of English, she came up to Blackie and pointed at his stomach, saying, "Too mucha spaghetti! Too mucha Coca-Cola!" We gave her some money and she ran off, but we'd never forget her lonely eyes.

And then it was time to say arrivederci. It had been a wonderful thirty days, but we were excited to return home to our families. On October 8TH we arrived back in Washington and were reunited with our loved ones.

The very day after we returned home, Blackie got a call from Morrie Haritan, a friend who owned the leading accounting firm in Washington. Morrie said they were starting a new bank and asked if Blackie would like to join them.

The seed for the enterprise had been planted earlier when Morrie was having lunch with Lou Paladini, a banker who handled the affairs of the late Floyd E. Davis, Sr., a prominent Washington businessman.

Following lunch, Lou and Morrie were walking back to their offices when they met up with the newly appointed Comptroller of the Currency, Mr. Saxon, and the Chief National Bank Examiner. They started to talk.

After listening to the conversation for awhile, Morrie asked two key questions: "How many people does it take to open a bank? And how much money is needed?"

Mr. Saxon replied, "It takes at least ten men of impeccable reputation who each have a net worth of at least a million dollars."

Morrie went back to his office burning with the idea of opening a new bank. A few days later he met with the well-known builder Charles

E. Smith, Nick Antonelli, and Kingdon Gould, great grandson of Jay Gould, the financier. They were all enthusiastic over opening a new bank, pledging stock totaling about three and a half million dollars.

When the directors first asked Blackie to join, we didn't even have a financial statement. But Morrie Haritan took over our books and put one together for us.

The application for the charter for Madison National Bank had been made earlier in March and a charter was granted in May. But the bank didn't open until December 2, 1962, when Nick's building was completed. Charles E. Smith was named chairman of the board.

Blackie was quite nervous before his first bank meeting. But with his new gray suit and yellow tie he looked the part of "the man in the gray flannel suit."

After the meeting, he said to me, "Boy, there's really a difference in old money and new. Kingdon Gould came in with tennis shoes fresh from a game, and his shoe strings didn't even match. He said his kids had lost one of the strings but it didn't seem to bother him a bit. If I'd dressed that way, I would have felt out of place. Guess it takes awhile to feel as secure as Kingdon."

Just the same, we were on our way now. Fifteen years had flown by quickly.

I thought back to my old dream of destiny and asked myself if it had been fulfilled. Immediately, deep inside myself, I knew that there was more to come.

VI

A Long Search

19

Expansion and Enterprise

IN 1963 THE WORLD'S TROUBLES WERE BUILDING UP. The Bay of Pigs fiasco had occurred and Fidel Castro was firmly entrenched with a Cuban dictatorship right off our Florida coast. Kennedy had made a strong stand against the communist buildup. He was much loved not only by Americans but by the world, particularly after his "Ich bin ein Berliner" speech.

Besides staying current with world affairs, we were doing more traveling and picking up ideas for Blackie's along the way. One trip was to San Juan, Puerto Rico, where we attended a parking convention with Nick Antonelli. While there, the president of the National Parking Association, Bill Barr, introduced us to Jules Lederer, husband of the columnist Ann Landers. Jules, who had just founded Budget Rent a Car, became friends with Blackie and Nick and offered them their pick of a Budget-Rent-a-Car franchise anywhere in the world. San Juan seemed very pleasant and so Blackie and Nick chose Puerto Rico.

In old San Juan a former convent is now a hotel called El Convento. Its restaurant has high ceilings, a wrap-around balcony, and a beautiful interior patio that is separated from an outside courtyard by a large, wrought-iron gate.

Blackie and I were dining there one night, enjoying steaming black bean soup with fresh chopped onions on the top. While we were eating, Blackie started to stare intently at his surroundings as though absorbing every detail. "Louie," he said eventually, "Do you see those balconies up there and the high ceilings? When I build the cocktail lounge I'm going to make it just like this."

Several months later, in October, we heard that the contents of the famous Capitol Theatre were for sale. We decided to find out what furnishings we could acquire for the future cocktail lounge.

Located in the fourteen-story National Press Building on F Street, the theater had opened in 1927 and had been named one of the ten most opulent theaters in the country. With its thirty-five hundred seats, double hydraulic lifts for the organ and orchestra, and gilt-encrusted lobbies, it deserved such a high ranking. Much of its furniture was thought to originate in an Austrian castle.

The auction would take place soon, so on a cool day we went to see the theater. It had been all torn up and its contents were labeled and ready to be sold. I felt a little nostalgic as I remembered the many movies and live shows we had enjoyed there. Our last visit had showcased Blackie's favorite dancer with the beautiful legs, Mitzi Gaynor. Still, although this was a sad occasion, it was a great opportunity to find some intriguing pieces for the restaurant while helping to keep a part of Washington's history alive.

As we looked through the rich and varied furniture, what interested Blackie most were the balustrades. They were finely wrought, each featuring the etched head of an exquisite lady.

"I've got to have these for my balcony in the cocktail lounge," he said to me. "And look at those hanging lights! They can be mounted from the high ceiling."

I agreed, and started to imagine what the new lounge would look like.

Blackie paused before a large, slightly damaged painting of Cupid. Pointing at a round hole in the canvas he said, "I'm ashamed to admit it to you, Louie, but I did that one Saturday afternoon when I was about sixteen. I was with some friends and that painting was hanging up by the men's room. I don't know why I'd do such a thing, but I had a cigarette in my hand and I walked up and burned a hole right in Cupid's belly button. I've got to have it so I can fix it up and clear my conscience."

Needless to say that was one of the several magnificent paintings we bought that afternoon, together with seven of the balustrades, two intricate gold tables, chandeliers of various types, five carved chairs, two sofas, and a divided settee that was perfect for the space between the men's and ladies' rooms.

We also had some stained-glass windows stored for the lounge from Nick Antonelli. Whenever he acquired a new piece of property, he would immediately apply for a permit to tear down its rundown building. Then he'd use the land as a parking lot until he would either build an apartment house or an office building.

Nick had bought the old Providence Hospital, and told us about the pretty stained-glass windows from the chapel dating back to June 15, 1844. We could have them if we wanted, he said.

Blackie was worried that someone would question him when he and his crew went to take down the windows, so Nick wrote a letter for him to show if asked. But no one ever inquired, and after dismantling the fine stained glass Blackie housed them across the street in the Colonial Warehouse until we could use them.

For two years we had already been storing a terrific old bar for the lounge as well. Blackie had heard from Chester Morris, a Cadillac salesman, that it was for sale from the O'Donnell seafood people in Maryland. He drove out to the farm and saw that the bar was a beauty, all hand carved and held together by wooden pegs. He bought it, and the next day our cabinet maker, Norman Cooper, carefully disassembled it and loaded it in a truck. We didn't have anywhere to store it, so Blackie set it on our roof and covered it with a waterproof tarpaulin.

Now with the acquisitions from the Capitol Theatre, we had everything gathered for the cocktail lounge. Blackie was ready to build it and to enlarge the kitchen. He got down to work, drawing up blueprints and deciding where to put our lovely finds. As he made progress he would change his original plans, improvising as he saw fit. In the end the blueprints were useful mainly to the plumbers because he had made so many changes. But he knew what he was doing, for when the lounge was completed its rich, welcoming atmosphere was more than we could have imagined.

Not long after the Capitol Theatre auction, the telephone rang during the restaurant's afternoon lull. It was our friend Pete Boinis, whom we had met through Joe Rinaldi. Pete and Joe had opened The Keg on Wisconsin Avenue, and as the name implies, they sold lots of beer and their customers were the young.

While operating The Keg, Pete was also a marketing man for Xerox 5000. Xerox machines were the latest technology and Pete was the top salesman. He had previously been a much heralded football star at the University of Maryland, eventually becoming a coach. But Pete had an entrepreneurial spirit and was determined to get into business for himself. The Keg, while a success, was not the only thing he wanted to accomplish.

Previously Joe had brought Pete to the Touchdown Club where Nick and Blackie were playing gin rummy. When Pete told Nick and Blackie of his dream to open a different type of dancing place with a live band, they were impressed. They told Pete to draw up the plans and find his location, and they would finance him through the Madison National Bank.

Pete found a great spot on Wisconsin and Van Ness Street. He named his new restaurant The Bastille and within a few weeks it was considered a success.

Then Pete ran into a problem, about which he was on the phone with Blackie. He said, "As you know, I finally got my restaurant opened and I'm doing really well. But now I need to find out what kind of percentages I'm supposed to have."

"What do you mean?" Blackie asked.

"Well, you know I'm new at this, but it seems that you must know things like what percentage should the rent be, and the payroll. How much should the food cost be?"

"Have you got a pencil there?"

"Yes, I'm sitting at my desk."

"Well rent should be about 6 percent. Let's see, food cost. I keep it at less than 34 percent. If it gets higher than that it blows all the profits."

"Liquor cost," Pete said. "How much should that be?"

"We'll have to break that down. Liquor itself should be 19 percent. Wine is more expensive and you don't sell that much. That ought to be 34 percent. Champagne is about the same as wine. Beer should be 18 percent. But if you keep the whole thing below 22 percent then you'll be in the right ball park. Remember, don't give any beer to the bartenders! Reckon on 5 percent for advertising and keep the payroll at 25 percent or below. Then count on no more than 10 percent for all the extras—insurance and stuff like that. Have you got it?"

"Yeah, well I hope so. I made a note of everything. You'll have to come and see my place."

"Pete, let me give you a bit of advice. Remember, you can't steal and grow."

"What did you say?"

"I said, you can't steal and grow."

"That's what I thought you said, and I don't intend to."

"Listen, Pete, I'll bring the One-thirty Club and we'll come and have lunch with you next week."

After Blackie hung up the phone, I said, "Pete will do well. He's very disciplined."

Nick, Blackie, and my instincts were sound; Pete's restaurant flourished. And it was right for the Madison Bank to finance him. After a few years he sold The Bastille for almost a half million dollars. Eventually, after owning and selling the popular Hunka Munka in Ocean City, he moved to Florida. He is a very successful businessman who owns a five-star restaurant in Boca Raton, aptly named Pete's, and counts Dave Thomas, founder of Wendy's, as his closest friend.

On a Friday afternoon toward the end of November it seemed to be a day like any other day. Blackie and Nick were in San Juan, Puerto Rico, for a meeting of their Budget-Rent-a-Car franchise and I was tending the restaurant. Having just received a call from Garfinckel's department store, I decided to go there to look at some items they had set aside for me.

I paid for my clothes, and just when I signed my check I heard a lady say, "The president has been shot!" I thought she certainly couldn't mean here in America—she must be talking about a foreign country.

But when I turned on my car radio I learned it was true, that the president had been shot. This was not a day like every other day, but November 22, 1963, a day that would go down in history.

Back at the restaurant, customers were gathered around the news ticker, not able to grasp what they had heard. Some looked sadly at the autographed picture of Kennedy hanging on the wall. Then the final word came—the president had died. Tearfully and immediately, everyone cleared out of the restaurant.

The phone rang. It was Blackie calling from the San Juan airport to see if the radio's reports of "el Presidente está muerto" were true. He and Nick arranged to take the next flight home.

Then I got a call from Gregory, who was a freshman at Blair Academy in New Jersey. He said he had been on the way to the library to see if there was a letter from home when he heard the dreadful news. I was so grateful he called so we could share the moment.

When I got home, BJ told me how he had been listening to his new transistor radio just as recess was just finishing. He said, "I heard the newsflash and rushed into the classroom, telling the teacher, 'The president has just been shot!' She got mad and made me stand in the corner. I tried my best to make her understand I wasn't making it up. But a minute later, another teacher came in and then she knew the truth."

We turned on the television and Dina, just a few years old, couldn't understand why everyone was crying. The television news became even more important as everyone gathered around to get the details. We watched with unbelief as Lee Harvey Oswald, the one reported to have shot the president, was himself shot by Jack Ruby.

A different feeling crept across America after the assassination of President Kennedy. We thought that it couldn't happen here, but it did and it changed the world. People felt like they had lost their heart, and a slump came over the restaurant for six weeks. Yet being in business, we had to carry on—and that's precisely what we did.

Over a year later, on Christmas day, 1964, Blackie was restless. We had been assembling property for an apartment/hotel complex at Nineteenth and N Streets, Northwest, and had just signed a note for $500,000. If we hadn't taken on the debt, we would have lost the possibility of the new building.

Blackie was worried about the additional payment and wanted to get started on the project immediately. I was busy in the kitchen baking apple pies and the kids were playing around the Christmas tree with their new toys.

"Louie, where's the telephone book?" Blackie asked.

"It's right over there, on the shelf of the small table. Why? Who will be working today?"

"Someone Jewish, probably. I'm going to call up every architect I can find until one answers. And that's who I'll pick."

I kept on cooking and heard him dialing number after number. I thought he was a little crazy, but eventually I heard him talking to someone, asking if he was working.

The fellow must have been, because Blackie asked for his address. He paused and replied, "The Esso building. Yeah, I know where it is."

Blackie hung up the phone, grabbed his heavy jacket, and told us he'd be back soon.

He returned just as we were preparing to have dinner. As he joined us he said, "Well, I went to that office and there was Elliott Gitlin cuddled up over a little electric heater because the heat in the building was off. I showed him the layout of the land and right away he came up with some good ideas. We're going to meet again early next week."

Blackie worked hard on implementing his plans for the hotel/apartment house. But in the end it took him four years before Embassy Square was up and running.

One day Blackie was out in front of the restaurant when a squad car drove up and a uniformed policeman stepped out. Just as Blackie was beginning to wonder what he had done wrong, the young rookie put out his hand and said, "Hi. My name is Bill Katapothis. As you can tell, I'm a Greek. If there's anything I can help you with, let me know."

Blackie told me later, "For a moment I thought they had caught up with me." He said with a sheepish laugh, "I haven't always had permits for everything I've done."

Bill Katapothis became a good friend, and eventually a godfather to Ulysses II's firstborn son.

It was November 1965, and we had owned the restaurant property for four years. Our seating capacity was now seven hundred and our sales were over a million dollars a year. The hub of the city—around Fourteenth and F Streets—had shifted our way, causing our property to double and triple in value. And inflation had worked in our favor as well.

One successful business enterprise seemed to spark off another. We had opened many new Washington restaurants: the Black Saddle, the Black Rose, the Black Bird, the Black Frisco, the Black Russian, and the Black Gun. And our many small coffee shops were our answer to the increasing number of people who wanted to eat on the run.

With so many business ventures to manage, Blackie was all consumed. He worked day and night while I looked after the children and the home, as well as tending to customers at the restaurant.

We had reached success, but I began to wonder at what price. I was deeply lonely, although I tried not to acknowledge it. Whenever I became blue or down, I would remember growing up during the grim days of the Depression. I would then push my heavy feelings aside and revel in our achievements. But even my optimistic nature couldn't bury the unnamed longings that would return and color my outlook. I began to wonder if I was missing out on a vital part of life that couldn't be reached through money or success. I thought back to my parents' faith in God, which was such an important part of their life. He didn't seem to play a role in mine anymore. And then a frightening incident made me aware that he was still looking after me.

It happened on a seemingly uneventful Saturday night. The house was quiet, for Blackie was on a fishing trip in Florida with Nick Antonelli, BJ was staying the night at a friend's house, and Greg was away at prep school. Carmen, Dina's nanny, was asleep in her room in the basement.

Around midnight I was awakened by a loud noise. Immediately I went into four-year-old Dina's room to check on her. She too had heard the noise and was awake but not crying. I picked her up and she snuggled into me, remaining quiet.

While still holding her, I went toward the stairs and looked down. My heart jumped when I saw a large man standing by the front door who was obviously demented. He was pounding one palm against the other and was staring up at us wild-eyed. His face reminded me of our employee, Cleveland—I had seen that manic look before.

Although I was petrified, I thought I could handle him. Then I realized with a jolt that this could be our last night on earth. I said to myself, "I must stay calm or I will rile him. He's big and powerful, and I must keep my wits about me."

Because I didn't want the man to come up the stairs I started to walk down toward him. All the while I was holding Dina tightly and whispering words of comfort—telling her to stay very quiet, which miraculously she did throughout the whole experience.

The intruder motioned for us to follow him toward the basement. Hearing us, Carmen came out of her room and then froze in silent fear. He indicated that she should go back in the room and that I was to follow. He didn't speak a word and he didn't take his eyes from mine. I sat on a chair holding Dina close while Carmen stood near the door. Meanwhile he had taken off his shoe and started banging it against the floor.

Surreptitiously I signaled to Carmen to go up the street and get our neighbor Alejandro Orfilla. As the big man continued to stare at me, Carmen disappeared out the door. When she left, he got up and grabbed the bedspread as if he was going to smother us.

Jumping up, with Dina still clinging to me tightly, I cried out in a loud, authoritative voice, "You wouldn't do that to your sister or mother and you're not going to do it to us."

I commanded him to lie down on the bed. He did. I reached over and turned on the television, but the screen only showed the test pattern. He stared at it, then once again started to get up. Again I commanded him to lie down. This went on for about ten minutes. He would begin to rise; I would order him to lie down. Each time—amazingly—he obeyed.

Finally, to my relief I heard noises upstairs. Alejandro obviously had called the police. Stealthily they came down the stairs and I slowly backed out of the doorway just as they appeared. It took six policemen to get the man out of the house, while another stayed behind and helped us move a heavy chest against the smashed-in door. We later discovered that the intruder was a sick soldier who had escaped from Mt. Alto Mental Hospital.

When it was all over Alejandro held the still-sleeping Dina and me in his arms, comforting us.

"Alejandro," I said with emotion, "I'm going to call you my vigilante from now on."

"I'm just glad I was able to help, Lou," he said.

This break-in was a truly terrifying moment in my life. I thanked God for sparing Dina and me, and I began to think more about him.

A week after Thanksgiving, a meeting at the James L. Dixon and Company moved my life into a disturbing direction. It seemed commonplace enough at the time, just a gathering to sign some real-estate papers for further expansion. But it was then that I met the famous Jeane Dixon, the seeress whose book was on the best-seller list and who had predicted the death of President Kennedy.

We met at the office of her husband, James Dixon, an attractive man who looked polished and successful. As we sat down, Blackie and Jimmy began to talk real estate and how wonderful it would be if downtown Washington could have high-rise buildings. Soon, I heard a woman's modulated voice speaking almost in a whisper. The voice was so intimate that I turned around and saw a tall slender woman wearing a navy-blue dress topped by a lace collar and with a gold cross about her neck. It was Jeane Dixon.

She was talking to another couple who were about to leave. "See you again soon and God bless you," she said, and then turned to Blackie. "So you're the creative restaurateur I've heard so much about. Blackie's is so beautiful. There's such a wonderful feeling there."

Blackie seemed slightly taken aback and smiled more than he usually did when flattered. Then she turned to me, feeling my arm as we greeted each other. I wasn't surprised, for someone had told me that she always took the person's arm she was introduced to in order to tune in on the person's vibrations. She continued to hold my arm and as we made small talk I felt that in some strange way she was having another conversation deep inside of herself.

Apparently satisfied with what she had gleaned, she took hold of Blackie's arm. Not really talking, she listened to Jimmy and Blackie, nodding assent now and then. Then she released Blackie's arm and turned back to me.

"Let's all go upstairs. There are some papers there to sign."

Blackie and I went into Jimmy's office while Jeane left to take a phone call. Jimmy handed the papers to Blackie to read, and Blackie studied them carefully. This deal was for a piece of property for the hotel we hoped to build one day right next to the restaurant.

Meanwhile, I couldn't help but hear Jeane's voice coming in from her office, and I thought how warm and encouraging she sounded. When she returned to us, I had just finished signing the papers. As Jimmy and Blackie continued talking about the property, Jeane beckoned me to come into her office.

"Your husband is a diamond in the rough," she said. "I get some of the vibrations flowing from him that I used to feel touching Mike Todd." Her eyes were disconcerting as they stared directly into mine. "Your future shows many changes!"

I felt a tightening in my throat, for I didn't particularly like changes. I smiled but said nothing to encourage her to tell me any more.

She said warmly, "I want to see you soon. Can we come to dinner Saturday night?"

I remembered that Blackie was going to Detroit over the weekend and told her so. She said, "Oh, that's all right. It's you I want to talk to."

Something about the way she said "you" and how she looked into my eyes made me uneasy. Yet I didn't know how to refuse her. "Fine," I said. "Suppose you and Jimmy come to Blackie's about seven."

"We'll be there, Loulie." She had already changed my name, and the one she had chosen was what my late brother Joel had called me when I was a little girl. Thinking of him, I felt sad. After Leona's death, Joel had gradually lost the will to live and was only fifty when he died.

As we all said our farewells, Jeane held onto my arm again. Her face held a strange expression when she did this, as if she were further confirming something that had come to her earlier. Because she appeared so interested in me, I wondered if I had found a friend. She seemed to be responding to my inner loneliness. When we left the office I glimpsed heavy clouds and noticed that the day had turned eerily dark. Why did I have such a sense of foreboding?

The next morning, Jeane sent over an autographed copy of her best-selling book, *The Gift of Prophecy*. I spent all evening and some of the next morning reading it. I found out that when she was just a little girl a gypsy fortune-teller had told her that she had a gift of prophecy. She began to tell people's fortunes and misfortunes from a very young age.

I was intrigued to read that President Roosevelt had talked to her six months before his death. He had sent for her to find out how long he had to live. I also learned of her special connections with congressmen and women, movie stars, and just plain people like me. As I read her book I built up an awe for her. Maybe she really did have access to hidden knowledge about the future.

As I walked into the Black Angus room to greet Jeane and her husband on Saturday night I was attentive and excited to see them.

"I spent yesterday and this morning reading your book, Jeane. I found it fascinating."

Obviously pleased, she replied, "My whole life has been fascinating, Loulie. Ever since I can remember, God has been so good to me. He's brought the most intriguing people my way. I've always used every opportunity to tell people what they should and should not be doing, for I feel this is what God wants me to do."

She then took hold of my arm again. "I can feel that you're in harmony with God. You're working every day. This business provides happiness for people and as long as you do the right thing and strive to help others, then you're in God's will."

I was intrigued, for this way of thinking was new to me. Perhaps what I had been longing for was a closer connection to God. Could Jeane help me find him?

We finished dinner and Jeane took my hand, saying, "I've already told you that there will be many changes in your life. I won't reveal any of them to you now. But later on, I will." Jimmy didn't seem to be listening as he tapped his fingers to the music and watched the people dancing.

In the glowing candlelight I found myself studying Jeane's eyes. They seemed to contain a new dimension that for the first time frightened me. I was too afraid to ask any questions.

Then she leaned closer to whisper in my ear. "There is something very important I want to tell you tonight. I hate to tell you this, but I must."

For a brief moment her eyes looked sad, and then she continued, "You know, Loulie, two people who work together have to respect each other. You have to share in the success too. You're as important as your husband."

I resisted her words, saying, "I've always believed that the bulk of the success should go to the husband. Being a man, he needs this more than a woman."

"You can't overlook it," she said. "Having mutual respect for each other in your personal and business life is the only way you can really be happy. There will come a time soon when you will, by a step you will take, assure yourself of more respect. It will be hard but you will take it."

This topic made me uncomfortable and I moved uneasily in my chair. There were times when Blackie didn't show me respect, but I always blamed it on his Greek upbringing and his old-world manners. He treated other people the same way.

When Jimmy excused himself, Jeane leaned close. "I have to tell you this quickly while Jimmy is gone. When we first met and I touched your arm, I knew I should warn you that you were facing some kind of physical danger. And now I'm convinced that my first impression was right. I don't know when it will happen but you will have trouble in your car, possibly by being assaulted. I see red, yes, I actually see blood in your car."

I was stunned. "An accident maybe?" I asked.

"I'm not sure," she said, knitting her brows and holding onto my arm firmly. Then her tone changed. "I see you coming out of it okay and having many wonderful things happen to you."

Jimmy returned and we left the restaurant. As we drove to their home on N Street, Jeane did most of the talking. With Jimmy there, I didn't feel free to ask any questions.

When we arrived at the front door, Jimmy got out first and I hastily asked Jeane, "How long before this thing happens?"

"Possibly six months. Maybe longer. It's hard to tell. You'll come out of it all right."

Later, as I lay in bed feeling very alone, my emotions were churning over Jeane's comments about Blackie's lack of respect. And her words of an assault and blood in my car truly chilled me.

As I lay there, I mumbled to myself, "Jeane is a world-famous seeress. She has talked to presidents. She told me I was doing God's will. Maybe I should be grateful for her prediction—it could save my life."

It took me quite awhile to fall asleep.

Over the next few months I seemed to have no peace. I suffered many sleepless nights wondering what would happen in my car and brooding over Jeane's remarks about Blackie. I tried to ignore what she had said, but I always seemed to come back to her predictions about danger as I was trying to fall asleep. Scenes of bloody accidents and a mangled car would unfold before my eyes, as much as I hated to see them. During the day, however, I would put the thoughts and concerns out of my mind while at home or the restaurant.

Early into the new year, 1966, I was able to forget Jeane's predictions while we celebrated a major business deal. The occasion was the day when three high-school dropouts and the grandson of a famous financier took over the landmark Mayflower Hotel. It was then the crown jewel of the hotel industry, and was the place that had so fascinated me when I first came to Washington.

The deal was made over the phone. Bill Cohen called Blackie one day and said, "Greek, how much do you want of the Mayflower?"

"I don't know. How much is left?"

"Probably 10 to 14 percent."

"Okay, I'll take whatever's left."

That was it—the $14 million sale was agreed. No lawyers were involved, except to draw up the final papers as they formed a company called Maywash. Deals were still made this way—just a word of agreement and a handshake.

The three high-school dropouts each had memories of the Mayflower. Blackie and Bill Cohen weren't allowed to enter through the front door because Blackie was a busboy and Bill collected the trash. Nick Antonelli had parked the customers' cars. But not so for their other partner, Kingdon Gould, great grandson of Jay Gould.

So it was a high point in their lives when as the new owners they entered through the front door of the historic Mayflower. They were the first to be local owners since the hotel's earliest history.

Meanwhile, Blackie and Nick gave up their Budget-Rent-a-Car franchise in Puerto Rico and Jules Lederer asked them if they wanted another franchise. Nick wasn't interested, but Blackie decided to take the whole of Switzerland along with a Swiss partner, Herb Mueller. After this, Blackie had many trips to Europe, and I accompanied him occasionally.

Winter passed, and on a beautiful day in April I was outside planting red petunias and Dina was having great fun in the dirt beside me. But I wasn't making progress, so I asked her to go play with her teddy bear, which was lying beside the car about ten feet away.

She did and I continued planting, loving the petunias because they grow so carefree and are so colorful all summer. Then a hornet came and frightened me when it took a nose-dive at my head. I have bitter memories of hornets. Once, picking raspberries as a little girl, I put my hand deep into a bush, not knowing that I was reaching into a hornet's nest. When I withdrew my hand, my arm was crawling with the little creatures. Frightened, I beat my hand to get them off and was stung eight times. Ever since, even the sound of them makes me panic.

I was so occupied with the pesky hornet that I failed to notice Dina entering our car. It wasn't until I turned toward the car that I saw her little blond head above the steering wheel. The hornet continued to plague me, and then suddenly I heard the familiar click of the gear shift. Cadillacs were then made so that they could slip out of gear without a key just by moving the lever from park to neutral. The car began to move slowly and I quickly forgot the hornet as I ran for the car door. I was sure I could open it and stop the car.

I reached the handle and pressed the lever, but the car was picking up so much speed from the steep hill that I couldn't open the door. I ran faster and faster, struggling to open it. Dina's little face was peering at me through the door window, a frightened look in her eyes. As I struggled with the handle, I began to cry.

The car seemed like a moving giant and I was helpless as it continued to go faster and faster. Then it moved away from me, running over my feet and cutting my legs. The pain seared my mind and I screamed, following the car down the hill, "My little girl! My little girl! Help! Help!"

Still running after the car, I saw and heard it crash into a neighbor's house—the loudest sound I'd ever heard. I thought surely Dina would be badly hurt. I finally got to the car door and flung it open. She had been thrown to the floor and was frightened and crying.

I leaned over the seat and grabbed her, lifting her into my arms. I held her close for a few moments, kissing and examining her. Nothing seemed broken. In her little-girl innocence, she said, realizing she must have done something dreadful, "I didn't mean to do it, Mommy!"

I held her, sobbing all the while. I was crying tears of happiness and joy now that she seemed all right.

"I don't hurt, Mommy, but you've got red all over you."

I looked down at my legs and over the front seat and saw blood everywhere. Jeane Dixon's words repeated in my mind, "Your blood will be in this car."

Then I heard some neighbors approaching and they took charge. When I was able, they helped me walk home and called Blackie. When he heard how much I was hurting, he decided we should go to the emergency room. Once there he held my hand and grew impatient after all the necessary papers were filled in. Finally, a doctor came and they took x-rays of my feet.

Following this, they brought me to an enclosed area where I began to cry and shake with chills. They said it was shock and that they would give me a sedative; I should just lie there a few hours and then I could go home. My legs looked ugly, but the x-rays revealed that nothing was broken.

Lying there in the hard, narrow cot, I reviewed the past six months since Jeane Dixon had made her prediction. I relived the fear I had felt each time I stepped into my car at night and I thought of how I would stay home from work rather than venture out as I grew more tense and nervous. I recalled how foolish Ulysses thought I was to take her words so seriously.

As I thought back over the months, I couldn't stop the tears. Then my tears turned to hysterical laughter. Then the tears began again and I laughed and cried until all the worry and fear inside seemed to dissolve. Jeane's prophecy had come and gone. It was all over.

I hoped something else was over too. Ever since Jeane's prediction, I had felt a presence close to me. It was nothing I could see, as many times I had turned around quickly trying to spot it but nothing was ever there. The presence wasn't frightening; it didn't hurt me but neither did it comfort me. Had I built up so much fear of Jeane's prediction that fear itself had become a real presence? Or had I unwittingly entered a spiritual realm with forces at work that I hadn't known existed?

I pondered the questions, and then it hit me. Her prediction had really come true! Not exactly in the way she said, but true, nevertheless. I wondered where this strange power came from. Was it from God?

On a Saturday night in November Blackie went to a stag Board of Trade dinner at the Sheraton Park Hotel. This was a very popular affair for the local businessmen and city officials to meet and socialize with each other.

I spent the evening at Blackie's, going through the twelve rooms greeting friends and acquaintances and introducing myself to new-comers. The evening sped by rapidly.

At nine-thirty I went upstairs to my office, eating a sandwich and drinking tea. My thoughts went to my family in California, whom I hadn't written for a long time. I poured out my thoughts and feelings to them and then wrote to Gregory, now seventeen, at Blair Academy.

It was ten-thirty and time to go home. I looked for stamps, but there were none. Hating to write letters and not mail them, I thought of the liquor store on the corner.

Downstairs I spoke briefly to Al, the cashier. "What does it look like tonight?"

"About fifteen hundred people." Al could tell from the dinner checks how much the headcount for the night would be.

I drove to the corner liquor store and was greeted by the owner and his wife.

"What are you doing out by yourself at this time of night?" he asked.

"Why Frank, this is my neighborhood. We've been here for twenty years!"

"Listen to me," he said. "Things have changed in the past twenty years. You shouldn't be walking around at night by yourself."

"I'm not walking around. I just stopped by for some stamps." The stamp-machine was working and I was soon applying stamps to the envelopes.

Frank's wife had fear in her voice. "We live in danger here every moment. There are so many robberies! We have our store up for sale. This used to be the greatest country in the world to have a business. Not so today!"

Then Frank, always demonstrative, drew his tweed jacket aside and showed me a gun stuck in his belt. "See, Lou, I keep my little friend with me at all times. There's another in that drawer for my wife. Look, I'll walk you to the car." Then he reached over and put three candy bars in my hand. "Take these home to the kids."

I put the letters and candy bars into my purse and with Frank in back of me, walked out to my new white sedan.

When I opened the door of my unlocked car, I looked into the barrel of a big, black gun. The large black man behind it had been hiding in the back seat. He reared up and said, "Get in or I'll shoot!"

I was so frightened that I backed up, falling down as I did. As I began to crawl away, I could see the man emerging from the car with the gun still pointing at me. Frank, standing near his store entrance, saw what was happening. He came forward right beside me and raised his gun at the man. With a trembling voice, he yelled, "Don't shoot her! Don't shoot!"

I felt my stockings being torn to shreds as I kept crawling toward the store entrance. Frank stood his ground and the man, now uncertain, put his gun back in his pocket and walked freely down the street. I turned to see his beige jacket disappear behind some buildings.

Frank helped me up and once inside, he said, "I wouldn't have done that for anyone else. Don't ever leave your car without locking it again!"

I poured out my thanks to him, telling him I owed him my life. I was shaking so much I could hardly get the words out.

Soon the police officers arrived and took a report. Then we rode around in the squad car to see if we could spot the man, but we saw no one who resembled him. We went to police headquarters to look through the mug shots. Nothing.

Blackie looked deeply concerned when he arrived at the police station to pick me up. He put his arms around me and hugged me, asking, "What's going on with you?"

"I don't know. Jeane Dixon predicted trouble with my car. I guess when she says you're going to have trouble, you really have trouble."

That night in bed I lay awake for hours, trying to understand what was happening. Did Jeane save me by preparing me for this encounter? How did she know that something was going to happen to me? Was it good to have this advance warning and all the agony that came with it? Did I instinctively do the right thing because of her prophecy? Could she lead me to God and to peace? If so, why were so many bad things happening to me? I struggled with these questions and finally fell asleep.

20

Respect, but Isolation

ON A COLD, RAINY AFTERNOON in late January 1967, I was feeling lonely and depressed as I stood staring through the glass doors of the New Orleans room at Blackie's. The room was closed until dinnertime and was quiet, save for the staccato sound of the raindrops on the window panes. Then the sound started to change as the rain turned to snow. Soon the heavy snow was clinging to the trees as I remembered other winters in another place and time.

I thought back to 1933, the height of the Depression. Mama and Papa were worried because the large stack of wood was nearly gone and the snow made it almost impossible to find more. Pa said he'd have to write a letter applying for Relief, which Mama explained was help from the government.

I remembered the morning when the food and blankets came. Inside the boxes and gunny sacks were cans of stew and prunes, grapefruit, and oranges. Although I was nine, I had never before held an orange. I sat on the chair and carefully peeled it, and a little spray shot out. The smell made my jaws ache.

I thought of the clean and bright blankets we had received and how warm and cozy they felt. Mama folded and unfolded them as though she couldn't believe they were ours.

That night in bed, wrapped up in the blanket with the most pink in it and my head resting on a clean pillowcase, I knew I had my first taste of luxury. It awakened in me dreams of all the beauty out there in the world. I prayed right then that when I grew up I would have clean, soft sheets and live in a beautiful house.

And now, not only did I have clean sheets, but I had a lovely round bed made especially for me with its silken sheets and lace pillows. I smelled the roasting of the meat and thought of all the food I had available—anything I wanted at my fingertips. My prayers for wealth and luxury had been answered beyond my wildest dreams.

My thoughts were interrupted as I realized that the waiters were beginning to set up the room for the dinner business. Remembering my family and past life had brought tears to my eyes, and I brushed them away in embarrassment.

On my way to the office upstairs, I was vividly conscious of all the things within the restaurant depicting my recent life: the pictures of when I was the Venus Queen in New Orleans; the framed copies of write-ups in newspapers and magazines of our business success and our socializing with famous figures; the mementos gathered from our around-the-world trip. Indeed we had so many things of interest that someone had said that when the museums are closed one can always go to Blackie's. My childhood dreams had come true far beyond anything I could have imagined.

I went inside the private quarters that Ulysses and I shared. He was away in Panama on another fishing trip with Nick Antonelli. Suddenly I felt a nostalgia steal into my heart. I had so much—was I terribly selfish to want more? Who could understand my frustration?

I paced the gold rug, then sat down at Ulysses' beautifully carved desk. Leaning back in his huge leather chair, I raised my legs and tried to rest, not wanting to worry about anything. Suddenly the intercom startled me. It was our secretary, Mary.

"Mrs. Auger, you have a call on 32. A Mrs. Shirley Peike."

Shirley was a close friend and confidant of Jeane Dixon.

"Hi, Lou, I just talked to Jeane. She wants to know if you'll have lunch with us tomorrow about one o'clock. She mentioned the Black Rose. Do you suppose we could eat there?"

I couldn't believe what I was hearing—she called just at the moment of my loneliness. With summoned restraint I said, "Tell Jeane I would love it. I'll meet both of you at the Black Rose around one."

That night I found it hard to sleep. I reviewed the past year and the car episodes. I certainly hadn't been my usual self with Ulysses. Constantly thinking about the prophecies had made me tense and nervous. I wasn't always available to him either, and often when he needed papers signed for new business deals he had to send them up to the house for my signature, which annoyed him. I had less stamina and was absent a lot of the time. I didn't smile and laugh as much—and once he brought it up, saying, "I don't hear you sing anymore."

I noticed some changes in him too, which I found disconcerting; for the first time he had become secretive. Sometimes when I approached his desk, he would hurriedly place papers in a drawer. Once when our secretary was absent and I sat at her desk, I began to check the files and saw that some new property and eight new restaurants had been put in his name alone. He had never done this before and I tried not to let it bother me, for I was certain that sooner or later he would include me.

But I started to become a little bitter that he would want to be separate from me. Was it because I hadn't been available to him when he needed signatures? I remember a customer saying to me, "You smile a lot, but it's only your mouth that moves."

As I drove to the Black Rose the next day, I was hoping that Jeane wouldn't give another of her knife-like predictions. Part of me wanted to hear what the future would hold, especially if it included happiness and peace. But I dreaded bad news. I wondered if I should tell her about Ulysses' secretiveness.

My mind was troubled with these thoughts when I entered the restaurant, and as I approached Jeane and Shirley I felt my inner confidence fading. I was shaking as I sat down and greeted them.

Jeane sensed my emotions, and her eyes changed quickly to a deep seriousness. "Loulie, I have thought about you so many times. You wouldn't believe how often I've prayed for you. I wanted to see you before, but the timing was not right."

As she fixed her eyes on mine, I became silent. Finally I answered quietly, "I was delighted when you called yesterday. I've thought about you a great deal too."

As we ate, I told Jeane about my experiences that had fulfilled her predictions. She listened intently, scowling a little now and then but saying nothing. After finishing her crab salad her eyes seemed to grow dark and her mouth hardened. "Loulie, that was just a minor prediction. I'm going to make another one that will startle you, but not today. When the time comes that I can tell it to you, I will bank my entire reputation on it happening."

As she looked directly at me, I suddenly felt weak. Then Jeane turned to Shirley, and said firmly, "Shirley, would you go powder your nose? I have things to discuss with Loulie."

Shirley gathered her things with a trace of a pout and left us.

Jeane turned directly to me. "Loulie, I only have thirty minutes to talk to you because I have a very important appointment and I must not be late. If you want me to help you, you must tell me what's eating you up. I know what it is, but I want to hear it from you first."

How could I tell her? I'd always kept my innermost thoughts private and now struggled to explain. "You work with your husband and so do I," I stammered. "You understand his worries just as I understand my husband's worries. Maybe Blackie has a reason for doing what he does and maybe I have no right to question his motives, but. . . ." I couldn't continue.

"Loulie, you can go on this way, feeling sorry for yourself, and you'll just end up retiring further and further in the corner until you'll be like a bird in the cage. You'll be old and you will never find your true self. I think I know what troubles you but I want you to tell me."

"But I feel disloyal talking about our personal problems."

"I know you do, but I believe that God has sent me to you to help you. You are not the first to have these problems. Remember, God uses me in this way."

When she said God had sent her, I melted. I felt like crying, for who was I for God to care about me?

"You know," I said, "Blackie and I have had our ups and downs, and until now we've been partners in everything and I've loved it. Being by his side is the only thing I really want. But now he has teamed up with a friend to form a separate corporation. They're building eight new restaurants. It's not the money so much, it's the feeling of separation and the lack of respect."

Tears fell, and Jeane took my arm, closed her eyes, and said, "Loulie, I get psychically that your husband, together with his friend, is not behaving properly. When they travel around, they have many different women." She paused.

"I urge you not to say anything to him about what I'm telling you. You're not to worry either, for wonderful things are in store for your future, but certain things must come to pass first. This you must understand—because Blackie is acting the way he is, he has moved out of harmony with God. Being out of harmony, he cannot think straight and that is why he is leaving you out of the properties and why you are growing apart in your marriage. I wish that I could talk to your husband and help him, but he is not ready to talk to me or anyone else. Not yet."

Then, still grasping my arm, she became enthusiastic.

"I told you there are changes ahead in your life. Big changes! The timing is not right for me to tell you all these things yet, but I get psychically that unless you act right now, you'll never be able to recover the properties he's taking from you."

Letting go of my arm she opened her purse and reached for her wallet, pulling a card from it and checking the phone number. She asked where a telephone extension was, and I motioned to a waitress to bring it.

In a few moments, I could hear her making arrangements for me to go see the lawyer whose card she held in her hand. As she spoke to him, she insisted that he see me the next day. She warned him to take good care of me, saying that I needed advice immediately.

Hanging up, she said, "You can trust this man. I hope you know that there are few lawyers you can trust in this town. Most would run right to Blackie and tell him everything."

I sighed, and she continued, "After you take certain steps, he is going to be very angry with you for a while, but someday he will thank you. I will tell you more later on. Timing is everything."

She looked at her watch and sprang up, saying, "Walk with me back to my office and return and get your car later, will you? We can talk on the way and I need the fresh air and exercise."

Jeane and I walked arm-in-arm to her office. She was so excited about what I was about to do and kept emphasizing that this was putting me on the threshold of a new life.

"Now smile, Loulie!" she exclaimed. "Whenever you're with me or away, I want you to smile. Most people wouldn't have the strength for me to talk to them like this, but I know you have. You've got to forget your life as it is now and learn to live in the future for it's going to be beautiful!"

By this time we had reached Erlebacher's Dress Shoppe on Connecticut Avenue and caught sight of a lovely baby-blue dress in the window.

"Loulie! That dress! That's the one for you. I'm late but let's go and look at it."

The dress was size six and fit me perfectly.

Jeane waited there until she was satisfied, then she whispered to me, "Now that dress will bring you luck. Every time you wear it, good things will come your way. Even after it gets worn out, keep it as your good-luck charm. Wear it on the day you face your husband about the properties and you're sure to win."

Being really late for her appointment now, she left me there at the store. Her parting words were, "Do exactly as the lawyer tells you. He's a good one and you can trust him."

That night, I felt even lonelier than I did the day before and needed two sleeping tablets to get to sleep. When Jeane was beside me telling me of the glorious future she could see, I almost believed that it could be possible. Alone in the bedroom, however, I remembered her statements about Ulysses and broke out in perspiration and fear.

The next day I walked into the lawyer's office. He was formerly at the Justice Department and was well known in Washington. His warm, friendly manner put me instantly at ease.

"Well now, Mrs. Auger, I know a great deal about the success you and your husband enjoy in this town, so you needn't go into your background. Just tell me about your present problem."

I explained that my husband and I had always been partners, that he was forming a new restaurant partnership without me, and that Jeane felt I needed to act.

"Will there be papers to sign?" he asked.

"Yes, there will be some guarantees for me to sign."

"Then you should simply refuse to sign any papers unless your name is included. Your husband can't make a move without your signature."

He paused as I digested his words.

He continued, "I believe Jeane is right in saying you must act at this particular time. If you refuse to face him now, there would be nothing I could do later but take legal action. You have an ace-in-the-hole now—the signatures—that you won't have later."

I walked out of the office feeling depressed. I felt like a traitor, but Jeane's words about my wonderful future buoyed me up. Still, I cried bitter tears all through the night and the next few days until Ulysses returned home from his trip.

As soon as I saw him, I felt strange and sensed a wall between us. Jeane's words came back to me about other women, but I didn't really believe there was any truth to them. Yet she had been right about other things, so how did I know? I was happy he was home, though, for the business was not the same without him. I loved him and didn't ever want to hurt him.

The business picture changed rapidly over the next few days. Blackie and Nick decided to take a third partner and were dividing the restaurants three ways instead of two.

Whenever I had a chance, I checked the constant flow of papers coming into the office about the change in the restaurant ownership. Sometimes I called the lawyer to check on a legal matter, but his advice remained the same.

Then the moment arrived. Papers were given to me to sign and I refused. Blackie was furious and exploded, pouring out angry words at me. I just sat there in my new blue dress, feeling terrible but resolved not to give in. It was true; Blackie could do nothing without my signature.

The day ended with my tears spilling everywhere, many angry words exchanged between us, and with us being more divided than we ever had been in our twenty-one years of marriage. But I won—I was brought in as a full partner. We were equal again as we had been when we first started out so humbly twenty years before.

Jeane was right, I gained respect that day. But I had lost something else—the closeness between my husband and me.

That night, I was awakened in the early hours of the morning. There standing before me was a ghostly apparition, white and shimmering, frightening yet fascinating. I started to scream, but as soon as I sat up in bed, it disappeared. I fell back, wondering what it could mean. Had my association with Jeane brought me into a dark world? I didn't want to think about it and took another sleeping pill.

During the weeks and months following the confrontation with Ulysses, I went through a time of even more confusion and loneliness. My happiness was gone, and little things set my nerves on edge.

My marriage, which had always been the center of my life, was now under tremendous pressure. All the joy had been stripped from it. I was caught up with a desire to see my future spelled out before me. Somehow I had latched onto a compelling, hidden power that seemed to be controlling my destiny and dragging me into strange paths.

It was Jeane who had introduced me to this power, which I thought was from God. I knew I needed God and wanted him back in my life. I wanted to be calm and strong, like Mama had always been.

My thoughts were often on our business. I had won a victory there, but I had lost my close relationship with Ulysses. The unity we had before had been born of travail. Now it was as if we had come to a fork in the road, and he was being pulled one way and I another. Had I done the right thing?

The two-and-a-half years since the first meeting in the Dixon office had been a time of fear, anxiety, and pain. Before Ulysses and I had been united in our struggles, such as not having a lease for many

years. But now that business was prospering, we seemed to be growing further and further apart.

In late March the plans for the new restaurants were taking off. We
were still using the trademark "black" in the names, but each restaurant would sport a different theme. For instance, the Black Beret would
be a book-lined lounge and the Black Tahiti would feature Polynesian
cuisine and dancing. The Black Greco would be a cafeteria, restaurant,
and supper club all in one, depending on the time of day. The new
restaurants would be located near office buildings in the downtown
area to serve the noontime office workers. And they would be close to
Nick's parking lots for convenience and accessibility in the evening.

In the midst of this busy business activity and continued strained
relations with Ulysses, Jeane arranged another luncheon meeting with
me. I hoped that now all my predicted bad experiences were in the past.
It was with real optimism that I left home dressed in the baby-blue
good-luck dress.

At Trader Vic's restaurant the headwaiter spotted me and took me
to Jeane.

"Loulie, we're meeting here today because the timing is right. Do
you remember how I talked to you about timing? I told you before that
when the time came for me to tell you about further changes in your life,
that I would call you. The timing is today! Isn't that exciting?"

She was indeed anxious to tell me something. I sat quietly, hoping
I was prepared to take whatever it was.

"I told you, Loulie, that you would make a move to gain yourself
more respect. You did that—you're more confident now. It shows in
your face and even in the way you walked in here."

She paused, lowered her eyes a few moments, and then startled
me.

"When you walked in here, Loulie, you were surrounded by a brilliant white aura. I see auras around some people. Yours is white and so
bright that I believe that you are under divine guidance. I see you rising
in some field. I don't know what it is, but you can never do it with your
husband. He doesn't like that sort of competition from you."

The waiter then brought us two orders of chicken salad topped
with chunks of pineapple. Just before we began to eat, Jeane said a short
prayer. The fact she said the prayer pleased me and I felt more relaxed.

When we finished eating, her eyes darkened and I felt my pulse increase—something important was coming.

"Loulie, you cannot trust men. They will lie their way out of everything they're guilty of."

"Really? I never quite felt that way."

"That's because you're a naive person. You trust because you are trustworthy." She paused. "You trust your husband, but you shouldn't. He lives a life about which you know nothing. You're alone most evenings, aren't you?"

"That's true."

"When your husband gets lonely, he finds company. He is searching for something. But what he doesn't realize is that he has it all in you. You have done all you can for him—there is nothing more you can do."

I was upset. The conversation had taken a sudden lurch—and her words felt like arrows that pierced my heart.

She was silent for a few moments, then continued. "I told you when I first saw you that there would be changes coming in your future. I don't know the exact timing, perhaps between two and four years from now. However, it's to your advantage that I tell you. Your husband does a good job of taking care of his own needs, but he doesn't try to take care of yours. You've got to be smart and watch everything that you sign, making sure you're always equal with him. Prepare yourself for the move he'll be making.

"There will come a woman in his life who will excite him and he will fall in love with her. He won't want to leave you for her, but she will insist. She will threaten to leave him if he doesn't marry her. When she does this, he will divorce you and marry her. I'll stake my reputation on this. You must prepare yourself for a divorce."

I sat in stunned silence as she continued.

"Soon after your husband is married again he will realize his mistake. I don't see his marriage lasting very long."

I started to speak, but suddenly her mood changed.

"There is great happiness coming into your life. Yes, you should rejoice for you will find happiness with someone else. You'll find someone to love and appreciate you. I'm trying to help you so that you can find this love. You can never be free until your husband leaves you. When he does, you should rejoice."

I knew Jeane felt she was doing me a great favor by foretelling my future, but her words brought me pain to the very center of my being. I was certainly not experiencing the peace of God that Papa was always talking about.

"When will all this happen?" I asked.

"After his marriage fails, he'll realize all the mistakes he's made, and that he really loved only you."

"Then why don't I just tell him everything you've said? Maybe he'd listen and avoid all these things that you say will happen to him."

Her eyes narrowed into thin slits and she tossed her head a little. I sensed that I had somehow violated her trust in me. Suddenly I regretted my words. Jeane was my friend, and with certain people she felt free to communicate her special knowledge.

I tried to make amends. "Jeane, I'm sorry. I'm just worried about my husband. I'd like to be able to help him."

She rested her hand on mine. "Loulie, I realize it will be lonely for you, living with him and knowing all that is going on. It will hurt and you will cry inside. But remember this—you have courage. If I didn't think you were strong I wouldn't have told you. You have to believe it is to your advantage to know."

At that moment I couldn't see any advantage in knowing all this. Suddenly there wasn't anything to hold on to and the tears came, running down my cheeks.

Jeane saw my agony and didn't speak for quite a few moments. Then she closed her eyes and folded her hands, as if in prayer. She began to smile, and leaned forward while whispering, "I just had a vision of your next husband. I saw a tall man next to you. He will not only love you, but he will appreciate you."

She paused, "Oh, he is definitely the right man for you and I would stake my reputation on this also."

I asked her what his name was and she responded at once, naming a very prominent businessman whom I knew well. David was one of our early customers when we first started in business, and was always considerate and kind to me. Her suggestion was not beyond the realm of possibility for he was recently divorced and was admired by many. Jeane saw that something in me responded to her suggestion.

"Loulie, I have told you about David because I truly believe that he is the one for you. In fact, I know it! But you must promise that you will never approach him. I may tell him about you in the proper time, for he has been searching for the right woman. When I tell him, he will know you are the one."

I came away from the luncheon deeply troubled. Though touched by Jeane's concern for me, I knew I was heading for many sleepless nights. Her prophecy of my marriage being doomed had an almost paralyzing effect and I felt trapped. Her words that happiness lay ahead with David were some comfort, but not much. I felt I was on a road I couldn't get off.

21

Still Searching

It was during January 1968 that my faith in Jeane Dixon was shaken. David married someone else. Jeane had been so sure that I would marry him after my husband divorced me, and she had been wrong.

She had an explanation, of course. David told her that he couldn't wait, especially as Jeane couldn't give him the exact timing when I would be available. She added, "He probably wasn't the one for you. But Loulie, I still see a tall, handsome man beside you, one who will love you as you've never been loved."

At that point, my thinking took a turn. If Jeane could be wrong in her prediction about David, then she could be wrong about Ulysses divorcing me. I would try to avoid her. I would also try to spend more time with my husband.

Weeks passed. On the evening of April 4, 1968, I was making my way to the restaurant to meet Ulysses for a quick sandwich and a movie. I was feeling hopeful, for I had told him that I wanted to be with him more in the evenings and we had agreed to go out once a week. To a certain degree I had been able to throw off Jeane's depressing prediction.

I executed a right turn off of Massachusetts Avenue onto Twenty-third Street, just as a newsbreak came on the car radio about a march on Washington. I sighed and turned off the radio. Washington had become a grim stage for demonstrations as the news media projected every incident into the living rooms across the nation and the world.

Once in the restaurant, Sam Changuris, our maître d', greeted me warmly. "It's good to see you," he said with a broad smile.

"Thank you, Sam," I said, returning the warmth. "Looks like business will be good tonight."

"Sure will. It's cherry blossom time, and that always brings in the people. Was the parking lot filled?"

"Just about," I replied.

"I think your husband is in the kitchen with the chef. Shall I tell him you're here?"

"Thanks, Sam, but I'll just mingle with the customers for a while."

Just then I heard a voice exclaiming, "Loulie! You're here!"

It had to be Jeane. No one else called me by that name, and I hadn't seen her for quite some time.

She beckoned me to her table. "Meet Nancy! This is her favorite restaurant. Every time she visits from California, she insists I bring her here. Please join us."

I sat down a bit reluctantly, wondering what would happen to my date with Ulysses.

As we talked, I noticed Jeane was observing me closely. Finally, she said, "You look different. What's new in your life?"

Before I could tell her about the disconcerting presence that seemed to surround me, disturbing my rest, the bell on the United Press news ticker rang.

"We're about to get an important newsflash," I said.

Jeane suddenly grew silent and bowed her head. Seconds later she said, "I knew it this afternoon—it's Martin Luther King! He has been shot. He's been shot in the head."

I sat speechless for a moment, then rose and tore the ticker tape from the cylinder. It read: "Martin Luther King was shot and killed today in Memphis, Tennessee—just after 6:00 by an assassin . . . he was shot in the head."

I was stunned by the news and thought almost immediately that if Jeane could make such a startling prediction as this, maybe she was right about Ulysses and me. I felt a dryness in my throat and dread in my heart as the familiar feeling of being trapped came over me.

I returned and spread the news before her. She put on her glasses and began to read just as Blackie approached the table.

"What's going on?" he asked. "What's the news?"

"It's Martin Luther King!" Jeane said. "He's been shot in the head! I got it psychically this afternoon. I told someone earlier today that this was going to happen."

Blackie leaned over Jeane's shoulder, reading the paper. For a brief moment she looked into his face and then turned slowly to me. A dark, strange look came into her eyes. It was as if she were saying, "I'm also right about you two!" A sharp arrow pierced my heart, and Blackie and I didn't have our date that night.

The next few weeks became known as the riots of 1968 as part of the Fourteenth Street corridor was burned and looted and the National

Guard was called out. A time of sadness, depression, and instability followed, not only in Washington but across the nation. The general mood was reflected in our volume, which was down a good 10 percent.

Jeane's accurate prediction of Martin Luther King's sudden death shook me to the core. It seemed to cement in me the belief that my marriage would end. I longed for peace, but it eluded me. I wanted to find God, but he seemed to be slipping further and further away from me.

In February Ulysses asked me to accompany him to Zurich for his annual board meeting, and I was eager to go with him. And although it was in the middle of the Cold War, we decided also to visit Moscow, which I had always dreamed of seeing.

I packed our clothes for deep winter. I loved to travel and was determined to forget Jeane Dixon and all her predictions and just live for the moment, to be with my husband and enjoy this exciting experience.

From Zurich we flew to the Wien Airport in Vienna, Austria, and there we awaited the departure of Aeroflot Flight 018 to Moscow. All the Russians around us wore fur hats. Several carried bags of whiskey, American cigarettes, and French perfume. One man who wore a brown fur hat and a black armband stood to the side. I noticed his sad eyes.

Flight 018 was delayed, although we could see the Aeroflot jet out on the field. Impatient, Blackie checked at the counter, but they didn't give a reason for the delay. Soon, however, we saw a small taxi drive across the field to the Aeroflot. Someone got out and boarded the plane, and within minutes our flight was announced.

When we finally arrived in Moscow, it was dark as we rode past what seemed to be endless apartment dwellers to the Berlin Hotel. We hurried to the dining room, for we were shivering, tired, and hungry. Seeing that most of the diners were drinking vodka, Blackie asked for the same, and then we ordered salmon, Berlin salad, and caviar.

While waiting to be served, we struck up a conversation with a young American, Tom Miller, who was spending three years going around the world. Together we listened to the orchestra playing American rock and roll and watched the dancers doing the twist—just as we had eight years previously. We began to feel brighter and happier.

Returning to our room, we took a good look around. There was a bath, which I started to run immediately, and a front room with a high ceiling and chandelier. The beds were two small cots, but I liked their firmness.

The bulb in the lamp beside the table was out, so Blackie climbed up on the desk to borrow a ceiling bulb. He couldn't reach it, so he put a table on top of the desk and clambered up. We noticed then that the chandelier was the most attractive thing in the time-worn room.

The next morning Blackie and I stood peering out the window, watching hundreds of people bundled up with scarves, mittens, fur hats, and boots walking briskly down the street. Some were standing in line to shop at the market. Later we realized that every store, restaurant, and public bath had long lines of people outside.

We stopped at the new skyscraper Russian Hotel where there was a dollar store for tourists only. We told our guide that in America, the citizens come first. She replied that Russia needs the foreign currency.

Blackie bought a muskrat hat for $14 and three rabbit fur hats for $8. I asked about Russian sable, and our guide answered with a sniff, "Only the Czar's wife wore sable." But I did find some black-enamel boxes to purchase for gifts. The artists who painted them had been icon painters before the government closed the churches.

When Blackie and I returned to our hotel to dress for dinner, I noticed that it was difficult to see in the mirror. Wondering why, we looked up and saw that the chandelier had been changed. Tom said later that we had monkeyed with the microphone when we changed bulbs. We were glad it was our last night there.

When we flew from Moscow to Paris on Air France, we noted such a contrast from our experiences in Russia. We saw a woman ahead of us trying to give the flight attendant some enlarged American dollar bills. She must have saved the bills in a can for they had rust marks on them. The attendant refused, saying they were outdated, but Blackie bought them from her immediately.

When we returned home, we framed the dollars and placed them at the entrance of Blackie's, a good souvenir to remind us how some have to buy their freedom.

It was the autumn of 1969, one of my favorite times of year. Yellow pumpkins and big red apples were piled high in the marketplaces.

Leaves were a kaleidoscope of gold and red and the cool, fresh air seemed to awaken people's appetites. We continued to be busy at Blackie's and were nearing the end of our five-year expansion of the new restaurants. The Black Crystal and Blackie's Virginia had opened successfully. And the Black Horse Tavern in the Embassy Square hotel had received rave reviews from people who loved the beautiful wood paneling, rich leather, and choice antiques. We were feeding about twenty-five thousand daily throughout "Blackie's Circuit," as we called it, and bringing in around $8 million a year. Our business just kept on booming as I remained tormented about the future.

One day in October I was at Blackie's, bantering with our customers, when I was called to the phone. "Shirley Peike wants to speak to you."

"Jeane has asked me to invite you to accompany her to Los Angeles. She's going to be autographing her new book on reincarnation."

The trip sounded interesting, but I wondered if I should risk another time with her. Hadn't her predictions brought enough turmoil into my life?

Shirley continued, "You'll be leaving next Friday and returning on Monday. By the way, she says to tell you she has a real surprise for you. There's someone important she wants you to meet."

Perhaps Jeane would tell me of good times to come. I was intrigued and told her I'd check it out with Blackie.

When Blackie walked in shortly thereafter, his face was flushed from the chilly air and his hair was a little askew. That little curl that never would stay in place was dangling over his forehead and his brown eyes were shining.

"You waited for me!" he said.

"Yes," I said, returning his smile. "Jeane Dixon has invited me to go to Los Angeles with her next weekend. She's promoting her new book. Do you think I should go?"

He hesitated only a moment as he shuffled through his papers. "It's okay with me."

Then he surprised me by saying, "You remember Mike Mouratidis who was in the office the other day? Well, he says he's stuck with some fur coats. I haven't bought you anything for a long time. Look at the two he has and if you like them, go ahead and get them."

For a moment he looked at me just like in the old days and my heart skipped a beat. I leaned over the big red velvet chair and kissed him on the side of his face and he turned and hugged me in return, holding me closely. It was a much-needed moment and I left the office humming a tune.

On the following Friday morning I felt light and adventurous to be traveling to California with Jeane and her secretary, Alice Braemer. But my joy was short-lived, for as soon as we settled down in the plane, Jeane leaned over and whispered, "I went through my tarot cards last night and I can tell you for sure that the break in your marriage is going to happen soon."

As my heart sank, my mind was in conflict and I was sorry I had come. My relationship with Ulysses was better, and yet here was Jeane saying our marriage would soon be over. This seemed so negative and destructive. Yet I'm sure she thought she was helping me. Indeed I had heard her say over and over, "I am God's instrument to help people."

She also made it clear that she would share the prophecies she received only with those whom she chose to, but after that she would not "carry" that person. Each recipient had to find their own way to deal with her words. I found this difficult, and part of me hoped I could just escape from it all, but I felt a need to be with her that I couldn't explain to anyone.

The day after arriving in California we drove to a large department store where Jeane was to autograph her books. As we breezed along the freeways, I grew nostalgic remembering our wedding at the Marriage Manor and our first year of marriage there in California. Now, twenty-three years later, I wondered what was happening to us.

I tried to put my worries behind me as we entered the large room where hundreds were waiting for Jeane. As she signed her books I watched with fascination. She touched some people to feel their vibrations but others she ignored. Many tried to linger but the push of the people kept the line going. It occurred to me that she was like an idol, and it seemed a little pathetic. I started to wonder what I was doing here.

After the signing was over and we returned to the hotel, Jeane said, "Tomorrow is a very important luncheon. I have placed you next to a world-famous astrologer from London. His specialty is timing. In regard to your divorce, he will tell you 'when.' "

The tone of her voice frightened me a little. Still, being naturally optimistic, I hoped he would come out with something different than Jeane's prediction.

At lunch the next day, the hotel's ballroom was awhirl with beautifully dressed people including many famous movie stars, the most important of whom sat at the head table with Jeane. I noticed the man seated on my left observing me closely. As I turned toward him he touched my arm softly. "My name is Ghandi. I am a special friend of Jeane's. I would very much like to talk to you."

"You must be the one Jeane wanted me to meet."

He half smiled, and said, "The only time I can see you is five o'clock this afternoon. Here's my address." He paused. "Also, please give me your birth date and the exact time of your birth."

"My birthday is October fifth, but as to the exact time of the day, I don't know."

Later, I rapped on Ghandi's door right on time, feeling a little nervous and furtive. I was hoping he would see something good in my marriage, and not a divorce.

Ghandi opened the door and motioned for me to sit in a chair by his desk. He was a short dark man with closely cropped hair and ears that lay flat against his head. It seemed his whole being was surrounded by a strange dim light and I found it very hard to look into his eyes.

He got right to business, pulling out several lined pieces of paper along with a chart with stars and other markings all over it.

"As soon as I saw you today," he began, "I knew we were destined to meet. Let me begin by saying that you have a very interesting life before you. Take October now. This month is nearly over, but I want to show you your 'down' days and your 'up' days. See this date? There you probably had aches and pains in your legs and feet." Then he pointed to a three-day span. "On these days you felt strong and well. Now here you had a real bright day. I put a star on that one."

I was startled. "That was last Thursday when Jeane invited me to come to California and my husband bought me two fur coats."

He smiled smugly. "It's all right here in the stars. Every important move you will ever make is right here. But before I speak to you further, let me look at your palms."

Obediently, I held out my hands for him to examine.

"See, this is your life line. Mmmm—a good long life. And here's your health line. Very good! And here's your marriage line." He scowled and his dark face became even darker. Then he re-examined my left hand and jotted something in his notebook.

"Frankly," he said in his crisp Indian accent, "I can't pinpoint it right now but next year at this time I will be able to tell you the exact day when your husband will tell you that he will leave you."

Not giving me a chance to speak, he continued, "I'm going to be in New York in January. I would like for you to meet me there. Then I will be coming to Washington next September or October. When I'm there I want you to arrange for me to meet with your husband. This will further help me determine exactly when your marriage will break up."

I arranged for a meeting in New York and he gave me the address of a hotel close to Grand Central station. I paid him the two-hundred-dollar fee for the twenty-minute session. He said that he would send me my November chart to guide me through the month, and then a new chart each month following.

When I returned to the hotel, Jeane asked me how the meeting went, saying, "I have placed you in good hands. Ghandi is one of the greatest astrologers in the world. He will help you get through this."

Then she paused, sighing. "I have to turn you over to him because I'm overwhelmed by people and my work. I hope you understand."

I was reflective on the plane ride back to Washington, thinking about the monthly charts the astrologer would send me. I was hoping against hope to hear something positive from him as he mapped out my future. Then a question arose in my mind. Could Jeane and Ghandi be working together? Why were they both so convinced that my marriage would soon be dissolved? Perhaps I should be wary of them both.

But despite my doubts, in January I went to New York as arranged.

Ghandi's office was in a dark and old hotel. He gave me my new astrology chart and told me that he would be coming to Washington in ten months, in October. He made me promise that I would arrange for him to see Blackie so that he could pinpoint the exact time of our breakup. I felt myself slipping further and further into despair. It was as if I had lost that spark that always made me rise up, and as if I had no will of my own.

It was August and nearly a year had passed since my trip to LA with Jeane. I was desperate for the predictions to bring forth something positive, although they never seemed to. But on a warm day at Orly Airport outside of Paris, I turned my thoughts to my family. Dina was dressed in her matching gold and blue coat and dress as we bounced and rode on the moving walkway. We were passing through on our way to Athens.

"Mommy," she exclaimed, "look how fast we can walk!"

I smiled at her, sensing her excitement, for she was anxious to see her brothers, whom we were meeting under the specific instructions of my husband. Gregory, now twenty-one, had been working at the Dorchester Hotel in London after attending the famous Ecole Hotelaire in Lausanne, Switzerland. This was the same hotel school that Conrad Hilton's son had attended. Ulysses II, who no longer wanted to be called BJ, was seventeen and had just finished his freshman year at Maret School in Washington.

Blackie, being a strong Greek father, was wary of the developing drug scene and detested rock music. Pot, we discovered, was no longer just a thing to cook in and Mary Jane didn't stand for an innocent young girl. We knew the meaning of "Raindrops Keep Fallin' on my Head" but were shocked to learn that "Lucy in the Sky with Diamonds" glorified LSD.

Blackie was determined to remove Ulysses from this scene, where many young people were protesting Vietnam, going on peace marches, and defying authority. Thus he had convinced Gregory to go to Athens for the summer to be with Ulysses and to oversee the opening of a new restaurant along with Juan, a partner of Blackie's. My assignment was to assist them in finding an apartment and to enroll Ulysses in the American Community School just outside Athens.

When Dina and I arrived and I saw the unhappy faces of my sons, I knew my trip to Greece would center on trying to bring harmony to our family. We had rented a cabin by the sea, not far from Athens, so the boys could snorkel, swim, and go boating when off from work.

The next morning Dina and I enjoyed a walk on the beach and a swim in the cool, clear water before her brothers arrived. Gregory and Ulysses came around eleven, dragging in their snorkeling equipment.

For a while we ate our late breakfast, enjoying the food and each other. Then Gregory asked, "What's going on? Why did Dad decide to open up a restaurant—was it just so that he could send us here and get us out of the way?"

"Oh no," I responded. "Juan is a friend of your Father's who married a young Greek girl from Athens. She just couldn't adjust to life in Washington so Juan begged Dad to set him up a restaurant here. Your dad agreed."

Ulysses asked, "Did Dad check him out? We think he's stealing."

"Stealing!" I exclaimed.

"Yes, stealing," Gregory replied. "We're keeping our eyes on him, and if we get the goods on him, we're taking him to court."

As I tried to digest this, Ulysses fixed his eyes on me and asked, "Is it true that I can't go home to get my car and return to my school?"

The pent-up hurt and anger came bursting out, and his voice broke. He had already been in Athens since late June, and I sensed he was getting tired of it. The only thing I could do was to give him a straight answer.

"Sorry, Ulysses. Your father wants me to arrange for the two of you to find an apartment and to enroll you in the American School."

Greg chimed in, "And I suppose that means I can't go back to my job in London either."

I nodded, saying, "Dad wants you here to oversee the restaurant."

Deeply upset, they reared up from the table, giving Dina a brush of a kiss and stumbling over their snorkeling equipment as they left. We could hear the roar of the motor as they took off, leaving Dina crying. A precious moment had been shattered.

At the beginning of the third week, Dina and I grew tired of the sun and the water. Missing city life, we drove to Athens and checked into the Hilton. A few days later, we met the boys at the new restaurant. With them was our friend Mike Mouratidis.

"Mike," I exclaimed, "How good to see you!"

"And you too," he said, giving us a kiss.

He chuckled a bit as he said, "Do you know what your sons did? They followed Juan home last night, putting socks across their license plates so that he wouldn't recognize the car. Turns out Juan has been living in a grand house and even has a Mercedes! It doesn't seem he's been putting your money toward the restaurant. We've hired a lawyer and are taking Juan to court."

When the day in court came, I went along, although I couldn't understand the high Greek being spoken. As bribes were rampant we weren't too surprised when the case was settled with both sides losing. Although the evidence seemed clear, we didn't get our money back. So effectively Juan got away with it.

When it came time for Ulysses to enroll at the American School, he wouldn't let me go with him, saying he could handle it himself. I knew he was still upset about not being able to return to Washington. Meanwhile Gregory had enrolled in a Greek language school. They had found a large, furnished apartment in Kolonaki and now were all set, so my daughter and I returned to Washington.

Once home, Dina and I were on our way to buy her school wardrobe when the phone rang. It was Myrtle, calling from San Diego. After a few pleasantries, she got to the point.

"Louie, I have some bad news. It's Maria—she's very ill. If you want to see her alive, you'd better come right now."

"No one told me she was sick."

"Well, it happened so quickly. She found out a few months ago that she had colon cancer. When they operated, it had spread all over."

My heart deeply troubled, I left Dina with her father and Carmen, her nanny, and took the first available plane to San Diego. There to meet me was Myrt. As we hugged each other, she said, "Maria is close to the end. I think we should go directly to the hospital," she said.

When we arrived there, I checked to make sure I had brought the autographed book by Jeane on reincarnation. I hoped to explain to Maria that she would soon be coming back in a different body and not to worry. I also had a pearl and ruby bracelet to give her.

We walked into her hospital room and saw Maria, who was propped up on pillows. She had lost all of her lovely hair and was wearing a brown wig. Her beautiful eyes lit up as we came into the room. They were large and luminous, yet filled with peace. And her face, so thin and so fragile, was radiant.

I said to myself, "How can she be so peaceful?"

We embraced, so glad to see each other. I loved her dearly, remembering how calm and wise she had always been. Staring at her, I recalled that time years before in our Mankato home when I was just twelve years old. She had looked across the dining room table and said, not sadly, "I'm going to die young one day—for a purpose."

I didn't answer her then because I couldn't understand what she meant and she probably didn't either. And now here she was, barely fifty.

As I hugged her, I shuddered at how thin and fragile she was. "What happened?" I asked.

"I don't know. I was feeling a little tired and then I noticed blood. By the time I got to the doctor, it was too late. But don't worry. I'm going to a far better place."

"What do you mean?"

"You know, heaven!"

"Heaven? Maria, I brought you Jeane Dixon's book on reincarnation. She explains all about what happens. You'll be coming back!"

I took the book and the bracelet from my purse and put the book beside her bed while attempting to put the bracelet on her wrist.

She took one look at Jeane's book and threw it on the floor. She thanked me for the bracelet and then very gently asked me to sit in the chair close to her. As she looked into my eyes and held my hands, she said softly, "Where I'm going, the gates are made of pearls. The streets are all gold. I have no need of this bracelet. You keep it."

She coughed then and I could see how weak she was. She pressed the bracelet back into my hand and drew me closer. Her beautiful shining eyes met mine. "Remember this! Man has once to die and then the judgment. You need Jesus."

Saying this took great effort and I had to help her lay back on the pillows. She released my hand and grimaced in pain.

The nurse came then, for it was already time for us to go. I looked back at her on the bed. Her eyes were closed and she was pale and extremely weak. I was sorry that she hadn't wanted the book or the bracelet. It seemed I wasn't any help to her.

Most of my immediate family were waiting for me downstairs. I joined Myrtle and Weldon, Hazel and Arnie, Bertha and Jay, and Chris and Lorna in the cafeteria.

I hadn't seen any of them for quite a few years. They were all my family but I had moved so far away from them—and not only in terms of geography. Consequently there was a little strangeness between us. I sat rather quietly, for Maria's words had made a stunning impression on me.

Chris was now a Pentecostal minister. His children with Hurler's syndrome had lived much longer than expected—Darlene had died in late 1964 at the age of twenty-three, and Dale died shortly thereafter. Doctors said that their lives had been extended because they had received so much love. Chris asked, "Well, Louie, where have you been gallivanting this year and what have you been doing?"

"Well, I just returned from a month in Athens and when I go back home, I'll return to work. Our restaurant business is still really growing."

Unimpressed, he asked, "But what have *you* been doing?"

"Well, I've been studying."

"Studying what?"

"I'm a friend of Jeane Dixon and she's introduced me to astrology, reincarnation, the works of Edgar Cayce, and so on. We shouldn't be so worried about Maria—she'll be back."

"Be back?" he asked with alarm.

"Sure. Edgar Cayce says that's what 'born again' means. He explains that a person is born again and again until they reach perfection."

Chris had an incredulous expression on his face as he looked at me in disbelief. "Reincarnation! This is what you've been studying!"

He stared at me in shocked amazement for a while and then began to laugh. He laughed so hard, in fact, that he fell off his chair. When he pulled himself together, he said with empathy and a touch of compassion, "You are the most completely lost person I have ever seen."

My pride reared, and I said, "At least half the people in this country are lost then." I thought to myself, "Chris, in that cloistered world of yours, what do you know?" Our conversation ended and family activities took over.

Soon thereafter my sister died, but her words to me would not.

On the way back to Washington, Maria's words haunted me. I had almost forgotten how to pray. I did believe in God—but Jesus! He seemed so outdated. I hadn't thought much about him since I was a child.

But on the following Thursday, when I was driving Blackie to his weekly board meeting for the Madison National Bank, the idea came to me to stop in at St. Matthews Cathedral. Once inside the beautiful brick building I wandered about, seeing many places to light candles.

I finally lit one right in front of the statue of Mary holding the baby Jesus. Placing the candle in the slot, I knelt and prayed, "Jesus, my sister says I need you. Please help me. Please show me who you are."

I meant the prayer from my heart. If indeed this Jesus did listen to people, then maybe he would hear me. I couldn't think of anything else to say, except to thank him for hearing me. I put money in the poor box and left. I repeated this prayer many times that month.

22

A New Joy

WE HAD FINISHED THE FIVE-YEAR EXPANSION of the new restaurants by the autumn of 1970. The Black Rooster Pub was a hit with its British ales, pub sandwiches, and dart boards. The Black Circus was also promising, especially because of the offbeat entertainment we were planning. We hosted the internationally known guitarist Charlie Byrd in early 1971 and were looking forward to featuring a new trio, "The Runners," better known as Washington Redskins runningbacks Henry Dyer, Charley Harraway, and Larry Brown.

Of the new restaurants, the Black Ulysses was one of the larger ones, seating nearly four hundred in its various rooms. The name came about when Blackie and I drove by the building site with Dina. When Blackie and I were discussing what we should call the restaurant, Dina asked, "Why not Ulysses?" We agreed with her, and made the Black Ulysses an authentic Greek restaurant, hiring Gus Balourdos from Ithaca, Greece, as our chef. We had fun highlighting the Greek theme, and even had a welcoming card at each table that said: "We have endeavored to bring a typical Athenian Restaurant to Washington. In doing so we have allowed organized confusion and disorganization to permeate at the Ulysses."

Back at our flagship, Blackie's House of Beef, we were approaching our twenty-fifth year. We were planning on celebrating by lowering the price of our prime rib dinner from $4.75 to $2.95 for the month before Thanksgiving.

As we were making these anniversary plans, the day came on October 7, 1971, for the meeting between Blackie and Ghandi. I stationed myself close to the front desk so I could keep my eye out for Ghandi. When he arrived, I escorted him upstairs.

After their meeting, I went up to the office, somewhat leery of what Blackie might say and wondering if he'd be angry.

"That guy!" he said, shaking his head.

"What do you mean?"

"Well, he's pretty good. He hit the nail on the head many times."

I wondered what he meant by that as I made my way to my own appointment. Once there, he got down to business immediately, seeming immensely pleased with himself. "I have mapped out your husband's chart as well as yours. I now can give you the date when he is going to tell you."

I sighed and sunk into a chair. "Did you talk to him about me?"

"I can't tell you that, but here is the date. It is the Sunday after Thanksgiving at precisely four o'clock in the afternoon."

I mentally figured out that I had about seven weeks to go.

He said, "We have to get busy."

"Get busy?"

"Yes, you must make sure you get most of everything." Now he really was excited. "We can beat the drums—that comes from ancient Egypt. If we beat the drums, you can get nearly everything."

His words really upset me. "I don't want you to beat any drums. I don't want most of everything. I want only what is fair."

Ghandi noticed my change in mood and said, "I'm going to prove to you how right I am. I told your husband this and now I am going to tell you. Exactly at one P.M. on Monday after the first week in November, Blackie will fly into a terrible rage. You'll see it, and when you do, you'll believe and know that I am right."

I paid him four hundred dollars and left.

I felt really depressed, thinking how my life had lost all zest and meaning.

That night I had a vivid dream in which I was at my church, St. Sophia Greek Orthodox Cathedral. I looked around and everyone in the congregation, including Father John, was yawning. Just then I dropped my diamond wedding ring. After picking it up, I held it up to the light and saw such beauty—a lovely house with bright flowers and a lush green lawn. The dream seemed to say that if I didn't give up, in the end I would see great beauty. It stayed vividly before me, strengthening me to keep going.

A few weeks later my friend of many years, Janet Ballas, called me. I hadn't spoken to her for quite a while, so we decided to meet for coffee.

We embraced, and Janet said, "I'm so sorry to hear about your sister. How are you taking it?"

"Okay, I guess." I looked down at my coffee and was quiet.

Janet paused and asked, "How's Jeane Dixon? Have you seen her lately?"

"Yes, indeed. I even went to California with her awhile ago . . . I guess it's been a year already."

"How did that go?" she asked, with a suspicious tone in her voice.

"Oh, we had a great time. She introduced me to a world-famous astrologer."

"Astrologer!" Janet exclaimed.

"Yes, he has been uncannily right about everything."

Her look was incredulous. "Why have you gone so far away from your parents' faith—from your roots?"

"Janet, you just don't understand!"

"Don't understand! Look, I used to know you when you were just a normal person. Remember that far back? Now, you're off somewhere, living in the future. What ever happened to the 'now' of life? Why don't you turn your back on all that stuff and walk away?"

How could I make her understand that I was not free to walk away? It was as if I was caught in a web, and every attempt to get out of it just brought more frustration. I was falling deeper and deeper and there didn't seem to be any way out. Talking about it didn't help.

Janet and I parted quickly.

The first weekend in November, Ulysses and I spent the weekend in Ocean City with friends. On Monday morning we drove back to Washington, arriving at Blackie's at exactly 12:45. We were all in good humor.

Inside I was rejoicing. Ghandi had predicted that on this day at exactly one P.M. my husband would fly into a terrible rage. It just wasn't going to happen, I told myself.

Together we went up to the office and ordered roast beef sandwiches, coleslaw, and iced tea and coffee. Just before the food was served, Mary buzzed, telling Blackie he had a telephone call. It was our real-estate agent, Mike Zarpas.

As Blackie listened his face began to turn red and he swore.

"Akers knew I was assembling that property for my hotel. He had no business buying that piece right in the middle! What good is that one piece going to do him?"

He banged down the phone, his face contorted in anger, and let fly a stream of profanity.

I looked at my watch—one P.M.

As Thanksgiving approached, I became more and more despondent even as business at the restaurant was booming. Our anniversary special had hit a nerve, and we were serving two thousand people on a Saturday night. We decided to extend the special through the end of the year.

Even as I surveyed the crowds, I dreaded the upcoming confrontation with Ulysses after Thanksgiving. Ghandi had been right about the rage at one o'clock, so I believed he'd also be right about Sunday at four. I began to become obsessed with that date, and couldn't get it out of my mind.

Before the holiday, Ulysses suggested, "Why don't we go to the beach house for Thanksgiving? Let's get out of here—just the three of us.

Dina was delighted. She was hoping to run and play on the shore and collect shells. We usually enjoyed the beach so much, but this weekend I couldn't take in the quiet beauty because of the dreaded deadline. My legs felt like lead, my heart was heavy, and my nerves were on edge.

Thanksgiving dinner was delicious and we rested on both Thursday and Friday. Late Saturday morning we heard a rap on the door downstairs. It was Richard, an old friend. He seemed lonely, and I was glad to welcome him.

I made lunch for the four of us, preparing cold turkey sandwiches with cranberry sauce on pumpernickel bread. We finished up the pumpkin pie, topped with vanilla ice cream. While serving the coffee and cleaning up the kitchen, I could hear Richard say to Ulysses, "You know, when I got the divorce I thought that everything was going to be wonderful. But it isn't. I miss my kids. And how do I know what my next wife will be like? I don't like dating all these strangers. I guess that the simple life of marriage is best after all."

Ulysses was silent.

That night, Ulysses fell asleep in bed watching the news. I turned off the television and lay down next to him. All was quiet, except for the pounding of the surf and the beating of my heart. "This is my last night with him," I lamented. "Tomorrow at four he'll tell me that he's going to leave."

I leaned over and kissed him lightly, barely touching his gray-black hair. Tears ran down my cheeks and I buried my face in the pillows to quiet my sobs. For nearly five years I had endured the bondage of seeking the future. I had been tortured with the thoughts that the predictions would come true while desperately hoping they wouldn't. Now in just a few more hours it would be over.

As I couldn't sleep, I got up and pulled a robe about me and walked out on the small terrace overlooking the ocean, shivering from the damp air. Too cold to stay outside, I went back to bed. Another hour went by and the clock read one A.M.

"I can do nothing," I murmured. I stuffed my hand in my mouth to keep from crying out while my tears soaked the pillow.

Somehow I made it through the night, and after breakfast we cleaned the house, getting ready to leave. Dina was fussing, unhappy about having to return to the city. My mind was only on the clock. We left at 2:30—an hour and a half to go, I thought silently.

As we rode along, there was a profound silence in the car. Dina had fallen asleep in the back seat with Raggedy Ann in her arms. I sighed, wondering how a divorce would affect her.

At a few minutes to four, Blackie pulled over to the side of the road. My mouth felt dry from tension, but all he said was, "You drive."

This was so unexpected—he was always the one to drive on the highway.

"All right," I answered, sliding across to the driver's seat.

There were just a few moments to go. "Here it comes," I thought. "But why does he want me driving?"

Exactly at four o'clock, he reached over and turned on the radio—to Oral Roberts. Oral's message was on the problem of broken homes and divorce. I couldn't believe the timing and relevance to our situation.

Ulysses didn't say a word. For the first time I could ever remember, he listened to the hour-long preaching and music without switching it off.

Instead of feeling a great sense of relief, I felt stunned. So much of my emotion and energy had been projected toward this four P.M. hour, but it hadn't happened. Ghandi had staked his reputation on it and I had suffered so much preparing for it—and it hadn't happened!

I felt a sudden oppression come upon me; it was as if I had slipped into total darkness. During the days that followed, this blackness would not leave me. I watched over Dina's school routine, tried to care for the house, and do everything needed at the restaurant, but the dark cloud hung over me wherever I went. I lacked all enthusiasm for living.

A week later, I drove Blackie to Madison National Bank for his board meeting and once again stopped off at St. Matthews Cathedral. There I knelt in front of the statue.

"Jesus, I feel so lost and alone. Please help me get out of this black hole I'm in." I put more dollars than usual in the poor box and left.

Although darkness had settled on me like a tent, Christmas was near and I had Dina to consider. I pushed myself to get through the holiday.

Then on the day before Christmas, we received a call from a friend, Angelo Puglisi, who reported seeing Ulysses and Gregory in a nearby hotel. We called them, and they were eager to come home. Having had their fill of Athens, they had saved their money and bought their own tickets. Blackie was upset with them at first, but we both were impressed with their creativity and resourcefulness. Besides, it was Christmas and we were so glad to see them.

After New Year's, when everyone was asleep, I arose quietly and sat alone in my dressing room. Feeling as if I were sinking deeper and deeper into darkness, I looked at all the stuff I had been so engrossed in. Astrology—that had failed. Jeane Dixon—a strange woman, seemingly loving, yet totally obsessed by her own predictions and trying to play God. Edgar Cayce's books—I couldn't even understand now what I saw in them.

I thought in the beginning that I was reaching God through all this stuff, but it didn't lead me to him.

A couple days later, the phone rang. It was Jeane Dixon.

"Loulie, how have you been?"

"Just fine," I lied.

"I'm leaving for Hawaii tomorrow. Can we have lunch today? Tomorrow is my birthday but I really want to celebrate it today with you. Tomorrow I'll be on the plane."

Without enthusiasm, I agreed to meet her. We ate at the Black Tahiti, and it was a strained lunch. We both knew something had changed. As I looked across at her, I thought, "What am I doing with this woman? She might mean well, but what have I to do with her?"

I tried to listen to what she was saying, but her words no longer made any impression on me. We sat silently as if there was nothing more to talk about. I didn't tell her of Ghandi's failure, for it didn't seem to matter anymore. We kissed each other goodbye, both knowing that a change had occurred in our relationship.

That night when I fell asleep I had two vivid dreams. In the first a woman who looked just like Maria appeared before me like ashes rising from an ashtray. She stood right before my face, saying, "You must come over here. Your dad needs you."

I said, "I will—I'll come."

I awoke then with thoughts of suicide. When I fell asleep again, I saw a skeleton sitting in my car. It was beckoning me to come with a bony finger.

I snapped, almost audibly. "I'm coming, I'm coming. Don't rush me!"

I remained awake for the rest of the night. I thought of Blackie's new bottle of sleeping pills—the perfect way out. Tomorrow, though, I would go to work and settle some things. Maybe I'd make out a will and give some of my friends the little articles they liked. Then tomorrow evening I would just go to sleep forever. It would be a fitting ending to these last five years of torment and pain.

I wanted to look extra special that Tuesday, January 5, 1971, for it was to be my last personal appearance. It was a busy day at Blackie's and there were many people to talk to.

Around 12:30 the assistant manager approached me. "Two lovely-looking women are asking to see you. They're in the Boot Hill room."

I peaked through the doorway and recognized Windsor Elliott, a former Vogue model I had met a year before. She had tried to tell me about her religious conversion but I hadn't been interested. Now she was asking to see me again. Because this was my last day I wanted to be kind, so I went to her table and she introduced me to her friend Ruth McBride.

We started talking and they asked about my life, seeming genuinely to care. They had a gentle air about them. Their eyes resembled deep pools of peace, just like Maria's. To my surprise I found myself telling them about my dreams from the night before, leaving out only my plans for that very evening. I also mentioned some of the things that Jeane Dixon and Ghandi had predicted.

Ruthie remarked, "It sounds like you've really been searching."

"Yes", I said, "I suppose I have."

She paused for a moment and then continued gently, "Lou, I know you've been looking for God. I know you're sincere. But you are not going about it the right way." Both women were looking at me and their eyes were kind and loving.

She continued, "There are two spiritual territories. One is good, the other evil. The evil one pretends to be good, but it isn't. It is full of fear and darkness and it's like a trap. Once you're in it you can't get out. It belongs to Satan, who is real, even if you don't think he is. The other realm, which is much more powerful, belongs to God. His arena is full of light and truth. He's the one who can give you peace."

Pausing again, Ruthie gave me a long look. I was fascinated by what she had said but felt a little uncomfortable under her steady gaze.

"Lou," she said, "You've wandered into the wrong camp."

Suddenly it seemed very noisy in the restaurant. Ruthie asked, "Can we talk somewhere where it's quiet?"

"A friend of mine has an apartment nearby and she's out of town," I replied. "I have a key so we could meet over there. I can't get away until just before three—could we meet then?"

Windsor shook her head. "I'm terribly sorry, but I'm going to Europe tomorrow for three months and I haven't even begun to pack..." She trailed off abruptly.

I caught Ruthie looking purposefully at Windsor. "Lou," Ruthie said, "I'm sure we'll be able to meet you at three." Later on I learned that she had kicked Windsor under the table because she felt that it was so important to talk with me.

Later, at the apartment, when we were all seated comfortably and sipping tea, Windsor told me her story. She had been a Vogue cover girl, earning a six-figure salary modeling in New York and Paris. While engaged to a French baron, she went with him to a party at the apartment of his friend, Salvador Dali. Scores of Paris's glittering "Who's Who" were there, and in the center of the room pacing restlessly among the guests was a magnificent cheetah on a long, gold chain.

"As I watched the cheetah," Windsor said, "I noticed that he had been declawed and detoothed, and I realized that this graceful, strong animal had become a tragic caricature of what he'd been created to be. I studied the guests as they moved restlessly from one fleeting conversation to the next and was struck by the parallel. Somehow, I thought, *we too* have become tragic caricatures of what we were created to be.

"I flew back to New York the next day determined to search for answers to the flood of questions the party had opened up."

As Windsor continued, I learned that when she was home in her upper East Side apartment she did something that she had never done before—she flipped open her mother's Bible and was riveted by the first words she read: "For what does it profit a man if he gain the whole world and lose his own soul?"

Windsor said, "I felt like I had been shot through the heart. That sentence summed up my dilemma exactly."

Later, when she was visiting a friend on Long Island, she was invited to watch the Billy Graham Crusade being televised from Madison Square Garden. Billy was preaching on John 3, Jesus saying that we must be born again. She was convinced by what she heard, and particularly the need to be born again—not physically of course, but spiritually. She heard Billy talk of God's love. That God sent his only son to die for us. That his son, Jesus, did die, and then rose from the dead. She heard and put her faith in God. Her spirit was made alive and she became a follower of Jesus Christ.

As Windsor was speaking I glanced quickly from her to Ruthie. The same look of peace that I had seen before was still there. I carried on listening, fascinated by the story.

"I felt I needed to pursue the one thing that mattered," Windsor said, "So to the surprise of my agent and friends, I left modeling and closed my New York apartment."

As Windsor spoke, I set my tea aside and wondered how she could step away from such success. She continued by telling me of her move to Washington, D.C., where she had discovered a thriving network of young professionals whose faith was central to their lives. They worked in law, on Capitol Hill, or in the arts, and although they worshiped in many different churches, a common bond held them together.

Windsor wanted to open the doors of this world to other young professionals who struggled with the hollowness she'd felt so keenly that night in Paris, so that they too could know Jesus. She rented a small embassy, which she called Trinity House, and began hosting dinner parties and guest speakers.

When she finished I said, "God may have changed you, but I don't think he can help me." I thought to myself that nobody could help me, and that I was hopelessly stuck.

Windsor replied, "Lou, this goes back to what Ruthie was saying in the restaurant. You wandered into the demonic camp. You have been dabbling in the dark side of the supernatural, in the realm of the occult. Getting into this realm always leads toward destruction and the death of the soul."

"Occult?" I asked. I was horrified at the thought.

Windsor continued, "The word occult means hidden knowledge. I know you didn't know what you were doing, but through the astrology, tarot cards, psychic phenomena, and the other things that you told us you were involved in, you've opened the door for demonic forces to guide and shape your future."

I was shocked by her words. I didn't like the sound of this at all. I protested, "But Jeane Dixon believes in God. She prays all the time. And she goes to church."

"She's sadly deceived," Windsor continued. "In the Bible God warns his children to beware of the *curse* of the occult, especially astrology and psychic phenomenon. The occult acts like a lure that draws you in to greater and greater darkness.

"You have been around those who use all of the right words and seem to be messengers of God but they're counterfeits. They mix God-talk with deadly evil, many times unwittingly. They often believe they are helping people, while all the time they are opening them up to be destroyed."

As Windsor spoke, my emotions were in turmoil. Tenseness settled across my shoulders.

"Lou," Windsor's voice was gentle, "Tell me. Did good come out of your relationships with these people and the things you did? Did they bring you peace and freedom or did you feel oppressed?"

I thought of Jeane once more. She was a friend who said she wanted to help me. But the result was negative as she steered me toward astrology, reincarnation, séances, and people like Ghandi. I remembered the darkness and despair that had settled over me, and the feeling that I couldn't escape from the road I was on.

Before I answered I had to ask a question. "What about reincarnation?"

Ruthie reached for her Bible and read Hebrews 9:27, "Man has once to die, and then the judgment." The same scripture that my beloved Maria had quoted!

Ruthie spoke again, "Lou, Satan has death as his final goal, but God always wants to lead us into life. He has wonderful plans for us. He doesn't want to hurt or destroy us. He brings hope and gives us a future—he gives us the way out."

The way out! That's what I had been looking for all the time—the way out!

I remained silent and thought about my plan to take the sleeping pills that night, then realized they couldn't be God's way out. But I still wasn't sure that anyone could help me. Then I remembered Mama's words, "I have placed you in God's hands." I recalled all the prayers I had lifted to Jesus in St. Matthew's Cathedral. Was this his answer?

As I thought about Jesus, my beautiful children came to mind. I never wanted to hurt or leave them. Could Windsor and Ruthie's words be true? I looked into Windsor's eyes and asked, "Could Jesus really help me?"

"Yes, he can," she replied. "I promise you. Just as he changed my life, I know that he can change yours." She paused and then asked gently, "Would you like to pray?"

An inner battle seemed to rage inside me for several moments. The tension in my shoulders increased. I wanted to be free of everything that had dragged me down for the last five years, like the predictions that left me scared and depressed. Could Jesus do this? I realized I really didn't want to take those sleeping pills tonight—I wanted to live! I said, "Yes, go ahead, let's pray. But I don't know what to say."

Windsor's lovely face grew soft. "We could pray the main things and you could pray after us and add whatever you'd like in your own words."

She reached out and took my hand and I prayed along with her: "Father, I come to you in Jesus' name. I am sorry for my sins and that I wandered into the occult to try to find my future. Forgive me, and please come into my heart and live your life in me. I accept your sacrifice for my sins. I renounce the devil and all of his works. Please show me your plans for my life."

As I prayed an indescribable peace came over me. The tension lifted. Tears of gratitude poured down my cheeks. In the space of a moment, I felt completely changed.

"Windsor! Ruthie!" I exclaimed through my tears. "What's happened? I was heading one direction just a few moments ago, and now I feel all new!"

"It says in Scripture that when anyone is joined to Christ he is a new being: The old is gone, the new has come." Ruthie was beaming with joy and excitement as she spoke. "Your sins have been forgiven, Lou. You feel different because you've been 'born again.' Your spirit has been made alive by the Spirit of God living in you."

"I can hardly believe this is happening to me," I said.

"And now," Ruthie continued, her face shining, "Jesus lives inside you and you have a relationship with both him and God the Father. Does Jesus ever love you!"

Suddenly I remembered the church meetings that had been held in our home in Mankato. I remembered hiding upstairs while they were all singing in the front room. The words of one song came flooding back.

"There is power, power, wonder working power/in the precious Blood of the Lamb."

Again I felt peace flood over me like a warm blanket. I realized that this is what I'd always been searching for. I felt so different—as though I was back to the real me!

More memories came flooding back. "Ruthie, Windsor, did I tell you that my mother was a Christian and prayed for all us children? And when I was twelve I went to a Baptist Bible camp. The minister asked all who wanted to receive Christ to raise their hands, and I raised mine. Could it be that Jesus has been with me through all of this stuff, and that he was just waiting for me to get to the end of myself?"

I paused for a moment to wipe my eyes. "I wanted to step out of all of this—the astrology, fortune telling, and everything else—but I couldn't. It was as if I were entangled in a web."

Windsor answered, "You *were* caught in a web. And Jesus is the only name in heaven or earth that is powerful enough to set you free. 'If the Son sets you free, you will be free indeed.'"

"It all seems so foolish now," I said. "How did I get so involved in all of this darkness? Papa would've been very disappointed."

Ruthie then said, "Lou, there's something you must do when you get home. You must burn all the occult books, your astrology charts, all Edgar Cayce material, and everything you have been studying. All of Jeane Dixon's books. Burn all your good-luck charms and trinkets and buddhas and anything that has to do with the occult."

I agreed, and they left me with a scripture to learn and meditate on: "Greater is he who is in me [the Lord Jesus] than he who is in the world [Satan]" (1 John 4:4).

How I rejoiced as I drove home to the house where I had left in such despair just a few hours before. As I walked in, I exclaimed: "Wow, this house is mine! Now I can enjoy it—it all looks so different!"

The flowers on the table were beautiful and fragrant. Lifting up my hands and singing, I told the Lord it was his house.

Then I ran outside to find Dina and her friend Evy. Dina's blue eyes were bright and her cheeks were red from the cool air. I hugged her close, praying silently, "Lord, she is your little girl. I give her to you." I hugged Evy, too, and promised to pray for her.

Another old song came to mind: "Amazing grace, how sweet the sound/that saved a wretch like me." As I sang, tears of joy rolled down my face. I had never felt so free.

Ulysses came home around nine P.M., much earlier than usual. I fixed his dinner and brought it up to our bedroom. Bubbling over, I tried to tell him what had happened to me, but he was hungry and wanted to watch the news. Seeing him so engrossed, I realized that just as I couldn't talk with him about the psychic world before, now I couldn't talk to him about Jesus either. So I began to pray for him.

When everyone was asleep, I went to the bookshelves in my dressing room and gathered up everything that spoke of the occult. I carried it all downstairs and lit a fire in the fireplace, singing all the while. Into the fire went the Edgar Cayce books. Then I lifted up my astrology charts, I said, "Thank you, Lord, that I don't have to live by this horrible stuff anymore! I'm going to live in the 'now' of life, not in the future."

As I tore up Jeane Dixon's books, I said a prayer for her. I destroyed all of the good-luck charms I could find.

As I watched everything burn I said, "This was the devil's plan to destroy me, but you, Lord, have your plans for me. Whatever they are, I promise you that I will follow them to the best of my ability."

Then I thought of the blue good-luck dress that was hanging in my storage closet. Creeping up the three flights of stairs to the attic, I removed it, then quietly opened the front door and threw it into the trash can. When I came back inside, it was as if the house sighed with relief.

About a week later, my joy was gone. Just like that, the dark feelings were back. With Windsor in Europe, I called Ruthie at Trinity House.

"I have been gloriously happy but lately strange things have been happening to me."

"Like what?" she asked.

"I'm being dragged down again. I feel a weight upon my head. Sometimes it's hard to say the name of Jesus."

She sounded concerned as she said, "I'd like to see you, Lou, and I'd like you to meet a friend of mine. He's an expert at praying for people who have been in the occult so that they get completely free. Can you come over this afternoon?"

I agreed to be there at three o'clock.

All that day, as I drove the car and then later as I went about my work in the restaurant, I kept repeating, "Greater is he who is in me than he who is in the world."

While at work, my mind was bombarded with thoughts against going to Trinity House. Instead, I had a strong desire to go shopping. When it was nearly three o'clock I decided to skip my meeting.

Just then I was called to the phone. It was Ruthie, wanting to confirm our meeting.

"No, I don't think I'm going to come."

"What do you mean?" she asked.

"Well, I'm all right and I don't want to trouble you. Also, I have some important shopping I must do."

"I want to see you, Lou; I think it's important. Please come."

It was 3:15 when I rapped on the door of Trinity House. Ruthie and Charles were waiting. I began to shake and grew very cold. To my surprise I wanted to flee but I kept repeating, "Greater is he who is in me than he who is in the world."

Charles explained that by giving my life to Jesus I belonged to him. However the lingering effects of the demonic activity in my life had to be cleaned up.

His words reminded me of buying the Sea-Land Tavern so long ago. When we signed the papers it was ours, but it needed a thorough cleaning and remodeling before it was ready for business. I smiled at the memory.

Charles then asked me to think of anyone I needed to forgive. I replied that to the best of my ability I forgave everyone and promised to continue to forgive if I remembered painful incidents from my past. I also asked God to forgive me for getting involved in spiritual things that were not of him.

Then we prayed. Charles asked the Lord to set me free from everything that was trying to bring me down or destroy me, as well as from all the effects of being involved unwittingly in the occult. As soon as we said, "Amen," I felt different. It was as though I had just gone through a carwash where I had been soaped and scrubbed and had come out the other side all clean and shiny! Ruthie quoted the scripture that summed up the feeling exactly, "If the Son sets you free, then you will be free indeed."

A flood of relief washed over me. I began to thank God for his goodness. And to think—I had nearly gone shopping!

As the days went on I endured times that were difficult, when I felt oppressed. But when I said the name of Jesus I knew that I was free. I was also benefiting from meeting new brothers and sisters in Christ. Ruthie took me to various Bible study meetings where I learned the importance of prayer and studying God's word, and she also introduced me to well-known Christian leaders. Sharing my story with others was an exhilarating and liberating experience, and I realized how profoundly grateful I was to those through whom I had passed literally from death to life.

When Jeane returned from Hawaii, she called and asked if we could have lunch. I hesitated, but decided to go. I thought that perhaps if I shared my experiences with her, I could help her get out of the occult.

We met at our Black Beret restaurant. As I walked down the stairs, I could see Jeane sitting with two priests. I was a bit surprised, but kept my resolve to tell her about my conversion. In the past she would always have something to say to me, but this time I wanted to do the talking.

As I sat down and listened to their conversation, I was saddened to realize that neither of the priests seemed to condemn Jeane for all of her dark activities. Nor did they talk about Jesus.

After a short time, I said to Jeane, "I've received new life through the Lord Jesus Christ. He saved me from death, for just when I had decided to end it all, he sent two delightful women to share his love and truth with me."

I told her of my new freedom and joy of living fully in the present, now that I had left the occult behind. I also said how tarot cards and fortune telling were not of God but were actually of the enemy, Satan.

As I was speaking I felt a heavy weight around me. At times it even felt like I was receiving physical blows. I kept repeating to myself, "Greater is he who is in me than he who is in the world."

Jeane didn't receive my words and one of the priests seemed to look at me with displeasure. But the other one agreed with what I had said and remarked to Jeane, "You know, I think she's right."

As I looked at Jeane to see how she would react, I saw tears spring into her eyes. She seemed convicted by what the priest had said, but didn't want to hear anymore. The lunch was soon over, and when we said goodbye I knew I would never again have lunch with her.

When I got home, I was singing an old favorite from my childhood: "He walks with me, he talks with me, he tells me I am his own. And the joy we share as we tarry there none other has ever known." As I thought about the lunch, I decided to write Jeane a letter. In it I said, "I hope that you will find Jesus just as I did."

Then I called Ruthie and told her what had happened. She said, "I've been praying for you nonstop all day. Now I know why!"

With a clear and restored mind, I was now able to focus my attention on my family. Gregory found an apartment and became manager of the Black Beret. And Ulysses II moved to the top floor of our house, but we were unable to find space in any of the local schools for him.

Not many days later, we received a call from our old friend Fishbait Miller, the much-loved Doorkeeper of the House of Representatives. He wanted to know if Ulysses II would like to become a page for Congressman McMillan at the Capitol. He would make about four hundred dollars a month, plus his schooling, which would begin at six in the morning. The one condition was that he cut his hair.

He wasn't happy when I drove him to the barber shop and waited outside. His parting words were, "I'm going to tell them how I want it cut."

We met Fishbait at the congressman's office. Ulysses was well qualified and it was arranged. Then Fishbait told me to wait while he took Ulysses to another room. Thirty minutes later Ulysses appeared again—this time with a regular GI haircut and a frown on his face.

But God had answered my prayer for both boys, and Dina now had her brothers close at hand. I had found my way back to the "now" of living, and life was once again becoming rich and full.

V

Joy amid Challenge

23

Travels, Travails, and Triumphs

IN 1973, AN ARTICLE APPEARED in the *Washington Post* entitled, "This Blackie Likes to Build," which featured a photograph of him adding onto the restaurant yet again. But the restaurant wasn't the only object of his creative energies. One morning in March he said to me, "You know, I've been building up that restaurant too much. Let's spend some time working on the house."

"Sounds good," I said. "What would you like to do?"

"Well, Dina's twelve years old now and the boys are growing up. We should have a place for them to swim. Let's put in a pool."

Our first call was made to Elliott Gitlin, the architect whom Blackie had found that Christmas nearly ten years ago. We asked him to come to the house and see if a pool could be added.

We met one morning over coffee, and Elliott in his slow, methodical way took out his pencil and began to draw, working with Blackie to create what Blackie had in mind. They collaborated together well, bouncing ideas off of each other and making modifications as they went along.

One thing they agreed on was to erect a wall that would extend along the street and enclose the area. As I heard them speak of it I looked out at my nice green lawn where the kids liked to run and play ball, realizing that it would all disappear. Although I was sad to lose the space, I knew a swimming pool would be even better.

After Blackie and Elliott had agreed on the plans, Blackie said to me, "Louie, I don't know what this is going to cost all together, but I'm just going to plow right into it."

I trusted that it would work out in the end, but I braced myself for the upheaval of the coming months.

We began construction on June 1. Blackie had called up Jack Lyon of Lyon Construction Company to come out to the house. After assessing the area, Jack said, "Do you know how many truckloads we're going to have to pull out of here?"

Blackie replied, "No, just go ahead and do it."

For days the trucks with the big front endloaders would pull up the street and dig the ever larger hole. The neighbors were nice about it, but the dust that was flying everywhere was certainly a hassle for them.

While the building was going on, we were also planning a trip to China. President Nixon had opened up the door to the long-closed country by sending a diplomatic mission to Peking and inviting the Chinese to send a delegation to Washington. When the Chinese diplomats had been due to arrive in Washington, the White House had called the Mayflower, asking us to accommodate the Chinese until they could find a permanent place to live.

In return, we were given permission to tour China—a childhood dream of mine. I could still vividly remember dangling my feet in the Rapidan River and saying to Myrtle, "When I grow up, I want to see the world. I want to go to China."

In spite of our home being completely torn up, we made our plans with our friends from the Mayflower. With us would be fellow owners Nick and Gwenn Antonelli and Thorne and Hannah Gould, Thorne being Kingdon's son. (Kingdon couldn't go because as a former Ambassador to Luxembourg he would have outranked the highest U.S. liaison officer in China, who at that time was George Bush Sr.) The general manager and his wife, Bill and Penny Hulett, also joined us. Because Bill Cohen had recently died no one represented him. We left Norman Cooper in charge of the renovation and Dina with her nanny.

So it was in January 1974 that Blackie and I were sitting with our traveling companions on the terrace of the Carlton Hotel overlooking the glorious harbor of Hong Kong.

Bill Hulett remarked, "You know, the day that the White House called I nearly flipped. During my whole lifetime we've heard nothing but bad news of China. But then when the Chinese came through the doors of the Mayflower, all dressed the same in their blue Mao jackets, they looked so ordinary and innocent. It seemed hard to connect them with the millions killed in the communist purges."

Thorne asked, "How did the Chinese react when you asked if we could go to China?"

Bill answered, "They hesitated just a little, for there haven't been American tourists in China before. Oh, there were politicos and others, but not just plain tourists. Apparently they called their man in Peking and he gave us permission."

We bought our roundtrip ticket for Kwangchow (Canton), first stopping in Shumchun just across the border. There we had to lay everything out for customs. As we stood waiting for their agents to look at our stuff, I saw the familiar communist sign: "WORKERS OF THE WORLD, UNITE."

The Chinese custom agents were especially interested in Blackie and the four watches we had bought for the kids in Tokyo.

"Why do you need four watches? Are you going to sell them?" they asked, also suspiciously eyeing his wad of dollar bills held together with a rubber band. Wherever Blackie traveled, he made sure he had at least a hundred dollars in single bills so that he could tip easily.

"No," Blackie said, "I'm not going to sell them. They're gifts for my children."

The agents counted and recounted his money, writing everything down and explaining that he must keep an accurate account of what he spent so that his money would balance on his way out of the country.

Nick asked Blackie, "Why do they give you such a hard time? Whenever I go through customs with you no matter what country it is, you're the one they pick on."

"I don't know," Blackie said. "I must fit the wrong profile."

Just then, our Chinese guide appeared. He said, "My name is Tungseh. You are the Mayflower Group. Welcome to China. I am from the China travel service and will be your guide in Canton."

We boarded the Canton Kowloon Express for the ninety-mile trip. As we sat in the no-frills train with the sing-song music in the background, we broke out in smiles. We were actually on our way.

Penny, always enthusiastic, said, "Look! It's just like in the movies! They're working in the rice patties with their coolie hats and black silk outfits. They even have shoulder poles."

We noticed that we were not being received with much friendliness on the train. But we were as new to them as they were to us. Bill said, "They're not used to Americans, and we're probably too exuberant. Let's see what this China travel book has to say."

"Look," he said, "It says 'don't pull a girl's pigtail.' "

Just then a young girl with a long black pigtail appeared with a tray of covered porcelain cups of green tea. When she bent over to serve us, her long pigtail brushed Blackie's hand. We all stifled a laugh.

Bill went on reading, " 'Don't call waiters "boy." They are to be called "tungchih," meaning comrade.' We ought to learn that word."

We read down the list. Penny said, "Look, it says 'don't talk politics'. And 'don't bring in subversive literature, particularly Bibles.' "

Blackie read, "And 'don't be too talkative. If you pursue a subject and get a blank expression, drop the subject at once.' "

We thought about the freedoms Americans enjoy as we sped along. Then the train came to a halt at the Canton railroad station. A bus was waiting for us, and as we made our way to board it we noticed throngs of people, all dressed in similar dark clothes.

As we drove along, weaving in and out of the bicycles, horse-drawn carts, and motor bikes, Tungseh said, "You are going to be staying at the new Tung Feng Hotel."

The hotel was new, but Blackie looked it over with distress. Standing in the corridor on the way to our room, he said, "Look, the tiles end here and start up there in a new color. The colors don't even blend. They must have run out of that color."

"Well," I said, "That's what happens when the government runs everything."

"Hope it never happens to us."

The next morning we greeted Tungseh with "ni hao," meaning hello, and he smiled. "Today," he said, "you will be briefed on a collective ivory-carving factory."

When we got to the factory we were taken to a small room, probably the former owner's office. We were served green tea in covered porcelain cups as the manager of the collective spoke to us. Behind him hung a picture of Chairman Mao Tse-tung, his round face and penetrating eyes bearing down on us.

"This factory was once owned by one man." The manager paused, expecting us to think that that was wrong. "Now this is known as a collective."

Nick, who was next to me, whispered, "Wonder where the stuckee went."

The manager continued, "You will see the workers very happily working at their jobs."

We entered the immense factory, where row after row of workers sat under the ever-present picture of Chairman Mao. They used special instruments to carve out figures from the ivory, making beautiful birds, dogs, cats, and even bracelets. All seemed completely absorbed in their work and rarely even looked our way. If they were happy or not, it didn't show.

We watched for awhile, but I was extremely aware of the dust from all of the carving. It nearly stopped our breathing.

Gwenn said, "Guess we can't buy anything here, but aren't those little carved animals exquisite?"

"Yes," I said, "but I can't wait for the fresh air." We stepped out the door and took a good, deep breath.

A couple days later we boarded the train for Shanghai and marveled at the verdant landscape we were passing through. The hanging trees shrouded with mist were even more beautiful against the silhouettes of the gray-green mountains. We saw what looked like fields of rice, winter-wheat, and green rapeseeds growing profusely right up to the city of Shanghai.

Tungseh did not accompany us, but we would be met by another person from the China travel service. As soon as we stepped from the train we saw a young man smiling and carrying a sign saying, "The Mayflower Group." We wondered how he could have missed us.

As we rode to the fourteen-story Peace hotel, our new guide, Hui, was talkative and enthusiastic. "Welcome," he said. "Welcome to Shanghai! Shanghai means on the sea. This city is our gateway to the world. We are just twelve miles North of the Yangtze River. We are located on the Hwang Pu River, near Soochow Creek."

We nodded to him, happy to be here although we weren't too familiar with the geography. As we entered the hotel, Blackie noticed the small rug at the entrance, which had probably been there for thirty years. Although it was black with dirt, it wasn't at all worn. Blackie was intrigued, and said, "Got to get some of these rugs."

The next morning we dressed and went downstairs. I was wearing my fur coat, but if I read the glances correctly, it was attracting disdainful looks. Blackie was wearing his leather coat and Greek fishermen's hat, but he wasn't very warm. All of the Chinese had on varying shades of the padded coats.

Bill said, "Why don't we all buy those blue coats—it'll appear better to them and maybe we'll be warmer."

We consulted with Hui, who seemed pleased with the idea. He took us to the impressive Bund Avenue, built largely by the British. The local department store was packed with Chinese customers trying on their shoes and coats. There we saw racks of the heavily padded blue coats with deep pockets and hoods. Although the clothes we saw looked functional, they lacked all beauty.

Bill tried on his coat first, and it made him look twice his size. As he pulled up the hood and covered his face, we couldn't tell him from the other people around us. We all laughed with glee.

Just as we were walking out of the store, I spotted some flat Chinese shoes and tried on a pair. They were ugly, made of black corduroy with rubber soles, but felt comfortable and especially on the foot I had hurt previously. Now, decked out in my coat with the hood up and the shoes on my feet, I could pass for any Chinese.

The next day we asked Hui where we could buy some of the Chinese rugs. When he said we should go to the Friendship store located on Nanking Road, we remembered that all foreigners had to buy from specialty stores, just as in Russia. Hui had obtained special permission for us to buy our coats in the department store.

We found the large Friendship store and were amazed at how beautiful everything was. We saw blue porcelain pots of all shapes and sizes, many kinds of carpets, large porcelain fish bowls, hand-carved teak wooden chests, matching beds and couches, and intricate dining-room tables and chairs. We had seen similar things in Tokyo, but not at these prices.

A hand-wrought Chinese screen caught my eye. "Blackie," I said, "please buy this for Dina. Look, it has three horses running down the side. I've never seen anything like it."

Dina was at a horse-loving stage, and we got her the screen at the unbelievable price of $125.00.

We bought all the gifts we needed and then some. The set of dishes that first caught my eye was just $100.00 for a complete twelve-person setting, hand painted and edged in gold. Gwenn and I each bought a set.

When it came time to pay, Nick and Blackie presented their traveler's checks to the comrades. But the Chinese didn't understand our dollars, let alone travelers checks.

"Go to bank!" they said. But our guide had left us and we didn't know where the bank was. In sparse English, one of the girls directed Nick and Blackie to the local bus and wrote them a sign that read, "Bank of China." Blackie and Nick squeezed onto the crowded bus and returned more than an hour later.

Blackie painted a vivid picture of the experience. "We showed the driver the sign and he let us off at the bank. Fortunately, some of the workers understood English, and we gave them the invoice bill and travelers checks. You should have heard all the commotion as they checked over the travelers checks to make sure they were authentic. Then they had to convert the value from dollars to their juans. Never heard so much chatter."

Nick chimed in, "You should've seen them. The little girl who seemed to be the boss counted out the money first."

Blackie said, "Yeah, she counted it, and then she handed it to a tall Chinese fellow who studied us while he bent over counting the money. Then the guy next to him counted it. Then another fellow, and another girl."

Nick said, "Must've been eight different people counting the money."

Blackie said, "Yeah, and then they handed it to me to count again. I said, 'Count again! Eight people counting is enough!'"

He shook his head, and continued, "It was hard to get all of the money into our pockets. We had to hold our coats together to keep it from falling out. Good thing there weren't any pickpockets on the bus."

The comrade at the store came over and Blackie handed her the juans. He stood and patiently watched her counting the money again. She gave him quite a few juans in change. We filled out the bill of lading carefully, writing in our home address and that of Shapiro Shipping in Baltimore, because everything had to go through customs before we could claim it anyway.

A few days later we said goodbye to Hui and flew to Peking (Beijing), the capital of China for over a thousand years.

Bill said, "We're now sixteen thousand miles from home."

"How do you know?" Blackie asked.

Bill pulled out his book, "It says so right here."

At the Peking International Airport two guides introduced themselves, a young woman, Chi, and a young man, Wang.

We smiled at them as they helped us gather up our luggage and directed us to the minibus. Once again we drove through the bicycle-laden streets, and Wang said, "You will be staying at the Peking Hotel."

At this point, we weren't concerned with the hotel so much for we were too excited about where we were. The "forbidden city" held such mystery, and it seemed a dream to be able to walk on the Great

Wall after China had been closed off for such a long time. This was the subject of our discussion as we went down for dinner.

We ordered mostly western, and as we ate, I thought I saw some fellow Americans across the room.

"I think those are Americans over there," I said to Blackie.

"I don't think so," he replied, "there's not supposed to be any others over here."

Nick said, "Sure looks like it."

I said, "I'm going to go ask." I got up and said with a smile, "Excuse me, but are you Americans?"

"Sure are. Who are you?"

"Well, according to the Chinese, we're the first tourists in China. The Chinese delegation stayed at our Mayflower Hotel in Washington and now we're visiting in return."

"Well, we're part of the American Liaison Group over here. I'm Emile Morin and this is my wife, Anne."

"Wait a moment, let me get my husband over here," I said, motioning to Blackie.

When he came over, I said, "This is my husband, Blackie Auger."

"Are you with the restaurant, Blackie's?"

"Yes—I'm Blackie."

"Know how many times we've been in your restaurant! So good to meet you."

Emile and Anne had finished their dinner, so they came and joined us. We had a lovely time discussing our Chinese adventures together.

The next day we received invitations to lunch at the American Liaison residence located in the embassy section. Mr. and Mrs. George Bush were currently the head of our Liaison Group in China, but they had been called away. In their place were Mr. and Mrs. Jensen. Imagine our surprise when they took one look at us and said, "Oh, hi Blackie! Hi Louie!" It turned out that their son and our son Ulysses were classmates at Maret School. What a small world to meet friends over here in Peking!

We had an interesting time, but as the walls had ears we did not discuss China itself. After our lunch, we left the Jensens, whose parting remark was, "You've got a real treat in store for you, walking on the Great Wall. Have a great time! Hope to see you back in Washington."

The following morning we visited the Peking Zoo and saw the cuddly black and white pandas that are found only in Northern China. Our guides left us alone in the afternoon, and we walked down the Street of Heavenly Peace (Tienan Avenue), which is considered to be the world's longest avenue, to the Great Hall of the People, which faces Tienanmen Square (Gate of Heavenly Peace).

Bill said, "The book says that it only took ten months to build this entire area."

Blackie said, "With all these millions of people, you could build anything almost overnight. They certainly look like willing workers, too."

Nick said, "Look at that huge picture of Chairman Mao. He must be the god around here."

Bill said, "Yeah, and if you don't believe it, just say something bad about his little red book."

We were awed by the square, and were stunned years later to remember our time there when in the summer of 1989 we heard about the student protests and saw the lone protester courageously standing in front of a column of Red Army tanks, willing to give his life for the cause of democracy. Tragically, five thousand civilians died in that protest as the army quashed the prodemocracy movement.

The next day we were scheduled to visit the Great Wall. We drove forty-two kilometers north of Peking and then made our way to the Pata Ling mountains. Wang explained, "The wall is thirty feet high and twenty-five feet wide with forty guard towers at regular intervals. No other structure in the world is as big."

Bill said, "When we went to the moon, our astronauts could see it."

Wang continued, telling us that over eleven million men labored for a decade during the Chin Dynasty just to join the existing portions. The wall was built to keep the northern nomads out of agricultural China.

I wore my flat Chinese shoes to climb up the stone steps. Not all of us made it to the top, as Penny was six months pregnant and Blackie got too breathless from the height. Bill and I reached the top first and stood together singing "Tie a Yellow Ribbon to the Old Oak Tree" at the top of our lungs.

People brushed against us, some standing and listening, but we didn't care. Something made us want to sing, for here we were, the first American tourists in communist China. We had read of all the atrocities and the bloodshed to set up this form of government. Maybe we were singing for all those who had died. Or maybe we were singing for ourselves, that we could walk out of here free.

For whatever reason, we sang for all we were worth and didn't want to stop as we looked out over the many more miles of the winding wall. Forced by time to return, we finally came down to join the others.

A couple days later it was nearly time to leave China. I was getting very bored with my clothes, and in particular the blue coat with its four-inch padding and the flat Chinese shoes. Having had my hair fixed, I decided to put on makeup and wear my regular shoes and fur coat.

But when I came down to breakfast, Chi gave me a disdainful look and turned her back on me. I could have ignored her since I'd probably never see her again. But I realized that I must have looked like all the capitalists whom she had been trained to hate, rolled into one.

I stood still for a moment, thinking how to handle the situation. Then I excused myself, went back up to the room, and put on my Chinese shoes and the blue coat. When I came down, I looked straight at her and smiled, and I saw a vulnerable side to her as she smiled back.

Later on, as we were driving to our last dinner at the original Peking Duck restaurant, Chi sat beside me and we had a nice conversation. I told her of my faith in God and she said that she didn't particularly like Buddhism. She didn't make any derogatory comments about the Christian faith, which I might have expected. I let the subject drop, but silently breathed a prayer for her.

The next morning we were eating breakfast in the hotel dining room just before the bus would take us to the international airport. As we were sitting at the table, the manager of the Peking Hotel sent for Bill Hulett.

When he returned, Blackie asked, "What did they want?"

"Well, you know they have the same problems over here that we have back home—how to train and keep good culinary people. I told them it was a worldwide problem. They're still operating the hotel like sixty to seventy years ago, so I set up a typical hotel organizational chart."

Blackie asked, "What do you mean?"

"Didn't you notice all the people on our floor? The guy who makes your bed might also clean your room, help with your telephone call, and do room service. They've got to break it down to a system."

Bill paused and said, "They've got a long way to go. Hope I helped them a little."

Our trip had ended. We had been gone from our family for three weeks now and the thrill of getting home enlivened us though we were quite tired. As we landed at National Airport, we felt like we had been gone a year, and it looked as if Dina had grown an inch. We gave her a heart-shaped box of candy for the Valentine's Day we had missed and told her of the special screen that would be coming. And Greg and Ulysses loved their watches.

We were also interested to see all the progress on the house. Norman had been doing a fine job overseeing the work, including the pool, which was nearly ready. We were now beginning to work on the interior, and had hired Ray Bates to work with the decorators. Work continued.

The news of the moment was Watergate. As the hearings droned on, Senator Sam Ervin, with his southern drawl and commonsense ways, filled the television screens as he methodically probed to reveal the cover-up. It was a sad day for the country on August 9, 1974, when President Richard M. Nixon, his family beside him, announced he was stepping down. By the afternoon, we had a new president, Gerald M. Ford, who was the first person to be both vice president and president without being elected to office.

Life in the capital and at Blackie's went right on. One hot day in late summer I was standing at the front desk after the lunch rush was over when two young men walked into the front door. Their faces were rather stern, and I could guess from their briefcases that they were probably lawyers. They looked as though they had just graduated from Yale or Harvard.

The short, stocky one with tortoise-shell glasses spoke first. "We're here to see Mr. Auger. Is he in?"

His colleague nodded at me, all the while holding the same serious expression.

As I had the time, I took them up to the office, wondering what they wanted. I said to our secretary, "Mary, these two young men want to see Mr. Auger."

Mary asked them, "Well, what do you want to see him about?"

The lawyer who had spoken previously responded again, this time more forcefully. "We're here from the Coca-Cola Company, and we need to speak with Mr. Auger."

Mary rang the buzzer and gave Blackie the message. He came out from his office with a friendly look and invited them in. I went along too.

Blackie sat down, lit a cigarette, and asked, "What can I do for you?"

"We've been around to your carryout restaurants and the other restaurants. . . . I believe that there are thirteen in all. . . ." The lawyer paused a moment, checked his notes, and continued, "Yes, there are thirteen. We're here to tell you that we have carefully documented every Coca-Cola sale you've made in the past few weeks, and you have misrepresented us."

Blackie started to lose his good humor and asked, "What the hell are you talking about?"

The other lawyer drew out a yellow sheet of paper from his briefcase and said, "We have proof here, Mr. Auger, that many customers came into your places and asked for Coca-Cola, but they were given Pepsi-Cola or Diet Rite. You have misrepresented our product."

"What do you mean?"

"Well customers ask for a Coke, and your workers—mostly Spanish—give them any kind of cola. The Coca-Cola Company plans on suing you if this is not corrected, as the public demands Coca-Cola."

Blackie just stared at them for a moment but I could see his blood pressure rising. Without saying a word to the young men, he picked up the telephone and buzzed for Mary.

She came in and he said, "Write a memo right now and get ahold of all of our managers. Tell them that I want all of the Coca-Cola products thrown out of all of the carryout shops, all of the restaurants—everywhere. I don't want any Coca-Cola products sold anywhere, and especially here at Blackie's! Find out how much we owe them and pay them off. I'm through with them."

The guys stood up. "You can't do that. We told you, the public demands Coca-Cola!"

"Yeah, well I'm going to find out if they do or not." He said to Mary, "Get Billy Martin at Pepsi-Cola on the line and tell him to fill up all our places with Pepsi."

The two young lawyers had changed their attitude. When they came in they were very sure of themselves, but when they left they were shaking their heads, shocked at Blackie's swift reaction.

As they walked out, Blackie said, "If you would have sent a nice public relations person, we could have talked it over and I would have cooperated, but I'm not going to be intimidated by you or the company!"

Two weeks later, the two lawyers returned. As they approached Mary, Blackie could see them for he had his office door open. He called out, "What do you want now?"

They went into his office, saying, "We went by your Black Horse Tavern and they're still selling Coca-Cola there."

Blackie, not bothering with the intercom system, yelled to Mary, "Get Peter Laricos on the phone!"

Peter Laricos was our flamboyant manager of the popular Black Horse Tavern at our Embassy Square hotel. He had many friends in the Hollywood crowd, including Bob Hope.

"Peter," Blackie said. "Understand that you're still selling Coca-Cola there. I want you to put every bottle of Coke you've got out on the sidewalk right now. Tell the delivery man to come and pick them up, and stop all orders of any kind to the Coca-Cola Company. I don't want to see even one of their products around."

Blackie hung up and asked, "Are you satisfied now?"

The lawyers nodded and left. But they came back a third time, carrying with them a thick notebook. They showed Blackie all the lawsuits that the Coca-Cola Company had undertaken, saying, "Coca-Cola has never lost a case. They're going to sue you for misrepresenting them."

Blackie was furious, but all he said was, "Well, I've been to the man with the black robe before."

In the fall of 1974, in the midst of conducting his business deals and consulting with our lawyers regarding the Coca-Cola case, Blackie seemed preoccupied. After dinner one day, he shared what was on his mind by posing a single question to Gregory: "Do you think you can handle it?"

"Handle what?"

"Blackie's."

"Yes, I do," Greg replied with confidence.

Our eldest son had proven himself with managing the Black Rooster Pub for a couple years. He had taken it over in 1972 when the manager quit on the spur of the moment. She was a brunette beauty, and when Greg stepped in the male customers were still looking for her. They were less than thrilled with the new manager, and one patron even named him "SOB" for "son of Blackie."

Greg had a tough time living down the name, but soon the customers respected him for his transformation of the pub. Though the Black Rooster had none of the history of British pubs, Greg set up dart boards, imported Guinness Stout and English ale, and patterned it on the London pubs he had frequented while working in that great city. The Black Rooster became one of the most popular places on L Street.

Now it was time for him to turn his eyes and dreams on our flagship restaurant. With managing it came unusual experiences, like the one he recounted to me not long after he took over.

He said, "I was standing at the front desk and there was a waiting line of about forty-five minutes. I was so busy taking names and answering questions that I didn't have time to look up. I was feeling a little harassed and didn't dare put anyone in front of another, or there'd be a fight.

"A fellow continued to stand in front of the desk. He said to me very firmly, 'You don't understand. I need a table for two.'

"He wouldn't budge. He said the same thing again, 'I need a table for two.' Finally I looked up and saw the face of Rock Hudson.

"I said to him immediately, 'I do understand. Come with me.' Rock so wowed the rest of the people that nobody said a word. After all, who is going to keep Rock Hudson waiting?"

Our day in court over soft drinks came in 1975. The judge heard the case of Coca-Cola, that customers asking for Coca-Cola were given some other cola. Then he heard our defense, which was that Coke was a generic term and that foreign managers thought that every cola was called "Coke."

Blackie was called to the stand. Facing him were the two counselors from Coca-Cola we had met on previous occasions, plus another one in an expensive suit who did all the talking.

While on the witness stand, Blackie had an inspiration. At the appropriate moment he asked permission to speak. "Your honor, if you will give me another name for a BAND-AID, I'll do anything you want."

The judge thought awhile, looking up to the ceiling. Then he said to the Coca-Cola lawyers, "Let me see the consent agreement."

They handed it up to the judge. He glanced through it, crossing off some things. Then he handed it down to Don Cefaratti, our lawyer, for him to read. Don also marked across certain words, and handed the document back up to the judge. As he handed it back, Blackie could see that nearly everything had been crossed off.

The judge examined it again and handed it to the Coca-Cola counselor. "See if this meets with your approval."

The end decision was that we were to print on every napkin, menu, and placemat, "WE DO NOT SELL COCA-COLA PRODUCTS." Incidentally, the public has never demanded Coca-Cola.

Greg had hired his friend Toto to work with him as assistant manager at Blackie's, and together they became suspicious of one of our cashiers. Carl was an older man who appeared dull and drab but seemed to have a sharp mind for figures.

No matter where we would be traveling, each night Blackie would call in to the restaurant and ask, "What kind of business are we doing?"

Carl could always give him an estimate of the amount of sales, and it would closely fit the total at the end of the evening.

This uncanny ability seemed odd to Greg and Toto. They began to keep an eye on Carl, and noticed that he always carried a brown paper bag when he left the restaurant each night. Wondering what was in the bag, Greg and Toto followed him to the parking lot. Just as Carl was getting into his car, he stumbled. The paper bag opened and many guest checks fluttered to the ground. Carl scrambled to pick them up and put them back in the paper bag.

Greg asked Toto, "Should we nab him now, or should we follow him and see where he goes?"

They decided not to wait. They had Carl arrested and he wound up in jail. Greg figured that he stole at least five thousand dollars just that week, and perhaps over a million dollars in nine years.

Several months later, in early 1976, Greg had plans for establishing a dancing place at Blackie's. He had the concept all worked out—he would rearrange the back part of the restaurant, put in a good sound system, and play music of the fifties and sixties to attract his generation.

He had decided on the name while visiting Denver with a friend from his Black Rooster days, Bill Caldwell, whose father owned the King Coil Mattress Company. Greg took Bill around to his old haunts from when he attended the Denver Hotel Restaurant School, including the highest point of the Front Range mountains. As they stood overlooking the grand city of Denver, Greg remarked, "Haven't been back here for years. It's just like deja vu standing here."

Bill replied, "Deja vu? Sounds like a good name for that dancing place you keep talking about at Blackie's."

Greg agreed. Later he went to his father with his idea: "I'd like to put a place to dance in the New Orleans room called Deja Vu. It's pretty back there and there's plenty of space. I'll need about forty-five thousand dollars to put in the sound system."

Blackie blew up. "Do you think I want all those young kids coming into this restaurant and tearing things up?"

It was a fight, but Greg stood his ground. Over the following weeks I noticed that little by little Greg was changing the room, including the addition of a large dance floor. His father was so busy with other things that he failed to see the not-so subtle changes.

Greg continued to ask Blackie about his idea. One day in late May we were standing out in front of the restaurant, ready to go to the airport for another board meeting in Zurich. Greg said, "Dad, I haven't given up my idea for a place to dance. What I need is forty-five thousand dollars to put in a good sound system."

All I heard was the resounding answer, "No, you're not going to do it!" as Blackie got into the taxi and slammed the door. He mumbled about it all the way to the airport.

We were gone for ten days. When we returned about nine o'clock in the evening on Friday, June 4th, there was a crowd of people lined up on M Street. Blackie said, "What's going on—hope there's not a fire."

We entered through the front door of Blackie's and walked back to Deja Vu. The room was totally filled with dancers moving to the beat of the sensational music. There wasn't even anywhere to stand. As we looked in, a young man spotted Blackie and said, "I'm from the White House. Can you get me a table?"

Blackie looked around and didn't see a free table anywhere. He said, "Well I'm Blackie, and even I can't get a table."

Deja Vu was a success from the moment Greg opened the doors—without a loan from his father. A month later, on July 4, 1976, the new dancing spot hosted a party for the two hundredth anniversary of the United States. The room was bulging with people who were dancing and celebrating. Greg had proven himself again, and Blackie admitted that the idea was a hit. It remains popular to this day.

Our sons were increasingly running the restaurants while Blackie focused on other enterprises and I stood on the sidelines, praying and cheering. I was also enjoying the house, which had taken forty-three months to complete. It was finally finished on December 5, 1976, just in time for a beautiful Christmas.

24

Battles and Buildings

Business downstairs had its troubles, like the Coca-Cola incident, but the deal-making business in the office upstairs had its share of fussarias too. For instance, in early 1978 Blackie wanted to refinance the loan on Embassy Square. Previously he had secured the loan through Bankers Trust in an unusual way.

He had sold the ground to them for $1.5 million and leased the use of it for a yearly rent of 6 percent of the value, which amounted to $80,000 a year. In addition, the lease had a provision for the ground to be reappraised every twenty years as if it were an empty piece of land. Then, for the actual building on the site, he secured a loan of $3.5 million at 6 percent interest.

When Blackie wanted to refinance the loan on the building, he found out he was unable to do so because of the ground lease. To refinance the loan, Blackie would have to find out what the ground would be reappraised at.

When he had it appraised it came in excess of $10 million. Since the lease called for the rent to be 6 percent of the appraised value, the rent would climb to $600,000 per year. Blackie had to act right away, and not wait for the next twenty-year lender's appraisal. If he did we would surely lose the property then, for the rent would be exorbitant.

Blackie called Norman Hecht at Madison Bank. "Norman, I need a sharp finance guy to help me out of a real dilemma."

"There's a real sharp guy from Poland I'll put you in touch with, Leon Segal. Heard he was educated in Germany following the war. People say he's a genius at financing."

When Blackie met with him, Leon said in his heavy accent, "There's only one thing to do to solve this problem. We have to buy the land back, and we have to refinance the building in order to secure the land. Hopefully we can buy back the ground at the same $1.5 million."

With interest rates at 16 percent and still rising under President Carter, the situation looked grim. But then Leon learned that Bankers Trust would refinance their own loans that carried an interest rate of 6 percent. He arranged a new loan with Bankers Trust for $5.7 million to buy the land and refinance the building.

After the deal was made, Leon said to Blackie, "God must have been watching over you. If the bank had asked for a reappraisal of the land prior to accepting the payment, the deal would never have been made."

Blackie and Leon had a toast with Courvoisier, and Blackie said, "You're pretty good, Leon, a real financial strategist. I would have hated to lose Embassy Square."

Later in 1978 we found ourselves engaged in a battle with the U.S. Immigration and Naturalization Service. We had been in contact with the INS since 1972, when we had a Taiwanese chef working at the Black Tahiti for whom we wanted to get a green card. Yu-Ching Ting had found his way to us from Taipei, and unbeknownst to us presented us with a fake Social Security card. We hired him, but we notified our lawyer Jack Wasserman that he was a good employee and that we wanted to help him get his green card.

On April 19, 1972, Wasserman petitioned the INS for Yu-Ching Ting, who had been a chef in China. The petition stated that no one in this country could do the required cooking that was needed. Another advertisement was put in the paper for that type of cook, but no one suitable answered. Thus the petition was approved and Yu-Ching Ting received his green card.

Jack Wasserman was an excellent attorney, and was known in town as "the immigration lawyer." His aim was to figure out a way to accommodate anyone who wanted to come and work in the United States. He petitioned the INS many times for us, not only for our Chinese restaurant but for the Black Ulysses, our Greek restaurant.

We remained in close contact with the INS. A couple years after obtaining Yu-Ching Ting's green card, Blackie met with two INS agents who asked if he had any illegal aliens working for him. He replied, "My employees all have Social Security cards. If they have the card, it's legal for me to let them work. You can check the payroll records and see for yourselves."

My family, celebrating our fortieth wedding anniversary in 1986. From the left, Gregory II, Alison and Ulysses II, me and Ulysses, Dina and her husband, Frank, and Gregory's wife, Margaret.

Blackie and me with our special friend, Vice President Hubert H. Humphrey.

My dreams of wearing a sparkling white gown were finally realized when I was named the New Orleans Queen Venus for Mardi Gras, 1962.

Friends and pages at the Venus Ball: Messrs. John Krisko, Vinton Lee, Angelo Puglisi, William G. Barr, John Kalivritinos, D. F. (Nick Antonelli), Mayor Victor Schiro, Joseph Rinaldi, Ted Britt, Blackie Auger, and Mike Zarpas. In front, the tired and restless pages.

Gregory's family: Gregory III, Margaret, Alexander, Gregory II, and Bridgette.

Ulysses II's family: Annabel-Rose, Nicholas, Ulysses II, Alison, Ulysses III, and James.

Dina's family: Franciscos, Dina, Vassiliki, Dina II, and Frank Economides.

If the INS had a specific question about the official residence of a particular worker, sometimes Blackie would give them the employee's address. There weren't any problems until 1976, when an INS agent whom Blackie knew came into the restaurant with some other officials. All of a sudden they started chasing our workers, causing chaos in the restaurant. Blackie felt betrayed and told the INS agents that they'd need a warrant to come in next time.

Two years later, in March 1978, we endured another raid—this one two hours long, starting at six P.M. We learned later that the agents had been staking out the restaurant for days, looking for wetbacks—illegal aliens who came mostly from El Salvador, risking their lives to cross the border from Mexico.

The young immigrants came to us with eager faces and scared eyes, and unbeknownst to us, false Social Security numbers. They needed work and we were short-handed. We paid them the minimum wage until some learned English and rose through the ranks. Some worked as dishwashers, others as cleanup people, and some we trained as busboys. Depending on their experience, we hired them to paint, attend to the grounds, or maintain the corner parking lot at Twenty-second and M.

The March 30TH raid was extremely disruptive to our customers, and Blackie burned within, vowing to seek justice. He sought $100,000 in damages against the INS, and in October Judge Louis Oberdorfer, a U.S. District Court judge, ruled in our favor in a case that became known as Blackie's I, saying that the raid was "unreasonable and unlawful" as the INS search warrant had authorized them only to search for property, not people. We sighed with relief at the ruling.

On other fronts, we had been assembling the property surrounding Blackie's for many years with the dream of building a hotel over it. As Gregory once pointed out, "We have to build the hotel, because no matter what we do, the Blackie's roof always leaks." Blackie was deeply involved with the realization of this dream and also the contemplated renovation of the Mayflower Hotel to its original grandeur.

Although we owned the land for a hotel, in order to borrow the money to erect the actual building we needed to find a flag—a name hotel. Blackie contacted the Sheraton and several other chains in the search for the right partner.

Then Gary Wilson, the CFO of Marriott Corporation, came to see Blackie about Marriott managing the Mayflower. The Maywash group, as the owners of the Mayflower were called, included Richard Cohen, the son of the now deceased Bill Cohen, Kingdon Gould, Nick Antonelli, and Blackie, along with several other minor partners.

But it was too late for the Mayflower to be given over to Marriott because the Mayflower group, with Kingdon Gould as spokesman, had just announced that, "As owners, we are committed to the idea that the Mayflower Hotel must continue to be an asset to the city, and we will maintain for many years to come the standard of excellence for which it has become famous."

After a six-month feasibility study and many discussions with the Joint Committee on Landmarks, the owners had committed themselves to the restoration of the historic hotel. The Maywash group had acquired a new partner, Stouffer Hotels, under a twenty-year contract.

The Stouffer company heralded the Mayflower as the flagship of their expanding hotel chain and cooperated with the owners to restore this hotel fully. By now, our old friend and former manager of the Mayflower, Bill Hulett, had become president of Stouffer Hotels. He sent Tom Lee, general manager of the Stouffer Hotel in Westchester County, New York, to work with the Mayflower group.

Although Marriott wasn't able to run the Mayflower, Blackie was pleased that Gary Wilson had approached him, for he had another idea. He said to him, "I'd like for you to run the hotel I'm building right over my restaurant. Do you think Marriott would be interested in being the flag?"

Wilson arranged a meeting with Blackie and the decision-making people at Marriott. They seemed very interested and said that they would conduct a feasibility study and get back with Blackie. Indeed, the study revealed that our area, the West End, would be a positive location for a hotel.

The partnership was agreed and the story was released to the press on May 13, 1978: "Marriott Corporation and restaurateur Blackie Auger announced yesterday they will build a 350-room hotel at 22ND and M Streets N.W., beside and above Blackie's House of Beef. The hotel will be the first built in Washington by Marriott, which was founded here fifty years ago."

The Marriott Corporation had long desired a hotel in Washington, but they were a little leery about the complications of dealing with the District government. They were, however, also considering a hotel on Pennsylvania Avenue in connection with the new Convention Center.

When we began the digging for the hotel, the right side of our kitchen began to sink even though the retaining wall had been built on deep cement caissons. It was disconcerting to walk into the kitchen as it made one feel a bit woozy. But soon the problem was corrected and the process of building began in earnest.

The immigration saga continued in November 1978, when we were on our way home from our quarterly meeting of Budget Rent a Car in Zurich. While in the baggage department of National Airport waiting for our luggage, Blackie saw a fellow reading the *Washington Post*. Glancing over the guy's shoulder, he thought he saw a headline and picture of Blackie's House of Beef.

He said to me, "Got to find a copy of the *Washington Post*."

Sure enough, on the front page was a picture of the INS agents chasing our employees and arresting them right in front of the restaurant. The story read: "As immigration officials walked through the restaurant shortly before the luncheon crowds arrived, workers could be seen charging out of the front door and sprinting down the street with investigators in hot pursuit."

We hailed a taxi and Blackie thundered, "Go to Twenty-second and M, Blackie's."

We heard that the incident occurred just after eleven o'clock when our staff was getting ready for the busy lunch. The roast beef and Virginia ham had been brought outside, and the carver was dressed in his whites and sharpening his knife. The busboys were removing the ketchup from the refrigerator, counting out the tablecloths and napkins, and doing the myriad other tasks. The servers were ready and the customers were starting to stream in.

What the customers and staff didn't know was that a black INS truck was parked in the alley, leading to the back door, and another one hovered outside the front door. There were ten INS investigators in all, along with two lawyers and a press spokesmen. And the *Washington Post* had been alerted in advance.

Suddenly the INS agents came through the doors yelling, "Immigration!" There was pandemonium, people flying everywhere, and customers not understanding what was happening. The agents grabbed our son, Ulysses, just as if he were a wetback. He fought free, screaming at them in English, and they let him go immediately.

The busboys ran in every direction with the immigration officials in hot pursuit. The illegals hid anywhere they could find. Later, we found some crouched in the freezers, the walk-in boxes, the trash room, and upstairs in the locker rooms. Some got away and we never saw them again. Most were grabbed by the agents.

Fourteen immigrants were booked, and some were sent back to their countries. Others, however, were returned to us. We learned later that the INS carried out the search using a type of civil warrant they had never used before; this one was based on civil procedures, rather than criminal. Several INS agents told the *Washington Post* that they had been "crippled" by the October ruling, and so they decided to try out a new type of civil warrant. Not surprisingly, the first place they raided was Blackie's.

But Blackie and Jack Wasserman contended that Judge Oberdorfer's ruling, recent Supreme Court decisions, and the Fourth Amendment of the U.S. Constitution didn't allow the use of general search warrants to arrest people. They began to plan new legal action immediately, and in December filed a suit against four INS officials.

Wasserman said the reasons behind the INS investigation were discriminatory, such as observations that several people employed at Blackie's spoke Spanish, appeared to be of Hispanic descent, or had "foreign-style haircuts."

The ruling on the lawsuit didn't occur until October 4, 1979. In a case that became known as Blackie's II, Judge Oberdorfer struck down as unconstitutional the INS's November search and said that we had substantial constitutional rights at stake in protecting ourselves from these illegal searches. He said that the INS warrant used "appears to grant the searching officers a 'roving commission' to search the premises, limited only by their subjective judgments about what persons in the United States without legal authority look like." He also said that the INS "created commotion in Blackie's by entering with a squad-size force, interrogating suspects, seizing them and removing them from the restaurant."

Judge Oberdorfer ruled that in the future, the INS could only enter Blackie's with a precise description of the people for whom it is searching. Also, it must have a magistrate appraise the possible effect a search would have on the others in the restaurant. We were hoping that our troubles with the INS were behind us.

Of course we had no idea at the time that the immigration rulings of the late seventies under Judge Oberdorfer wouldn't stand. In 1981 a U.S. Court of Appeals eased the procedures for immigration agents to raid businesses in the District of Columbia. Jack Wasserman was determined to take the case to the Supreme Court. But tragically, just as he was putting the case together, he became ill and died of cancer at the age of sixty-eight. We were saddened by his death, and especially that he wouldn't be able to pursue his dream.

Wasserman's law firm assigned the case to a young man in the firm, Tom Elliot. He asked for a writ of certiorari to the U.S. Court of Appeals in order to move this case upward. But the circuit judges presiding denied the rehearing of the case, which happens in ninety out of a hundred cases.

Even so, our case was cited again and again in immigration-related lawsuits and case warrants around the country. One was close to home. When Blackie and his One-thirty group were enjoying lunch at Tom Sarris's steakhouse, Blackie kidded Tommy, "You've got a lot of aliens around here. I can spot them anywhere."

A few days later the INS actually did raid Tom, and Blackie was one of the first people to hear about it.

Tom said, "You louse! You sicked the INS on me!"

"No, I didn't," Blackie protested.

"Yes, you did. When they came in with a warrant, it had your name on it."

Blackie couldn't make Tom understand that "Blackie's II" was now the standard and would be cited on every case warrant across the country, similar to the Miranda decision. He called his lawyer, Paul Varoutsos, and Paul explained it to him.

It was only years later, in 1986, that there was a major overhaul of the immigration law. When Congress understood the dilemma that employers were facing regarding who could work and what documents were needed, they instituted a new law requiring prospective employees to fill out an I-9 form, which came in effect after May 5, 1986. This document states that the employer has checked every new employee's authorization to work in this country, which could include a U.S. passport, green card, Social Security card, or driver's license.

The INS visited us after the law was implemented, this time not to raid our restaurant but to explain the new law. And some top officials even gave us a plaque when they attended a dinner held at Blackie's of the American Immigration Lawyers Association. Those whom we had fought we were now pleased to serve.

Meanwhile, one cloudy day in 1980, Blackie was returning from the Madison Bank meeting. He pulled up to the stoplight at Connecticut and M and saw Dimitri Mallios, our lawyer, waiting to cross the street.

Dimitri called out, "How'd you like to buy thirty-nine Ponderosa restaurants?"

Blackie responded, "Sure, I might consider it. I need more work for my son, Ulysses. Tell the guy to come see me."

Blackie told me about it when he got home. "Ulysses is so filled with energy and anxious to keep moving," he said. "I'll look into these Ponderosa restaurants—they'll be Ulysses' college education."

Blackie had dropped out of Central High School, which is now Cardoza, in the ninth grade. He tended to disdain higher education, saying that if you didn't have it in you to be successful, no amount of formal education would help. If you had the natural ability, why waste time?

The day came when Ulysses had wanted to go to college. His father had told him, "If you will work your way through and pay for it yourself, I'll give you all the money back when you finish." Ulysses declined the offer and instead threw himself into his work. He had worked in the family business while growing up, doing every possible job as Gregory had done before him. He had been a broiler cook, carver, butcher, expediter, and even assistant chef.

Then when Ulysses had turned twenty in 1973, his father had transferred him to the Black Ulysses, our cafeteria by day and Greek nightclub by night. Blackie was growing weary of running this place. The belly dancers were threatening to sue and the Greek customers were increasingly demanding.

Tired of all the politics, Blackie said to Ulysses, "I've had this Greek place for too long. What else can we do with it?"

"Put in rock and roll music, Dad. Lots of young people are looking for a nice place to dance. Deja Vu has worked out well, but this will be for the younger crowd."

"All right, see what you can do with it."

Chris Petropolis was still the general manager for the cafeteria by day, but Ulysses renamed the restaurant "Bojangles" and introduced dancing at night to the music of the sixties and seventies. Ulysses' youthful energy knew no bounds and for a time he enjoyed running the place, turning it into a success. While there he even met his future wife, Alison Hawthorne, the great-great-granddaughter of Nathaniel Hawthorne.

Over the years Ulysses' influence grew, and Blackie was counting on him more and more. Eventually he took over the entire group of restaurants, reporting directly to his father. Ulysses changed many of the names, as he didn't want them all to begin with the word "black." For instance, the Black Rose became Ha' Penny Lion and the Black Greco became Abbey Road.

Ulysses hired an assistant, and now in the summer of 1980 he was still complaining to his father that the company could be growing more. So without too much deliberation, Blackie made the financial arrangements and bought the thirty-nine Ponderosas on January 29, 1981.

When we first acquired them, the thirty-three restaurants in Maryland and six in Virginia were grossing $25 million. All went well for the first few months, for budget steak houses were popular just before we bought them. But as we learned later, the Ponderosa people were clever to sell them when they did, for the restaurants began plunging in sales.

Interest rates had risen to 16 percent under President Carter and the cost of borrowing money was out of sight. Gasoline was in short supply, and the price per gallon rose. And inflation hit, along with rising interest rates. Unemployment continued to increase and people weren't eating out as much. Retired people on a fixed income and blue-collar workers, the majority of our business, were affected most. Ponderosas, Rustlers, Sizzlers, and the Golden Coral steak houses all dropped in sales.

Also, the Ponderosa restaurant buildings had been built twenty years before and were starting to look old and tired. They hadn't been constructed well in the first place, and now many of the roofs began to leak. The biggest fear was that it would rain on a Friday, the biggest sales day, and leak on the customers. Even the sidewalks were breaking up near to the front door. In short, our hastily bought business was a boondoggle.

A couple months before acquiring the Ponderosas, on November 2, 1980, a very young, beautiful bride walked down the aisle of Saint Sophia Cathedral, her father's arm around her slender waist. At nineteen Dina had fallen in love with the man with whom she wanted to spend her life. How could I say she was too young to marry, as I had met Blackie at just seventeen?

When Dina was about fifteen, she had said to me, "Mama, I want to marry a man with long legs who comes from a large family." I didn't pay much attention then, as young girls say lots of things.

But just four years later, she met Frank, a tall, young man with long legs. He came from a large Greek family whom we had known even before Dina was born. We were thrilled with their love and their commitment to each other, and celebrated their wedding at the Mayflower Hotel, dancing until dawn. Dina's childhood friend, Evelyn Kokinos, was her maid of honor.

Other things were changing on the family front. One painful day, after making a great success of Blackie's and Deja Vu, Gregory walked out. He had clearly been mulling over plans for his future and was waiting for the right time to approach his father.

"Dad, I want to further my education and go to the next level. I want to get a degree in business."

His father was not happy. His face darkened and he began to scowl. Blackie couldn't understand why Greg wasn't satisfied with his work in the restaurant and Deja Vu, especially as they were both so successful.

Without thinking, Blackie shot out the first thing that came into his head, "Well, if you do, you're going to have to do it on your own. I've spent all I'm going to spend on your education."

Needless to say, they didn't part on friendly terms.

Greg took out a government student loan and was accepted into the MBA program of George Washington University. Besides being a full-time student, he became a waiter at Dominique's. The owner, Monsieur D. Ermo, hired him and immediately called him, "Monsieur Blackie."

Customers who recognized Greg would ask, "Did your father buy this, too?"

He'd answer, "No, I'm just a waiter here and Diane is my boss. If you want to sit in my station, ask Diane." Diane was the popular maître d' and everyone in town seemed to know her.

Greg worked there for almost a year before he decided to team up with his friend Toto, who'd quit his job as assistant manager at Blackie's the same time as Greg. Toto's mother-in-law had some money and was willing to back them, so they decided to look for a restaurant to run together.

Separately Greg and Toto went out to search for the right small cafe or restaurant to buy. Greg lived in a small apartment close to the university that was located on the Metro blue line. He worked out that if he could find a restaurant located on the blue line, thereby saving valuable time, he could make enough money to see him through school without having to borrow any more.

I remember how excited he was as he called me one day. "Mom!" he said, "I checked out every restaurant on the blue line. I'd go in and ask the owner if he wanted to sell. He'd see me with my blue jeans on and think I wasn't serious. More than one threw me out. But when I was almost to the end of the line on Capitol Hill, I walked into a place called McQuires. The guy was so anxious to sell that he practically handed the place over to me! It's just a small Irish pub. The chef is known for his fried chicken."

As Greg was a full-time student, Toto opened up in the morning and Greg took over as soon as his classes were finished. The restaurant employed one chef, one bartender, and one waitress.

The place was low on dishes—low on everything—but it did have steady customers and a loyal following. However it was hard going and after salaries there was very little profit. They were on COD with all the vendors and were even beginning to lag behind with their sales tax and the rent. Greg talked over the situation with his pretty brunette girlfriend, Margaret, who later became his wife.

"Margaret, I made Deja Vu a success. I know I can do the same here."

She agreed, and encouraged him to keep working at it.

He was planning for the upcoming St. Patrick's Day and wanted to make it a hit. For the one night he hired a disc jockey to play Irish music, and then sent placards around the neighborhood to announce the celebration.

When the evening was over he said to Margaret, "Look—one night's sales gave us enough money to pay the bills! We can get caught up now."

As they celebrated Greg was struck with an idea. "Margaret, I could give up the MBA, go on with this restaurant, and make a fair living. What do you think?"

They talked about it and decided that sticking it out with graduate school would be best in the long run.

Eventually Greg sold out to Toto, but just before he did the food critic for the Capital Hill Rag came in. Once in a while the chef disappeared on one of his "toots" and this was one of those nights. Greg was stuck in the kitchen and Margaret was nervous out front, trying to tell the critic that the chef was making something special for him. Whatever

Greg made, the critic must have been pleased. He gave McQuire's a good review.

Just before Greg graduated, he called me.

"How's school?" I asked.

He had messed around a bit when his father was paying for his education, but it was different now that he was funding himself. He said to me, "Fine. The other day only one other student showed up in the economics class and the professor said we could skip it. I stood up and said, 'No, we're not! I'm working hard to pay for this tuition and I want you to teach me.' "

"What did he do?"

"He taught the class!"

I laughed to myself and thought, "That's my boy!"

It was a hot summer's day in 1982 when I peered into Greg's small office. He had finished his MBA, graduated from George Washington University, married Margaret, and had come back to work for Auger Enterprises. He was in the office fighting off the creditors of the struggling Ponderosa chain while Ulysses handled the day-to-day management.

Greg's new Hewlett Packard 67 computer screen was dancing with numbers, and I noticed he was furrowing his brow. Seeing me, he called out, "Mom, come on in. I want to show you something."

"Good morning, Greg. How are we doing?"

"How are we doing; just terrible! It's as if we're losing a Mercedes a week—sixty thousand dollars—just as if we were sending it over a cliff."

Before I could respond, his phone rang. It appeared to be one of the many creditors. Greg tried to get the fellow off the line, but he was adamant and wanted to be heard out.

Greg hung up the phone and started to say something, but the phone rang again. He had to take several more calls while paging through the Ponderosa reports before he could talk with me. Finally he said, "Look here—we're losing a fortune. Boy, I don't remember them teaching us at business school what to do when the bottom drops out."

As sales continued to decline and cash sales shrunk, the sheriff often showed up to grab the sales-tax money, removing the cash right from the registers in the midst of regular business.

Ulysses would get calls from the managers: "Help—the police are here and they're taking all the money for the back taxes! I don't have any money to operate the store. What should I do?"

Ulysses would tell them, "Use your own money until we can get over there and refund you. Whatever you do, don't close the store!"

When money started to dry up, Ulysses implemented stringent controls for purchasing. He had to juggle each order, for he couldn't spend more than the money we had on hand. The Ponderosas had lost their credit, so Ulysses had to transfer the money by wire before the meat company would ship the order.

Meanwhile, our Washington Marriott hotel had opened on Gregory's birthday, March 13, 1981. We had a huge party and invited many friends, celebrating the fruitfulness of the years of sweat and strain. Also, the renovation of the Mayflower was in high gear. The whole city seemed grateful, including this mention in the *Washington Post*: "The Mayflower has a great opportunity to develop an identity, to become as great and enchanting a period piece of the 1920s as other hotels are in the 1890s. We hope the new owners understand this and that their modernization will not attempt to change the Mayflower into something it isn't."

This was the exact feeling of the owners. They had hired Intradesign, a firm with headquarters in Los Angeles, who worked from old photographs, historical descriptions of the period, and magazine and newspaper articles to restore the original feel of the twenties. They removed the black paint that was used for blackout purposes over the entrance during World War II. They refurbished the entire hotel—the kitchen, furniture, fixtures, and nearly all of the equipment. The renovation cost a total of $65 million, and the hotel became like new.

President Reagan wrote a congratulatory letter to them on November 7, 1983:

> I am delighted to send my warm congratulations to all those gathered to celebrate the Mayflower Hotel's recognition by the National Register of Historic Places.
>
> As the Mayflower completes one of the most extensive private restoration projects undertaken in the District of Columbia, this special moment serves as a fitting tribute to a landmark of Washington.

The Mayflower has been among the centerpieces of
the social and political life of the Nation's Capital for more
than half a century. It has housed important figures and
hosted significant business, civic, political and governmental
events.

Again, congratulations on this moment of historical
importance for the community and our nation.

Later in 1983, I stopped by Ulysses II's desk one day. I noticed that his
thick, black hair had a few more sprinkles of gray. "How are you doing,
Ulysses?"

He looked agitated. "If we don't advertise and use coupons," he
said, "we don't do any business. But when we advertise, we just barely
break even."

The Ponderosa menu ranged from just a dollar for a sandwich to
$4.99 for a complete dinner. We were advertising that a family of four
could eat out for twenty dollars.

One thing happened after another, making the situation turn from
bad to worse. Next the snows came and the roads to the restaurants
were blocked. Ulysses said, "I can't afford to pay for the snowplows to
clean out the parking lots, and if I close the Ponderosas, I'll lose over a
quarter of a million dollars just this weekend. What can we do?"

It seemed a no-win situation. The bills kept piling higher and
higher.

Later on Greg said to me, "Mom, does Dad know that we're losing
almost two Mercedes a week now? It's getting worse!"

It was past time for action. We called the people at Rustler steak
houses, and in July of 1985 they approached us to buy out the Ponderosas. But with so much debt, they didn't want to buy them just then.
They sent Ken Tambaschi, a young director of operations, to work
directly for Ulysses and added a training manual from the Rustlers.

We entered into a deal where they would fly the Rustler flag over
eleven of the Ponderosas to start, and then one by one over all thirty-
nine. The Rustlers would handle the marketing for a franchise fee, and
all of the Ponderosas would eventually become Rustlers.

In the end, the Rustlers purchased the stores from us, although it
took a long time to pay the trail left by all the debts. By the time we
sold them completely, which took ninety days, we were back to losing
just one Mercedes a week.

When it was all over, Blackie said to Dimitri, "Ulysses had a college education all right. I could have flown him back and forth to Harvard by helicopter for all the money it cost me."

In the summer of 1985 I was concerned about Blackie. I noticed that whenever he picked up something heavy, he'd clutch at his chest. He had been experiencing heart pains since the trip to China and was taking nitroglycerin.

When in 1974 he had asked for Dr. George Economos's opinion, the doctor was conservative and had said, "Look, I've checked you out and you're not that bad. The heart bypass is a relatively new surgery, and I don't want you to be a guinea pig. Let's wait until you really need it, and then we'll go in."

Now, ten years later, Blackie had what we thought was a routine appointment on June 18 with Dr. James Bacos at the Washington Hospital Center. Just before we left the house, Blackie said, "I'm going to leave my watch at home, and I'm only going to take a few dollars."

"Why?" I asked. "Don't you think you're coming back after the appointment?" I was only half-joking, but I sensed a seriousness in Blackie. Inwardly, he had suspicions that his time had come.

He had a stress test taken, and afterward Dr. Bacos said to me, "Better get a few things together for him. I'm going to take him in right now."

In the end, Blackie had a quadruple bypass and was in the hospital for a week. It was difficult for him to be grounded, but through it all he began to understand that he needed to slow down and appreciate life. Even so, he didn't lessen the pace as there was just too much to do. His main focus was to assemble the real estate on the corner of Twenty-second and M.

The last piece of property that we needed in order to own the entire block was located on the corner of Twenty-third and M. This corner was owned by a gentleman named Dave, who was a nice guy except for his demands of $3.6 million if Blackie Auger wanted to buy his land. It was a ridiculous price, as his property only measured two row houses, but it was the corner and Blackie needed it to complete the picture.

Ted Pedas came in the restaurant one day and went up to see Blackie. Ted and his brother Jim were trained as lawyers, but their real love was the cinema, not law. Their most famous theater was located close to us, the Circle Theatre at Washington Circle and Pennsylvania Avenue, specializing in classic foreign films.

Ted said, "Blackie, you've got the whole block except for the corner of Twenty-third and M. You need it, don't you?"

"I do, but the guy is holding me up without a gun. I'd be crazy to pay his amount no matter how much I might want the corner."

"Listen, I'll tell you what. I know the guy pretty well and we get along fine. He's a hard-working man who works for the District but runs a little cafe there on the corner. He comes in at lunchtime and waits on tables and takes cash in his work clothes. If you want, I'll go and talk to him—I'll be the straw."

"Go ahead, but don't mention my name. He doesn't like me much."

Ted went to Dave's cafe and said to him, "This is too much work. Why don't you just sell it?" But the guy was reluctant and wouldn't budge.

Ted approached him many times over the coming months, but Dave clung to the three-and-a-half million figure. Ted remained patient and casually mentioned that when Dave got ready to sell, he would give him a million dollars for the corner. Dave wouldn't agree to anything, but Ted continued to see him. Dave stuck to his high figure.

Then one Saturday morning in the summer of 1986, Ted and his family were planning on driving out to the country for a short vacation. Just before they were ready to leave, the telephone rang. It was Dave.

"Ted, my wife's sick. She has bad kidneys and needs an operation. I'm going to take you up on your offer—I'll take a million dollars for the ground and the chattel. Can you come right over? I'll sign the paper."

Ted made out a blank law reporter sales contract for a million dollars and met with Dave. Then he realized that he ought to have Blackie's approval. He told Dave he'd meet him again in an hour. Dave said, "My wife's at Sibley Hospital, which is where I'll be. Meet me there in an hour if you're serious, and we'll make a deal."

I was at home when Ted called, asking for Blackie.

"He's down at the Touchdown Club," I said. "You can reach him there."

Ted walked into the smoke-filled club and saw Blackie playing gin with Nick Antonelli, Mike Zarpas, Larry Sinclitico, and a few others.

Ted called to Blackie, "Look, I filled out this contract for the corner, but I thought I better get your approval before signing."

"What, the guy called you?"

"Yeah, his wife is sick. He's willing to sell."

"How much?"

"A million."

Blackie grumbled and said, "It's still too much, but sign it and don't let the guy out of your sight."

Ted met Dave at Sibley Hospital and they signed the paper on the hood of Ted's car. As Ted later remarked, "This is where patience and good timing paid off."

I thought back to the day in 1956 when we bought our first piece of ground, the Chinese laundry. The price then was $7,500. We had just paid a million, but now we owned the whole block. The real estate market had certainly come a long way in thirty years.

A few months later, Blackie spotted Dimitri Mallios at the corner of Connecticut and M. As Blackie stopped for the light he called out, "Hey, Dimitri, how are you doing?"

Dimitri was surprised but pleased. "Hey there! I want to talk to you. How'd you like to get into the telephone business?"

Blackie paused and replied, "Well, now that Ulysses has had his education with the Ponderosas, I'm sure he's ready for something that he'd really like. Let's talk about it."

As Blackie drove off he remembered that at this very corner six years earlier Dimitri had told him about the Ponderosa restaurants. Maybe this deal would turn out better.

Later on, Blackie and Dimitri met, and Dimitri described the opportunity. He knew of two men, John Bolus and John Mason, who wanted to start a telephone company and needed a strong partner with deep pockets. The telephone industry had once been in the hands of a small group, but since the break-up of the Bell System monopoly in 1984 it had suddenly become an open field.

Ulysses II, anxious to direct his energy at something other than our restaurants, met with the two partners to explore the possibilities. It seemed a good match, especially for Ulysses, who had always loved any kind of electronics. The new Cleartel Company set up their offices in our Colonial Storage building across from the restaurant.

At the same time, another opportunity in the telephone business opened up when a well-respected acquaintance, Tom Domenici, told Blackie, "A lottery for cell phones is about to happen. It's in the hands of some lawyers just across the street, and all the legal work and engineering has been completed. Would you be interested?"

Although Blackie didn't completely understand what was involved, he trusted Tom's judgment and decided to play along. They went over to the lawyers' offices and Blackie paid the required money to participate.

After signing the papers, Blackie said to me, "You know these cell phones are just like Dick Tracy phones. I don't think they'll be any good for at least twenty years."

I thought about how much technology had moved on since I was a little girl on the farm when we didn't even have a phone at the farmhouse.

A few days later, the drawing took place. We were linked into many other partners and learned that we had a share of nineteen cities all over the country, from Spokane, Washington, to Jacksonville, Florida.

In a few days, offers for thousands of dollars began to pour in to buy us out. With the accumulation of funds from the sale of these lottery winnings, Blackie invested the money into Cleartel and Ulysses was on his way. The only catch was that the telephone business seemed to eat money, and for the first few years Cleartel needed the support of Auger Enterprises to stay afloat.

The eighties under President Reagan had shown much growth and expansion. Our business enterprises were going well and we were making a lot of progress. Our biggest development over the ten years, however, had been in our family. In 1980, I had a dream while at a spa in Florida with my friend Janet Ballas. In my dream I opened up the lower drawer of the buffet in the dining room and saw a basket full of chickens.

After waking up, I described the dream to Janet and said, "I didn't see a mother hen there. I think I'm going to have lots of grandchildren."

When we arrived home we were greeted with the news that Ulysses II and Alison were expecting a child. It was the beginning of a busy decade that saw the birth of nine grandchildren. Interestingly, four of them were born a day apart and all on a Sunday: Ulysses III was born on Sunday August 9, 1981; a year later Franciscos was born on

Sunday, August 8, 1982; another year later Bridgette was born on Sunday, August 7, 1983; and then Alexander was born on Sunday, August 6, 1988.

My other grandchildren, Nicholas, Gregory, James, Vassiliki, and Annabel, were born in the same period of time. (My tenth, Constandina, known as Chewy, was born on Valentine's Day in 1991.) It seemed like the good times would go on forever.

25

Downturn, Recession, or Worse?

AS WE ENTERED THE LAST DECADE OF THE CENTURY, no one believed that the real estate business was headed off the edge of a cliff. There had been some early warning signs, but we thought it might be just a downturn that in time would reverse.

But in the summer of 1990, Jeff Arpin, a senior account manager from our lender, Citicorp, requested a meeting with us. Jeff had worked with Blackie since 1983, when he was fresh out of business school. I remember being at the front desk when Jeff first came in to see Blackie. I assumed that Jeff, representing such an influential corporation, would not be easily dismayed. However, he seemed a little nervous when he came in. With Blackie in meetings with visitors upstairs, I had lunch with Jeff and enjoyed his tremendous sense of humor.

After our meal we went up to the office, and I introduced Jeff to Blackie. Blackie was busy and didn't pay much attention to him for the first few moments. While still shifting papers, Blackie muttered a hello. Then, looking at Jeff out of the corner of his eye, he asked, "Are you book smart or street smart?"

Jeff was quick, and responded, "I'm working on the street-smart part."

Blackie sized him up and grunted, "Okay." Then he launched into a rather long speech about how people with fancy degrees don't really know anything about business. I could see that Jeff, although somewhat intimidated, took a great interest in the office surroundings and in Blackie himself. He seemed excited by the challenge of working with this respected but formidable businessman.

During the subsequent years, Blackie and Jeff's relationship matured and they developed an easy rapport, which sometimes transcended business matters. Most of their conversations were based on starting new ventures and acquiring new properties and hotels.

Over time, Jeff came to see Blackie as someone with a unique perspective on real estate because he understood what would and wouldn't work in real terms. Jeff knew that Blackie would take account of the mundane matters, like where a person would alight from a car and therefore where the building's door should be and which way it should swing open. And Jeff respected Blackie's honesty and openness.

But now in the beginning of 1990, Jeff and Blackie had a different edge to their discussions. While throughout the early years and after, their conversations had usually been positive and exciting with Citicorp as our ally, now the tone seemed to have changed. There were signs that a downturn in the real estate market—and subsequently the hotel business—was threatening the whole country. Jeff said quietly to Blackie, "The word is out that this downturn could be very serious."

By August things were deteriorating rapidly, and Jeff became increasingly concerned. He phoned Blackie and said, "I want to call a meeting with your whole family—you and Mrs. Auger and Gregory, Ulysses, and Dina."

We all assembled in a private room at the Washington Marriott. As we sat around the table, Jeff stood before a flip chart and drew a picture of a little row boat. In it he put two stick figures and asked, "Do you know who this is?"

We shook our heads.

He said to Blackie, "That's you and your wife when you started the restaurant, driving the little row boat. The two of you used to row around and do whatever you wanted. As the years went by, you added more people, but you didn't realize that you needed a bigger boat. You packed them all in the little row boat and you both kept rowing and rowing. Now you've got all kinds of people working for you, but you're still running your business from the same small boat."

Jeff flipped the page and drew a picture of a large ship. "What you have now is not a row boat but an ocean liner. You've got many different types of businesses—real estate, restaurants, hotels, and even a telephone company—which measure assets in the hundreds of millions. To move your ship forward you're still using two little oars. But it's not as maneuverable as it was in the past, and even the waters have changed."

Blackie asked for some coffee and held his face in his hands. He refused to look at Jeff.

Jeff continued, "By this I mean that today's world is not as honest as it was when you used to make deals with a handshake. That was fine in the beginning, but now you need to see things with different eyes. You need to do things differently. We're in the midst of a storm, and your ship is in trouble. We've been hoping that the bad weather would pass, but it seems to be turning into a real squall. In order to set your course straight you're going to need to recruit some outside help."

He paused, still looking at Blackie. "In fact, you're going to need to release your grip on the steering wheel as the main captain."

Blackie seemed to be jolted by Jeff's words. His favorite remark had always been, "I just look in the mirror and shake my head yes or no, and then do what I want," so he didn't like to hear that he needed to counsel with others and change the way of operating the businesses. In fact, he started to get a headache and decided to leave.

When we got home, I could tell that Blackie was consumed with the day's conversation and Jeff's assessment. He said to me, "Hell, we've lived through the riots of '68 and all that other stuff. I think he's over-doing it."

"I don't know," I responded. "It seems kind of serious to me."

From sheer necessity, we continued to have similar consultations with Jeff throughout the fall. As a banker who had large commitments from our family, he needed to understand what were the motivating factors behind the various ventures. For instance, he would ask what collateral was substantiating this property or that enterprise and who was responsible to handle this or that.

Jeff's questions created a lot of tension as deep emotional attachments came to the surface. Every motive and every issue had to be delved into and needed to be open to every member of the family, the partners, and key employees. The very nature of the conversations led to discord and for the first time, we discussed how to handle a family business and who should be in charge of what entity.

But the discussions also had light moments. At one of the meetings, Jeff said, "Our whole office calls the fax machine the flax machine after you. And what used to be the sub prime rate now is the subterranean prime, just like you always say."

"I may get my words mixed up," Blackie replied, "but you know what I'm talking about."

They had their little jokes, but Jeff had his company in mind and underneath was very serious.

We knew from our discussions with Jeff that the situation was not improving, and so the week before Thanksgiving Gregory took action. He called up his longtime friend, Bill Caldwell, who lived in Los Angeles.

After some small talk, Greg volunteered, "Bill, we're in real trouble. Could you come as soon as possible?" Ulysses II also called Bill, reiterating the message. Bill responded by catching the red eye to Washington the following week, and we held our meeting in the Washington Marriott on the day before Thanksgiving.

Early in the morning, Bill, though tired from traveling through the different time zones, met with Gregory and Ulysses to outline the broad issues. We arrived several hours later on that very cold morning, and after our greetings, settled in to hear what Bill had to say. Looking very serious, he stood at the easel and unhesitatingly delineated the various challenges we faced. The first issue he raised was the question of the health of the Madison National Bank, for any trouble at the bank would affect all the other loans and partnerships.

In 1963 the bank had been created by and for people in business, and especially those in real estate. The vision was to enable would-be entrepreneurs to explain their ideas, plans, and challenges to their banking representative, who as a fellow entrepreneur would understand the possibilities of the intended businesses.

Now with the threat to the real-estate sector, the bank could be hit hard. And with Blackie the largest shareholder and a board member for twenty-eight years, we would also be greatly affected.

After some discussion, Bill asked, "How much trouble do you think the bank is in?"

Blackie seemed to be losing patience. "I'm telling you, Madison will be all right. Let's move on."

Bill hesitated, but realized that Blackie was in no mood for further talk about the bank. He then took us through the other partnerships and assets. We decided that the most urgent matter to resolve was the Mayflower Hotel. The partners who then owned it included Blackie, Kingdon Gould and his son, Kingdon Gould III, and Richard Cohen. The massive renovation of the historic hotel had long been completed but now the property was losing money.

The Mayflower group had a potential buyer in the Stouffer Hotel Company, a subsidiary of the Nestle Corporation in Switzerland, which had managed the hotel since 1981 when it had gained a 12 percent ownership stake. The deal, however, was moving slowly because the partners were unable to come to a mutual decision about a sale price.

Bill said, "Blackie, you guys need to get together and agree on a price for the Mayflower. If you can sell that hotel, one of our big problems will be solved."

Blackie responded, "Well, Jeff's been on my neck about it too. Why don't you and I see what we can do?"

"Glad to. Let's arrange a time as soon as possible."

Bill then turned to Gregory and said, "We need to come up with a five-year forecast to plot out our future direction. Let's get it in order so that we can present it to Jeff. You know that he's got Citicorp hounding him."

"Okay. I'll get it started."

It was clear by the end of the day that Bill, who was tremendously qualified, would be vital to negotiating the troubled times ahead. He agreed to the herculean task of flying back and forth weekly between Los Angeles and Washington for the next six months.

When Bill returned to Washington after Thanksgiving to begin the assignment, the first thing that greeted him was correspondence from First American Bank saying that they were taking control of all their loans with Madison Bank, and ours in particular. Of our half-dozen loans, the two largest were the $9.5 million unsecured loan for the Mayflower and the $1.8 million loan on the Stouffer Hotel at National Airport. First American said they were putting all of the loans in default. Blackie was shocked that First American would not work with us.

We responded by using Blackie's contacts at the bank to set up a meeting with the executive vice president of First American. When on December 6, 1990, Blackie and Bill entered his office, they met his fury. "How did we ever set up this meeting?" he demanded. Later we learned that this was the first time since he had been a credit officer that he had experienced customer contact. He was tense and hostile, but during the course of the meeting Blackie and Bill managed to charm him. By the end, they had worked out a plan to prioritize repayment of the loan. The executive then referred Blackie and Bill to one of his lieutenants, as he made it clear he didn't want to have any more personal contact with them.

Of the First American loans, the one that concerned us the most was the Mayflower partnership loan. We had not paid interest on it for seven months, which is why First American, in order to satisfy the federal bank regulators, had been forced to classify the loan. Our lender was demanding that we bring this interest current or they would file an action.

We weren't the only ones in trouble. We began to receive faxes from friends who were in the same situation. The faxes would come in the form of cartoons, and one in particular featured a shark with the following words beneath: "Notes coming due." We all learned the meaning of the proverb that states, "The borrower is servant to the lender."

In the meantime, however, we and our partners were still trying to finalize the sale of the Mayflower to Stouffer Hotels. We were all on tenterhooks because if First American had classified our loans, they would have jeopardized the sale. Amazingly, two days before Christmas the partners came to an agreement with the Stouffer company on the sale of the Mayflower, including funding the delinquent interest.

At the end of the day of negotiations, Bill remarked to Blackie, "The agreement to sell the Mayflower was a good Christmas present, wasn't it?"

"Yeah, I guess it was. First American could have made mincemeat out of us."

Just when the negotiations on the Mayflower were nearly settled, another headache came along when Sovran Bank sent a default letter to the partnership of 1255 Twenty-second Street, of which we owned about 22 percent. The bank said that the loan of $19 million plus accrued interest was in default and was due immediately. The partnership's major challenge was that the 103,000 square-foot office building had no tenants and no prospects for any. But the bigger problem for us was that although we owned only a small percent of the partnership, Blackie, as general partner, had guaranteed the entire loan. This gave the bank significant leverage in trying to negotiate a solution.

The partnership and bank later reached a loggerhead because, on the one hand, the partnership decided that they would not fund the interest due the bank individually, and, on the other, the bank was unwilling to lend any more money. This set the stage for protracted negotiations. (Miraculously, Bill and Blackie, with the help of lawyer Richard Levin, were able at the end of July 1991 to restructure this loan.)

We set up a meeting with Jeff Arpin on January 6, 1991, at which we presented our plan for that year. Our loans with Citicorp on a half-dozen hotels and on the land at the corner of Twenty-second and M Street totaled in excess of $100 million; our plan for 1991 showed a negative cash flow of over $6 million. Although Jeff appeared concerned, he thought that a solution could be worked out.

Jeff said that Citicorp would respond by the end of January with a proposal that would restructure the loans and would provide enough working capital for us to meet our cash requirements. But in the intervening three weeks, several events happened that delayed the bank's decision.

The first concerned our dear friend Nick Antonelli, who was the managing partner of several of our partnerships. I noticed that he hadn't been looking too happy when he would come into the restaurant. Then Blackie said to me, "Nick said that he's probably going to have to file Chapter Seven bankruptcy, and that the media will have a heyday with it."

Indeed, several weeks later, on February 8, 1991, the *Washington Post* reported that Nick had the largest individual bankruptcy ever to appear in the Washington area, estimated to be between $200 and $250 million. When Blackie read the article, he said, "If we're not careful, it could happen to us too."

I said, "I think with the Lord and Bill's help, we'll be able to work it out."

Blackie kind of shrugged, but I really believed we would come through all right.

The second event was positive—the completion of the sale of the Mayflower Hotel. The Nestle Corporation finalized the purchase of the historic landmark for a little over $100 million.

After the papers were finally signed, I said to Blackie, "Kind of sad, isn't it, since you guys were the ones who did all of the renovation work." I patted his arm and kissed him on the cheek.

"Yep, but that's the way it goes," he responded.

Then Blackie opened the mail a few days later and we received a shock. The FDIC, which had taken over the National Bank of Washington, had sent him a formal notice demanding that he pay a $2.15 million unsecured loan or face possible 'forced liquidation.'"

Almost the same time, the FDIC sent the Madison Bank a formal letter in which the regulators demanded a plan for recapitalization. Without such a plan, they threatened seizure of the bank by the government.

We were stunned by the letters and decided to call a meeting with Jeff to discuss the situation. We knew that Jeff was going through a time of transition and wondered if he'd like to work with us through our challenges. We met in Blackie's office on January 17, which happened to be the night that the Gulf War broke out. As we flicked on the television to CNN to see what was happening, we were surprised to see Peter Arnet giving a report from Baghdad. Only a few weeks previously he had come into Blackie's for a meal, and now he was in the midst of the latest international conflict.

While being caught up in the drama of the war and discussing the possibility of Jeff working with us, a big rat jumped off the balcony and scampered across the floor. We were totally shocked, as we had never seen a rat in the building before. Blackie, with his Greek superstition, thought it was a bad sign, and it ended our conversations with Jeff about him working with us. We found out a few weeks later that Jeff was definitely leaving his position, and that therefore Citicorp would not respond to our situation until a new loan officer was in place.

During these nerve-wracking times, we as a family drew closer together. I watched as Gregory, Ulysses, and Dina began to talk more, and I saw how they came to understand what their positions were, what part they needed to play, and what their talents and obligations were. Blackie himself did not feel too well, and needed to rest more often.

As we were trying to restructure our loans and survive the major recession of the early nineties, unbeknownst to us, our lenders were trying to do the same thing. With the exception of Riggs Bank, every major lender in Washington would eventually either be taken over by the FDIC or merged with another bank from outside the area. For instance, in early 1991, Citicorp was given notice by the FDIC that they were under "regulatory watch" and needed a capital infusion. We read in the February 23RD edition of the *Washington Post* that thirty-five-year-old Prince Alaweed Al Saud from Saudi Arabia had stepped in with $590 million to purchase 15 percent of the Citicorp stock.

Sovran Bank was also placed under regulatory watch, and just forty-eight hours after we completed the refinancing of the 1255 Twenty-second Street building, Sovran Bank was sold to Nations Bank. First American Bank was seized by the FDIC and its senior officers were indicted for bank fraud.

Jimmy Moshovitis called saying, "What's going on? The rules are changing before our eyes, and all the names of the banks are becoming something else. The people we used to look to are gone, and now all these new people have come in. All they want is money—there's no give and take."

Then Norman Hecht called from the bank and Blackie put the call on the speakerphone. "Blackie, we got a letter from the FDIC saying that Madison is in trouble. They seem determined to get rid of our bank. We've done our best but I intend to fight."

We were affected by the new banking rules, which Nicholas Brady, the Secretary of the Treasury under President Bush, was instituting. Under the new regulations, banks were required to post collateral for borrowings and were strongly urged to borrow directly from the federal government rather than from other banks. In addition, the requirements for the capitalization of banks were changed. The definition of capital was modified and restricted, and the amount of capital required was increased.

In early 1991, a young federal examiner in charge of supervising Madison's loans came to the office, and Blackie and I had lunch with her. Her job was to revalue all of our property, so she looked around at the business and the Marriott Hotel. Although she was only twenty-seven years old, the exercise of her responsibilities had an immense effect. She greatly devalued our property, and in particular the Washington Marriott. Overnight we lost $20 million in value.

As a result, our loan on the Marriott became substandard and we were almost in default. In previous downturns in the economy, examiners would allow financial institutions time to correct situations. But under the new rules, the loans had to be taken care of immediately. There was no compassion or flexibility on the part of what we considered to be very inexperienced examiners.

Over a period of just three years, the federal examiners had radically changed their point of view about the bank. In 1989, they had declared that even though the Madison directors were large borrowers from the bank, the directors were also the largest depositors and they always had more money on deposit than what they borrowed. In addition, the examiners said that Madison had one of the strongest bank boards in the area and that the directors themselves were some of the bank's best customers. But now in 1991 they criticized the very board of directors they had earlier praised, claiming that Madison was filled with inappropriate insider loans.

In April and early May, the young examiner and her colleagues met weekly with Madison's board. In one of the last meetings, the directors personally committed to contributing $10 million in new capital and to an additional $20 million within thirty days. But the examiners stated through their representative that they would not wait, refusing to honor the efforts of the board to save their beloved bank.

Just before the bank closed, Madison had a particularly busy day. The *Washington Post* reported that the examiners considered the long line to be a run on the bank, which not surprisingly brought about a self-fulfilling prophecy. People became concerned about their deposits and started taking money out. The negative reporting caused a run on the bank.

It was a heart-rending moment on May 10, 1991, when federal regulators closed the bank. With Blackie the bank's largest shareholder, we lost more money than anyone else. After the day's meeting with Norman Hecht and some of the others, Blackie came back to the restaurant and told the server to give him a bottle of Heineken Beer and a shot of Courvoisier. As I sat down with him, he said, "This is one of the saddest days of my life. It's almost worse than the war. We all did our best, and it's hard to believe that the bank could go down. I never dreamed it was possible."

I didn't say anything because I couldn't believe it either.

Madison's failure was the second collapse of a bank in the nation's capital in a year; it followed the failures of a half-dozen local savings and loans affected by the bust in the commercial real estate market. The federal government sold Madison to Signet Banking Corporation of Virginia for $18 million and took responsibility for approximately $11 million of unsecured debt.

In early June, Robert Clarke, the Comptroller of the Currency, was quoted in the *Washington Post* as saying that the bank's directors and Signet had not received preferential treatment. And although the OCC had discovered problems, "none of these problems appeared to be life-threatening . . . so long as the economy kept the bank buoyed."

In the weeks and months to come I would often see Blackie sitting quietly, kind of brooding. I knew what he was thinking—he was so used to going to the bank every Thursday, and he missed it. It was like a boyhood dream that had come and gone, and he couldn't get accustomed to the feeling of loss. He really loved that bank.

By early 1992, Citicorp changed our loan officer again and then reneged on their verbal commitment to lend us additional money for working capital. Without this, we faced a severe cash crunch. And because of the economic downturn, all of our assets had been devalued by some 40 to 60 percent. On paper, it looked like our liabilities exceeded our assets and that we had no net worth. Bill's six-month assignment had now stretched into years with no end in sight.

In light of the lack of working capital, we had to come up with another plan. At one of our regular consultations, Bill said, "The hotel industry has been hit the hardest. We need to concentrate on the hotels and try to get them straight. We should focus on the Washington Marriott, as it's the only hotel without a Citicorp loan. If we can keep the Marriott safe and reconstruct the debt, maybe we can borrow on it and pay off some of the bills."

Blackie said strongly, "I will not borrow on the Marriott."

"I really think it's the only way out," Bill replied. "We've got to consider it."

Even though Blackie didn't agree, he began to mull it over.

In the midst of all the tension and uncertainty of the real-estate market, we were glad to have a change of pace in September 1992. Blackie opened a letter which I had received from Mankato High School that said, "Please come to the fiftieth anniversary of the 1942 class." He read it out loud to me, and without me asking, he said, "I'm going with you."

A couple days later we were in the boardroom with Bill Caldwell and Richard Levin. I said to them, "We're going back to my fiftieth reunion from high school!"

Bill looked at me with a sly smile and said, "But you don't look a day over forty!"

"Yeah, sure Bill," I said.

Bill became serious. "You know, when my mother was ill I was with her at the Mayo Clinic. If you two are going to Mankato, you should stop at Mayo."

Richard added, "Blackie, that's the right place for you. You haven't been feeling well, and you keep complaining about that funny pain in your stomach. You must go—promise me that you won't go to Minnesota without going to the Mayo Clinic."

I agreed. "Ulysses, you know they're right. You should have your blood pressure checked out and tell the doctors about your headaches."

Blackie asked, "How can we go there when we don't even know anyone? Don't we need some kind of connection?"

I said, "You know, there's a friend of ours whose husband has been there. I'll give him a call and see if he'll refer us to his doctor."

Later I called Mr. Economides from Cyprus who was very gracious. He called his Dr. Miller and arranged for us to go to the Mayo Clinic after my reunion.

It had been twenty-five years since I had last attended a high-school reunion. Because I had left home so quickly after graduating, I didn't think anyone would remember me. But then the editor of the *Mankato Free Press,* Ken Berg, called and asked for an interview. He came to Washington and later did a nice full-page spread on this once small-town girl and her husband. So this time when I went to Minnesota, my former classmates knew a bit more about us. We enjoyed being with them, but Blackie wasn't feeling very well. We left for Rochester and checked in at the Mayo Clinic on my birthday, October 5, 1992.

I passed my exam quickly, but when they took a CAT scan of Blackie, one doctor spotted a small shadow in the area of the pancreas. They conferred with us in a small room, and the doctor said, "If it's in the pancreas, I can't promise you anything. We'll just have to sew him up."

We had heard that cancer of the pancreas would spread so fast that if a person lived six months it would be a miracle. Blackie and I looked at one another and quietly walked hand-in-hand down the corridor to the hotel. There didn't seem much to say.

I notified the three kids to come and also called Dr. Economos. Even though he himself was suffering from lung cancer, he insisted on meeting us at the hospital. The following morning we all gathered in the cold operating room while they wheeled Blackie away. We waited for hours in the intensive care unit, and finally were told that Blackie was beginning to wake up. Tending him was a lovely nurse who didn't have the most beautiful face. As he came out of the anesthetic, he looked right at her and said, "Keeta the moutra" (Look at that face).

Gregory chuckled, and said, "Oh, he's going to be fine."

The final analysis was that if I hadn't graduated when I did, hadn't been from Minnesota, and if Bill and Richard hadn't insisted we go to the Mayo Clinic, the encapsulated cancer in the pancreas probably would have broken through. Also, when they removed the spleen, they found it had a non-Hodgkin's lymphoma tumor which also was encapsulated. And ten years previously Blackie had had a carcinoid in the bowel. Looking at his charts, the doctor summed it up, "Blackie, you dodged the bullet three times. The good thing is that each of the cancers has been different."

I thanked God for all of these factors and thought how blessed we were. We returned to Washington for Blackie's recuperation, only now he had to contend with diabetes since the partial removal of his pancreas.

Our business problems remained, and Blackie was beginning to realize that he could no longer be a one-man show.

One day Gregory decided to again broach the subject of bringing Tom Lee on board. "Do you remember when I told you about Tom Lee who helped us with the Mayflower negotiations? He was Bill Hulett's assistant in Cleveland. He's had plenty of experience, and he even managed the Stouffer hotel in Westchester, New York. Maybe I could get him to come down here and help us get the hotels straight."

Blackie had been thinking over Greg's suggestion and responded positively.

Greg continued, "You know the Renaissance chain was sold and he didn't want to go along with the new company. Maybe he has time to come and help us out. How about if I give him a call?"

Blackie agreed, and Gregory made the call. Although Tom was working for the city of Cleveland, he had some spare time and was willing to come. He started working for us, flying back and forth at least one day a week from his home in Cleveland.

With Blackie unable to be fully at the helm, we needed to grasp the whole picture and look ahead to the future. We decided to have a special meeting with Tom to discuss the overall business strategy. We met in the board room at our Stouffer Hotel in Virginia with Blackie, Greg, and Ulysses at one end of the table and Tom and I at the other.

Tom was familiar with the many problems of the various businesses. Before the meeting, he had drawn up a plan that called for the consolidation of the restaurants, the hotels, the construction, the maintenance company, and the real estate under one umbrella. He prepared graphs and a proposal on just how all of this could be accomplished. Everything except Cleartel was included, for this was completely under the direction of Ulysses II.

Blackie listened to the plan and studied the graphs. He frankly was not too strong since his operation, and didn't feel very well. When

Tom finished speaking, nobody said anything for quite a long time, for we hadn't thought of structuring the business all together.

Blackie broke the silence. "The man that can handle all of this hasn't been born yet."

We all chuckled at this remark, but Gregory and Ulysses felt that that man who could oversee it was sitting in our midst. They exchanged glances and thanked Tom.

Ulysses asked Tom if he would wait outside a moment. Then he said, "Dad, Tom's our man. If we can persuade him, he would be the best."

Greg added, "His contract for the city of Dayton will be up in March."

Tom was out in the lobby getting ready to leave, but Ulysses called him back in.

Blackie said, "I didn't realize you were talking about yourself."

Tom looked surprised. "I wasn't. I don't intend to do this."

Gregory said, "Well, we'll have to wait and see."

We left the meeting thinking that this would be the perfect solution. And indeed, over time Blackie began to call on Tom more and more. Then on December 23RD, Ulysses had a Dell computer system delivered to Tom in Ohio, with a note that said: "If you're going to work with us, you're going to have to learn this. Merry Christmas."

He took that computer seriously, and by the next week he was toting his laptop on his trips to Washington.

Tom began to work with us three and four days a week, each time staying in the Embassy Square Suites hotel, while finishing off his commitments in Ohio. He was proving to be the man we needed.

Ulysses and Greg had lunch with Tom, and Tom told them that he would be coming to us fulltime in May of 1993. Now we had two fine people, Bill Caldwell as Chief of Finance, and Tom Lee as Chief Operating Officer, flying back and forth from different parts of the United States.

We celebrated Blackie's seventy-second birthday in September 1993 with the U.S. Army Rangers and the British Commandos in Italy. We were all together at the Chiungi Pass, which overlooks the plain of Naples and is four thousand feet high, to commemorate the fiftieth anniversary of the Allied victory.

The guys were remembering back to the Ranger victory there in September 1943, which had started the successful rout of the Nazis from Italy. With us was Van T. Barfoot, who had been awarded the Congressional Medal of Honor, and Phil Stern, the celebrated photographer.

The only remaining building at this strategic site is a restaurant called La Violetta. Inside we climbed steps to the second floor and took in the lovely surroundings. The pink tablecloths and matching flowers belied the blood of thousands of warriors who had fought and died there since ancient Roman times.

We feasted on the local cuisine and enjoyed the wine of the area (vino rosso locali di tavaio). Our meal was topped off with foaming cups of cappuccino. What a contrast to fifty years before.

Later on we laid wreaths at the various tombs of the well-kept graveyards. Row upon row of the brave men, too young to die, stood out before us. There was not a dry eye among us.

It took a year for Bill Caldwell and Steve Powers, a former executive from the Madison Bank, to negotiate the $100 million deal with Citicorp. This agreement allowed us to retain Embassy Square and the hotel at National Airport, but we sold the BWI Marriott to Citicorp along with the Stouffer hotel in Valley Forge, Pennsylvania. After these negotiations were settled, Steve left us and went to work for Marriott.

We decided that it was time to take our loans out of Citicorp. We began prolonged meetings with Lehman Brothers of New York, who were impressed with our team and the unity of direction among the family. In the end they not only refinanced our existing debt but lent us enough money to refurbish our properties.

Tom and Gregory took over all of the operations, and especially the three remaining hotels. One day Blackie said to Tom, "If you had been here all along, we probably could have retained all of the hotels."

"Well, we'll never know," Tom replied.

Tom and Gregory decided it would be best to remove the Stouffer name from the Washington National Airport hotel and get a new flag. After interviewing almost all of the management companies, they decided it would be best if we managed the property ourselves and franchised it to a national chain. We were able to strike an unusual deal with Hilton hotels, which included a loan of $1.5 million for capital improvements. We learned later that Hilton never loaned money for capital improvements, and that we were the first and only case.

Remodeling the hotel proved to be a wise decision. Gregory became the general manager and within two years we were able to sell the property for $37.5 million. Prior to Lehman Brothers taking over Citicorp, it had been valued at less than $20 million.

Lehman Brothers gave us the opportunity to reposition both the Embassy Square Suites and the Hilton in the market place, but their loan was for only two years with a one-year extension. This forced us to refinance the property in a very short time. Through Bill's investment banking contacts, he was able to arrange for Donaldson, Lufkin, and Jenrette to refinance the Marriott Hotel and our Embassy Square hotel. This new arrangement and the sale of the Hilton brought in enough money to repay all of our outstanding obligations, including those to the FDIC. Our Controller of many years, Joe Tatusko, said, "Thank God," and breathed a sigh of relief.

It had taken great effort on everyone's part, but now perhaps we could take a deep breath and continue to conduct business. But none of us would ever forget our near collapse. We had made it through, with God's help.

The years around the turn of the decade were emotionally intense both business-wise and personally. In the late eighties and mid-nineties, all of my remaining siblings died except my brother Marlin. Pearl had cancer and Hazel went of a stroke when she was eighty-six. I was comforted by the knowledge that they were believers and had made their peace with God.

But because we had been so close in age, I found Myrtle's death more difficult. She and Weldon had been in Baja, Mexico, where they loved to go fishing. One night Myrtle had unbearable stomach pains and was extremely sick. She went to the local hospital where they operated on her and discovered she had cancer.

I went to see Myrt many times and we prayed together on the phone. She was an exercise enthusiast and would play tennis and go running even though she knew she was dying. She said, "You can keep the body strong even if you are sick!" It caught up with her though, and she died when she was sixty-nine, a year after being diagnosed.

Chris, the Pentecostal minister, died in a very similar way to Papa. He and Lorna were going shopping and he was waiting for her on the terrace. When Lorna appeared, he had slumped to the ground. He never regained consciousness. Later, Lorna said he looked very peaceful.

So it was sad but no surprise when I received a phone call telling me that my sister Bertha had only a short time to live. I left immediately for California, taking with me my nine-year-old granddaughter, Vassiliki, Dina and Frank's daughter. Vassiliki wanted to meet her mother's favorite aunt, if only briefly.

Dimpled and blue-eyed Bertha was the one who loved to sing and play the piano. She was always happy and would see the bright side to a situation. She could laugh and laugh over almost anything. She took in stray cats and dogs, was rarely sick, and had never had an operation of any kind.

Bertha was eighty-three when she hurt her shoulder falling off a ladder. She called to tell me what she'd done and then said, "Don't ever climb up on a ladder," laughing. She had made a joke of it! But her daughter Sue, who was a nurse, was not pleased with her healing progress and took her for a CATscan. They found that she was riddled with cancer.

On her very last night, she requested that we all sing along with her two sons, Gary and Bruce, as they played their guitars. Her husband Jay wrapped her pink robe lovingly about her shoulders as he wheeled her into the living room. I sat close to her and she held my hand.

In a weak voice she said, "Louie, let's sing the old song." I immediately knew what she wanted, "The Old Rugged Cross." This was the song we sang when we moved from the farm to Mankato. As we sang, all the memories rushed back. Bertha herself sang softly, but so sweetly.

She had not eaten in many days, and the next day she wanted only to sleep so Vassiliki, Marlin, and I went to Sea World. When we returned, Bertha had slept peacefully right into the next world, surrounded by her loved ones.

In the plane going home I realized how glad I was that Vassiliki had been with me and wondered what she would remember of her visit. I found out a few years later when she was entering the ninth grade and had to write an essay as part of her application to high school. To my delight she wrote about visiting her Great Aunt Bertha. And she wrote beautifully.

I realized that some things were passing but others were being passed on. Long ago the Lord had given me the desire to write. He had also given it to Vassiliki.

26

Passing it On

SINCE 1972, ULYSSES II HAD SPENT many lonely nights checking out our restaurants, but his heart had never fully been in it. He had always loved electronics, and now he needed to focus all of his energy on his Cleartel telephone company as it was growing more and more. Bill Caldwell, too, was leaning toward the Internet field, although he remained our finance officer. With most of our business problems settled, however, he had more time available for other ventures. So he and Ulysses became increasingly immersed in this emerging field.

It had been apparent at the planning meeting in early January 1991 that Cleartel needed to stand on its own, so a plan was implemented that would allow the company to break even on a cash basis in 1991. From that point until 1996, Cleartel required no further cash infusions while it expanded its operations up and down the Atlantic seaboard. Ulysses also bought out his partners and hired a new chief operating officer, Ron Burlinson.

In early 1997, I was in the office when Ulysses came by. He had been very busy with the expansion of Cleartel, and now he seemed a little anxious.

"What's the matter?" I asked.

"I want to talk to Dad."

"He just went out," I replied. "What's up?"

"Well, I wanted to tell him about a couple who have an Internet company that we think we can buy. It's one of the original Internet companies."

"What's the name of it?"

"CAIS Internet. It's not your ordinary Internet company—it's a first-tier company."

After this last remark, he looked at me as if I wouldn't comprehend what he was saying. True, I didn't understand very much, but the

Internet seemed to be where the world of business was going and I was interested.

Just then Blackie came in and I said, "Ulysses wants to talk to you about something. I'd like to hear more about it as well."

Blackie didn't wait, but asked Ulysses, "How are the telephones?"

"Well, with all of the cell phones around today, the telephone business is suffering. I need to get into something else."

"What do you have in mind?"

"Remember when we hooked up with GTE Codetel? They've asked me if Cleartel could help them develop an Internet product for their customers. So Ron Burlinson and I've been looking for an Internet company, and I think we've found one. It's owned by a husband and wife team in Virginia."

"What's it called?" Blackie asked.

"CAIS, which stands for Capital Area Internet Service. We're lucky to have found it, because most Internet companies have already commercialized. But this one is just waiting to be developed. I'd like to buy it, Dad, and all I need is a little financial help."

Blackie asked, "Why haven't they expanded, and who are they anyway?"

"They're known as a carrier's carrier."

"What the heck does that mean?"

"It means," Ulysses answered, "that they are a first-tier company. They are the first point of access for all the companies who want to get on the Internet. They aren't just an ordinary Internet company.

"I have to make up my mind quickly, because right now they're negotiating with Cable & Wireless, and you know what a large telecommunications company they are. But we think that CAIS would like to sell it to us."

Blackie asked, "How much money are you talking about?"

Ulysses kind of half-smiled, a little afraid to give the figure, but then he said, "I need five million dollars."

Blackie looked at me and asked, "What do you think?" Then he said, "What does Bill think of the deal?"

"Bill knows it's right for us. We can see that the telephone business is going down and we desperately need this company."

Knowing how enthusiastic Ulysses was to get going, we did some research into the company and the Internet business overall. We began to see what a good opportunity it was and how right it was for Ulysses. Our next step was to figure out how to come up with the money.

It took some fancy footwork from Blackie to finance this acquisition. He finally worked out a line of credit for $2 million from First Union Bank, which he personally guaranteed, as well as a personal loan from a bank in Panama. The principals took back a $2 million note which made the entire purchase price $5 million.

Not long after the purchase of the company, Ulysses came by the office again. Flashing his nice smile, he said, "I'm really curious to meet this guy."

"What guy?" I asked.

"Well, I've heard about a graduate of MIT who was buying a T-1—a 1.5 megabit connection—for his house. You don't know what that means, do you?"

"No, but tell me more."

"Well, it's a highly unusual capacity to go into a house, no matter how big the house is. The guy's name is David Goodman, and I'm going to meet him here for lunch today."

"Good. When you bring him in, let me know. I'd like to say hello to him."

In truth I had no idea what Ulysses was talking about, but later at the restaurant was introduced to a tall, thin man with glasses. As far as I could tell, he looked like a very brainy guy.

I learned that David had discovered and patented a technology that he claimed would allow voice, data, and even video to travel simultaneously over existing copper wires in any building. He said that someone could talk on the telephone, work on a computer with a high-speed dedicated connection (up to ten b/d), and watch television all at the same time.

Ulysses was impressed and immediately grasped the commercial possibilities that this technology could open up. He explained his vision for it with great enthusiasm.

Over the next few months, Ulysses and David had many discussions that eventually resulted in a final contract in April 1997. At the stroke of the pen, CAIS became the exclusive worldwide licensee for David's patent, which was ultimately named Overvoice.

Overvoice, however, needed to be proven. We thought immediately of the real-estate developers, the Charles E. Smith Company, and in particular, Bobby Kogod, with whom we had enjoyed a strong relationship over the years. Ulysses spoke with Bobby and in August they began a trial of the technology within the Smith Company. Over the next six months, seventy-eight apartments in a Virginia complex were wired with it.

In the late summer of 1997 I received an invitation for my fifty-fifth high-school reunion. Blackie saw it and said, "I want to come with you again."

When we arrived in Minneapolis later in September, Marlin and his wife Georgine were there to meet us. We left the hustle and bustle of Minneapolis and before long were driving along the Minnesota River, which ties into the Mississippi River. As we entered Le Sueur from Highway 169 we mused over the Green Giant who stands proudly above the road. This was the internationally known valley of the Jolly Green Giant!

We approached Garden City, where I had been born. All that was left to mark our farm was the river, which flowed serenely on. Nearing Mankato, we passed the old Hubbard Mill and went onto Front Street where the Saulpaugh Hotel used to stand. It had been torn down, and even the bridge that crossed the river right next to it had been replaced.

Marlin remarked, "I remember when I got my first driver's permit in 1941. It cost me thirty-five cents."

"Times have sure changed," I said.

That evening we went to the reunion dinner with my class. We were more acquainted now. The former president of our class, a take-charge guy right from grade school, was the emcee and we listened to a classmate sing Broadway hits. As we joined in to sing the familiar tunes I looked around at the faces, remembering little incidents of the past. Most of the people had stayed in Mankato so they were close friends, but I was still an outsider, just like I had been when I left. But although I was a stranger, I knew that my roots were sunk deep into the rich Minnesota soil. I may have tried to get away from them, but they wouldn't let me go. The dreams of destiny that had pursued me in my childhood and beyond had been fulfilled. But only in part, for I still felt there was more to come.

The next morning we took a ride up past the Mankato High School and went through the downtown section. The dime store where I had worked to earn my ticket out of town had long been torn down. After heading out of the downtown area we neared Mama's house and saw that a reddish bungalow now stood in its place. The little store on the corner where they had so kindly given us credit was now a decorating studio. There was little left that I remembered from my youth, except for the house across the street.

There was to be a picnic beside the lake, but before heading there we decided to go to the cemetery to see my father and mother. I looked down at the graves, knowing that their souls were elsewhere and that only their remains were below the markers. Still, as I said hello, I saw their faces and remembered times past—Mama spilling the gravy on her stomach, and Papa digging out the yard to make way for plumbing. I remembered Mama putting me into God's hands and Papa giving me his blessing, which had followed me all of my life. I sighed and breathed a prayer of thanks for their lives.

We browsed through the tombstones and found the oldest one, dated 1788–1861. Further on was a gravestone from 1865 for the Jewett family. Five names were listed, after which it said, "Whole family killed by the Indians."

We left the cemetery and made our way to the class picnic. As we drove on the highway, I asked Georgine, "Why aren't there rows of corn anymore? Looks like the corn is growing close together, like all the seeds are just thrown everywhere."

"Corn is no longer planted in rows, except for sweetcorn," she replied. "Now it's planted in full."

Then I saw the big round bales of hay lying out in the fields, surrounded by the rich green grass. It all looked so neat and tidy. As we continued along the highway, I enjoyed glimpsing the tall cattails by the river and the golden rods and red sumac decorating the countryside.

On our last day we stopped at Marlin and Georgine's summer house at the edge of Lake Jefferson, which is seventy-five miles south of Minneapolis. We stood by the front of the house and watched a muskrat come swimming down the lake.

As we were looking over the lake, Marlin said, "I've decided that I'm going to stay here the winter. I want to see if I can take it."

"What do you mean?" I asked.

"Well, I just hate to leave Minnesota. The guys up at the restaurant stay all year, and I want to stay too."

Georgine said, "Not me—I'm going to California. It could be sixty degrees below zero here, and I just can't stand that."

But Marlin had set his jaw, just like our father used to do. I knew there would be no changing his mind.

Before we said farewell to Marlin and Georgine, they showed us around their beautiful little town. We saw the Rohlfing Hardware Store, the Rohlfing Laundromat, and the Rohlfing Grocery Store, all run by the same family.

Marlin said, "I want to show you their hardware store that operates on the honor system. After you've picked out what you want, you take it three stores down to their grocery store and pay there."

I stood in front of the hardware store and saw that they sold Trustworthy Hardware. Seemed appropriate.

Marlin continued, "Only lately did they put in a television monitor, but before that there wasn't any surveillance at all. Strictly the honor system, and they haven't lost anything yet."

Blackie said, "Do you know how long that would last in D.C.?"

Marlin just laughed, "You're not living in the right place. We trust one another around here."

We had a great time in this peaceful place, and then returned to Washington, quite refreshed.

In October, Ulysses II called Blackie with good news. "Dad, Overvoice worked at the Smith Company—they're really happy with it. So now we're ready to move. Next month we're going to the hotel-motel show in New York to introduce it. There we'll meet some of the big boys."

"Well, I wish you luck. Let me know how it goes."

When Bill and Ulysses were at the hotel-motel show, one of the people they met was Stan Julien from Microsoft. He became so excited about the technology that he invited Bill and the general manager of CAIS, Evans Anderson, to attend their introduction of high-speed Internet trials to the hotel industry in San Diego.

At that meeting, CAIS was introduced to a company called ATCOM. This start-up had a server solution that worked with Overvoice to provide high-speed Internet access to hotels. As a result of this meeting, Microsoft, ATCOM, and CAIS entered into an agreement to have trials with six hotels located in San Diego, Seattle, and Washington, D.C.

While all of this was going on, Blackie and I decided to take a cruise in February 1998 off the coast of Mexico. Before we left, Blackie said to Dina, "I don't feel very well, and I really don't feel like going. But we bought the tickets, so I'd better go."

After Dina told me about this conversation, I said to Blackie, "If you don't want to go, it's all right with me."

"No, let's go. Maybe it will do me good."

We joined our old friends Connie and Helen Valanos, Lou Economos (whose husband Dr. George Economos had died on February 16, 1994), and others, and boarded the cruise ship in Fort Lauderdale. When we boarded, Blackie bought a bottle of vodka because he thought it might elevate his mood.

Later on, our friend Taki Fotos joined us in our cabin. I sat on the bed and watched the two of them drinking toasts to each other, reminiscing over past experiences. We didn't know it then, but the vodka combined with all of the medicines Blackie was taking would have a profound effect.

Blackie continued to complain about not feeling well over the next few days and didn't touch the rest of the vodka. He tried his best to keep up with everyone else but was continually drained. I hoped that seeing Dina's dear friend Evy and her family in Cancun would pick up his spirits. But as the ship docked near Cancun, Blackie looked gray and tired.

The next day was Valentine's Day, and we disembarked in the Bahamas. As we walked around enjoying the atmosphere, Blackie told me to buy some jewelry as a gift, which I did while he sat on a bench nearby. When I returned to him he was pale and soaked in perspiration. We immediately walked back to the ship and he went to bed.

A couple hours later he hadn't improved and I knew I had to take some action. Earlier I had noticed a wheelchair just sitting in the foyer not far from our room. As I set Blackie in it, I said, "I'm taking you down to the infirmary."

I was trying my best to push him along the thick carpet, but he was heavy and I was not making very good progress. Just then our friend Frank Athanison and his wife came along and saw me struggling. Frank said, "Lou, let me push."

We made our way down to the infirmary. When we wheeled Blackie in, he was completely soaked with perspiration and looked like he was about to pass out. The nurse immediately put him on a hospital bed and called the ship's doctor. When he got there, he looked at Blackie and said, "Don't worry, I think it's just a bad cold. We'll give him some antibiotics and let him sleep."

After they gave him the medicine, he fell fast asleep. They kept him there the night, and early in the morning, I went down to see how he was.

"How are you?" I asked, looking into his sleepy eyes.

"What am I doing down here?" he asked. "I want to go back to the room."

"No, you need to stay here so that they can keep an eye on you. Have they been monitoring your diabetes?"

The nurse responded, "Yes, we've been checking on him regularly."

I convinced him to stay and spent the morning there with him. By noon I went up to lunch, and while there I was paged and told to come down to the infirmary immediately.

When I got there one of the stewards said, "Your husband is very sick. In order for us to take him to the nearest hospital, we will need his passport and his medical papers. We've already called the Coast Guard."

I was stunned and asked, "Why? What's happened so quickly?"

The doctor spoke up, "We can't handle him here—we're just not equipped. He's having heart failure, and we believe by the sound of his breathing that he has double pneumonia."

I was totally shocked. I couldn't believe that such a serious thing could happen on a vacation. As I gave them the passport and papers I asked if I could go too. They said they wouldn't know until the helicopter came.

By two o'clock, it seemed the whole ship was watching my husband being taken up by hoist into the helicopter, which was hovering over us noisily. Blackie was completely medicated and later would remember nothing of it. There was no room for me to go along, so I had to wait until the next day until we disembarked in Fort Lauderdale.

From there I flew to Key West and checked into a small motel near the hospital. I went quickly to find him, but he was so drugged and full of medicine that he hardly knew I was there. His lungs were being pumped and he was on life support. I asked to see the doctor immediately.

The doctor said, "After examining him, I believe he has double pneumonia. Also, his heart continues to fail. I noticed that he takes a lot of medicine. Has he been drinking anything lately?"

"Yes, actually he did have quite a bit of vodka a few days ago."

"Well, with all the medicine he's been taking, it's very dangerous for him to consume any kind of liquor, particularly in large quantities."

I asked, "How serious is this?"

"It's very serious. Your husband will be staying here for some time. We've given him heavy antibiotics and something for his pain. We are keeping him heavily sedated as we pump the liquid out of his lungs."

"Are you also monitoring his diabetes?"

"Of course. We saw his tag and we're checking him continually."

I notified the kids and they came two days later. They were very upset to see their father completely on life support and unable to talk or to walk. He had always been so strong, but now there he lay.

On the tenth day, Gregory insisted that we move him from this hospital as soon as possible. We called the Cleveland Clinic in Fort Lauderdale, where we were acquainted with Dr. Bush, Blackie's heart doctor. He said, "I'll take care of him. You get him up here."

As I packed our clothes, I put Blackie's shoes in the suitcase and wondered if he would ever walk in them again. It was a poignant moment, but I knew I had to be strong, and that the Lord would help me to keep going through all the uncertainty and questions.

We arranged for a helicopter to transport Blackie, and then Gregory, Dina, and I flew to Fort Lauderdale where we met the ambulance at the hospital. Dr. Bush placed Blackie in the intensive care unit immediately.

The next day Dr. Bush called me in. "Mrs. Auger, after carefully examining your husband, I have determined that he has had a stroke. I am going to have him examined by Dr. Hanson, who is a neurologist, and he will talk to you about what you can expect. We have his heart stabilized."

All of this sad news made me feel very tired and drained. I met with Dr. Hanson, and he said very clearly, "People who have had a stroke need to feel loved. You must surround your husband with love, for when a person has a stroke, he loses his will to live. You must make him want to live."

I told the kids what Dr. Hanson had said.

Gregory said, "We won't have any problem doing that."

Dina added, "Dad knows how much we love him."

Gregory and Dina couldn't stay with me fulltime, but they and Ulysses visited periodically over the course of the forty days. Their spouses, Margaret, Frank, and Alison, came when they were able to. In the beginning, Blackie didn't rally and sometimes he didn't know they were there, but I, and many of his friends, went to the hospital every day. Dr. Peter Neff, who was teaching at a Florida university, came over and was a good support as well.

Blackie remained totally on life support for three weeks. Even after he regained consciousness, he couldn't speak or write his name. It looked bad and I nearly gave up hope, but I prayed all the while.

After a month, Blackie gradually regained his speech. Then it was a great day when he could once again write his name. After five weeks, he was transferred to the Holy Cross Rehabilitation Hospital and I knew we were out of the woods.

One day when I went in to visit him, he said, "Boy, I thought it was the end today."

"Why? What happened?

"Well, when I woke up, there was a priest standing over my bed. I was startled, and I asked him, 'Has my time come?' I thought he was giving me the last rites, but actually it was just Holy Communion."

We laughed, and I said, "Ulysses, you've been through so much. I'm sure your time is not yet."

Blackie shared the room with a Jewish gentleman who was learning to walk after a hip replacement. He and Blackie got along very well, and enjoyed talking and joking with each other.

The hospital was located close to a Greek store, so one day Dina and I went there and bought avgolemono soup. We got enough soup for Blackie and his roommate. While they were enjoying it, Greg, Dina, and I met with a psychiatrist across from their room. He questioned us about Blackie's mental state to ascertain how much damage the stroke had done. As we were finishing the meeting, we heard the sound of choking and then saw Blackie jumping up out of bed and walking down the hall to get the nurse. The psychiatrist saw his quick movements and said, "If he can walk like that we'll discharge him tomorrow, because the insurance won't cover him any longer."

After we had returned to our apartment in Florida and Blackie was recuperating, Greg and Dina and Frank came for another visit.

Gregory handed Blackie a write-up and a menu and said, "Look at this, Dad. You have an opportunity to give up Blackie's. Smith and Wollensky—that big company from New York—have come to see me, and they've offered to take it over. Of course they will gut it completely and turn it into what they want, but they'll give us fifty thousand dollars clear each month to lease the whole place. What do you think?"

Blackie answered, "Who are Smith and Wollensky? I've never heard of them."

"Well, take a look at this and see what you think. They also have a restaurant in Miami that we could visit if you want to know more."

After Greg and Dina and Frank had left, we had dinner at the restaurant in Miami with Dr. Peter Neff. It was quite good, but their style was so different from ours that Blackie couldn't imagine the restaurant being like it. Later on, Blackie and I talked about how it would be if we gave up the restaurant. After being identified with it for such a long time, it would seem strange for us to let it go.

"We'd have the money but having someone else in Blackie's doesn't seem right. It belongs in our family," Blackie said. "Greg and Dina have so much talent. Do you think that they could team up together, since Ulysses has his business? Maybe we should let them take the restaurant and remodel the whole thing."

"That's a good idea, if Dina can spare the time," I said. I thought of her growing family and the successful real estate and remodeling business that she and Frank had built up together.

Before returning to Washington in April, we had a visit from Ulysses II and Alison. Blackie asked Ulysses how the trials had gone for Overvoice.

Ulysses was surprised that he even remembered. He answered, "They were very positive. They're going to release the results at the trade show in Los Angeles in June. I think we're beginning to grow. The Overvoice technology can't lose."

He continued, "We had to hire an outside private investor named Ted Ammon. You've heard of him—he's the CEO of Big Flower Press. We sold 3 percent of the company to him for $4 million. We need to enter the high-yield market and raise $150 million to finance our business plan, so we hired ING and Montgomery Security to assist us. We've been working with the lawyers, accountants, and investment bankers, and now we're ready to enter the market by the first week of August."

His father let out a small sigh.

Ulysses continued enthusiastically, "We were able to get a bridge loan from ING for $7.5 million. All we need is another million so that the company can operate until the year end."

As I heard this I thought of Blackie's saying, "I bought a ticket to the dance, and now I have to dance." Blackie said to Ulysses, "If you're sure that that's all it will take, I'll give it to you so that the company can keep going."

"Well, I didn't want to bother you with this right now, but you know this kind of business moves fast. We're going to make it, Dad, don't worry. We're getting to know the right people, and they like our product."

While Blackie was recouping, we had the restaurant and CAIS to think about. Then at Easter time, we returned to Washington. Blackie was saddled with a cane, but apart from that, he was doing quite well.

After a couple weeks at home, Blackie said to me, "I've decided. Louie, you remember how we talked about Blackie's? Let's do what we said—let's turn over the restaurants, hotels, and all the business to the kids. We'll make a trust and give them everything. I want Gregory and Dina to run the restaurants and hotels. Mind you, Dina will probably only want to do this part of the time because of raising her family and working with Frank in the business. But that's fine because Greg has the qualifications and talent to run the day-to-day operations. I'm sure he'll do an excellent job. And Ulysses has his own company. This way the three of them will be well set and can carry on the business. Let's keep Blackie's and let Greg and Dina remodel it."

Ulysses II continued to market the Overvoice technology to both the apartment and hotel industries. In September of 1998, CAIS was told about a trial at the Anaheim Hilton Hotel using copper wiring to provide high-speed Internet access to the guests. The experience had been less than satisfactory, which prompted the hotel to approach CAIS.

Within seventy-two hours, CAIS deployed their Overvoice technology on the copper wires. The guests' Internet access was now perfect, so the other company was asked to withdraw from the trial. CAIS began negotiating a longterm agreement to provide the technology among the whole Hilton Hotel chain, which owned or operated 225 hotels in North America, including Bill's favorite, the Beverly Hilton in Beverly Hills, California.

Amid the negotiations, Bill called one evening about nine o'clock. "Well, they signed the agreement about ten minutes ago. They're also going to throw in our television connection along with the Internet hookup. The man I was dealing with was so negative all day. I tried to work on him, but he wouldn't even crack a smile. He was impossible, and I was just too tired. Then suddenly his attitude changed—he agreed on everything and signed the contract."

I said to Bill, "I prayed for you and Ulysses all day. I just knew how important this meeting was."

"Yes, we needed the deal with Hilton in order to go public."

The time leading up to going public was filled with activity and excitement. Blackie and I stood on the sidelines, learning all the lingo we weren't familiar with while Ulysses and Bill traveled from city to city. In each place they would put on what they called their "dog and pony show," in which they demonstrated their product.

May 20, 1999, was the date of the initial public offering. Ulysses, Alison, and Bill went to Bear Stearns in New York where they had set the price of the initial offering at nineteen dollars per share.

We were thrilled to watch Bill Caldwell being interviewed on CNN as our stock CAIS was displayed on the Nasdaq board.

Later Ulysses called and said, "Well, I think I've made up for the Ponderosa restaurants now. I just picked up $130 million today."

We all laughed. Even though that debacle hadn't been his fault, I would say to Dimitri Mallios that Ulysses had indeed gained a Harvard education.

Little by little Blackie was recuperating. Even so, by now he had a new name. The doctor himself had said, "He's as strong as a bull—just like Lazarus. It's as if he has risen from the dead." Friends followed the doctor's lead and began to call him Lazarus.

One day the name acquired even more significance. Blackie was checking on matters at the bank and asked, "Why was all this money removed from my account?"

The banker investigated and stunned Blackie with his reply: "The Social Security Administration has stopped your Social Security checks. It looks as though they've marked you dead."

Although it took awhile to straighten out the bureaucratic mess, with Blackie having to appear in person with a witness, we laughed over the situation and thought of Mark Twain's quip of "Rumors of my demise have been greatly exaggerated." This turned out to be one of the best stories that Blackie told from his ordeal.

On a beautiful summer's day shortly afterward, Gregory came to see us at the house. As we sat together on the porch he shared his and Dina's plans for the restaurant. We talked about the changes that were taking place in the neighborhood, and how our former big lot, which we had bought house by house over a period of some thirty years, was now the building site for the splendor of a Ritz Carlton.

Gregory said, "Look, Dad, we need to place ourselves in the market for all these new customers in the West End. Think of all the hotels that have come here since we first built the Marriott just twenty years ago!"

He and Dina were eager to get on with remodeling the restaurant and arranged to meet with our architect Elliott Gitlin to devise a design strategy. We agreed. A couple of weeks later we gathered in Elliott's office, along with Tom Lee, our chief operating officer, and were amazed as they laid out their plans—they were superb.

As we poured over them, Gregory had one request. "Dad, with your high blood pressure, you won't be able to stand it when we begin to tear Blackie's apart. Promise us that you won't go into the restaurant until it's all finished."

Blackie sighed. "Okay. I'll agree—I won't go in there until you're done. But I'll be keeping my eye on the figures."

We didn't go into the restaurant until a year later when Greg and Dina invited me and not their father. They wanted me to be the advance party to soften the blow. I went with friends, Jimmy Pedas and his wife Wanda, who picked me up at the house.

When we entered the restaurant the change was so complete that I was shocked. It was only three-quarters finished, but what frustrated me was that my favorite fireplace, which had come from a mansion in Philadelphia, had been torn down. I was very attached to that fireplace and I didn't think the replacement was half as attractive.

I lashed out at Gregory. There stood my tall, proud son, calm and resolute; he listened to everything I had to say and then said, "Mother, you're only seeing part of the picture."

His calmness put me at ease. He was right. I had barely looked around at the rest of the place, but his face spoke more than his words. I saw the joy he felt at the work he and Dina, along with designer Lou Battistone, had done.

I began then to take in the big picture; the way they had hung the magnificent gates from the Evelyn Walsh McLean estate; the way they had used furniture that had once belonged to the Emperor Maximillian. This wonderfully carved table and the equally impressive chairs were set in a private room that featured a view of the new wine cellar boasting thirty-six hundred bottles.

In the area where desserts were being displayed I found the top of the ornate mantle I so loved. It fit perfectly. The new bar was intriguing with its stained-glass ceiling and modern lights. It managed to be both relaxing and exciting at the same time. And the restrooms were so beautiful that Blackie got a call from Jimmy Pedas who wanted to know if he could make reservations for dinner in the men's room!

I sat down at the table with Gregory and Dina and looked into their proud faces. I felt ashamed of my pettiness and they seemed to understand.

I said to them, "One thing I don't want is for your success to go to your heads." We began to laugh. How wonderful it is when tension turns to laughter and joy prevails.

Not too long after my visit to the restaurant Carl Lehmann, Blackie's Army Ranger friend, called him. "Blackie, can you meet me at the restaurant? I want to talk over the Ranger convention that's coming up in New Orleans."

Blackie agreed and called Greg. "I'm coming down to meet a friend."

I wasn't sure how my husband would react to all the changes in the restaurant. When we entered I noticed his face was pleased, especially when he walked toward the new shining copper, steel, and brass kitchen that was partially visible from almost any area of the restaurant. And at the entrance to the kitchen was a life-sized photograph of Blackie that had been taken in our first Minute Grill, showing him carrying a tray of dishes into the kitchen. The waiters passed this point constantly, and I'm sure that first waiter inspires them all!

After taking it all in, Blackie turned to me and said, "They really did a great job. I guess I knew all along that they were capable of it."

I agreed.

The team of Greg, Dina, and Tom had plenty of work to do. They tore down the old Blackie's Country in Springfield, Virginia, and with Elliot designed the Marriott Courtyard, which was due to be finished in September 2001. They polished up some of the restaurants we had and completely remodeled others. They took over all the things that Blackie used to do. Now we had the pleasure of just watching them implement their plans.

One day, Blackie and I sat quietly out on the porch, enjoying the moment. Our family business had been taken over and signed in trust to the three children. Gregory was now President of Blackie's House of Beef, Inc., and in charge of day-to-day operations, Dina was Vice President and Secretary, working several days a month, and Ulysses II was

Chairman of CAIS and had Bill Caldwell working with him. Along with Tom Lee, Greg and Dina were finishing up the remodeling of Blackie's Deja Vu Again, a place for the more sophisticated to dance, also on Twenty-second Street. We've been at that location now for over fifty-five years—that's a lot of time!

Blackie and I knew that although we were much older than when we began, we were indeed blessed to be together and to have a fine family. But I also knew in my heart that if I had not turned to the Lord when I did, this family would have had a very different ending.

Blackie's friends still call him Lazarus. He continues to be strong and can walk with the addition of a cane, which he's fighting to get rid of. He's passed on the running of the business, but he still stays involved. As Gregory remarked to Ulysses and Dina, "Dad turned the business over to us all right, but in everything I do, I always feel Dad's eye on me."

Yes, his eye will keep following them, and so will my prayers.

Acknowledgements

THIS BOOK HAS BEEN INCUBATING for many years. I've started and stopped it—and then begun it again numerous times. It was as if I couldn't give up on it, since it was a childhood dream.

Kids with big imaginations think a lot of things. Did I really see what I thought I saw so long ago in Minnesota? I was eight years old and the sky was filled with big, thick snowflakes—just enough to make everything look beautiful. Delighted, I lay back on a log and gazed up at the heavens, but all I could see was snow coming fast into my face. I opened my mouth and let the flakes fall in. Then to my complete amazement, I saw a book open up in the sky above me and I thought, "I'm going to write a book!"

I ran inside to tell Mama and then began to make up stories about everything. For Christmas when money was scarce I would read Mama a story I had written. All through the intervening years I had the deep sense that I would write a book; the thought colored and added excitement to my life.

Just before my sister Myrtle died I asked her if she remembered me running into the house and telling Mama that I was going to write a book. She was my last eyewitness and I needed to know if my memory had been playing tricks on me.

She was very weak, but she said to me, "Yes, I remember it like it was yesterday."

Originally *My Life with Blackie the Greek* was two books. It was my son-in-law, Frank Economides, who suggested joining them together. I agreed. Around that time a talented young editor named Amy Boucher Pye came into the restaurant. She wanted to hold her wedding rehearsal dinner at Blackie's; I needed a discerning eye to help oversee combining the manuscripts. A successful partnership was born. She has been invaluable to me. As an added bonus she was from Minnesota and we developed a lasting kinship. She had married a Londoner and moved there and so we corresponded by email and fax. Near the end of the book she became too busy with her work in London to continue with the project.

On the very day that Amy told me of her schedule constraints, another talented young woman was introduced to me by my daughter Dina. Although recently arrived in Washington, D.C. from England, Geraldine Buckley was not a stranger. Her brother's children are friends with all of our grandchildren. She too is an editor and writer, and has worked with me in the final stages of this book. We both feel that she was brought in by God's plan.

I would like to thank my friends Ruthie McBride and Windsor Elliott for their friendship, prayers, and the important role they have played in my life. It is with their blessings that I have recounted their part in my story.

There are many others I would like to thank: Janet Ballas for her friendship and encouragement; also Ted Pedas, who phoned me one day when I was feeling discouraged and told me he was halfway through the manuscript and found it riveting; Tammy Baird and Allen Cannon for all their work running around to make copies and helping me to keep the computer working; my neighbor Amy Ballard for catching errors; Colonel Frank Athanason who suggested the name of the book and his wife Vickie for correcting the Greek spelling; and George Cokinos and Harry Magafan for spreading their enthusiasm for the book among the Greek community. Bless you all!

I would also like to thank Cappy Shannon, Vivian Kalavritinos, Shirlie Ornstein, Mary Zarpas, and all the many friends who have been sources of encouragement over the years. I couldn't include all their names, although I wanted to.

I wish to thank my children: Gregory who told me, "It's your book, Mom, write what you like," and for his wife Margaret who was so enthusiastic about the project. For Ulysses II, who said, "Go ahead Mom, but I won't read it for another twenty years," and Alison who seemed to agree with him. I knew what they meant because they were shy about stories being written about them. And for Frank and Dina, who gave me many good suggestions and stuck with me all the way.

Lastly, I am very grateful for my husband, Ulysses (Blackie), who put up with all the times I was at the computer, who was always enthusiastic about the book, and who diligently checked every point to make sure it really happened the way I said it did. With all my heart I thank him for his patience and his love.

Gregory Auger

Margaret Auger

Ulysses Auger II

Alison Auger

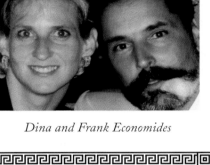
Dina and Frank Economides

Thank You for Being a Part of our Life's Journey

Richard Levin

Tom Lee

Ted and Lea Pedas

Jimmy Pedas

Bill Caldwell

Gwenn Antonelli

"Nick" Antonelli

Wanda Pedas

George Cokinos

Thank You for Being a Part of our Life's Journey

Harry Magafan

John T. Pappas

Dr. George Economos and wife, Stavroula (Lou)

Col. Frank Athanason

Pete Boinis

Millie and Angelo Puglisi

Joe Tatusko

Norman Hecht

John Deoudes

Vivien Kalivritinos

John Kalivritinos

Leon Segal

Janet Ballas

Niece, Phylis Comer

Niece, Ruth Battle

Chef Claude Rodier

Amy Boucher Pye
Editor

Chef
Gus Daskalakis

Amb. Alejandro
Orfila

Geraldine Buckley
Editor

Dino Economides

Mike and Mary
Zarpas

Elliott Gitlin

George Panagus

Irene and George
Pappas

Blackie's sister,
Margaret Tzafferis

Blackie's sister,
Harriet Maroulis

Ruth McBride

Father John
Tavlarides

Dimitri Mallios

Dr. Peter Neff

Taki Fotis

Niece,
Sue Nestika

Helen Valanos

Connie Valanos

Evelyn Kokinos
Acuná

Blackie's House of Beef became just Blackie's after the $5 million renovation in 2001.